The Lost Coast
and Other Sharon McCone Stories
Marcia Muller

Stark House Press • Eureka California

For Greg Shepard, publisher extraordinaire

THE LOST COAST AND OTHER SHARON McCONE STORIES

Published by Stark House Press
1315 H Street
Eureka, CA 95501, USA
griffinskye3@sbcglobal.net
www.starkhousepress.com

THE LOST COAST
Copyright © 2026 by Marcia Muller. (See Acknowledgements for original copyright information.)

Published by arrangement with the author. All rights reserved under International and Pan-American Copyright Conventions.

ISBN: 979-8-88601-176-0

Cover and text design by Mark Shepard, shepgraphics.com

PUBLISHER'S NOTE
This is a work of fiction. Names, characters, places and incidents are either the products of the author's imagination or used fictionally, and any resemblance to actual persons, living or dead, events or locales, is entirely coincidental.

Without limiting the rights under copyright reserved above, no part of this publication may be reproduced, stored, or introduced into a retrieval system or transmitted in any form or by any means (electronic, mechanical, photocopying, recording or otherwise) without the prior written permission of both the copyright owner and the above publisher of the book.

First Stark House Press Edition: January 2026

"Marcia Muller is the founding 'mother' of the contemporary female hard-boiled private eye."
—Sue Grafton

"An intelligent, compassionate woman—independent yet feminine, not just another female image of Marlowe and company." —*Chicago Sun-Times*

"For devotees of the hard-boiled school, McCone is the best of a recent spate of female detectives."
—*San Francisco Review of Books*

"Marcia Muller is one of the most consistently solid series writers around." —*Alfred Hitchcock's Mystery Magazine*

"Muller continues to reveal new facets of character in her San Francisco P.I., Sharon McCone." —*Publishers Weekly*

"Those encountering Muller's work for the first time will be inspired to read all of the previous McCone books."
—*Booklist*

"Muller undoubtedly remains one of today's best mystery writers." —*Associated Press*

"Muller maintains her exemplary high standards: great female private eye, smooth flowing narrative, and riveting plot." —*Library Journal*

"The action never stalls ... For crime aficionados, Marcia Muller is always a welcome name, one to rely on when you want a sure thing." —*BookPage*

"She is one of those rare series authors who never lets her characters grow stale or trite." —*BookReporter.com*

"Muller remains the best." —*San Diego Union-Tribune*

TABLE OF CONTENTS

Preface 7
Deceptions 10
All the Lonely People 28
The Place That Time Forgot 40
Somewhere in the City 54
Silent Night 69
Benny's Space 82
The Lost Coast 98
The Holes in the System 117
Knives at Midnight 136
Up at the Riverside 155
Irrefutable Evidence 170
Telegraphing 185
Tell Me Who I Am 196
April 13 212
Scamming the Scammer 227
The McCone Files 239
Bibliography 258

ACKNOWLEDGMENTS

"Deceptions". Copyright © 1981 by Marcia Muller. Originally published in Ä Matter of Crime #1.

"All the Lonely People." Copyright © 1989 by Marcia Muller. Originally published in Sisters in Crime.

"The Place That Time Forgot." Copyright © 1990 by Marcia Muller. Originally published in Sisters in Crime #2.

"Somewhere in the City." Copyright © 1990 by Marcia Muller. Originally published in The Armchair Detective.

"Silent Night." Copyright © 1990 by Marcia Muller. Originally published in Mistletoe Mysteries.

"Benny's Space." Copyright © 1992 by Marcia Muller. Originally published in A Woman's Eye.

"The Lost Coast." Copyright © 1994 by Marcia Muller. Originally published in Deadly Allies.

"The Holes in the System," "Irrefutable Evidence," "Telegraphing." Copyright © 1996, 2005, 2009 by Marcia Muller. Originally published in Ellery Queen's Mystery Magazine.

"Knives at Midnight." Copyright © 1996 by Marcia Muller. Originally published in Guilty as Charged.

"Up at the Riverside." Copyright © 1999 by Marcia Muller. Originally published in Irreconcilable Differences.

"Tell Me Who I Am." Copyright © 2016 by Marcia Muller. Originally published as Grand Central Publishing eBook.

"April 13." Copyright © 2020 by Marcia Muller. Originally published in Deadly Anniversaries.

"Scamming the Scammer." Copyright © 2024 by Marcia Muller. Originally published in Shamus and Anthony Commit Capers.

"The McCone Files." Copyright © 1995 by Marcia Muller. Originally published in The McCone Files in two parts, "The Last Open File" and "File Closed."

PREFACE

Sharon McCone made her first book-length appearance in 1977 (*Edwin of the Iron Shoes*), but it was almost a decade before she appeared in short-story form, due to my early discomfort with writing short fiction. In a novel, one can include many events, relevant or irrelevant, and then as the plot develops, pick and choose—tossing out some, retaining others. But a story requires a tight construction from the very first, and my construction abilities were shaky to say the least. Time and practice have helped me to sharpen my skills, and I hope these stories reflect this.

As the series progressed, a number of major characters emerged: Ted Smalley, the All Souls Legal Cooperative secretary and later officer manager of McCone Investigations. Hank Zahn, Sharon's best friend from her college days at U.C. Berkeley and founder of the San Francisco based law firm. Zahn's wife Ann-Marie Altman and their adopted daughter, Habiba Hamid; Greg Marcus, a homicide lieutenant who took great pleasure in antagonizing McCone. Hy Ripinsky, her lover and eventual husband. Best friend Rae Kelleher joined the cooperative as Sharon's assistant, later followed her to Pier 24 1/2 when she set up her own firm, and still later married her former brother-in-law, country music star Ricky Savage.

And then there were the families, both adopted and blood-related. When McCone found out upon her father's death that she was not the natural child of the couple who raised her, she began a search for her identity that led her to an Indian reservation in Montana where artist Elwood Farmer resided and later to Boise, Idaho, and her birth mother Saskia Blackhawk, a powerful Indian rights attorney, as well as to a half sister, Robin, and a problematical half brother, Darcy.

Locations also play a major role in the McCone series. San Francisco is a scenically and ethnically diverse place, as is all of California. The offerings in this collection are set against such backgrounds as Fort Point beneath the Golden Gate Bridge; seamy and prosperous areas throughout the city; both sides of the US/Mexican border; the Russian River; Mammoth Lakes in isolated Inyo County; and the lonely, windswept Pacific coast near the Oregon border. The Moccasin Telegraph, which extends among Indians throughout the country via telephone wires, is not precisely a place, but often seems to be in its capacity for uniting members of the indigenous tribes.

Various real-life events, most notably the great San Francisco

Earthquake of 1990, have provided background for the novels and stories. A series of murders of indigenous women, turf wars in the city's Mission District, duels among gang members, scams and other intrigues—they've all been fuel for investigation.

The best fuel for fiction, however, is the characters: rich and poor; criminals and victims; honest and conniving; peaceable and murderous; evil and altruistic. They're all included in this volume, and I hope you'll enjoy reading about them.

—Marcia Muller,
Petaluma, California
May 2, 2025

The Lost Coast
and Other Sharon McCone Stories
Marcia Muller

DECEPTIONS

San Francisco's Golden Gate Bridge is deceptively fragile-looking, especially when fog swirls across its high span. But from where I was standing, almost beneath it at the south end, even the mist couldn't disguise the massiveness of its concrete piers and the taut strength of its cables. I tipped my head back and looked up the tower to where it disappeared into the drifting grayness, thinking about the other ways the bridge is deceptive.

For one thing, its color isn't gold, but rust red, reminiscent of dried blood. And though the bridge is a marvel of engineering, it is also plagued by maintenance problems that keep the Bridge District in constant danger of financial collapse. For a reputedly romantic structure, it has seen more than its fair share of tragedy: some eight hundred-odd lost souls have jumped to their deaths from its deck.

Today I was there to try to find out if that figure should be raised by one. So far I'd met with little success.

I was standing next to my car in the parking lot of Fort Point, a historic fortification at the mouth of the San Francisco Bay. Where the pavement stopped, the land fell away to jagged black rocks; waves smashed against them, sending up geysers of salty spray. Beyond the rocks the water was choppy, and Angel Island and Alcatraz were mere humpbacked shapes in the mist. I shivered, wishing I'd worn something heavier than my poplin jacket, and started toward the fort.

This was the last stop on a journey that had taken me from the toll booths and Bridge District offices to Vista Point at the Marin County end of the span, and back to the National Parks Services headquarters down the road from the fort. None of the Parks Service or bridge personnel—including a group of maintenance workers near the north tower—had seen the slender dark-haired woman in the picture I'd shown them, walking south on the pedestrian sidewalk about four yesterday afternoon. None of them had seen her jump.

It was for that reason—plus the facts that her parents had revealed about twenty-two-year-old Vanessa DiCesare—that made me tend to doubt she actually had committed suicide, in spite of the note she'd left taped to the dashboard of the Honda she'd abandoned at Vista Point. Surely at four o'clock on a Monday afternoon *someone* would have noticed her. Still, I had to follow up every possibility, and the people at the Parks Service station had suggested I check with the rangers at Fort Point.

I entered the dark-brick structure through a long, low tunnel—called a sally port, the sign said—which was flanked at either end by massive wooden doors with iron studding. Years before I'd visited the fort, and now I recalled that it was more or less typical of harbor fortifications built in the Civil War era: a ground floor topped by two tiers of working and living quarters, encircling a central courtyard.

I emerged into the court and looked up at the west side; the tiers were a series of brick archways, their openings as black as empty eyesockets, each roped off by a narrow strip of plastic strung across it at waist level. There was construction gear in the courtyard; the entire west side was under renovation and probably off limits to the public.

As I stood there trying to remember the layout of the place and wondering which way to go, I became aware of a hollow metallic clanking that echoed in the circular enclosure. The noise drew my eyes upward to the wooden watchtower atop the west tiers, and then to the red arch of the bridge's girders directly above it. The clanking seemed to have something to do with cars passing over the roadbed, and it was underlaid by a constant grumbling rush of tires on pavement. The sounds, coupled with the soaring height of the fog-laced girders, made me feel very small and insignificant. I shivered again and turned to my left, looking for one of the rangers.

The man who came out of a nearby doorway startled me, more because of his costume than the suddenness of his appearance. Instead of the Parks Service uniform I remembered the rangers wearing on my previous visit, he was clad in what looked like an old Union Army uniform: a dark blue frock coat, lighter blue trousers, and a wide- brimmed hat with a red plume. The long saber strapped to his waist made him look thoroughly authentic.

He smiled at my obvious surprise and came over to me, bushy eyebrows lifted inquiringly. "Can I help you, ma'am?"

I reached into my bag and took out my private investigator's license and showed it to him. "I'm Sharon McCone, from All Souls Legal Cooperative. Do you have a minute to answer some questions?"

He frowned, the way people often do when confronted by a private detective, probably trying to remember whether he'd done anything lately that would warrant investigation. Then he said, "Sure," and motioned for me to step into the shelter of the sally port.

"I'm investigating a disappearance, a possible suicide from the bridge," I said. "It would have happened about four yesterday afternoon. Were you on duty then?"

He shook his head. "Monday's my day off."

"Is there anyone else here who might have been working then?"

"You could check with Lee—Lee Gottschalk, the other ranger on this shift."

"Where can I find him?"

He moved into the courtyard and looked around. "I saw him start taking a couple of tourists around just a few minutes ago. People are crazy: they'll come out in any kind of weather."

"Can you tell me which way he went?"

The ranger gestured to our right. "Along this side. When he's done down here, he'll take them up that iron stairway to the first tier, but I can't say how far he's gotten yet."

I thanked him and started off in the direction he'd indicated.

There were open doors in the cement wall between the sally port and the iron staircase. I glanced through the first and saw no one. The second led into a dark hallway; when I was halfway down it, I saw that this was the fort's jail. One cell was set up as a display, complete with a mannequin prisoner; the other, beyond an archway that was not much taller than my own five-foot-six, was unrestored. Its waterstained walls were covered with graffiti, and a metal rafting protected a two-foot-square iron grid on the floor in one corner. A sign said that it was a cistern with a forty-thousand-gallon capacity.

Well, I thought, that's interesting, but playing tourist isn't helping me catch up with Lee Gottschalk. Quickly I left the jail and hurried up the iron staircase the first ranger had indicated. At its top, I turned left and bumped into a chain link fence that blocked access to the area under renovation. Warning myself to watch where I was going, I went the other way, toward the east tier. The archways there were fenced off with similar chain link so no one could fall, and doors opened off the gallery into what I supposed had been the soldiers' living quarters. I pushed through the first one and stepped into a small museum.

The room was high-ceilinged, with tall, narrow windows in the outside wall. No ranger or tourists were in sight. I looked toward an interior door that led to the next room and saw a series of mirror images: one door within another leading off into the distance, each diminishing in size until the last seemed very tiny. I had the unpleasant sensation that if I walked along there, I would become progressively smaller and eventually disappear.

From somewhere down there came the sound of voices. I followed it, passing through more museum displays until I came to a room containing an old-fashioned bedstead and footlocker. A ranger, dressed the same as the man downstairs except that he was bearded and wore granny glasses, stood beyond the bedstead lecturing to a man and a woman who were bundled to their chins in bulky sweaters.

"You'll notice that the fireplaces are very small," he was saying, motioning to the one on the wall next to the bed, "and you can imagine how cold it could get for the soldiers stationed here. They didn't have a heated employees' lounge like we do." Smiling at his own little joke, he glanced at me. "Do you want to join the tour?"

I shook my head and stepped over by the footlocker. "Are you Lee Gottschalk?"

"Yes." He spoke the word a shade warily.

"I have a few questions I'd like to ask you. How long will the rest of the tour take?"

"At least half an hour. These folks want to see the unrestored rooms on the third floor."

I didn't want to wait around that long, so I said, "Could you take a couple of minutes and talk with me now?"

He moved his head so the light from the windows caught his granny glasses and I couldn't see the expression in his eyes, but his mouth tightened in a way that might have been annoyance. After a moment he said, "Well, the rest of tour on this floor is pretty much self-guided." To the tourists, he added, "Why don't you go on ahead and I'll catch up after I talk with this lady."

They nodded agreeably and moved on into the next room. Lee Gottschalk folded his arms across his chest and leaned against the small fireplace. "Now what can I do for you?"

I introduced myself and showed him my license. His mouth twitched briefly in surprise, but he didn't comment. I said, "At about four yesterday afternoon, a young woman left her car at Vista Point with a suicide note in it. I'm trying to locate a witness who saw her jump." I took out the photograph I'd been showing to people and handed it to him. By now I had Vanessa DiCesare's features memorized: high forehead, straight nose, full lips, glossy wings of dark-brown hair curling inward at the jawbone. It was a strong face, not beautiful but striking—and a face I'd recognize anywhere.

Gottschalk studied the photo, then handed it back to me. "I read about her in the morning paper. Why are you trying to find a witness?"

"Her parents have hired me to look into it."

"The paper said her father is some big politician here in the city."

I didn't see any harm in discussing what had already appeared in print. "Yes, Ernest DiCesare—he's on the Board of Supes and likely to be our next mayor."

"And she was a law student, engaged to some hotshot lawyer who ran her father's last political campaign."

"Right again."

He shook his head, lips pushing out in bewilderment. "Sounds like she had a lot going for her. Why would she kill herself? Did that note taped inside her car explain it?"

I'd seen the note, but its contents were confidential. "No. Did you happen to see anything unusual yesterday afternoon?"

"No. But if I'd seen anyone jump, I'd have reported it to the Coast Guard station so they could try to recover the body before the current carried it out to sea."

"What about someone standing by the bridge railing, acting strangely, perhaps?"

"If I'd noticed anyone like that, I'd have reported it to the bridge offices so they could send out a suicide prevention and rescue team." He stared almost combatively at me, as if I'd accused him of some kind of wrongdoing, then seemed to relent a little. "Come outside," he said, "and I'll show you something."

We went through the door to the gallery, and he guided me to the chain link barrier in the archway and pointed up. "Look at the angle of the bridge, and the distance we are from it. You couldn't spot anyone standing at the rail from here, at least not well enough to tell if they were acting upset. And a jumper would have to hurl herself way out before she'd be noticeable."

"And there's nowhere else in the fort from where a jumper would be clearly visible?"

"Maybe one of the watchtowers on the extreme west side. But they're off limits to the public, and we only give them one routine check at closing."

Satisfied now, I said, "Well, that about does it. I appreciate your taking the time."

He nodded and we started along the gallery. When we reached the other end, where an enclosed staircase spiraled up and down, I thanked him again and we parted company.

The way the facts looked to me now, Vanessa DiCesare had faked this suicide and just walked away—away from her wealthy old-line Italian family, from her up-and-coming liberal lawyer, from a life that either had become too much or hadn't been enough. Vanessa was over twenty-one; she had a legal right to disappear if she wanted to. But her parents and her fiancé loved her, and they also had a right to know she was alive and well. If I could locate her and reassure them without ruining whatever new life she planned to create for herself, I could feel I'd performed the job I'd been hired to do. But right now I was weary, chilled to the bone, and out of leads. I decided to go back to All Souls and consider my next moves in warmth and comfort.

All Souls Legal Cooperative is housed in a ramshackle Victorian on one of the steeply sloping side-streets of Bernal Heights, a working-class district in the southern part of the city. The co-op caters mainly to clients who live in the area: people with low to middle incomes who don't have much extra money for expensive lawyers. The sliding fee scale allows them to obtain quality legal assistance at reasonable prices—a concept that is probably outdated in the self-centered 1980s, but is kept alive by the people who staff All Souls. It's a place where the lawyers care about their clients and a good place to work.

I left my MG at the curb and hurried up the front steps through the blowing fog. The warmth inside was almost a shock after the chilliness at Fort Point; I unbuttoned my jacket and went down the long deserted hallway to the big country kitchen at the rear. There I found my boss, Hank Zahn, stirring up a mug of the navy grog he often concocts on cold November nights like this one.

He looked at me, pointed to the rum bottle, and said, "Shall I make you one?" When I nodded, he reached for another mug.

I went to the round oak table by the windows, moved a pile of newspapers from one of the chairs, and sat down. Hank added lemon juice, hot water, and sugar syrup to the rum; dusted it artistically with nutmeg; and set it in front of me with a flourish. I sampled it as he sat down across from me, then nodded my approval.

He said, "How's it going with the DiCesare investigation?"

Hank had a personal interest in the case; Vanessa's fiancé, Gary Stornetta, was a long-time friend of his, which was why I, rather than one of the large investigative firms her father normally favored, had been asked to look into it. I said, "Everything I've come up with points to it being a disappearance, not a suicide."

"Just as Gary and her parents suspected."

"Yes. I've covered the entire area around the bridge. There are absolutely no witnesses, except for the tour bus driver who saw her park her car at four, got suspicious when it was still there are seven, and reported it. But even he didn't see her walk off toward the bridge." I drank some more grog, felt its warmth, and began to relax.

Behind his thick horn-rimmed glasses, Hank's eyes became concerned. "Did the DiCesares or Gary give you any idea why she would have done such a thing?"

"When I talked with Ernest and Sylvia this morning, they said Vanessa had changed her mind about marrying Gary. He's not admitting to that, but he doesn't speak of Vanessa the way a happy husband-to-be would. And it seems an unlikely match to me—he's close to twenty years older than she."

"More like fifteen," Hank said. "Gary's father was Ernest's best friend, and after Ron Stornetta died, Ernest more or less took him on as a protege. Ernest was delighted that their families were finally going to be joined."

"Oh, he was delighted all right. He admitted to me that he'd practically arranged the marriage. 'Girl didn't know what was good for her,' he said. 'Needed a strong older man to guide her.'" I snorted.

Hank smiled faintly. He's a feminist, but over the years his sense of outrage has mellowed; mine still has a hair trigger.

"Anyway," I said, "when Vanessa first announced she was backing out of the engagement, Ernest told her he would cut off her funds for law school if she didn't go through with the wedding."

"Jesus, I had no idea he was capable of such ... Neanderthal tactics."

"Well, he is. After that Vanessa went ahead and set the wedding date. But Sylvia said she suspected she wouldn't go through with it. Vanessa talked of quitting law school and moving out of their home. And she'd been seeing other men; she and her father had a bad quarrel about it just last week. Anyway, all of that, plus the fact that one of her suitcases and some clothing are missing, made them highly suspicious of the suicide."

Hank reached for my mug and went to get us more grog. I began thumbing through the copy of the morning paper that I'd moved off the chair, looking for the story on Vanessa. I found it on page three.

> The daughter of Supervisor Ernest DiCesare apparently committed suicide by jumping from the Golden Gate Bridge late yesterday afternoon.
>
> Vanessa DiCesare, 22, abandoned her 1985 Honda Civic at Vista Point at approximately four p.m., police said. There were no witnesses to her jump, and the body has not been recovered. The contents of a suicide note found in her car have not been disclosed.
>
> Ms. DiCesare, a first-year student at Hastings College of Law, is the only child of the supervisor and his wife, Sylvia. She planned to be married next month to San Francisco attorney Gary R. Stornetta, a political associate of her father....

Strange how routine it all sounded when reduced to journalistic language. And yet how mysterious—the "undisclosed contents" of the suicide note, for instance.

"You know," I said as Hank came back to the table and set down the fresh mugs of grog, "that note is another factor that makes me believe she staged the whole thing. It was so formal and controlled. If they had samples of suicide notes in etiquette books, I'd say she looked one up and copied it."

He ran his fingers through his wiry brown hair. "What I don't understand is why she didn't just break off the engagement and move out of the house. So what if her father cut off her money? There are lots worse things than working your way through law school."

"Oh, but this way she gets back at everyone, and has the advantage of actually being alive to gloat over it. Imagine her parents' and Gary's grief and guilt—it's the ultimate way of getting even."

"She must be a very angry young woman."

"Yes. After I talked with Ernest and Sylvia and Gary, I spoke briefly with Vanessa's best friend, a law student named Kathy Graves. Kathy told me that Vanessa was furious with her father for making her go through with the marriage. And she'd come to hate Gary because she'd decided he was only marrying her for her family's money and political power."

"Oh, come on. Gary's ambitious, sure. But you can't tell me he doesn't genuinely care for Vanessa."

"I'm only giving you her side of the story."

"So now what do you plan to do?"

"Talk with Gary and the DiCesares again. See if I can't come up with some bit of information that will help me find her."

"And then?"

"Then it's up to them to work it out."

The DiCesare home was mock-Tudor, brick and half-timber, set on a corner knoll in the exclusive area of St. Francis Wood. When I'd first come there that morning, I'd been slightly awed; now the house had lost its power to impress me. After delving into the lives of the family who lived there, I knew that it was merely a pile of brick and mortar and wood that contained more than the usual amount of misery.

The DiCesares and Gary Stornetta were waiting for me in the living room, a strangely formal place with several groups of furniture and expensive-looking knickknacks laid out in precise patterns on the tables. Vanessa's parents and fiancé—like the house—seemed diminished since my previous visit: Sylvia huddled in an armchair by the fireplace, her gray-blond hair straggling from its elegant coiffure; Ernest stood behind her, haggard-faced, one hand protectively on her shoulder. Gary paced, smoking and clawing at his hair with his other hand. Occasionally he dropped ashes on the thick wall-to-wall carpeting, but no one called it to his attention.

They listened to what I had to report without interruption. When I finished, there was a long silence. Then Sylvia put a hand over her eyes and said, "How she must hate us to do a thing like this!"

Ernest tightened his grip on his wife's shoulder. His face was a conflict of anger, bewilderment, and sorrow.

There was no question of which emotion had hold of Gary; he smashed out his cigarette in an ashtray, lit another, and resumed pacing. But while his movements before had merely been nervous, now his tall, lean body was rigid with loosely controlled fury. "Damn her!" he said. "Damn her anyway!"

"Gary." There was a warning note in Ernest's voice.

Gary glanced at him, then at Sylvia. "Sorry."

I said, "The question now is, do you want me to continue looking for her?"

In shocked tones, Sylvia said, "Of course we do!" Then she tipped her head back and looked at her husband.

Ernest was silent, his fingers pressing hard against the black wool of her dress.

"Ernest?" Now Sylvia's voice held a note of panic.

"Of course we do," he said. But his words somehow lacked conviction.

I took out my notebook and pencil, glancing at Gary. He had stopped pacing and was watching the DiCesares. His craggy face was still mottled with anger, and I sensed he shared Ernest's uncertainty.

Opening the notebook, I said, "I need more details about Vanessa, what her life was like the past month or so. Perhaps something will occur to one of you that didn't this morning."

"Ms. McCone," Ernest said, "I don't think Sylvia's up to this right now. Why don't you and Gary talk, and then if there's anything else, I'll be glad to help you."

"Fine." Gary was the one I was primarily interested in questioning, anyway. I waited until Ernest and Sylvia had left the room, then turned to him.

When the door shut behind them, he hurled his cigarette into the empty fireplace. "Goddamn little bitch!" he said.

I said, "Why don't you sit down."

He looked at me for a few seconds, obviously wanting to keep on pacing, but then he flopped into the chair Sylvia had vacated. When I'd first met with Gary this morning, he'd been controlled and immaculately groomed, and he had seemed more solicitous of the DiCesares than concerned with his own feelings. Now his clothing was disheveled, his graying hair tousled, and he looked to be on the brink of a rage that would flatten anyone in its path.

Unfortunately, what I had to ask him would probably fan that rage. I braced myself and said, "Now tell me about Vanessa. And not all the stuff about her being a lovely young woman and a brilliant student. I heard all that this morning—but now we both know it isn't the whole truth, don't we?"

Surprisingly he reached for a cigarette and lit it slowly, using the time to calm himself. When he spoke, his voice was as level as my own. "All right, it's not the whole truth. Vanessa *is* lovely and brilliant. She'll make a top-notch lawyer. There's a hardness in her; she gets it from Ernest. It took guts to fake this suicide ...."

"What do you think she hopes to gain from it?"

"Freedom. From me. From Ernest's domination. She's probably taken off somewhere for a good time. When she's ready she'll come back and make her demands."

"And what will they be?"

"Enough money to move into a place of her own and finish law school. And she'll get it, too. She's all her parents have."

"You don't think she's set out to make a new life for herself?"

"Hell, no. That would mean giving up all this." The sweep of his arm encompassed the house and all the DiCesares's privileged world.

But there was one factor that made me doubt his assessment. I said, "What about the other men in her life?"

He tried to look surprised, but an angry muscle twitched in his jaw.

"Come on, Gary," I said, "you know there were other men. Even Ernest and Sylvia were aware of that."

"Ah, Christ!" He popped out of the chair and began pacing again. "All right, there were other men. It started a few months ago. I didn't understand it: things had been good with us; they still *were* good physically. But I thought, okay, she's young, this is only natural. So I decided to give her some rope, let her get it out of her system. She didn't throw it in my face, didn't embarrass me in front of my friends. Why shouldn't she have a last fling?"

"And then?"

"She began making noises about breaking off the engagement. And Ernest started that shit about not footing the bill for law school. Like a fool I went along with it, and she seemed to cave in from the pressure. But a few weeks later, it all started up again—only this time it was purposeful, cruel."

"In what way?"

"She'd know I was meeting political associates for lunch or dinner, and she'd show up at the restaurant with a date. Later she'd claim he was just a friend, but you couldn't prove it from the way they acted. We'd go to a party and she'd flirt with every man there. She got sly and secretive about where she'd been, what she'd been doing."

I had pictured Vanessa as a very angry young woman; now I realized she was not a particularly kind one, either.

Gary was saying, "... the last straw was on Halloween. We went to a costume party given by one of her friends from Hastings. I didn't want to go—costumes, young crowd, not my kind of thing—and so she was angry with me to begin with. Anyway, she walked out with another man, some jerk in a soldier outfit. They were dancing ...."

I sat up straighter. "Describe the costume."

"An old-fashioned soldier outfit. Wide-brimmed hat with a plume, frock coat, sword."

"What did the man look like?"

"Youngish. He had a full beard and wore granny glasses."

Lee Gottschalk.

The address I got from the phone directory for Lee Gottschalk was on California Street not far from Twenty-fifth Avenue and only a couple of miles from where I'd first met the ranger at Fort Point. When I arrived there and parked at the opposite curb, I didn't need to check the mailboxes to see which apartment was his; the corner windows on the second floor were ablaze with light, and inside I could see Gottschalk, sitting in an armchair in what appeared to be his living room. He seemed to be alone but expecting company, because frequently he looked up from the book he was reading and checked his watch.

In case the company was Vanessa DiCesare, I didn't want to go barging in there. Gottschalk might find a way to warn her off, or simply not answer the door when she arrived. Besides, I didn't yet have a definite connection between the two of them; the "jerk in a soldier outfit" *could* have been someone else, someone in a rented costume that just happened to resemble the working uniform at the fort. But my suspicions were strong enough to keep me watching Gottschalk for well over an hour. The ranger *had* lied to me that afternoon.

The lies had been casual and convincing, except for two mistakes—such small mistakes that I hadn't caught them even when I'd later read the newspaper account of Vanessa's purported suicide. But now I recognized them for what they were: the paper had called Gary Stornetta a "political associate" of Vanessa's father, rather than his former campaign manager, as Lee had termed him. And while the paper mentioned the suicide note, it had not said it was *taped* inside the car. While Gottschalk conceivably could know about Gary managing Ernest's campaign for the Board of Supes from other newspaper accounts, there was no way he could have known how the note was secured—except from Vanessa herself.

Because of those mistakes, I continued watching Gottschalk, straining my eyes as the mist grew heavier, hoping Vanessa would show up or that he'd eventually lead me to her. The ranger appeared to be nervous: he got up a couple of times and turned on a TV, flipped through the channels, and turned it off again. For about ten minutes, he paced back and forth. Finally, around twelve-thirty, he checked his watch again, then got up and drew the draperies shut. The lights went out behind them.

I tensed, staring through the blowing mist at the door of the apartment building. Somehow Gottschalk hadn't looked like a man who was going to bed. And my impression was correct: in a few minutes he came through the door onto the sidewalk carrying a suitcase—pale leather like the one of Vanessa's Sylvia had described to me—and got into a dark-colored Mustang parked on his side of the street. The car started up and he made a U-turn, then went right on Twenty-fifth Avenue. I followed. After a few minutes, it became apparent he was heading for Fort Point.

When Gottschalk turned into the road to the fort, I kept going until I could pull over on the shoulder. The brake lights of the Mustang flared, and then Gottschalk got out and unlocked the low iron bar that blocked the road from sunset to sunrise; after he'd driven through he closed it again, and the car's lights disappeared down the road.

Had Vanessa been hiding at drafty, cold Fort Point? It seemed a strange choice of place, since she could have used a motel or Gottschalk's apartment. But perhaps she'd been afraid someone would recognize her in a public place, or connect her with Gottschalk and come looking, as I had. And while the fort would be a miserable place to hide during the hours it was open to the public—she'd have had to keep to one of the off-limits areas, such as the west side—at night she could probably avail herself of the heated employees' lounge.

Now I could reconstruct most of the ongoing scenario: Vanessa meets Lee; they talk about his work; she decides he is the person to help her fake her suicide. Maybe there's a romantic entanglement, maybe not; but for whatever reason, he agrees to go along with the plan. She leaves her car at Vista Point, walks across the bridge, and later he drives over there and picks up the suitcase....

But then why hadn't he delivered it to her at the fort? And to go after the suitcase after she'd abandoned the car was too much of a risk; he might have been seen, or the people at the fort might have noticed him leaving for too long a break. Also, if she'd walked across the bridge, surely at least one of the people I'd talked with would have seen her—the maintenance crew near the north tower, for instance.

There was no point in speculating on it now, I decided. The thing to do was to follow Gottschalk down there and confront Vanessa before she disappeared again. For a moment I debated taking my gun out of the glovebox, but then decided against it. I don't like to carry it unless I'm going into a dangerous situation, and neither Gottschalk nor Vanessa posed any particular threat to me. I was merely here to deliver a message from Vanessa's parents asking her to come home. If she didn't care to respond to it, that was not my business—or my problem.

I got out of my car and locked it, then hurried across the road and down the narrow lane to the gate, ducking under it and continuing along toward the ranger station. On either side of me were tall, thick groves of eucalyptus; I could smell their acrid fragrance and hear the fog-laden wind rustle their brittle leaves. Their shadows turned the lane into a black winding alley, and the only sound besides distant traffic noises was my tennis shoes slapping on the broken pavement. The ranger station was dark, but ahead I could see Gottschalk's car parked next to the fort. The area was illuminated only by small security lights set at intervals on the walls of the structure. Above it the bridge arched, washed in fog-muted yellowish light; as I drew closer I became aware of the grumble and clank of traffic up there.

I ran across the parking area and checked Gottschalk's car. It was empty, but the suitcase rested on the passenger seat. I turned and started toward the sally port, noticing that its heavily studded door stood open a few inches. The low tunnel was completely dark. I felt my way along it toward the courtyard, one hand on its icy stone wall.

The doors to the courtyard also stood open. I peered through them into the gloom beyond. What light there was came from the bridge and more security beacons high up on the wooden watchtowers; I could barely make out the shapes of the construction equipment that stood near the west side. The clanking from the bridge was oppressive and eerie in the still night.

As I was about to step into the courtyard, there was a movement to my right. I drew back into the sally port as Lee Gottschalk came out of one of the ground-floor doorways. My first impulse was to confront him, but then I decided against it. He might shout, warn Vanessa, and she might escape before I could deliver her parents' message.

After a few seconds I looked out again, meaning to follow Gottschalk, but he was nowhere in sight. A faint shaft of light fell through the door from which he had emerged and rippled over the cobblestone floor. I went that way, through the door and along a narrow corridor to where an archway was illuminated. Then, realizing the archway led to the unrestored cell of the jail I'd seen earlier, I paused. Surely Vanessa wasn't hiding there....

I crept forward and looked through the arch. The light came from a heavy-duty flashlight that sat on the floor. It threw macabre shadows on the waterstained walls, showing their streaked paint and graffiti. My gaze followed its beams upward and then down, to where the grating of the cistern lay out of place on the floor beside the hole. Then I moved over to the railing, leaned across it, and trained the flashlight down into the well.

I saw, with a rush of shock and horror, the dark hair and once-handsome features of Vanessa DiCesare.

She had been hacked to death. Stabbed and slashed, as if in a frenzy. Her clothing was ripped, there were gashes on her face and hands, she was covered with dark smears of blood. Her eyes were open, staring with that horrible flatness of death.

I came back on my heels, clutching the railing for support. A wave of dizziness swept over me, followed by an icy coldness. I thought: he killed her. And then I pictured Gottschalk in his Union Army uniform, the saber hanging from his belt, and I knew what the weapon had been.

"God!" I said aloud.

Why had he murdered her? I had no way of knowing yet. But the answer to why he'd thrown her into the cistern, instead of just putting her into the bay, was clear: she was supposed to have committed suicide; and while bodies that fall from the Golden Gate Bridge sustain a great many injuries, slash and stab wounds aren't among them. Gottschalk could not count on the body being swept out to sea on the current; if she washed up somewhere along the coast, it would be obvious she had been murdered—and eventually an investigation might have led back to him. To him and his soldier's saber.

It also seemed clear that he'd come to the fort tonight to move the body. But why not last night, why leave her in the cistern all day? Probably he'd needed to plan, to secure keys to the gate and fort, to check the schedule of the night patrols for the best time to remove her. Whatever his reason, I realized now that I'd walked into a very dangerous situation. Walked right in without bringing my gun. I turned quickly to get out of there ....

And came face-to-face with Lee Gottschalk.

His eyes were wide, his mouth drawn back in a snarl of surprise. In one hand he held a bundle of heavy canvas. "You!" he said. "What the hell are you doing here?"

I jerked back from him, bumped into the railing, and dropped the flashlight. It clattered on the floor and began rolling toward the mouth of the cistern. Gottschalk lunged toward me, and as I dodged, the light fell into the hole and the cell went dark. I managed to push past him and ran down the hallway to the courtyard.

Stumbling on the cobblestones, I ran blindly for the sally port. Its doors were shut now—he'd probably taken that precaution when he'd returned from getting the tarp to wrap her body in. I grabbed the iron hasp and tugged, but couldn't get it open. Gottschalk's footsteps were coming through the courtyard after me now. I let go of the hasp and ran again.

When I came to the enclosed staircase at the other end of the court, I started up. The steps were wide at the outside wall, narrow at the inside. My toes banged into the risers; a couple of times I teetered and almost fell backwards. At the first tier I paused, then kept going. Gottschalk had said something about unrestored rooms on the second tier; they'd be a better place to hide than in the museum.

Down below I could hear him climbing after me. The sound of his feet—clattering and stumbling—echoed in the close space. I could hear him grunt and mumble: low, ugly sounds that I knew were curses.

I had absolutely no doubt that if he caught me, he would kill me. Maybe do to me what he had done to Vanessa....

I rounded the spiral once again and came out on the top floor gallery, my heart beating wildly, my breath coming in pants. To my left were archways, black outlines filled with dark-gray sky. To my right was blackness. I went that way, hands out, feeling my way.

My hands touched the rough wood of a door. I pushed, and it opened. As I passed through it, my shoulder bag caught on something; I yanked it loose and kept going. Beyond the door I heard Gottschalk curse loudly, the sound filled with surprise and pain; he must have fallen on the stairway. And that gave me a little more time.

The tug at my shoulder bag had reminded me of the small flashlight I keep there. Flattening myself against the wall next to the door, I rummaged through the bag and brought out the flash. Its beam showed high walls and arching ceilings, plaster and lathe pulled away to expose dark brick. I saw cubicles and cubbyholes opening into dead ends, but to my right was an arch. I made a small involuntary sound of relief, then thought, *Quiet!* Gottschalk's footsteps started up the stairway again as I moved through the archway.

The crumbling plaster walls beyond the archway were set at odd angles—an interlocking funhouse maze connected by small doors. I slipped through one and found an irregularly shaped room heaped with debris. There didn't seem to be an exit, so I ducked back into the first room and moved toward the outside wall, where gray outlines indicated small high-placed windows. I couldn't hear Gottschalk any more—couldn't hear anything but the roar and clank from the bridge directly overhead.

The front wall was brick and stone, and the windows had wide waist-high sills. I leaned across one, looked through the salt-caked glass, and saw the open sea. I was at the front of the fort, the part that faced beyond the Golden Gate; to my immediate right would be the unrestored portion. If I could slip over into that area, I might be able to hide until the other rangers came to work in the morning.

But Gottschalk could be anywhere. I couldn't hear his footsteps above the infernal noise from the bridge. He could be right here in the room with me, pinpointing me by the beam of my flashlight....

Fighting down panic, I switched the light off and continued along the wall, my hands recoiling from its clammy stone surface. It was icy cold in the vast, echoing space, but my own flesh felt colder still. The air had a salt tang, underlaid by odors of rot and mildew. For a couple of minutes the darkness was unalleviated, but then I saw a lighter rectangular shape ahead of me.

When I reached it I found it was some sort of embrasure, about four feet tall, but only a little over a foot wide. Beyond it I could see the edge of the gallery where it curved and stopped at the chain link fence that barred entrance to the other side of the fort. The fence wasn't very high—only five feet or so. If I could get through this narrow opening, I could climb it and find refuge....

The sudden noise behind me was like a firecracker popping. I whirled, and saw a tall figure silhouetted against one of the seaward windows. He lurched forward, tripping over whatever he'd stepped on. Forcing back a cry, I hoisted myself up and began squeezing through the embrasure.

Its sides were rough brick. They scraped my flesh clear through my clothing. Behind me I heard the slap of Gottschalk's shoes on the wooden floor.

My hips wouldn't fit through the opening. I gasped, grunted, pulling with my arms on the outside wall. Then I turned on my side, sucking in my stomach. My bag caught again, and I let go of the wall long enough to rip its strap off my elbow. As my hips squeezed through the embrasure, I felt Gottschalk grab at my feet. I kicked out frantically, breaking his hold, and fell off the sill to the floor of the gallery.

Fighting for breath, I pushed off the floor, threw myself at the fence, and began climbing. The metal bit into my fingers, rattled and clashed with my weight. At the top, the leg of my jeans got hung up on the spiked wire. I tore it loose and jumped down the other side.

The door to the gallery burst open and Gottschalk came through it. I got up from a crouch and ran into the darkness ahead of me. The fence began to rattle as he started up it. I raced, half-stumbling, along the gallery, the open archways to my right. To my left was probably a warren of rooms similar to those on the east side. I could lose him in there ....

Only I couldn't. The door I tried was locked. I ran to the next one and hurled my body against its wooden panels. It didn't give. I heard myself moan in fear and frustration.

Gottschalk was over the fence now, coming toward me, limping. His breath came in erratic gasps, loud enough to hear over the noise from the bridge. I twisted around, looking for shelter, and saw a pile of lumber lying across one of the open archways.

I dashed toward it and slipped behind, wedged between it and the pillar of the arch. The courtyard lay two dizzying stories below me. I grasped the end of the top two-by-four. It moved easily, as if on a fulcrum.

Gottschalk had seen me. He came on steadily, his right leg dragging behind him. When he reached the pile of lumber and started over it towards me, I yanked on the two-by-four. The other end moved and struck him on the knee.

He screamed and stumbled back. Then he came forward again, hands outstretched toward me. I pulled back further against the pillar. His clutching hands missed me, and when they did he lost his balance and toppled onto the pile of lumber. And then the boards began to slide toward the open archway.

He grabbed at the boards, yelling and flailing his arms. I tried to reach for him, but the lumber was moving like an avalanche now, pitching over the side and crashing down into the courtyard two stories below. It carried Gottschalk's thrashing body with it, and his screams echoed in its wake. For an awful few seconds the boards continued to crash down on him, and then everything was terribly still. Even the thrumming of the bridge traffic seemed muted.

I straightened slowly and looked down into the courtyard. Gottschalk lay unmoving among the scattered pieces of lumber. For a moment I breathed deeply to control my vertigo; then I ran back to the chain link fence, climbed it, and rushed down the spiral staircase to the courtyard.

When I got to the ranger's body, I could hear him moaning. I said, "Lie still. I'll call an ambulance."

He moaned louder as I ran across the courtyard and found a phone in the gift shop, but by the time I returned, he was silent. His breathing was so shallow that I thought he'd passed out, but then I heard mumbled words coming from his lips. I bent closer to listen.

"Vanessa," he said. "Wouldn't take me with her...."

I said, "Take you where?"

"Going away together. Left my car ... over there so she could drive across the bridge. But when she ... brought it here she said she was going alone...."

So you argued, I thought. And you lost your head and slashed her to death.

"Vanessa," he said again. "Never planned to take me ... tricked me ..."

I started to put a hand on his arm, but found I couldn't touch him. "Don't talk any more. The ambulance'll be here soon."

"Vanessa," he said. "Oh God, what did you do to me?"

I looked up at the bridge, rust red through the darkness and the mist. In the distance, I could hear the wail of a siren.

Deceptions, I thought.

Deceptions ...

ALL THE LONELY PEOPLE

"Name, Sharon McCone. Occupation ... I can't put private investigator. What should I be?" I glanced over my shoulder at Hank Zahn, my boss at All Souls Legal Cooperative. He stood behind me, his eyes bemused behind thick horn-rimmed glasses.

"I've heard you tell people you're a researcher when you don't want to be bothered with stupid questions like 'What's a nice girl like you ...'"

"*Legal* researcher." I wrote it on the form. "Now—'About the person you are seeking.' Age—does not matter. Smoker—does not matter. Occupation—does not matter. I sound excessively eager for a date, don't I?"

Hank didn't answer. He was staring at the form. "The things they ask. Sexual preference." He pointed at the item. "Hetero, bi, lesbian, gay. There's no place for 'does not matter.'"

As he spoke, he grinned wickedly. I glared at him. "You're enjoying this!"

"Of course I am. I never thought I'd see the day you'd fill out an application for a dating service."

I sighed and drummed my fingertips on the desk. Hank is my best male friend, as well as my boss. I love him like a brother—sometimes. But he harbors an overactive interest in my love life and delights in teasing me about it. I would be hearing about the dating service for years to come. I asked, "What should I say I want the guy's cultural interests to be? I can't put 'does not matter' for everything."

"I don't think burglars *have* cultural interests."

"Come on, Hank. Help me with this!"

"Oh, put film. Everyone's gone to a movie."

"Film." I checked the box.

The form was quite simple, yet it provided a great deal of information about the applicant. The standard questions about address, income level, whether the individual shared a home or lived alone, and hours free for dating were enough in themselves to allow an astute burglar to weed out prospects—and pick times to break in when they were not likely to be on the premises.

And that apparently was what had happened at the big singles complex down near the San Francisco-Daly City line, owned by Hank's client, Dick Morris. There had been three burglaries over the past five months, beginning not long after the place had been leafleted by All the Best

People Introduction Service. Each of the people whose apartments had been hit were women who had filled out application forms; they had had from two to ten dates with men with whom the service had put them in touch. The burglaries had taken place when one renter was at work, another away for the weekend, and the third out with a date whom she had also met through Best People.

Coincidence, the police had told the renters and Dick Morris. After all, none of the women had reported having dates with the same man. And there were many other common denominators among them besides their use of the service. They lived in the same complex. They all knew one another. Two belonged to the same health club. They shopped at the same supermarket, shared auto mechanics, hairstylists, dry cleaners, and two of them went to the same psychiatrist.

Coincidence, the police insisted. But two other San Francisco area members of Best People had also been burglarized—one of them male—and so they checked the service out carefully.

What they found was absolutely no evidence of collusion in the burglaries. It was no fly-by-night operation. It had been in business ten years—a long time for that type of outfit. Its board of directors included a doctor, psychologist, a rabbi, a minister, and a well-known author of somewhat weird but popular novels. It was respectable—as such things go.

But Best People was still the strongest link among the burglary victims. And Dick Morris was a good landlord who genuinely cared about his tenants. So he put on a couple of security guards, and when the police couldn't run down the perpetrator(s) and backburnered the cases, he came to All Souls for legal advice.

It might seem unusual for the owner of a glitzy singles complex to come to a legal services plan that charges its clients on a sliding-fee scale, but Dick Morris was cash-poor. Everything he'd saved during his long years as a journeyman plumber had gone into the complex, and it was barely turning a profit as yet. Wouldn't be turning any profit at all if the burglaries continued and some of his tenants got scared and moved out.

Hank could have given Dick the typical attorney's spiel about leaving things in the hands of the police and continuing to pay the guards out of his dwindling cash reserves, but Hank is far from typical. Instead he referred Dick to me. I'm All Souls's staff investigator, and assignments like this one—where there's a challenge—are what I live for.

They are, that is, unless I have to apply for membership in a dating service, plus set up my own home as a target for a burglar. Once I started "dating," I would remove anything of value to All Souls, plus Dick would station one of his security guards at my house during the hours I was away from there, but it was still a potentially risky and nervous-making proposition.

Now Hank loomed over me, still grinning. I could tell how much he was going to enjoy watching me suffer through an improbable, humiliating, *asinine* experience. I smiled back—sweetly.

"'Your sexual preference.' Hetero." I checked the box firmly. "Except for inflating my income figure, so I'll look like I have a lot of good stuff to steal, I'm filling this out truthfully," I said. "Who knows—I might find someone wonderful."

When I looked back up at Hank, my evil smile matched his earlier one. He, on the other hand, looked as if he'd swallowed something the wrong way.

My first "date" was a chubby little man named Jerry Hale. Jerry was *very* into the singles scene. We met at a bar in San Francisco's affluent Marina district, and while we talked, he kept swiveling around in his chair and leering at every woman who walked by. Most of them ignored him but a few glared; I wanted to hang a big sign around my neck saying, "I'm not really with him, it's only business." While I tried to find out about his experiences with All the Best People Introduction Service, plus impress him with the easily fenceable items I had at home, he tried to educate me on the joys of being single.

"I used to be into the bar scene pretty heavily," he told me. "Did all right too. But then I started to worry about herpes and AIDS—I'll let you see the results of my most recent test if you want—and my drinking was getting out of hand. Besides, it was expensive. Then I went the other way—a health club. Did all right there too. But goddamn, it's *tiring*. So I then joined a bunch of church groups—you meet a lot of horny women there. But churches encourage matrimony, and I'm not into that."

"So you applied to All the Best People. How long have you—?"

"Not right away. First I thought about joining AA, even went to a meeting. Lots of good-looking women are recovering alcoholics, you know. But I like to drink too much to make the sacrifice. Dear Abby's always saying you could enroll in courses, so I signed up for a couple at U. C. Extension. Screenwriting and photography."

My mouth was stiff from smiling politely, and I had just about written Jerry off as a possible suspect—he was too busy to burglarize anyone. I took a sip of wine and looked at my watch.

Jerry didn't notice the gesture. "The screenwriting class was terrible—the instructor actually wanted you to write stuff. And photography—how can you see women in the darkroom, let alone make any moves when you smell like chemicals?"

I had no answer for that. Maybe my own efforts at photography accounted for my not having a lover at the moment....

"Finally I found All the Best People," Jerry went on. "Now I really do all right. And it's opened up a whole new world of dating to me—eighties-style. I've answered ads in the paper, placed my own ads too. You've always got to ask that they send a photo, though, so you can screen out the dogs. There's Weekenders, they plan trips. When I don't want to go out of the house, I use the Intro Line—there's a phone club you can join, where you call in for three bucks and either talk to one person or on a party line. There's a video exchange where you can make tapes and trade them with people so you'll know you're compatible before you set up a meeting. I do all right."

He paused expectantly, as if he thought I was going to ask how I could get in on all these eighties-style deals.

"Jerry," I said, "have you read any good books lately?"

"Have I ... *what?*"

"What do you do when you're not dating?"

"I work. I told you, I'm in sales—"

"Do you ever spend time alone?"

"Doing what?"

"Oh, just being alone. Puttering around the house or working at hobbies. Just thinking."

"Are you crazy? What kind of a computer glitch are you, anyway?" He stood, all five-foot-three of him quivering indignantly. "Believe me, I'm going to complain to Best People about setting me up with you. They described you as 'vivacious,' but you've hardly said a word all evening!"

Morton Stone was a nice man, a sad man. He insisted on buying me dinner at his favorite Chinese restaurant. He spent the evening asking me questions about myself and my job as a legal researcher; while he listened, his fingers played nervously with the silverware. Later, over a brandy in a nearby bar, he told me how his wife had died the summer before, of cancer. He told me about his promise to her that he would get on with his life, find someone new, and be happy. This was the first date he'd arranged through All the Best People; he'd never done anything like that in his life. He'd only tried them because he wasn't good at meeting people. He had a good job, but it wasn't enough. He had money to travel, but it was no fun without someone to share the experience with. He would have liked to have children, but he and his wife had put it off until they'd be financially secure, and then they found out about the cancer....

I felt guilty as hell about deceiving him, and for taking his time, money, and hope. But by the end of the evening I'd remembered a woman friend who was just getting over a disastrous love affair. A nice, sad woman who wasn't good at meeting people; who had a good job, loved to travel, and longed for children ...

Bob Gillespie was a sailing instructor on a voyage of self-discovery. He kept prefacing his remarks with statements such as, "You know, I had a great insight into myself last week." That was nice; I was happy for him. But I would rather have gotten to know his surface persona before probing into his psyche. Like the two previous men, Bob didn't fit any of the recognizable profiles of the professional burglar, nor had he any great insight into how All the Best People worked.

Ted Horowitz was a recovering alcoholic, which was admirable. Unfortunately, he was also the confessional type. He began every anecdote with the admission that it had happened "back when I was drinking." He even felt compelled to describe how he used to throw up on his ex-wife. His only complaint about Best People—this with a stern look at my wineglass—was that they kept referring him to women who drank.

Jim Rogers was an adman who wore safari clothes and was into guns. I refrained from telling that I own two .38 Specials and am a highly-qualified marksman, for fear it would incite him to passion. For a little while I considered him seriously for the role of burglar, but when I probed the subject by mentioning a friend having recently been ripped off, Jim became enraged and said the burglar ought to be hunted down and shot.

"I'm going about this all wrong," I said to Hank.

It was ten in the morning, and we were drinking coffee at the big round table in All Souls's kitchen. The night before I'd spent hours on the phone with an effervescent insurance underwriter who was going on a whale-watching trip with Weekenders, the group that god-awful Jerry had mentioned. He'd concluded our conversation by saying he'd be sure to note in his pocket organizer to call me the day after he returned. Then I'd been unable to sleep and had sat up hours longer, drinking too much and listening for burglars and brooding about loneliness.

I wasn't involved with anyone at the time—nor did I particularly want to be. I'd just emerged from a long-term relationship and was reordering my life and getting used to doing things alone again. I was fortunate in that my job and my little house—which I'm constantly remodeling—filled most of the empty hours. But I could still understand what Morton and Bob and Ted and Jim and even that dreadful Jerry were suffering from.

It was the little things that got to me. Like the times I went to the supermarket and everything I felt like having for dinner was packaged for two or more, and I couldn't think of anyone I wanted to have over to share it with. Or the times I'd be driving around a curve in the road and come upon a spectacular view, but have no one in the passenger seat to point it out to. And then there were the cold sheets on the other side of a wide bed on a foggy San Francisco night.

But I got through it, because I reminded myself that it wasn't going to be that way forever. And when I couldn't convince myself of that, I thought about how it was better to be totally alone than alone *with* someone. That's how *I* got through the cold, foggy nights. But I was discovering there was a whole segment of the population that availed itself of dating services and telephone conversation clubs and video exchanges. Since I'd started using Best People, I'd been inundated by mail solicitations and found that the array of services available to singles was astonishing.

Now I told Hank, "I simply can't stand another evening making polite chitchat in a bar. If I listen to another ex-wife story, I'll scream. I don't want to know that these guys' parents did to them at age ten that made the whole rest of their lives a mess. And besides, having that security guard on my house is costing Dick Morris a bundle he can ill afford."

Helpfully Hank said, "So change your approach."

"Thanks for your great suggestion." I got up and went out to the desk that belongs to Ted Smalley, our secretary, and dug out a phone directory. All the Best People wasn't listed. My file on the case was on the kitchen table. I went back there—Hank had retreated to his office—and checked the introductory letter they'd sent me; it showed nothing but a post-office box. The zip code told me it was the main post office at Seventh and Mission streets.

I went back and borrowed Ted's phone book again, then looked up the post office's number. I called it, got the mail-sorting supervisor, and identified myself as Sharon from Federal Express. "We've got a package here for All the Best People Introduction Service," I said, and read off the box number. "That's all I've got—no contact phone, no street address."

"Assholes," she said wearily. "Why do they send them to a P. O. box when they know you can't deliver to one? For that matter, why do you accept them when they're addressed like that?"

"Damned if I know. I only work here."

"I can't give out the street address, but I'll supply the contact phone." She went away, came back, and read it to me.

"Thanks." I depressed the disconnect button and redialed.

A female voice answered with only the phone number. I went into my Federal Express routine. The woman gave me the address without hesitation, in the 200 block of Gough Street near the Civic Center. After I hung up I made one more call: to a friend on the *Chronicle*. J. D. Smith was in the city room and agreed to leave a few extra business cards with the security guard in the newspaper building's lobby.

All the Best People's offices took up the entire second floor of a renovated Victorian. I couldn't imagine why they needed so much space, but they seemed to be doing a landslide business, because phones in the offices on either side of the long corridor were ringing madly. I assumed it was because the summer vacation season was approaching and San Francisco singles were getting anxious about finding someone to make travel plans with.

The receptionist was more or less what I expected to find in the office of that sort of business: petite, blond, sleekly groomed, and expensively dressed, with an elegant manner. She took J. D.'s card down the hallway to see if their director was available to talk with me about the article I was writing on the singles scene. I paced around the tiny waiting room, which didn't even have chairs. When the young woman came back, she said Dave Lester would be happy to see me and led me to an office at the rear.

The office was plush, considering the attention that had been given to decor in the rest of the suite. It had a leather couch and chairs, a wet bar, and an immense mahogany desk. There wasn't so much as a scrap of paper or a file folder to suggest anything resembling work was done there. I couldn't see Dave Lester, because he had swiveled his high-backed chair around toward the window and was apparently contemplating the wall of the building next door. The receptionist backed out the door and closed it. I cleared my throat, and the chair turned toward me.

The man in the chair was god-awful Jerry Hale.

Our faces must have been mirror images of shock. I said, "What are *you* doing here?"

He said, "You're not J. D. Smith. You're Sharon McCone!" Then he frowned down at the business card he held. "Or is Sharon McCone really J. D. Smith?"

I collected my scattered wits and said, "Which are you—Dave Lester or Jerry Hale?" I added, "I'm a reporter doing a feature article on the singles scene."

"So Marie said. How did you get this address? We don't publish it because we don't want all sorts of crazies wandering in. This is an exclusive service; we screen our applicants carefully."

They certainly hadn't screened me; otherwise they'd have uncovered numerous deceptions. I said, "Oh, we newspaper people have our sources."

"Well, you certainly misrepresented yourself to us."

"And you misrepresented yourself to *me*."

He shrugged. "It's all part of the screening process, for our clients' protection. We realize most applicants would shy away from a formal interview situation, so we have the first date take the place of that."

"You yourself go out with *all* the women who apply?"

"A fair amount, using a different name every time, of course, in case any of them know each other and compare notes." At my astonished look he added, "What can I say? I like women. But naturally I have help. And Marie"—he motioned at the closed door—"and one of the secretaries check out the guys."

No wonder Jerry had no time to read. "Then none of the things you told me were true? About being into the bar scene and the church groups and the health club?"

"Sure they were. My previous experiences were what led me to buy Best People from its former owners. They hadn't studied the market, didn't know how to make a go of it in the eighties."

"Well, you're certainly a good spokesman for your own product. But how come you kept referring me to other clients? We didn't exactly part on amiable terms."

"Oh, that was just a ruse to get out of there. I had another date. I'd seen enough to know you weren't my type. But I decided you were still acceptable; we get a lot of men looking for your kind."

The "acceptable" rankled. "What exactly is my kind?"

"Well, I'd call you ... introspective. Bookish? No, not exactly. A little offbeat? Maybe intense? No. It's peculiar ... you're peculiar—"

"Stop right there!"

Jerry—who would always be god-awful Jerry and never Dave Lester to me—stood up and came around the desk. I straightened my posture. From my five-foot-six vantage point I could see the beginnings of a bald spot under his artfully styled hair. When he realized where I was looking, his mouth tightened. I took a perverse delight in his discomfort.

"I'll have to ask you to leave now," he said stiffly.

"But don't you want Best People featured in a piece on singles?"

"I do not. I can't condone the tactics of a reporter who misrepresents herself."

"Are you sure that's the reason you don't want to talk with me?"

"Of course. What else—"

"Is there something about Best People that you'd rather not see publicized?"

Jerry flushed. When he spoke, it was in a flat, deceptively calm manner. "Get out of here," he said, "or I'll call your editor."

Since I didn't want to get J. D. in trouble with the *Chron,* I went.

Back at my office at All Souls, I curled up in my ratty armchair—my favorite place to think. I considered my visit to All the Best People; I considered what was wrong with the setup there. Then I got out my list of burglary victims and called each of them. All three gave me similar answers to my questions. Next I checked the phone directory and called my friend Sandy in the billing office at Pacific Bell.

"I need an address for a company that's only listed by number in the directory," I told her.

"Billing address, or location where the phone's installed?"

"Both, if they're different."

She tapped away on her computer keyboard. "Billing and location are the same: two-eleven Gough. Need anything else?"

"That's it. Thanks—I owe you a drink."

In spite of my earlier determination to depart the singles scene, I spent the next few nights on the phone, this time assuming the name of Patsy Newhouse, my younger sister. I talked to various singles about my new VCR; I described the sapphire pendant my former boyfriend had given me and how I planned to have it reset to erase old memories. I babbled happily about the trip to Las Vegas I was taking in a few days with Weekenders, and promised to make notes in my pocket organizer to call people as soon as I got back. I mentioned—in seductive tones—how I loved to walk barefoot over my genuine Persian rugs. I praised the merits of my new microwave oven. I described how I'd gotten into collecting costly jade carvings. By the time the Weekenders trip was due to depart for Vegas, I was constantly sucking on throat lozenges and wondering how long my voice would hold out.

Saturday night found me sitting in my kitchen sharing ham sandwiches and coffee by candlelight with Dick Morris's security guard, Bert Jankowski. The only reason we'd chanced the candles was that we'd taped the shades securely over the windows. There was something about eating in total darkness that put us both off.

Bert was a pleasant-looking man of about my age, with sandy hair and a bristly mustache and a friendly, open face. We'd spent a lot of time together—Friday night, all day today—and I'd pretty much heard his life story. We had a lot in common: he was from Oceanside, not far from where I'd grown up in San Diego; like me, he had a degree in the social sciences and hadn't been able to get a job in his field. Unlike me, he'd been working for the security service so long that he was making a decent wage, and he liked it. It gave him more time, he said, to read and to fish. I'd told him life story, too: about my somewhat peculiar family, about my blighted romances, even about the man I'd once had to shoot. By Saturday night I sensed both of us were getting bored with examining our pasts, but the present situation was even more stultifying.

I said, "Something has *got* to happen soon."

Bert helped himself to another sandwich. "Not necessarily. Got any more of those pickles?"

"No, we're out."

"Shit. I don't suppose if this goes on that there's any possibility of cooking breakfast tomorrow? Sundays I always fix bacon."

In spite of my having wolfed down some ham, my mouth began to water. "No," I said wistfully. "Cooking smells, you know. This house is supposed to be vacant for the weekend."

"So far no one's come near it, and nobody seems to be casing it. Maybe you're wrong about the burglaries."

"Maybe ... No, I don't think so. Listen: Andie Wyatt went to Hawaii; she came back to a cleaned-out apartment. Janie Roos was in Carmel with a lover; she lost everything fenceable. Kim New was in Vegas, where I'm supposed to be—"

"But maybe you're wrong about the way the burglar knows—"

There was a noise toward the rear of the house, past the current construction zone on the back porch. I held up my hand for Bert to stop talking and blew out the candles.

I sensed Bert tensing. He reached for his gun at the same time I did mine.

The noise came louder—the sound of an implement probing the back-porch lock. It was one of those useless toy locks that had been there when I bought the cottage; I'd left the dead bolt unlocked since Friday.

Rattling sounds. A snap. The squeak of the door as it moved inward.

I touched Bert's arm. He moved over into the recess by the pantry, next to the light switch. I slipped up next to the door to the porch. The outer door shut, and footsteps came toward the kitchen, then stopped.

A thin beam of light showed under the inner door between the kitchen and the porch—the burglar's flashlight. I smiled, imagining his surprise at the sawhorses and wood scraps and exposed wiring that make up my own personal urban-renewal project.

The footsteps moved toward the kitchen door again. I took the safety off the .38.

The door swung toward me. A half-circle of light from the flash illuminated the blue linoleum. It swept back and forth, then up and around the room. The figure holding the flash seemed satisfied that the room was empty; it stepped inside and walked toward the hall.

Bert snapped on the overhead light.

I stepped forward, gun extended, and said, "All right, Jerry. Hands above your head and turn around—slowly."

The flash clattered to the floor. The figure—dressed all in black—did as I said.

But it wasn't Jerry.

It was Morton Stone—the nice, sad man I'd had the dinner date with. He looked as astonished as I felt.

I thought of the evening I'd spent with him, and my anger rose. All that sincere talk about how lonely he was and how much he missed his dead wife. And now he turned out to be a common crook!

"You son of a bitch!" I said. "And I was going to fix you up with one of my friends!"

He didn't say anything. His eyes were fixed nervously on my gun.

Another noise on the back porch. Morton opened his mouth, but I silenced him by raising the .38.

Footsteps clattered across the porch, and a second figure in black came through the door. "Morton, what's wrong? Why'd you turn the lights on?" a woman's voice demanded.

It was Marie, the receptionist from All the Best People. Now I knew how she could afford her expensive clothes.

"So I was right about *how* they knew when to burglarize people, but wrong about *who* was doing it," I told Hank. We were sitting at the bar in the Remedy Lounge, our favorite Mission Street watering hole.

"I'm still confused. The Intro Line is part of All the Best People?"

"It's owned by Jerry Hale, and the phone equipment is located in the same offices. But as Jerry—Dave Lester, whichever incarnation you prefer—told me later, he doesn't want the connection publicized because the Intro Line is kind of sleazy, and Best People's supposed to be high-toned. Anyway, I figured it out because I noticed there were an awful lot of phones ringing at their offices, considering their number isn't published. Later I confirmed it with the phone company and started using the line myself to set the burglar up."

"So this Jerry wasn't involved at all?"

"No. He's the genuine article—a born-again single who decided to put his knowledge to turning a profit."

Hank shuddered and took a sip of Scotch.

"The burglary scheme," I went on, "was all Marie Stone's idea. She had access to the addresses of the people who joined the Intro Line club, and she listened in on the phone conversations and scouted out good prospects. Then, when she was sure their homes would be vacant for a period of time, her brother, Morton Stone, pulled the job while she kept watch outside."

"How come you had a date with Marie's brother? Was he looking you over as a burglary prospect?"

"No. They didn't use All the Best People for that. It's Jerry's pride and joy; he's too involved with the day-to-day workings and might have realized something was wrong. But the Intro Line is just a profit-making arm of the business to him—he probably uses it to subsidize his dating. He'd virtually turned the operation of it over to Marie. But he did allow Marie to send out mail solicitations for it to Best People clients, as well as mentioning it to the women he 'screened,' and that's how the burglary victims heard of it."

"But it still seems too great a coincidence that you ended up going out with this Morton."

I smiled. "It wasn't a coincidence at all. Morton also works for Best People, helping Jerry screen the female clients. When I had my date with Jerry, he found me ... well, he said I was peculiar."

Hank grinned and started to say something, but I glared. "Anyway, he sent Mort out with me to render a second opinion"

"Ye gods, you were almost rejected by a dating service."

"What really pisses me off is Morton's grieving-widower story. I really fell for the whole tasteless thing. Jerry told me Morton gets a lot of women with it—they just can't resist a man in pain."

"But not McCone." Hank drained his glass and gestured at mine. "You want another?"

I looked at my watch. "Actually, I've got to be going."

"How come? It's early yet."

"Well, uh ... I have a date."

He raised his eyebrows. "I thought you were through with the singles scene. Which one is it tonight—the gun nut?"

I got off the bar stool and drew myself up in a dignified manner. "It's someone I met on my own. They always tell you that you meet the most compatible people when you're just doing what you like to do and not specifically looking."

"So where'd you meet this guy?"

"On a stakeout."

Hank waited. His eyes fairly bulged with curiosity.

I decided not to tantalize him any longer. I said, "It's Bert Jankowski, Dick Morris's security guard."

THE PLACE THAT TIME FORGOT

In San Francisco's Glen Park district there is a small building with the words GREENGLASS 5 & 10¢ STORE painted in faded red letters on its wooden facade. Broadleaf ivy grows in planter boxes below its windows and partially covers their dusty panes. Inside is a counter with jars of candy and bubble gum on top and cigars, cigarettes, and pipe tobacco down below. An old-fashioned jukebox—the kind with colored glass tubes—hulks against the opposite wall. The rest of the room is taken up by counters laden with merchandise that has been purchased at fire sales and manufacturers' liquidations. In a single shopping spree, it is possible for a customer to buy socks, playing cards, off-brand cosmetics, school supplies, kitchen utensils, sports equipment, toys and light bulbs—all at prices of at least ten years ago.

It is a place forgotten by time, a fragment of yesterday in the midst of today's city.

I have now come to know the curious little store well, but up until one rainy Wednesday last March, I'd done no more than glance inside while passing. But that morning Hank Zahn, my boss at All Souls Legal Cooperative, had asked me to pay a call on its owner, Jody Greenglass. Greenglass was a client who had asked if Hank knew an investigator who could trace a missing relative for him. It didn't sound like a particularly challenging assignment, but my assistant, who usually handles routine work, was out sick. So at ten o'clock, I put on my raincoat and went over there.

When I pushed open the door I saw there wasn't a customer in sight. The interior was gloomy and damp; a fly buzzed fitfully against one of the windows. I was about to call out, thinking the proprietor must be beyond the curtained doorway at the rear, when I realized a man was sitting on a stool behind the counter. That was all he was doing—just sitting, his eyes fixed on the wall above the jukebox.

He was a big man, elderly, with a belly that bulged out under his yellow shirt and black suspenders. His hair and beard were white and luxuriant, his eyebrows startlingly black by contrast. When I said, "Mr. Greenglass?" he looked at me, and I saw an expression of deep melancholy.

"Yes?" he asked politely.

"I'm Sharon McCone, from All Souls Legal Cooperative."

"Ah, yes. Mr. Zahn said he would send someone."

"I understand you want to locate a missing relative."

"My granddaughter."

"If you'll give me the particulars, I can get on it right away." I looked around for a place to sit, but didn't see any chair.

Greenglass stood. "I'll get you a stool." He went toward the curtained doorway, moving gingerly, as if his feet hurt him. They were encased in floppy slippers.

While I waited for him, I looked up at the wall behind the counter and saw it was plastered with faded pieces of slick paper that I first took to be playbills. Upon closer examination I realized they were sheet music, probably of forties and fifties vintage. Their artwork was of that era anyway: formally dressed couples performing intricate dance steps; showgirls in extravagant costumes; men with patent-leather hair singing their hearts out; perfectly coiffed women showing plenty of even, pearly white teeth. Some of the song titles were vaguely familiar to me: "Dreams of You," "The Heart Never Lies," "Sweet Mystique." Others I had never heard of.

Jody Greenglass came back with a wooden stool and set it on my side of the counter. I thanked him and perched on it, then took a pencil and notebook from my bag. He hoisted himself onto his own stool, sighing heavily.

"I see you were looking at my songs," he said.

"Yes. I haven't really seen any sheet music since my piano teacher gave up on me when I was about twelve. Some of those are pretty old, aren't they?"

"Not nearly as old as I am." He smiled wryly. "I wrote the first in thirty-nine, the last in fifty-three. Thirty-seven of them in all. A number were hits."

"*You* wrote them?"

He nodded and pointed to the credit line on the one closest to him: "Words and Music by Jody Greenglass."

"Well, for heaven's sake." I said. "I've never met a songwriter before. Were these recorded too?"

"Sure. I've got them all on the jukebox. Some good singers performed them—Como, Crosby." His smile faded. "But then, in the fifties, popular music changed. Presley, Holly, those fellows—that's what did it. I couldn't change with it. Luckily, I'd always had the store; music was more of a hobby for me. 'My Little Girl'"—he indicated a sheet with a picture-pretty toddler on it—"was the last song I ever sold. Wrote it for my granddaughter when she was born in fifty-three. It was *not* a big hit."

"This is the granddaughter you want me to locate?"

"Yes. Stephanie Ann Weiss. If she's still alive, she's thirty-seven now."

"Let's talk about her. I take it she's your daughter's daughter?"

"My daughter Ruth's. I only had the one child."

"Is your daughter still living?"

"I don't know." His eyes clouded. "There was a ... an estrangement. I lost track of both of them a couple of years after Stephanie was born."

"If it's not too painful, I'd like to hear about that."

"It's painful, but I can talk about it." He paused, thoughtful. "It's funny. For a long time it didn't hurt, because I had my anger and disappointment to shield myself. But those kinds of emotions can't last without fuel. Now that they're gone, I hurt as much as if it happened yesterday. That's what made me decide to try to make amends to my granddaughter."

"But not your daughter too?"

He made a hand motion as if to erase the memory of her. "Our parting was too bitter; there are some things that can't be atoned for, and frankly, I'm afraid to try. But Stephanie—if her mother hasn't completely turned her against me, there might be a chance for us."

"Tell me about this parting."

In a halting manner that conveyed exactly how deep his pain went, he related his story.

Jody Greenglass had been widowed when his daughter was only ten and had raised the girl alone. Shortly after Ruth graduated from high school, she married the boy next door. The Weiss family had lived in the house next to Greenglass's Glen Park cottage for close to twenty years, and their son, Eddie, and Ruth were such fast childhood friends that a gate was installed in the fence between their adjoining backyards. Jody, in fact, thought of Eddie as his own son.

After their wedding the couple moved north to the small town of Petaluma, where Eddie had found a good job in the accounting department of one of the big egg hatcheries. In 1953, Stephanie Ann was born. Greenglass didn't know exactly when or why they began having marital problems; perhaps they hadn't been ready for parenthood, or perhaps the move from the city to the country didn't suit them. But by 1955, Ruth had divorced Eddie and taken up with a Mexican national named Victor Rios.

"I like to think I'm not prejudiced," Greenglass said to me. "I've mellowed with the years, I've learned. But you've got to remember that this was the mid-fifties. Divorce wasn't all that common in my circle. And people didn't marry outside our faith, much less form relationships out of wedlock with those of a different race. Rios was an illiterate laborer, not even an American citizen. I was shocked that Ruth was living with this man, exposing her child to such a situation."

"So you tried to stop her."

He nodded wearily. "I tried. But Ruth wasn't listening to me anymore.

She'd always been such a good girl. Maybe that was the problem—she'd been *too* good and it was her time to rebel. We quarreled bitterly, more than once. Finally I told her that if she kept on living with Rios, she and her child would be dead to me. She said that was just fine with her. I never saw or heard from her again."

"Never made any effort to contact her?"

"Not until a couple of weeks ago. I nursed my anger and bitterness, nursed them well. But then in the fall I had some health problems—my heart—and realized I'd be leaving this world without once seeing my grown-up granddaughter. So when I was back on my feet again, I went up to Petaluma, checked the phone book, asked around their old neighborhood. Nobody remembered them. That was when I decided I needed a detective."

I was silent, thinking of the thirty-some years that had elapsed. Locating Stephanie Ann Weiss—or whatever name she might now be using—after all that time would be difficult. Difficult, but not impossible, given she was still alive. And certainly more challenging than the job I'd initially envisioned.

Greenglass seemed to interpret my silence as pessimism. He said, "I know it's been a very long time, but isn't there something you can do for me? I'm seventy-eight years old; I want to make amends before I die."

I felt the prickle of excitement that I often experience when faced with an out-of-the-ordinary problem. I said, "I'll try to help you. As I said before, I can get on it right away."

I gathered more information from him—exact spelling of names, dates—then asked for the last address he had for Ruth in Petaluma. He had to go in the back of the store where, he explained, he now lived, to look it up. While he did so, I wandered over to the jukebox and studied the titles of the 78s. There was a basket of metal slugs on top of the machine, and on a whim I fed it one and punched out selection E-3, "My Little Girl." The somewhat treacly lyrics boomed forth in a smarmy baritone; I could understand why the song hadn't gone over in the days when America was gearing up to feverishly embrace the likes of Elvis Presley. Still, I had to admit the melody was pleasing—downright catchy, in fact. By the time Greenglass returned with the address, I was humming along.

Back in my office at All Souls, I set a skiptrace in motion, starting with an inquiry to my friend Tracy at the Department of Motor Vehicles regarding Ruth Greenglass, Ruth Weiss, Ruth Rios, Stephanie Ann Rios, or any variant thereof. A check with directory assistance revealed that neither woman currently had a phone in Petaluma or the surrounding communities. The Petaluma Library had nothing on them in their reverse street directory. Since I didn't know either woman's occupation, professional affiliations, doctor, or dentist, those avenues were closed to me. Petaluma High School would not divulge information about graduates, but the woman in records with whom I spoke assured me that no one named Stephanie Weiss or Stephanie Rios had attended during the mid- to late-sixties. The county's voter registration had a similar lack of information. The next line of inquiry to pursue while waiting for a reply from the DMV was vital statistics—primarily marriage licenses and death certificates—but for those I would need to go to the Sonoma County Courthouse in Santa Rosa. I checked my watch, saw it was only a little after one, and decided to drive there.

Santa Rosa, some fifty miles north of San Francisco, is a former country town that has risen to the challenge of migrations from the crowded communities of the Bay Area and become a full-fledged city with a population nearing a hundred thousand. Testimony to this is the new County Administration Center on its outskirts, where I found the Recorder's Office housed in a building on the aptly named Fiscal Drive.

My hour-and-a-half journey up there proved well worth the time: the clerk I dealt with was extremely helpful, the records easily accessed. Within half an hour, for a nominal fee, I was in possession of a copy of Ruth Greenglass Weiss's death certificate. She had died of cancer at Petaluma General Hospital in June of 1974; her next of kin was shown as Stephanie Ann Weiss, at an address on Bassett Street in Petaluma. It was a different address from the last one Greenglass had had for them.

The melody of "My Little Girl" was still running through my head as I drove back down the freeway to Petaluma, the southernmost community in the county. A picturesque river town with a core of nineteenth-century business buildings, Victorian homes, and a park with a bandstand, it is surrounded by little hills—which is what the Indian word *Petaluma* means. The town used to be called the Egg Basket of the World, because of the proliferation of hatcheries such as the one where Eddie Weiss worked, but since the decline of the egg- and chicken-ranching business, it has become a trendy retreat for those seeking to avoid the high housing costs of San Francisco and Marin. I had friends there—people who had moved up from the city for just that reason—so I knew the lay of the land fairly well.

Bassett Street was on the older west side of town, far from the bland, treeless tracts that have sprung up to the east. The address I was seeking turned out to be a small white frame bungalow with a row of lilac bushes planted along the property line on either side. Their branches hung heavy with as yet unopened blossoms; in a few weeks the air would be sweet with their perfume.

When I went up on the front porch and rang the bell, I was greeted by a very pregnant young woman. Her name, she said, was Bonita Clark; she and her husband Russ had bought the house two years before from some people named Berry. The Berrys had lived there for at least ten years and had never mentioned anyone named Weiss.

I hadn't really expected to find Stephanie Weiss still in residence, but I'd hoped the present owner could tell me where she had moved. I said, "Do you know anyone on the street who might have lived here in the early seventies?"

"Well, there's old Mrs. Caubet. The pink house on the corner with all the rosebushes. She's lived here forever."

I thanked her and went down the sidewalk to the house she'd indicated. Its front yard was a thicket of rosebushes whose colors ranged from yellows to reds to a particularly beautiful silvery purple. The rain had stopped before I'd reached town, but not all that long ago; the roses' velvety petals were beaded with droplets.

Mrs. Caubet turned out to be a tall, slender woman with sleek gray hair, vigorous-looking in a blue sweatsuit and athletic shoes. I felt a flicker of amusement when I first saw her, thinking of how Bonita Clark had called her "old," said she'd lived there "forever." Interesting, I thought, how one's perspective shifts....

Yes, Mrs. Caubet said after she'd examined my credentials, she remembered the Weisses well. They'd moved to Bassett Street in 1970. "Ruth was already ill with the cancer that killed her," she added. "Steff was only seventeen, but so grown-up, the way she took care of her mother."

"Did either of them ever mention a man named Victor Rios?"

The woman's expression became guarded. "You say you're working for Ruth's father?"

"Yes."

She looked thoughtful, then motioned at a pair of white wicker chairs on the wraparound porch. "Let's sit down."

We sat. Mrs. Caubet continued to look thoughtful, pleating the ribbing on the cuff of her sleeve between her fingers. I waited.

After a time she said, "I wondered if Ruth's father would ever regret disowning her."

"He's in poor health. It's made him realize he doesn't have much longer to make amends."

"A pity that it took until now. He's missed a great deal because of his stubbornness. I know; I'm a grandparent myself. And I'd like to put him in touch with Steff, but I don't know what happened to her. She left

Petaluma six months after Ruth died."

"Did she say where she planned to go?"

"Just something about getting in touch with relatives. By that I assumed she meant her father's family in the city. She promised to write, but she never did, not even a Christmas card."

"Will you tell me what you remember about Ruth and Stephanie? It may give me some sort of lead, and besides, I'm sure my client will want to know about their lives after his falling-out with Ruth."

She shrugged. "It can't hurt. And to answer your earlier question, I have heard of Victor Rios. He was Ruth's second husband; although the marriage was a fairly long one, it was not a particularly good one. When she was diagnosed as having cancer, Rios couldn't deal with her illness, and he left her. Ruth divorced him, took back her first husband's name. It was either that, she once told me, or Greenglass, and she was even more bitter toward her father than toward Rios."

"After Victor Rios left, what did Ruth and Stephanie live on? I assume Ruth couldn't work."

"She had some savings—and, I suppose, alimony."

"It couldn't have been much. Jody Greenglass told me Rios was an illiterate laborer."

Mrs. Caubet frowned. "That's nonsense! He must have manufactured the idea, out of prejudice and anger at Ruth for leaving her first husband. He considered Eddie Weiss a son you know. It's true that when Ruth met Rios, he didn't have as good a command of the English language as he might, but he did have a good job at Sunset Line and Twine. They weren't rich, but I gather they never lacked for the essentials."

It made me wonder what else Greenglass had manufactured. "Did Ruth ever admit to living with Rios before their marriage?"

"No, but it wouldn't have surprised me. She always struck me as a nonconformist. And that, of course, would better explain her father's attitude."

"One other thing puzzles me," I said. "I checked with the high school, and they have no record of Stephanie attending."

"That's because she went to parochial school. Rios was Catholic, and that's what he wanted. Ruth didn't care either way. As it was, Steff dropped out in her junior year to care for her mother. I offered to arrange home care so she might finish her education—I was once a social worker and know how to go about it—but Steff said no. The only thing she really missed about school, she claimed, was choir and music class. She had a beautiful singing voice."

So she'd inherited her grandfather's talent, I thought. A talent I was coming to regard as considerable, since I still couldn't shake the lingering melody of "My Little Girl."

"How did Stephanie feel about her grandfather? And Victor Rios?" I asked.

"I think she was fond of Rios, in spite of what he'd done to her mother. Her feelings toward her grandfather I'm less sure of. I do remember that toward the end Steff had become very like her mother; observing that alarmed me somewhat."

"Why?"

"Ruth was a very bitter woman, totally turned in on herself. She had no real friends, and she seemed to want to draw Steff into a little circle from which the two of them could fend off the world together. By the time Steff left Petaluma she'd closed off, too, withdrawn from what few friends she'd been permitted. I'd say such bitterness in so young a woman is cause for alarm, wouldn't you?"

"I certainly would. And I suspect that if I do find her, it's going to be very hard to persuade her to reconcile with her grandfather."

Mrs. Caubet was silent for a moment, then said, "She might surprise you."

"Why do you say that?"

"It's just a feeling I have. There was a song Mr. Greenglass wrote in celebration of Steff's birth. Do you know about it?"

I nodded.

"They had a record of it. Ruth once told me that it was the only thing he'd ever given them, and she couldn't bear to take that away from Steff. Anyway, she used to play it occasionally. Sometimes I'd go over there, and Steff would be humming the melody while she worked around the house."

That didn't mean much, I thought. After all, I'd been mentally humming it since that morning.

When I arrived back in the city I first checked at All Souls to see if there had been a response to my inquiry from my friend at the DMV. There hadn't. Then I headed for Glen Park to break the news about his daughter's death to Jody Greenglass, as well as to get some additional information.

This time there were a few customers in the store: a young couple poking around in Housewares; an older woman selecting some knitting yarn. Greenglass sat at his customary position behind the counter. When I gave him the copy of Ruth's death certificate, he read it slowly, then folded it carefully and placed it in his shirt pocket. His lips trembled inside their nest of fluffy white beard, but otherwise he betrayed no emotion. He said, "I take it you didn't find Stephanie Ann at that address."

"She left Petaluma about six months after Ruth died. A neighbor thought she might have planned to go to relatives. Would that be the Weisses, do you suppose?"

He shook his head. "Norma and Al died within months of each other in the mid-sixties. They had a daughter, name of Sandra, but she married and moved away before Eddie and Ruth did. To Los Angeles, I think. I've no idea what her husband's name might be."

"What about Eddie Weiss—what happened to him?"

"I didn't tell you?"

"No."

"He died a few months after Ruth divorced him. Auto accident. He'd been drinking. Damned near killed his parents, following so close on the divorce. That was when Norma and Al stopped talking to me; I guess they blamed Ruth. Things got so uncomfortable there on the old street that I decided to come to live here at the store."

The customer who had been looking at yarn came up, her arms piled high with heather-blue skeins. I stepped aside so Greenglass could ring up the sale, glanced over my shoulder at the jukebox, then went up to it and played "My Little Girl" again. As the mellow notes poured from the machine, I realized that what had been running through my head all day was not quite the same. Close, very close, but there were subtle differences.

And come to think of it, why should the song have made such an impression, when I'd only heard it once? It was catchy, but there was no reason for it to haunt me as it did.

Unless I'd heard something like it. Heard it more than once. And recently ...

I went around the counter and asked Greenglass if I could use his phone. Dialed the familiar number of radio KSUN, the Light of the Bay. My former lover, Don Del Boccio, had just come into the studio for his six-to-midnight stint as disc jockey, heartthrob, and hero to half a million teenagers who have to be either hearing-impaired or brain-damaged, and probably both. Don said he'd be glad to provide expert assistance, but not until he got off work. Why didn't I meet him at his loft around twelve-thirty?

I said I would and hung up, thanking the Lord that I somehow managed to remain on mostly good terms with the men from whom I've parted.

Don said, "Hum it again."

"You know I'm tone-deaf."

"You have no vocal capabilities. You can distinguish tone, though. And I can interpret your warbling. Hum it."

We were seated in his big loft in the industrial district off Third Street, surrounded by his baby grand piano, drums, sound equipment, books, and—a recent acquisition—a huge aquarium of tropical fish. I'd taken a nap after going home from Greenglass's and felt reasonably fresh. Don—a big, easygoing man who enjoys his minor celebrity status and also keeps up his serious musical interests—was reasonably wired. We were drinking red wine and picking at a plate of antipasto he'd casually thrown together.

"Hum it," he said again.

I hummed, badly, my face growing hot as I listened to myself.

He imitated me—on key. "It's definitely not rock, not with that tempo. Soft rock? Possibly. There's something about it ... that sextolet—"

"That what?"

"An irregular rhythmic grouping. One of the things that makes it stick in your mind. Folk? Maybe country. You say you think you've been hearing it recently?"

"That's the only explanation I can come up with for it sticking in my mind the way it has."

"Hmm. There's been some new stuff coming along recently, out of L.A. rather than Nashville, that might ...You listen to a country station?"

"KNEW, when I'm driving sometimes."

"Disloyal thing."

"I never listened to KSUN much, even when we ..."

Our eyes met and held. We were both remembering, but I doubted if the mental images were the same. Don and I are too different; that was what ultimately broke us up.

After a moment he grinned and said, "Well, no one over the mental age of twelve does. Listen, what I guess is that you've been hearing a song that's a variation on the melody of the original one: which is odd, because it's an uncommon one to begin with."

"Unless the person who wrote the new song knew the old one."

"Which you tell me isn't likely, since it wasn't very popular. What is it you're investigating—a plagiarism case?"

I shook my head. If Jody Greenglass's last song had been plagiarized, I doubted it was intentional—at least not on the conscious level. I said, "Is it possible to track down the song, do you suppose?"

"Sure. Care to run over to the studio? I can do a scan on our library, see what we've got."

"But KSUN doesn't play anything except hard rock."

"No, but we get all sorts of promos, new releases. Let's give it a try."

"There you are," Don said. "'It Never Stops Hurting.' Steff Rivers. Atlas

Records. Released last November."

I remembered it now, half heard as I'd driven the city streets with my old MG's radio tuned low. Understandable that for her professional name she'd Anglicized that of the only father figure she'd ever known.

"Play it again," I said.

Don pressed the button on the console and the song flooded the sound booth, the woman's voice soaring and clean. The lyrics were about grieving for a lost lover, but I thought I knew other experiences that had gone into creating the naked emotion behind them: the scarcely known father who had died after the mother left him; the grandfather who had rejected both mother and child; the stepfather who had been unable to cope with fatal illness and had run away.

When the song ended and silence filled the little booth, I said to Don, "How would I go about locating her?"

He grinned. "One of the Atlas reps just happens to be a good friend of mine. I'll give her a call in the morning, see what I can do."

The rain started again early the next morning. It made the coastal road that wound north on the high cliffs above the Pacific highway dangerously slick. By the time I arrived at the village of Gualala, just over the Mendocino County line, it was close to three and the cloud cover was beginning to break up.

The town, I found, was just a strip of homes and businesses between the densely forested hills and the sea. A few small shopping centers, some unpretentious eateries, the ubiquitous realty offices, a new motel, and a hotel built during the logging boom of the late 1800s—that was about it. It would be an ideal place, I thought, for retirees or starving artists, as well as a young woman seeking frequent escape from the pressures of a career in the entertainment industry.

Don's record-company friend had checked with someone she knew in Steff Rivers's producer's office to find out her present whereabouts, had sworn me to secrecy about where I'd received the information and given me an address. I'd pinpointed the turnoff from the main highway on a county map. It was a small lane that curved off toward the sea about a half mile north of town; the house at its end was actually a pair of A frames, weathered gray shingle, connected by a glassed-in walkway. Hydrangeas and geraniums bloomed in tubs on either side of the front door; a stained glass oval depicting a sea gull in flight hung in the window. I left the MG next to a gold Toyota sports car parked in the drive.

There was no answer to my knock. After a minute I skirted the house and went around back. The lawn there was weedy and uneven; it sloped down toward a low grapestake fence that guarded the edge of the ice-plant-covered bluff. On a bench in front of it sat a small figure wearing a red rain slicker, the hood turned up against the fine mist. The person was motionless, staring out at the flat, gray ocean.

When I started across the lawn, the figure turned. I recognized Steff Rivers from the publicity photo Don had dug out of KSUN's files the night before. Her hair was black and cut very short, molded to her head like a bathing cap; her eyes were large, long-lashed, and darkly luminous. In her strong features I saw traces of Jody Greenglass's.

She called out, "Be careful there. Some damn rodent has dug the yard up."

I walked cautiously the rest of the way to the bench.

"I don't know what's wrong with it," she said, gesturing at a hot tub on a deck opening off the glassed-in walkway of the house. "All I can figure is something's plugging the drain."

"I'm sorry?"

"Aren't you the plumber?"

"No."

"Oh. I knew she was a woman, and I thought ... Who are you then?"

I took out my identification and showed it to her. Told her why I was there.

Steff Rivers seemed to shrink inside her loose slicker. She drew her knees up and hugged them with her arms.

"He needs to see you," I concluded. "He wants to make amends."

She shook her head. "It's too late for that."

"Maybe. But he *is* sincere."

"Too bad." She was silent for a moment, turning her gaze back toward the sea. "How did you find me? Atlas and my agent know better than to give out this address."

"Once I knew Stephanie Weiss was Steff Rivers, it was easy."

"And how did you find *that* out?"

"The first clue I had was 'It Never Stops Hurting.' You adapted the melody of 'My Little Girl' for it."

"I what?" She turned her head toward me, features frozen in surprise. Then she was very still, seeming to listen to the song inside her head. "I guess I did. My God ... I *did.*"

"You didn't do it consciously?"

"No. I haven't thought of that song in years. I ... I broke the only copy of the record that I had the day my mother died." After a moment she added, "I suppose the son of a bitch will want to sue me."

"You know that's not so." I sat down beside her on the wet bench, turned my collar up against the mist. "The lyrics of that song say a lot about you, you know."

"Yeah—that everybody's left me or fucked me over as long as I've lived."

"Your grandfather wants to change that pattern. He wants to come back to you."

"Well, he can't. I don't want him."

A good deal of her toughness was probably real—would have to be, in order for her to survive in her business—but I sensed some of it was armor that she could don quickly whenever anything threatened the vulnerable core of her persona. I remained silent for a few minutes, wondering how to get through to her, watching the waves ebb and flow on the beach at the foot of the cliff. Eroding the land, giving some of it back again. Take and give, take and give ...

Finally I asked, "Why were you sitting out here in the rain?"

"They said it would clear around three. I was just waiting. Waiting for something good to happen."

"A lot of good things must happen to you. Your career's going well. This is a lovely house, a great place to escape to."

"Yeah, I've done all right. 'It Never Stops Hurting' wasn't my first hit, you know."

"Do you remember a neighbor of yours in Petaluma—a Mrs. Caubet?"

"God! I haven't thought of her in years either. How is she?"

"She's fine. I talked with her yesterday. She mentioned your talent."

"Mrs. Caubet. Petaluma. That all seems so long ago."

"Where did you go after you left there?"

"To my Aunt Sandra, in L.A. She was married to a record-company flack. It made breaking in a little easier."

"And then?"

"Sandra died of a drug overdose. She found out that the bastard she was married to had someone else."

"What did you do then?"

"What do you think? Kept on singing and writing songs. Got married."

"And?"

"What the hell is this and-and-and? Why am I even talking to you?"

I didn't reply.

"All right. Maybe I need to talk to somebody. That didn't work out—the marriage, I mean—and neither did the next one. Or about a dozen other relationships. But things just kept clicking along with my career. The money kept coming in. One weekend a few years ago I was up here visiting friends at Sea Ranch. I saw this place while we were just driving around, and ... now I live here when I don't have to be in L.A. Alone. Secure. Happy."

"Happy, Steff?"

"Enough." She paused, arms tightening around her drawn-up knees. "Actually, I don't think much about being happy anymore."

"You're a lot like your grandfather."

She rolled her eyes. "Here we go again!"

"I mean it. You know how he lives? Alone in the back of his store. He doesn't think much about being happy either."

"He still has that store?"

"Yes." I described it, concluding, "It's a place that's just been forgotten by time. *He's* been forgotten. When he dies there won't be anybody to care—unless you do something to change that."

"Well, it's too bad about him, but in a way he had it coming."

"You're pretty bitter toward someone you don't even know."

"Oh, I know enough about him. Mama saw to that. You think *I'm* bitter? You should have known her. She'd been thrown out by her own father, had two rotten marriages, and then she got cancer. Mama was a very bitter, angry woman."

I didn't say anything, just looked out at the faint sheen of the sunlight that had appeared on the gray water.

Steff seemed to be listening to what she'd just said. "I'm turning out exactly like my mother, aren't I?"

"It's a danger."

"I don't seem to be able to help it. I mean, it's all there in that song. It never *does* stop hurting."

"No, but some things can ease the pain."

"The store—it's in the Glen Park district, isn't it?"

"Yes. Why?"

"I get down to the city occasionally."

"How soon can you be packed?"

She looked over her shoulder at the house, where she had been secure in her loneliness. "I'm not ready for that yet."

"You'll never be ready. I'll drive you, go to the store with you. If it doesn't work out, I'll bring you right back here."

"Why are you doing this? I'm a total stranger. Why didn't you just turn my address over to my grandfather, let him take it from there?"

"Because you have a right to refuse comfort and happiness. We all have that."

Steff Rivers tried to glare at me but couldn't quite manage it. Finally— as a patch of blue sky appeared offshore and the sea began to glimmer in the sun's rays—she unwrapped her arms from her knees and stood.

"I'll go get my stuff," she said.

SOMEWHERE IN THE CITY

At 5:04 p. m. on October 17, 1989, the city of San Francisco was jolted by an earthquake that measured a frightening 7.1 on the Richter Scale. The violent tremors left the Bay Bridge impassable, collapsed a double-decker freeway in nearby Oakland, and toppled or severely damaged countless homes and other buildings. From the Bay Area to the seaside town of Santa Cruz some 100 miles south, 65 people were killed and thousands left homeless. And when the aftershocks subsided, San Francisco entered a new era—one in which things would never be quite the same. As with all cataclysmic events, the question "Where were you when?" will forever provoke deeply emotional responses in those of us who lived through it ....

WHERE I WAS WHEN: the headquarters of the Golden Gate Crisis Hotline in the Noe Valley district. I'd been working a case there—off and on, and mostly in the late afternoon and evening hours, for over two weeks—with very few results and with a good deal of frustration.

The hotline occupied one big windowless room behind a rundown coffeehouse on Twenty-fourth Street. The location, I'd been told, was not so much one of choice as of convenience (meaning the rent was affordable), but had I not known that, I would have considered it a stroke of genius. There was something instantly soothing about entering through the coffeehouse, where the aromas of various blends permeated the air and steam rose from huge stainless-steel urns. The patrons were unthreatening—mostly shabby and relaxed, reading or conversing with their feet propped up on chairs. The pastries displayed in the glass case were comfort food at its purest—reminders of the days when calories and cholesterol didn't count. And the round face of the proprietor, Lloyd Warner, was welcoming and kind as he waved troubled visitors through to the crisis center.

On that Tuesday afternoon I arrived at about twenty to five, answering Lloyd's cheerful greeting and trying to ignore the chocolate-covered doughnuts in the case. I had a dinner date at seven-thirty, had been promised some of the best French cuisine on Russian Hill, and was unwilling to spoil my appetite. The doughnuts called out to me, but I turned a deaf ear and hurried past.

The room beyond the coffeehouse contained an assortment of mismatched furniture: several desks and chairs of all vintages and materials; phones in colors and styles ranging from standard black touchtone to a shocking turquoise princess; three tattered easy chairs dating back to the fifties; and a card table covered with literature on health and psychological services. Two people manned the desks nearest the door. I went to the desk with the turquoise phone, plunked my briefcase and bag down on it, and turned to face them.

"He call today?" I asked.

Pete Lowry, a slender man with a bandit's mustache who was director of the center, took his booted feet off the desk and swiveled to face me. "Nope. It's been quiet all afternoon."

"Too quiet." This came from Ann Potter, a woman with dark frizzed hair who affected the aging-hippie look in jeans and flamboyant overblouses. "And this weather—I don't like it one bit."

"Ann's having one of her premonitions of gloom and doom," Pete said. "Evil portents and omens lurk all around us—although most of them went up front for coffee a while ago."

Ann's eyes narrowed to a glare. She possessed very little sense of humor, whereas Pete perhaps possessed too much. To forestall the inevitable spat, I interrupted. "Well, I don't like the weather much myself. It's muggy and too warm for October. It makes me nervous."

"Why?" Pete asked.

I shrugged. "I don't know, but I've felt edgy all day."

The phone on his desk rang. He reached for the receiver. "Golden Gate Crisis Hotline, Pete speaking."

Ann cast one final glare at his back as she crossed to the desk that had been assigned to me. "It has been too quiet," she said defensively. "Hardly anyone's called, not even to inquire about how to deal with a friend or a family member. That's not normal, even for a Tuesday."

"Maybe all the crazies are out enjoying the warm weather."

Ann half-smiled, cocking her head. She wasn't sure if what I'd said was funny or not, and didn't know how to react. After a few seconds her attention was drawn to the file I was removing from my briefcase. "Is that about our problem caller?"

"Uh-huh." I sat down and began rereading my notes silently, hoping she'd go away. I'd meant it when I'd said I felt on edge, and was in no mood for conversation.

The file concerned a series of calls that the hotline had received over the past month—all from the same individual, a man with a distinctive raspy voice. Their content had been more or less the same: an initial plaint of being all alone in the world with no one to care if he lived or died; then a gradual escalating from despair to anger, in spite of the trained counselors' skillful responses; and finally the declaration that he had an assault rifle and was going to kill others and himself. He always ended with some variant on the statement, "I'm going to take a whole lot of people with me."

After three of the calls, Pete had decided to notify the police. A trace was placed on the center's lines, but the results were unsatisfactory; most of the time the caller didn't stay on the phone long enough, and in the instances that the calls could be traced, they turned out to have originated from booths in the Marina district. Finally, the trace was taken off, the official conclusion being that the calls were the work of a crank—and possibly one with a grudge against someone connected with the hotline.

The official conclusion did not satisfy Pete, however. By the next morning he was in the office of the hotline's attorney at All Souls Legal Cooperative, where I am chief investigator. And a half an hour after that, I was assigned to work the phones at the hotline as often as my other duties permitted, until I'd identified the caller. Following a crash course from Pete in techniques for dealing with callers in crisis—augmented by some reading of my own—they turned me loose on the turquoise phone.

After the first couple of rocky, sweaty-palmed sessions, I'd gotten into it: become able to distinguish the truly disturbed from the fakers or the merely curious; learned to gauge the responses that would work best with a given individual; succeeded at eliciting information that would permit a crisis team to go out and assess the seriousness of the situation in person. In most cases, the team would merely talk the caller into getting counseling. However, if they felt immediate action was warranted, they would contact the SFPD, who had the authority to have the individual held for evaluation at S. F. General Hospital for up to seventy-two hours.

During the past two weeks the problem caller had been routed to me several times, and with each conversation I became more concerned about him. While his threats were melodramatic, I sensed genuine disturbance and desperation in his voice; the swift escalation of panic and anger seemed much out of proportion to whatever verbal stimuli I offered. And, as Pete had stressed in my orientation, no matter how theatrical or frequently made, any threat of suicide or violence toward others was to be taken with the utmost seriousness by the hotline volunteers.

Unfortunately I was able to glean very little information from the man. Whenever I tried to get him to reveal concrete facts about himself, he became sly and would dodge my questions. Still, I could make several assumptions about him: he was youngish, reasonably well-educated, and Caucasian. The traces to the Marina indicated he probably lived in that bayside district—which meant he had to have a good income. He listened to classical music (three times I'd heard it playing in the background) from a transistor radio, by the tinny tonal quality. Once I'd caught the call letters of the FM station—one with a wide-range signal in the Central Valley town of Fresno. Why Fresno? I'd wondered. Perhaps he was from there? But that wasn't much to go on; there were probably several Fresno transplants in his part of the city.

When I looked up from my folder, Ann had gone back to her desk. Pete was still talking in low, reassuring tones with his caller. Ann's phone rang, and she picked up the receiver. I tensed, knowing the next call would cycle automatically to my phone.

When it rang some minutes later, I glanced at my watch and jotted down the time while reaching over for the receiver. Four-fifty-eight. "Golden Gate Crisis Hotline, Sharon speaking."

The caller hung up—either a wrong number or, more likely, someone who lost his nerve. The phone rang again about twenty seconds later and I answered it in the same manner.

"Sharon. It's me." The greeting was the same as the previous times, the raspy voice unmistakable.

"Hey, how's it going?"

A long pause, labored breathing. In the background I could make out the strains of music—Brahms, I thought. "Not so good. I'm really down today."

"You want to talk about it?"

"There isn't much to say. Just more of the same. I took a walk a while ago, thought it might help. But the people, out there flying their kites, I can't take it."

"Why is that?"

"I used to ... ah, forget it."

"No, I'm interested."

"Well, they're always in couples, you know."

When he didn't go on, I made an interrogatory sound.

"The whole damn world is in couples. Or families. Even here inside my little cottage I can feel it. There are these apartment buildings on either side, and I can feel them pressing in on me, and I'm here all alone."

He was speaking rapidly now, his voice rising. But as his agitation increased, he'd unwittingly revealed something about his living situation. I made a note about the little cottage between the two apartment buildings.

"This place where the people were flying kites," I said, "do you go there often?"

"Sure—it's only two blocks away." A sudden note of sullenness now entered his voice—a part of the pattern he'd previously exhibited. "Why do you want to know about that?"

"Because ... I'm sorry, I forgot your name."

No response.

"It would help if I knew what to call you."

"Look, bitch, I know what you're trying to do."

"Oh?"

"Yeah. You want to get a name, an address. Send the cops out. Next thing I'm chained to the wall at S. F. General. I've been that route before. But I know my rights now; I went down the street to the Legal Switchboard, and they told me ..."

I was distracted from what he was saying by a tapping sound—the stack trays on the desk next to me bumped against the wall. I looked over there, frowning. What was causing that ... ?

"... gonna take the people next door with me ..."

I looked back at the desk in front of me. The lamp was jiggling.

"What the hell?" the man on the phone exclaimed.

My swivel chair shifted. A coffee mug tipped and rolled across the desk and into my lap.

Pete said, "Jesus Christ, we're having and earthquake!"

"... The ceiling's coming down!" The man's voice was panicked now.

"Get under a door frame!" I clutched the edge of the desk, ignoring my own advice.

I heard a crash from the other end of the line. The man screamed in pain. "Help me! Please help—" And then the line went dead.

For a second or so I merely sat there—longtime San Franciscan, frozen by my own disbelief. All around me formerly inanimate objects were in motion. Pete and Ann were scrambling for the archway that led to the door of the coffeehouse.

"Sharon, get under the desk!" she yelled at me.

And then the electricity cut out, leaving the windowless room in blackness. I dropped the dead receiver, slid off the chair, crawled into the kneehole of the desk. There was a cracking, a violent shifting, as if a giant hand had seized the building and twisted it. Tremors buckled the floor beneath me.

This is a bad one. Maybe the big one that they're always talking about.

The sound of something wrenching apart. Pellets of plaster rained down on the desk above me. Time had telescoped; it seemed as if the quake had been going on for many minutes, when in reality it could not have been more than ten or fifteen seconds.

Make it stop! Please make it stop!

And then, as if whatever powers-that-be had heard my unspoken plea, the shock waves diminished to shivers, and finally ebbed.

Blackness. Silence. Only bits of plaster bouncing off the desks and the floor.

"Ann?" I said. "Pete?" My voice sounded weak, tentative.

"Sharon?" It was Pete. "You okay?"

"Yes. You?"

"We're fine."

Slowly I began to back out of the kneehole. Something blocked it— the chair. I shoved it aside, and emerged. I couldn't see a thing, but I could feel fragments of plaster and other unidentified debris on the floor. Something cut into my palm; I winced.

"God, it's dark," Ann said. "I've got some matches in my purse. Can you—"

"No matches," I told her. "Who knows what shape the gas mains are in."

"... Oh, right."

Pete said, "Wait, I'll open the door to the coffeehouse."

On hands and knees I began feeling my way toward the sound of their voices. I banged into one of the desks, overturned a wastebasket, then finally reached the opposite wall. As I stood there, Ann's cold hand reached out to guide me. Behind her I could hear Pete fumbling at the door.

I leaned against the wall. Ann was close beside me, her breathing erratic. Pete said, "Goddamned door's jammed." From behind it came voices of the people in the coffeehouse.

Now that the danger was over—at least until the first of the aftershocks—my body sagged against the wall, giving way to tremors of its own manufacture. My thoughts turned to the lover with whom I'd planned to have dinner: where had he been when the quake hit? And what about my cats, my house? My friends and my co-workers at All Souls? Other friends scattered throughout the Bay Area?

And what about a nameless, faceless man somewhere in the city who had screamed for help before the phone went dead?

The door to the coffeehouse burst open, spilling weak light into the room. Lloyd Warner and several of his customers peered anxiously through it. I prodded Ann—who seemed to have lapsed into lethargy—toward them.

The coffeehouse was fairly dark, but late afternoon light showed beyond the plate-glass windows fronting on the street. It revealed a floor that was awash in spilled liquid and littered with broken crockery. Chairs were tipped over—whether by the quake or the patrons' haste to get to shelter I couldn't tell. About ten people milled about, talking noisily.

Ann and Pete joined them, but I moved forward to the window. Outside, Twenty-fourth Street looked much as usual, except for the lack of traffic and pedestrians. The buildings still stood, the sun still shone, the air drifting through the open door of the coffeehouse was still warm and muggy. In this part of the city, at least, life went on.

Lloyd's transistor radio had been playing the whole time—tuned to the station that was carrying the coverage of the third game of the Bay Area World Series, due to start at five-thirty. I moved closer, listening.

The sportscaster was saying, "Nobody here knows *what's* going on. The Giants have wandered over to the A's dugout. It looks like a softball game where somebody forgot to bring the ball."

Then the broadcast shifted abruptly to the station's studios. A newswoman was relaying telephone reports from the neighborhoods. I was relieved to hear that Bernal Heights, where All Souls is located, and my own small district near Glen Park were shaken up but for the most part undamaged. The broadcaster concluded by warning listeners not to use their phones except in cases of emergency. Ann snorted and said, "Do as I say but not ..."

Again the broadcast made an abrupt switch—to the station's traffic helicopter. "From where we are," the reporter said, "it looks as if part of the upper deck on the Oakland side of the Bay Bridge has collapsed onto the bottom deck. Cars are pointing every whichway, there may be some in the water. And on the approaches—" The transmission broke, then resumed after a number of static-filled seconds. "It looks as if the Cypress Structure on the Oakland approach to the bridge has also collapsed. Oh my God, there are cars and people—" This time the transmission broke for good.

It was very quiet in the coffeehouse. We all exchanged looks—fearful, horrified. This was an extremely bad one, if not the catastrophic one they'd been predicting for so long.

Lloyd was the first to speak. He said, "I'd better see if I can insulate the urns in some way, keep the coffee hot as long as possible. People'll need it tonight." He went behind the counter, and in a few seconds a couple of the customers followed.

The studio newscast resumed. "... fires burning out of control in the Marina district. We're receiving reports of collapsed buildings there, with people trapped inside ..."

The Marina district. People trapped.

I thought again of the man who had cried out for help over the phone. Of my suspicion, more or less confirmed by today's conversation, that he lived in the Marina.

Behind the counter Lloyd and the customers were wrapping the urns in dishtowels. Here—and in other parts of the city, I was sure—people were already overcoming their shock, gearing up to assist in the relief effort. There was nothing I could do in my present surroundings, but ...

I hurried to the back room and groped until I found my purse on the floor beside the desk. As I picked it up, an aftershock hit—nothing like the original trembler, but strong enough to make me grab the chair for support. When it stopped, I went shakily out to my car.

Twenty-fourth Street was slowly coming to life. People bunched on the sidewalks, talking and gesturing. A man emerged from one of the shops, walked to the center of the street and surveyed the facade of his building. In the parking lot of nearby Bell Market, employees and customers gathered by the grocery carts. A man in a butcher's apron looked around, shrugged, and headed for a corner tavern. I got into my MG and took a city map from the side pocket.

The Marina area consists mainly of early twentieth-century stucco homes and apartment buildings built on fill on the shore of the bay—which meant the quake damage there would naturally be bad. The district extends roughly from the Fisherman's Wharf area to the Presidio—not large, but large enough, considering I had few clues as to where within its boundary my man lived. I spread out the map against the steering wheel and examined it.

The man had said he'd taken a walk that afternoon, to a place two blocks from his home where people were flying kites. That would be the Marina Green near the Yacht Harbor, famous for the elaborate and often fantastical kites flown there in fine weather. Two blocks placed the man's home somewhere on the far side of Northpoint Street.

I had one more clue: in his anger at me he'd let it slip that the Legal Switchboard was "down the street." The switchboard, a federally-funded assistance group, was headquartered in one of the piers at Fort Mason, at the east end of the Marina. While several streets in that vicinity ended at Fort Mason, I saw that only two—Beach and Northpoint—were within two blocks of the Green as well.

Of course, I reminded myself, "down the street" and "two blocks" could have been generalizations or exaggerations. But it was somewhere to start. I set the map aside and turned the key in the ignition.

The trip across the city was hampered by near-gridlock traffic on some streets. All the stoplights were out; there were no police to direct the panicked motorists. Citizens helped out: I saw men in three-piece suits, women in heels and business attire, even a ragged man who looked to be straight out of one of the homeless shelters, all playing traffic cop. Sirens keened, emergency vehicles snaked from lane to lane. The car radio kept reporting further destruction; there was another aftershock, and then another, but I scarcely felt them because I was in motion.

As I inched along a major crosstown arterial, I asked myself why I was doing this foolhardy thing. The man was nothing to me, really—merely a voice on the phone, always self-pitying, and often antagonistic and potentially violent. I ought to be checking on my house and the folks at All Souls; if I wanted to help people, my efforts would have been better spent in my own neighborhood or Bernal Heights. But instead I was traveling to the most congested and dangerous part of the city in search of a man I'd never laid eyes on.

As I asked the question, I knew the answer. Over the past two weeks the man had told me about his deepest problems. I'd come to know him in spite of his self-protective secretiveness. And he'd become more to me than just the subject of an investigation; I'd begun to care whether he lived or died. Now we had shared a peculiarly intimate moment—that of being together, if only in voice, when the catastrophe that San Franciscans feared the most had struck. He had called for help; I had heard his terror and pain. A connection had been established that could not be broken.

After twenty minutes and little progress, I cut west and took a less-traveled residential street through Japantown and over the crest of Pacific Heights. From the top of the hill I could see and smell the smoke over the Marina; as I crossed the traffic-snarled intersection with Lombard, I could see the flames. I drove another block, then decided to leave the MG and continue on foot.

All around I could see signs of destruction now: a house was twisted at a tortuous angle, its front porch collapsed and crushing a car parked at the curb; on Beach Street an apartment building's upper story had slid into the street, clogging it with rubble; three bottom floors of another building were flattened, leaving only the top intact.

I stopped at a corner, breathing hard, nearly choking on the thickening smoke. The smell of gas from broken lines was vaguely nauseating—frightening, too, because of the potential for explosions. To my left the street was cordoned off; fire-department hoses played on the blazes—weakly, because of damaged water mains. People congregated everywhere, staring about with horror-struck eyes; they huddled together, clinging to one another; many were crying. Firefighters and police were telling people to go home before dark fell. "You should be looking after your property," I heard one say. "You can count on going seventy-two hours without water or power."

"Longer than that," someone said.

"It's not safe here," the policeman added. "Please go home."

Between sobs, a woman said, "What if you've got no home to go to any more?"

The cop had no answer for her.

Emotions were flying out of control among the onlookers. It would have been easy to feed into it—to weep, even panic. Instead, I turned my back to the flaming buildings, began walking the other way, toward Fort Mason. If the man's home was beyond the barricades, there was nothing I could do for him. But if it lay in the other direction, where there was a lighter concentration of rescue workers, then my assistance might save his life.

I forced myself to walk slower, to study the buildings on either side of the street. I had one last clue that could lead me to the man: he'd said he lived in a little cottage between two apartment buildings. The homes in this district were mostly of substantial size; there couldn't be too many cottages situated in just that way.

Across the street a house slumped over to one side, its roof canted at a forty-five-degree angle, windows from an apartment house had popped out of their frames, and its iron fire escapes were tangled and twisted like a cat's cradle of yarn. Another home was unrecognizable, merely a heap of rubble. And over there, two four-story apartment buildings leaned together, forming an arch over a much smaller structure ....

I rushed across the street, pushed through a knot of bystanders. The smaller building was a tumble-down mass of white stucco with a smashed red tile roof and a partially flattened iron fence. It had been a Mediterranean-style cottage with grillwork over high windows; now the grills were bent and pushed outward; the collapsed windows resembled swollen-shut eyes.

The woman standing next to me was cradling a terrified cat under her loose cardigan sweater. I asked, "Did the man who lives in the cottage get out okay?"

She frowned, tightened her grip on the cat as it burrowed deeper. "I don't know who lives there. It's always kind of deserted-looking."

A man in front of her said, "I've seen lights, but never anybody coming or going."

I moved closer. The cottage was deep in the shadows of the leaning buildings, eerily silent. From above came a groaning sound, and then a piece of wood sheared off the apartment house to the right, crashing onto what remained of the cottage's roof. I looked up, wondering how long before one or the other of the buildings toppled. Wondering if the man was still alive inside the compacted mass of stucco....

A man in jeans and a sweatshirt came up and stood beside me. His face was smudged and abraded; his clothing was smeared with dirt and what looked to be blood; he held his left elbow gingerly in the palm of his hand. "You were asking about Dan?" he said.

So that was the anonymous caller's name. "Yes. Did he get out okay?"

"I don't think he was at home. At least, I saw him over at the Green around quarter to five."

"He was at home. I was talking with him on the phone when the quake hit."

"Oh, Jesus." The man's face paled under the smudges. "My name's Mel; I live ... lived next door. Are you a friend of Dan's?"

"Yes," I said, realizing it was true.

"That's a surprise." He stared worriedly at the place where the two buildings leaned together.

"Why?"

"I thought Dan didn't have any friends left. He's pushed us away ever since the accident."

"Accident?"

"You must be a new friend, or else you'd know. Dan's woman was killed on the freeway last spring. A truck crushed her car."

The word "crushed" seemed to hang in the air between us. I said, "I've got to try to get him out of there," and stepped over the flattened portion of the fence.

Mel said, "I'll go with you."

I looked skeptically at his injured arm.

"It's nothing, really," he told me. "I was helping an old lady out of my building, and a beam grazed me."

"Well—" I broke off as a hail of debris came from the building to the left.

Without further conversation, Mel and I crossed the small front yard, skirting fallen bricks, broken glass, and jagged chunks of wallboard. Dusk was coming on fast now; here in the shadows of the leaning buildings it was darker than on the street. I moved toward where the cottage's front door should have been, but couldn't locate it. The windows, with their protruding grillwork, were impassable.

I said, "Is there another entrance?"

"In the back, off a little service porch."

I glanced to either side. The narrow passages between the cottage and the adjacent buildings were jammed with debris. I could possibly scale the mound at the right, but I was leery of setting up vibrations that might cause more debris to come tumbling down.

Mel said, "You'd better give it up. The way the cottage looks, I doubt he survived."

But I wasn't willing to give it up—not yet. There must be a way to at least locate Dan, see if he was alive. But how?

And then I remembered something else from our phone conversations....
I said, "I'm going back there."

"Let me."

"No, stay here. That mound will support my weight, but not yours." I moved toward the side of the cottage before Mel could remind me of the risk I was taking.

The mound was over five feet high. I began to climb cautiously, testing every hand- and foothold. Twice jagged chunks of stucco cut my fingers; a piece of wood left a line of splinters on the back of my hand. When I neared the top, I heard the roar of a helicopter, its rotors flapping overhead. I froze, afraid that the air currents would precipitate more debris, then scrambled down the other side of the mound into a weed-choked backyard.

As I straightened, automatically brushing dirt from my jeans, my foot slipped on the soft, spongy ground, then sank into a puddle, probably a water main was broken nearby. The helicopter still hovered overhead; I couldn't hear a thing above its racket. Nor could I see much: it was even darker back here. I stood still until my eyes adjusted.

The cottage was not so badly damaged at its rear. The steps to the porch had collapsed and the rear wall leaned inward, but I could make out a door frame opening into blackness inside. I glanced up in irritation at the helicopter, saw it was going away. Waited, and then listened ...

And heard what I had been hoping to. The music was now Beethoven—his third symphony, the *Eroica*. Its strains were muted, tinny. Music played by an out-of-area FM station, coming from a transistor radio. A transistor whose batteries were functioning long after the electricity had cut out. Whose batteries might have outlived its owner.

I moved quickly to the porch, grasped the iron rail beside the collapsed steps, and pulled myself up. I still could see nothing inside the cottage. The strains of the *Eroica* continued to pour forth, close by now.

Reflexively I reached into my purse for the small flashlight I usually kept there, then remembered it was at home on the kitchen counter—a reminder for me to replace its weak batteries. I swore softly, then started through the doorway, calling out to Dan.

No answer.

"Dan!"

This time I heard a groan.

I rushed forward into the blackness, following the sound of the music. After a few feet I came up against something solid, banging my shins. I lowered a hand, felt around. It was a wooden beam, wedged crosswise.

"Dan?"

Another groan. From the floor—perhaps under the beam. I squatted and made a wide sweep with my hands. They encountered a wool-clad arm; I slid my fingers down it until I touched the wrist, felt for the pulse. It was strong, although slightly irregular.

"Dan," I said, leaning closer, "it's Sharon, from the hotline. We've got to get you out of here."

"Unh, Sharon?" His voice was groggy, confused. He'd probably been drifting in and out of consciousness since the beam fell on him.

"Can you move?" I asked.

"... Something on my legs."

"Do they feel broken?"

"No, just pinned."

"I can't see much, but I'm going to try to move this beam off you. When I do, roll out from under."

"... Okay."

From the position at which the beam was wedged, I could tell it would have to be raised. Balancing on the balls of my feet, I got a good grip on it and shoved upward with all my strength. It moved about six inches and then slipped from my grasp. Dan grunted.

"Are you all right?"

"Yeah. Try it again."

I stood, grasped it, and pulled this time. It yielded a little more, and I heard Dan slide across the floor. "I'm clear," he said—and just in time, because I once more lost my grip. The beam crashed down, setting up a vibration that made plaster fall from the ceiling.

"We've got to get out of here fast," I said. "Give me your hand."

He slipped it into mine—long-fingered, work-roughened. Quickly we went through the door, crossed the porch, jumped to the ground. The radio continued to play forlornly behind us. I glanced briefly at Dan, couldn't make out much more than a tall, slender build and a thatch of pale hair. His face turned from me, toward the cottage.

"Jesus," he said in an awed voice.

I tugged urgently at his hand. "There's no telling how long those apartment buildings are going to stand."

He turned, looked up at them, said "Jesus" again. I urged him toward the mound of debris.

This time I opted for speed rather than caution—a mistake, because as we neared the top, a cracking noise came from high above. I gave Dan a push, slid after him. A dark, jagged object hurtled down, missing us only by inches. More plaster board—deadly at that velocity.

For a moment I sat straddle-legged on the ground, sucking in my breath, releasing it tremulously, gasping for more air. Then hands pulled me to my feet and dragged me across the yard toward the sidewalk—

Mel and Dan.

Night had fallen by now. A fire had broken out in the house across the street. Its red-orange flickering showed the man I'd just rescued: ordinary-looking, with regular features that were now marred by dirt and a long cut on the forehead, from which blood had trickled and dried. His pale eyes were studying me; suddenly he looked abashed and shoved both hands into his jeans pocket.

After a moment he asked, "How did you find me?"

"I put together some of the things you'd said on the phone. Doesn't matter now."

"Why did you even bother?"

"Because I care."

He looked at the ground.

I added, "There never was any assault rifle, was there?"

He shook his head.

"You made it up, so someone would pay attention."

"… Yeah."

I felt anger welling up—irrational, considering the present circumstances, but nonetheless justified. "You didn't have to frighten the people at the hotline. All you had to do was ask them for help. Or ask friends like Mel. He cares. People do, you know."

"Nobody does."

"Enough of that! All you have to do is look around to see how much people care about each other. Look at your friend here." I gestured at Mel, who was standing a couple feet away, staring at us. "He hurt his arm rescuing an old lady from his apartment house. Look at those people over by the burning house—they're doing everything they can to help the firefighters. All over this city people are doing things for one another. Goddamn it, I'd never laid eyes on you, but I risked my life anyway!"

Dan was silent for a long moment. Finally he looked up at me. "I know you did. What can I do in return?"

"For me? Nothing. Just pass it on to someone else."

Dan stared across the street at the flaming building, looked back into the shadows where his cottage lay in ruins. Then he nodded and squared his shoulders. To Mel he said, "Let's go over there, see if there's anything we can do."

He put his arm around my shoulders and hugged me briefly, then he and Mel set off at a trot.

The city is recovering now, as it did in 1906, and as it doubtless will when the next big quake hits. Resiliency is what disaster teaches us, I guess—along with the preciousness of life, no matter how disappointing or burdensome it may often seem.

Dan's recovering, too: he's only called the hotline twice, once for a referral to a therapist, and once to ask for my home number so he could invite me to dinner. I turned the invitation down, because neither of us needs to dwell on the trauma of October seventeenth, and I was fairly sure I heard a measure of relief in his voice when I did so.

I'll never forget Dan, though—or where I was when. And the strains of Beethoven's Third Symphony will forever remind me of the day after which things would never be the same again.

SILENT NIGHT

"Larry, I hardly know what to say!"

What I *wanted* to say was, "What am I supposed to do with this?" The object I'd just liberated from its gay red-and-gold Christmas wrappings was a plastic bag, about eight by twelve inches, packed firm with what looked suspiciously like sawdust. I turned it over in my hands, as if admiring it, and searched for some clue to its identity.

When I looked up, I saw Larry Koslowski's brown eyes shining expectantly; even the ends of his little handlebar mustache seemed to bristle as he awaited my reaction. "It's perfect," I said lamely.

He let his bated breath out in a long sigh. "I thought it would be. You remember how you were talking about not having much energy lately? I told you to try whipping up my protein drink for breakfast, but you said you didn't have that kind of time in the morning."

The conversation came back to me—vaguely. I nodded.

"Well," he went on, "put two tablespoons of that mixture in a tall glass, add water, stir, and you're in business."

Of course—it was an instant version of his infamous protein drink. Larry was the health nut on the All Souls Legal Cooperative staff; his fervent exhortations for the rest of us to adopt better nutritional standards often fell upon deaf ears—mine included.

"Thank you," I said. "I'll try it first thing tomorrow."

Larry ducked his head, his lips turning up in shy pleasure beneath his straggly little mustache.

It was late in the afternoon of Christmas Eve, and the staff of All Souls was engaged in the traditional gift exchange between members who had drawn each other's names earlier in the month. The yearly ritual extends back to the days of the co-op's founding, when most people were too poor to give more than one present; the only rule is Keep It Simple.

The big front parlor of the co-op's San Francisco Victorian was crowded. People perched on the furniture or, like Larry and me, sat cross-legged on the floor, oohing and aahing over their gifts. Next to the Christmas tree in the bay window, my boss, Hank Zahn, sported a new cap and muffler, knitted for him—after great deliberation and consultation as to colors—by my assistant, Rae Kelleher. Rae, in turn, wore the scarf and cap I'd purchased (because I can't knit to save my life) for her in the hope she would consign relics from her days at U. C. Berkeley to the trash can. Other people had homemade cookies and sinful fudge, special bottles of wine, next year's calendars, assorted games, plants, and paperback books. And I had a bag of instant health drink that looked like sawdust.

The voices in the room created such a babble that I barely heard the phone ring in the hall behind me. Our secretary, Ted Smalley, who is a compulsive answerer, stepped over me and went out to where the instrument sat on his desk. A moment later he called, "McCone, it's for you."

My stomach did a little flip-flop, because I was expecting news of a personal nature that could either be very good or very bad. I thanked Larry again for my gift, scrambled to my feet, and went to take the receiver from Ted. He remained next to the desk; I'd confided my family's problem to him earlier that week, and now, I knew, he would wait to see if he could provide aid or comfort.

"Shari?" My youngest sister Charlene's voice was composed, but her use of the diminutive of Sharon, which no one but my father calls me unless it's a time of crisis, made my stomach flip.

"I'm here," I said.

"Shari, somebody's seen him. A friend of Ricky's saw Mike!"

"Where? When?"

"Today around noon. Up there—in San Francisco."

I let out my breath in a sigh of relief. My fourteen-year-old nephew, oldest of Charlene and Ricky's six kids, had run away from their home in Pacific Palisades five days ago. Now, it appeared, he was alive, if not exactly safe.

The investigator in me counseled caution, however. "Was this friend sure it was Mike he saw?"

"Yes. He spoke to him. Mike said he was visiting you. But afterward our friend got to thinking that he looked kind of grubby and tired, and that you probably wouldn't have let him wander around that part of town, so he called us to check it out."

A chill touched my shoulder blades. "What part of town?"

"... Somewhere near City Hall, a sleazy area, our friend said."

A very sleazy area, I thought. Dangerous territory to which runaways are often drawn, where boys and girls alike fall prey to pimps and pushers ...

Charlene said, "Shari?"

"I'm still here, just thinking."

"You don't suppose he'll come to you?"

"I doubt it, if he hasn't already. But in case he does, there's somebody staying at my house—an old friend who's here for Christmas—and she knows to keep him there and call me immediately. Is there anybody else he knows here in the city?"

"... I can't think of anybody."

"What about that friend you spent a couple of Christmases with—the one with the two little girls who lived on Sixteenth Street across from Mission Dolores?"

"Ginny Shriber? She moved away about four years ago." There was a noise as if Charlene was choking back a sob. "He's really just a little boy yet. So little, and so stubborn."

But stubborn little boys grow up fast on the rough city streets. I didn't want that kind of coming-of-age for my nephew.

"Look at the up side of this Charlene," I said, more heartily than I felt. "Mike's come to the one city where you have your own private investigator. I'll start looking for him right away."

It had begun with, of all things, a moped that Mike wanted for Christmas. Or maybe it had started a year earlier, when Ricky Savage finally hit it big.

During the first fourteen years of his marriage to my sister, Ricky had been merely another faceless country-and-western musician, playing and singing backup with itinerant bands, dreaming seemingly improbable dreams of stardom. He and Charlene had developed a reproductive pattern (and rate) that never failed to astound me, in spite of its regularity: he'd get her pregnant, go out on tour, return after the baby was born; then he'd go out again when the two o'clock feedings got to him, return when the kid was weaned, and start the whole cycle all over. Finally, after the sixth child, Charlene had wised up and gotten her tubes tied. But Ricky still stayed on the road more than at home, and still dreamed his dreams.

But then, with money borrowed from my father on the promise that if he didn't make it within one more year he'd give up music and go into my brother John's housepainting business, Ricky had cut a demo of a song he'd written called "Cobwebs in the Attic of My Mind." It was about a lovelorn fellow who, besides said cobwebs, had a "sewer that's backed up in the cellar of his soul" and "a short in the wiring of his heart." When I first heard it, I was certain that Pa's money had washed down that same pipe before it clogged, but fate—perverse creature that it is—would have it otherwise. The song was a runaway hit, and more Ricky Savage hits were to follow.

In true *nouveau* style, Ricky and Charlene quickly moved uptown—or in this case up the coast, from West Los Angeles to affluent Pacific Palisades. There were new cars, new furniture and clothes, a house with a swimming pool, and toys and goodies for the children. *Lots* of goodies, anything they wanted—until this Christmas when, for reasons of safety, Charlene had balked at letting Mike have the moped. And Mike, headstrong little bastard that he was, had taken his life's savings of some fifty-five dollars and hitched away from home on the Pacific Coast Highway.

It was because of a goddamned moped that I was canceling my Christmas Eve plans and setting forth to comb the sleazy streets and alleys of the area known as Polk Gulch for a runaway ....

The city was strangely subdued on this Christmas Eve, the dark streets hushed, although not deserted. Most people had been drawn inside to the warmth of family and friends; others, I suspected, had retreated to nurse the loneliness that is endemic to this season. The pedestrians I passed moved silently, as if reluctant to call attention to their presence; occasionally I heard laughter from the bars as I went by, but even that was muted. The lost, drifting souls of the city seemed to collectively hold their breath as they waited for life to resume its everyday pattern.

I had started at Market Street and worked my way northwest, through the Tenderloin to Polk Gulch. Before I'd started out, I'd had a photographer friend who likes to make a big fee more than he likes to celebrate holidays run off a hundred copies of my most recent photo of Mike. Those I passed out, along with my card, to clerks in what liquor stores, corner groceries, cheap hotels, and greasy spoon restaurants I found open. The pictures drew no response other than indifference or sympathetic shakes of the head and promises to keep an eye out for him. By the time I reached Polk Street, where I had an appointment in a gay bar at ten, I was cold, footsore, and badly discouraged.

Polk Gulch, so called because it is in a valley that has an underground river running through it, long ago was the hub of gay life in San Francisco. In the seventies, however, most of the action shifted up Market Street to the Castro district, and the vitality seemed to drain out of the Gulch. Now parts of it, particularly those bordering the Tenderloin, are depressingly sleazy. As I walked along, examining the face of each young man I saw, I became aware of the hopelessness and resignation in the eyes of the street hustlers and junkies and winos and homeless people.

A few blocks from my destination was a vacant lot surrounded by a chain link fence. Inside gaped a huge excavation, the cellar of the building that had formerly stood there, now open to the elements. People had scaled the fence and taken up residence down in it; campfires blazed, in defiance of the NO TRESPASSING signs. The homeless could rest easy— at least for this one night. No one was going to roust them on Christmas Eve.

I went to the fence and grasped its cold mesh with my fingers, staring down into the shifting light and shadows, wondering if Mike was among the ragged and hungry ranks. Many of the people were middle-aged to elderly, but there were also families with children and a scattering of young people. There was no way to tell, though, without scaling the fence and climbing down there. Eventually I turned away, realizing I had only enough time to get to the gay bar by ten.

The transvestite's name was Norma and she—he? I never know what to call them—was coldly beautiful. The two of us sat at a corner table in the bar, sipping champagne because Norma had insisted on it. ("After all, it's Christmas Eve, darling!") The bar, in spite of winking colored lights on its tree and flickering bayberry candles on each table, was gloomy and semideserted; Norma's brave velvet finery and costume jewelry had about it more than a touch of the pathetic. She'd been sitting alone when I'd entered and had greeted me eagerly.

I'd been put in touch with Norma by Ted Smalley, who is gay and has a wide-ranging acquaintance among all the segments of the city's homosexual community. Norma, he'd said, knew everything there was to know about what went on in Polk Gulch; if anyone could help me, it was she.

The photo of Mike didn't look familiar to Norma. "There are so many runaways on the street at this time of year," she told me. "Kids get their hopes built up at Christmas time. When they find out Santa isn't the great guy he's cracked up to be, they take off. Like your nephew."

"So what would happen to a kid like him? Where would he go?"

"Lots of places. There's a hotel—the Vinton. A lot of runaways end up there at first, until their money runs out. If he's into drugs, try any flophouse, doorway, or alley. If he's connected with a pimp, look for him hustling."

My fingers tightened involuntarily on the stem of my champagne glass. Norma noticed and shook her elaborately coiffed head in sympathy. "Not a pretty thought, is it? But what do you see around here that's pretty—except for me?" As she spoke the last words, her smile became self-mocking.

"He's been missing five days now," I said, "and he only had fifty-some dollars on him. That'll be gone by now, so he probably won't be at the hotel, or any other. He's never been into drugs. His father's a musician, and a lot of his cronies are druggies; the kid actually disapproves of them. The other I don't even want to think about—though I probably will have to, eventually."

"So what are you going to do?"

"Try the hotel. Go back and talk to the people at that vacant lot. Keep looking at each kid who walks by."

Norma stared at the photo of Mike that lay face up on the table between us. "It's a damned shame, a nice-looking kid like that. He ought to be home with his family, trimming the tree, roasting chestnuts on the fire, or whatever other things families do."

"The American Christmas dream, huh?"

"Yeah." She smiled bleakly, raised her glass. "Here's to the American Christmas dream—and to all the people it's eluded."

I touched my glass to hers. "Including you and me."

"Including you and me. Let's just hope it doesn't elude young Mike forever."

The Vinton Hotel was a few blocks away, around the corner on Eddy Street. Its lobby was a flight up, over a closed sandwich shop, and I had to wait and be buzzed in before I could climb carpetless stairs that stank strongly of disinfectant and faintly of urine. Lobby was a misnomer, actually: it was more a narrow hall with a desk to one side, behind which sat a young black man with a tall afro. The air up there was thick with the odor of marijuana; I guess he'd been spending his Christmas Eve with a joint. His eyes flashed panic when I reached in my bag for my identification. Then he realized it wasn't a bust and relaxed somewhat.

I took out another photo of Mike and laid it on the counter. "You seen this kid?"

He barely glanced at it. "Nope, can't help you."

I shoved it closer. "Take another look."

He did, pushed it back toward me. "I said no."

There was something about his tone that told me he was lying—would lie out of sheer perversity. I could get tough with him, make noises about talking to the hotel's owners, mentioning how the place reeked of grass. The city's fleabags had come under a good bit of media scrutiny recently; the owners wouldn't want me to cause any trouble that would jeopardize this little goldmine that raked in outrageously high rents from transients, as well as government subsidized payments for welfare recipients. Still, there had to be a better way....

"You work here every night?" I asked.

"Yeah."

"Rough, on Christmas Eve."

He shrugged.

"Christmas night, too?"

"Why do you care?"

"I understand what a rotten deal that is. You don't think I'm running around here in the cold because I like it, do you?"

His eyes flickered to me, faintly interested. "You got no choice, either?"

"Hell, no. The client says find a kid, I go looking. Not that it matters. I don't have anything better to do."

"Know what you mean. Nothing for me at home, either."

"Where's home?"

"My real home, or where I live?"

"Both, I guess."

"Where I live's up there." He gestured at the ceiling. "Room goes with the job. Home's not there no more. Was in Motown, back before my ma died and things got so bad in the auto industry. I came out here thinking I'd find work." He smiled ironically. "Well, I found it, didn't I?"

"At least it's not as cold here as in Detroit."

"No, but it's not home either." He paused, then reached for Mike's picture. "Let me see that again." Another pause. "Okay. He stayed here. Him and this blond chick got to be friends. She's gone, too."

"Do you know the blond girl's name?"

"Yeah. Jane Smith. Original, huh?"

"Can you describe her?"

"Just a little blond, maybe five-two. Long hair. Nothing special about her."

"When did they leave?"

"They were gone when I came on last night. The owner don't put up with the ones that can't pay, and the day man, he likes tossing their asses out on the street."

"How did the kid seem to you? Was he okay?"

The man's eyes met mine, held them for a moment. "Thought this was just a job to you."

"... He's my nephew."

"Yeah, I guessed it might be something like that. Well, if you mean was he doing drugs or hustling, I'd say no. Maybe a little booze, that's all. The girl was the same. Pretty straight kids. Nobody's gotten to them yet."

"Let me ask you this: what would kids like that do after they'd been thrown out of here? Where would they hang out?"

He considered. "There's a greasy spoon on Polk, near O'Farrell. Owner's an old guy, Iranian. He feels sorry for the kids, feeds them when they're about to starve, tries to get them to go home. He might of seen those two."

"Would he be open tonight?"

"Sure. Like I said, he's Iranian. It's not his holiday. Come to think of it, it's not mine anymore, either."

"Why not?"

Again the ironic smile. "Can't celebrate peace-on-earth-good-will-to-men when you don't believe in it anymore, now can you?"

I reached into my bag and took out a twenty-dollar bill, slid it across the counter to him. "Peace on earth, and thanks."

He took it eagerly, then looked at it and shook his head. "You don't have to."

"I *want* to. That makes a difference."

The "greasy spoon" was called The Coffee Break. It was small—just five tables and a lunch counter, old green linoleum floors, Formica and molded plastic furniture. A slender man with thinning gray hair sat behind the counter smoking a cigarette. A couple of old women were hunched over coffee at a corner table. Next to the window was a dirty-haired blond girl; she was staring through the glass with blank eyes—another of the city's casualties.

I showed Mike's picture to the man behind the counter. He told me Mike looked familiar, thought a minute, then snapped his fingers and said, "Hey, Angie."

The girl by the window turned. Full-face, I could see she was red-eyed and tear-streaked. The blankness of her face was due to misery, not drugs.

"Take a look at the picture this lady has. Didn't I see you with this kid yesterday?"

She got up and came to the counter, self-consciously smoothing her wrinkled jacket and jeans. "Yeah," she said after glancing at it, "that's Michael."

"Where's he now? The lady's his aunt, wants to help him."

She shook her head. "I don't know. He was at the Vinton, but he got kicked out the same time I did. We stayed down at the cellar in the vacant lot last night, but it was cold and scary. These drunks kept bothering us. Mr. Ahmeni, how long do you think it's going to take my dad to get here?"

"Take it easy. It's a long drive from Oroville. I only called him an hour ago." To me, Mr. Ahmeni added, "Angie's going home for Christmas."

I studied her. Under all that grime, a pretty, conventional girl hid. I said, "Would you like a cup of coffee? Something to eat?"

"I wouldn't mind a Coke. I've been sponging off Mr. Ahmeni for hours." She smiled faintly. "I guess he'd appreciate it if I sponged off somebody else for a change."

I bought us both Cokes and sat down with her. "When did you meet Mike?"

"Three days ago, I guess. He was at the hotel when I got into town. He kind of looked out for me. I was glad; that place is pretty awful. A lot of addicts stay there. One OD'd in the stairwell the first night. But it's cheap and they don't ask questions. A guy I met on the bus coming down here told me about it."

"What did Mike do here in the city, do you know?"

"Wandered around, mostly. One afternoon we went out to Ocean Beach and walked on the dunes."

"What about drugs or—"

"Michael's not into drugs. We drank some wine, is all. He's ... I don't know how to describe it, but he's not like a lot of the kids on the streets."

"How so?"

"Well, he's kind of ... sensitive, deep."

"This sensitive soul ran away from home because his parents wouldn't buy him a moped for Christmas."

Angie sighed. "You really don't know anything about him, do you? You don't even know he wants to be called Michael, not Mike."

That silenced me for a moment. It was true: I really didn't know my nephew, not as a person. "Tell me about him."

"What do you want to know?"

"Well, this business with the moped—what was that all about?"

"It didn't really have anything to do with the moped. At least not much. It had to do with the kids at school."

"In what way?"

"Well, the way Michael told it, his family used to be kind of poor. At least there were some months when they worried about being able to pay the rent."

"That's right."

"And then his father became a singing star and they moved to this awesome house in Pacific Palisades, and all of a sudden Michael was in school with all these rich kids. But he didn't fit in. The kids, he said, were really into having things and doing drugs and partying. He couldn't relate to it. He says it's really hard to get into that kind of stuff when you've spent your life worrying about real things."

"Like if your parents are going to be able to pay the rent."

Angie nodded, her fringe of limp blond hair falling over her eyes. She brushed it back and went on. "I know about that; my folks don't have much money, and my mom's sick a lot. The kids, they sense you're different and they don't want to have anything to do with you. Michael was lonely at the new school, so he tried to fit in—tried too hard, I guess, by having the latest stuff, the most expensive clothes. You know."

"And the moped was part of that."

"Uh-huh. But when his mom said he couldn't have it, he realized what he'd been doing. And he also realized that the moped wouldn't have done the trick anyway. Michael's smart enough to know that people don't fall

all over you just because you've got another new toy. So he decided he'd never fit in, and he split. He says he feels more comfortable on the streets, because life here is real." She paused, eyes filling, and looked away at the window. "God, is it *real*."

I followed the direction of her gaze: beyond the plate glass a girl of perhaps thirteen stumbled by. Her body was emaciated, her face blank, her eyes dull—the look of a far-gone junkie.

I said to Angie, "When did you last see Mike ... Michael?"

"Around four this afternoon. Like I said, we spent the night in that cellar in the vacant lot. After that I knew I couldn't hack it anymore, and I told him I'd decided to go home. He got pissed at me and took off."

"Why?"

"Why do you think? I was abandoning him. I could go home, and he couldn't."

"Why not?"

"Because Michael's ... God, you don't know a thing about him! He's proud. He couldn't admit to his parents that he couldn't make it on his own. Any more than he could admit to them about not fitting in at school."

What she said surprised me and made me ashamed. Ashamed for Charlene, who had always referred to Mike as stubborn or bullheaded, but never as proud. And ashamed for myself, because I'd never really seen him, except as the leader of a pack jokingly referred to in family circles as "the little savages."

"Angie," I said, "do you have any idea where he might have gone after he left you?"

She shook her head. "I wish I did. It would be nice if Michael could have a Christmas. He talked about how much he was going to miss it. He spent the whole time we were walking around on the dunes telling me about the Christmases they used to have, even though they didn't have much money: the tree trimming, the homemade presents, the candlelit masses on Christmas Eve, the cookie decorating and the turkey dinners. Michael absolutely loves Christmas."

I hadn't known that either. For years I'd been too busy with my own life to do more than send each of the Savage kids a small check. Properly humbled, I thanked Angie for talking with me, wished her good luck with her parents, and went back out to continue combing the dark, silent streets.

On the way back down Polk Street toward the Tenderloin, I stopped again at the chain link fence surrounding the vacant lot. I was fairly sure Mike was not among the people down there—not after his and Angie's experience of the night before—but I was curious to see the place where they had spent that frightening time.

The campfires still burned deep in the shelter of the cellar. Here and there drunks and addicts lay passed out on the ground; others who had not yet reached that state passed bottles and shared joints and needles; one group raised inebriated voices in a chorus of "Rudolph, the Red-Nosed Reindeer." In a far corner I saw another group—two women, three children, and a man—gathered around a scrawny Christmas tree.

The tree had no ornaments, wasn't really a tree at all, but just a top that someone had probably cut off and tossed away after finding that the one he'd bought was too tall for the height of his ceiling. There was no star atop it, no presents under it, no candy canes or popcorn chains, and there was certain to be no turkey dinner tomorrow. The people had nonetheless gathered around it and stood silently, their heads bowed in prayer.

My throat tightened and I clutched at the fence, fighting back tears. Even though I spent a disproportionate amount of my professional life probing into events and behavior that would make the average person gag, every now and then the indestructible courage of the human spirit absolutely stuns me.

I watched the scene for a moment longer, then turned away, glancing at my watch. Its hands told me why the people were praying: Christmas Day was upon us. This was their midnight service.

And then I realized that those people, who had nothing in the world with which to celebrate Christmas except somebody's cast-off treetop, may have given me a priceless gift. I thought I knew now where I would find my nephew.

When I arrived at Mission Dolores, the neoclassical facade of the basilica was bathed in floodlights, the dome and towers gleaming against the post-midnight sky. The street was choked with double-parked vehicles, and from within I heard voices raised in a joyous chorus. Beside the newer early twentieth-century structure, the small adobe church built in the late 1700s seemed dwarfed and enveloped in deep silence. I hurried up the wide steps to the arching wooden doors of the basilica, then took a moment to compose myself before entering.

Like many of my generation, it had been years since I'd been even nominally a Catholic, but the old habit of reverence had never left me. I couldn't just blunder in there and creep about, peering into every worshipper's face, no matter how great my urgency. I waited until I felt relatively calm before pulling open the heavy door and stepping over the threshold.

The mass was candlelit; the robed figures of the priest and altar boys moved slowly in the flickering, shifting light. The stained glass window behind the altar and those on the side walls gleamed richly. In contrast, the massive pillars reached upward to vaulted arches that were deeply shadowed. As I moved slowly along one of the side aisles, the voices of the choir swelled to a majestic finale.

The congregants began to go forward to receive Communion. As they did, I was able to move less obtrusively, scanning the faces of the young people in the pews. Each time I spotted a teenaged boy, my heart quickened. Each time I felt a sharp stab of disappointment.

I passed behind the waiting communicants, then moved unhurriedly up the nave and crossed to the far aisle. The church was darker and sparsely populated toward the rear; momentarily a pillar blocked my view of the altar. I moved around it.

He was there in the pew next to the pillar, leaning wearily against it. Even in the shadowy light, I could see that his face was dirty and tired, his jacket and jeans rumpled and stained. His eyes were half-closed, his mouth slack; his hands were shoved between his thighs, as if for warmth.

Mike—no, Michael—had come to the only safe place he knew in the city, the church where on two Christmas Eves he'd attended mass with his family and their friends, the Shribers, who had lived across the street.

I slipped into the pew and sat down next to him. He jerked his head toward me, stared in openmouthed surprise. What little color he had drained from his face; his eyes grew wide and alarmed.

"Hi, Michael." I put my hand on his arm.

He looked at me as if he wanted to shake it off. "How did you ...?"

"Doesn't matter. Not now. Let's just sit quietly till mass is over."

He continued to stare at me. After a few seconds he said, "I bet Mom and Dad are really mad at me."

"More worried than anything else."

"Did they hire you to find me?"

"No, I volunteered."

"Huh." He looked away at the line of communicants.

"You still go to church?" I asked.

"Not much. None of us do anymore. I kind of miss it."

"Do you want to take Communion?"

He was silent. Then, "No. I don't think that's something I can do right now. Maybe never."

"Well, that's okay. Everybody expresses his feelings for... God, or whatever, in different ways." I thought of the group of homeless worshippers in the vacant lot. "What's important is that you believe in something."

He nodded, and then we sat silently, watching people file up and down the aisle. After a while he said, "I guess I do believe in something. Otherwise I couldn't have gotten through this week. I learned a lot, you know."

"I'm sure you did."

"About me, I mean."

"I know."

"What're you going to do now? Send me home?"

"Do you want to go home?"

"Maybe. Yes. But I don't want to be sent there. I want to go on my own."

"Well, nobody should spend Christmas Day on a plane or a bus anyway. Besides, I'm having ten people to dinner at four this afternoon. I'm counting on you to help me stuff the turkey."

Michael hesitated, then smiled shyly. He took one hand from between his thighs and slipped it into mine. After a moment he leaned his tired head on my shoulder, and we celebrated the dawn of Christmas together.

BENNY'S SPACE

Amorfina Angeles was terrified, and I could fully empathize with her. Merely living in the neighborhood would have terrified me—all the more so had I been harassed by members of one of its many street gangs.

Hers was a rundown side street in the extreme southeast of San Francisco, only blocks from the crime- and drug-infested Sunnydale public housing projects. There were bars over the windows and grilles on the doors of the small stucco houses; dead and vandalized cars stood at the broken curbs; in the weed-choked yard next door, a mangy guard dog of indeterminate breed paced and snarled. Fear was written on this street as plainly as the graffiti on the walls and fences. Fear and hopelessness and a dull resignation to a life that none of its residents would willingly have opted to lead.

I watched Mrs. Angeles as she crossed her tiny living room to the front window, pulled the edge of the curtain aside a fraction, and peered out at the street. She was no more than five feet tall, with rounded shoulders, sallow skin, and graying black hair that curled in short, unruly ringlets. Her shapeless flower-printed dress did little to conceal a body made soft and fleshy by bad food and too much childbearing. Although she was only forty, she moved like a much older woman.

Her attorney and my colleague, Jack Stuart of All Souls Legal Cooperative, had given me a brief history of his client when he'd asked me to undertake an investigation on her behalf. She was a Filipina who had emigrated to the states with her husband in search of their own piece of the good life that was reputed to be had here. But as with many of their countrymen and -women, things hadn't worked out as the Angeleses had envisioned: first Amorfina's husband had gone into the import-export business with a friend from Manila; the friend absconded two years later with Joe Angeles's life savings. Then, a year after that, Joe was killed in a freak accident at a construction site where he was working. Amorfina and their six children were left with no means of support, and in the years since Joe's death their circumstances had gradual been reduced to this two-bedroom rental cottage in one of the worst areas of the city.

Mrs. Angeles, Jack told me, had done the best she could for her family, keeping them off the welfare rolls with a daytime job at a Mission district sewing factory and nighttime work doing alterations. As they grew older, the children helped with part-time jobs. Now there were only two left at home: sixteen-year-old Alex and fourteen-year-old Isabel. It was typical of their mother, Jack said, that in the current crisis she was more concerned for them than for herself.

She turned from the window now, her face taut with fear, deep lines bracketing her full lips. I asked, "Is someone out there?"

She shook her head and walked wearily to the worn recliner opposite me. I occupied the place of honor on a red brocade sofa encased in the same plastic that had doubtless protected it long ago upon delivery from the store. "I never see anybody," she said. "Not till it's too late."

"Mrs. Angeles, Jack Stuart told me about your problem, but I'd like to hear it in your own words—from the beginning, if you would."

She nodded, smoothing her bright dress over her plump thighs. "It goes back a long time, to when Benny Crespo was ... they called him the Prince of Omega Street, you know."

Hearing the name of her street spoken made me aware of its ironic appropriateness: the last letter of the Greek alphabet is symbolic of endings, and for most of the people living here, Omega Street was the end of a steady decline into poverty.

Mrs. Angeles went on, "Benny Crespo was Filipino. His gang controlled the drugs here. A lot of people looked up to him; he had power, and that don't happen much with our people. Once I caught Alex and one of my older boys calling him a hero, I let them have it pretty good, you bet, and there wasn't any more of *that* kind of talk around this house. I got no use for the gangs—Filipino or otherwise."

"What was the name of Benny Crespo's gang?"

"The *Kabalyeros*. That's Tagalog for Knights."

"Okay—what happened to Benny?"

"The house next door, the one with the dog—that was where Benny lived. He always parked his fancy Corvette out front, and people knew better than to mess with it. Late one night he was getting out of the car and somebody shot him. A drug burn, they say. After that the *Kabalyeros* decided to make the parking space a shrine to Benny. They roped it off, put flowers there every week. On All Saints Day and the other fiestas, it was something to see."

"And that brings us to last March thirteenth," I said.

Mrs. Angeles bit her lower lip and smoothed her dress again.

When she didn't speak, I prompted her. "You'd just come home from work."

"Yeah. It was late, dark. Isabel wasn't here, and I got worried. I kept looking out the window, like a mother does."

"And you saw ...?"

"The guy who moved into the house next door after Benny got shot,

Reg Dawson. He was black, one of a gang called the Victors. They say he moved into that house to show the *Kabalyeros* that the Victors were taking over their turf. Anyway, he drives up and stops a little way down the block. Waits there, revving his engine. People start showing up; the word's been put out that something's gonna go down. And when there's a big crowd, Reg Dawson guns his car and drives right into Benny's space, over the rope and the flowers.

"Well, that started one hell of a fight—Victors and *Kabalyeros* and folks from the neighborhood. And while it's going on, Reg Dawson just stands there in Benny's space acting macho. That's when it happened, what I saw."

"And what was that?"

She hesitated, wet her lips. "The leader of the *Kabalyeros,* Tommy Dragón—the Dragon, they call him—was over by the fence in front of Reg Dawson's house, where you couldn't see him unless you were really looking. I was, 'cause I was trying to see if Isabel was anyplace out there. And I saw Tommy Dragón point this gun at Reg Dawson and shoot him dead."

"What did you do then?"

"Ran and hid in the bathroom. That's where I was when the cops came to the door. Somebody'd told them I was in the window when it all went down and then ran away when Reg got shot. Well, what was I supposed to do? I got no use for the *Kabalyeros* or the Victors, so I told the truth. And now here I am in this mess."

Mrs. Angeles had been slated to be the chief prosecution witness at Tommy Dragón's trial this week. But a month ago the threats had started: anonymous letters and phone calls warning her against testifying. As the trial date approached this had escalated into blatant intimidation: a fire was set in her trash can; someone shot out her kitchen window; a dead dog turned up on her doorstep. The previous Friday, Isabel had been accosted on her way home from the bus stop by two masked men with guns. And that had finally made Mrs. Angeles capitulate; in court yesterday, she'd refused to take the stand against Dragón.

The state needed her testimony; there were no other witnesses, Dragón insisted on his innocence, and the murder gun had not been found. The judge had tried to reason with Mrs. Angeles, then cited her for contempt—reluctantly, he said. "The court is aware that there have been threats made against you and your family," he told her, "but it is unable to guarantee your protection." Then he gave her forty-eight hours to reconsider her decision.

As it turned out, Mrs. Angeles had a champion in her employer. The owner of the sewing factory was unwilling to allow one of his longterm workers to go to jail or to risk her own and her family's safety. He brought her to All Souls, where he held a membership in our legal-services plan, and this morning Jack Stuart asked me to do something for her.

What? I'd asked. What could I do that the SFPD couldn't to stop vicious harassment by a street gang?

Well, he said, get proof against whoever was threatening her so that they could be arrested and she'd feel free to testify.

Sure, Jack, I said. And exactly why *hadn't* the police been able to do anything about the situation?

His answer was not surprising: lack of funds. Intimidation of prosecution witnesses in cases relating to gang violence was becoming more and more prevalent and open in San Francisco, but the city did not have the resources to protect them. An old story nowadays—not enough money to go around.

Mrs. Angeles was watching my face, her eyes tentative. As I looked back at her, her gaze began to waver. She'd experienced too much disappointment in her life to expect much in the way of help from me.

I said, "Yes, you certainly are in a mess. Let's see if we can get you out of it."

We talked for a while longer, and I soon realized that Amor—as she asked me to call her—held the misconception that there was some way I could get the contempt citation dropped. I asked her if she'd known beforehand that a balky witness could be sent to jail. She shook her head. A person had a right to change her mind, hadn't she? When I set her straight on that, she seemed to lose interest in the conversation; it was difficult to get her to focus long enough to compile a list of people I should talk with. I settled for enough names to keep me occupied for the rest of the afternoon.

I was ready to leave when angry voices came from the front steps. A young man and woman entered. They stopped speaking when they saw the room was occupied, but their faces remained set in lines of contention. Amor hastened to introduce them as her son and daughter, Alex and Isabel. To them she explained that I was a detective "helping with the trouble with the judge."

Alex, a stocky youth with a tracery of mustache on his upper lip, seemed disinterested. He shrugged out of his high school letter jacket and vanished through a door to the rear of the house. Isabel studied me with frank curiosity. She was a slender beauty, with black hair that fell in soft curls to her shoulders; her features had a delicacy lacking in those of her mother and brother. Unfortunately, bright blue eyeshadow and garish orange lipstick detracted from her natural good looks, and she wore an imitation leather outfit in a particularly gaudy shade of purple. However, she was polite and well-spoken as she questioned me about what I could do to help her mother. Then, after a comment to Amor about an assignment that was due the next day, she left through the door her brother had used.

I turned to Amor, who was fingering the leaves of a philodendron plant that stood in a stand near the front window. Her posture was stiff, and when I spoke to her she didn't meet my eyes. Now I was aware of a tension in her that hadn't been there before her children returned home. Anxiety, because of the danger her witnessing the shooting had placed them in? Or something else? It might have had to do with the quarrel they'd been having, but weren't arguments between siblings fairly common? They certainly had been in my childhood home in San Diego.

I told Amor I'd be back to check on her in a couple of hours. Then, after a few precautionary and probably unnecessary reminders about locking doors and staying clear of windows, I went out into the chill November afternoon.

The first name on my list was Madeline Dawson, the slain gang leader's widow. I glanced at the house next door and saw with some relief that the guard dog no longer paced in its yard. When I pushed through the gate in the chain link fence, the creature's whereabouts became apparent: a bellowing emanated from the small, shabby cottage. I went up a broken walk bordered by weeds, climbed the sagging front steps, and pressed the bell. A woman's voice yelled for the dog to shut up, then a door slammed somewhere within, muffling the barking. Footsteps approached, and the woman called, "Yes, who is it?"

"My name's Sharon McCone, from All Soul's Legal Cooperative. I'm investigating the threats your neighbor, Mrs. Angeles, has been receiving."

A couple of locks turned and the door opened on its chain. The face that peered out at me was very thin and pale, with wisps of red hair straggling over the high forehead; the Dawson marriage had been an interracial one, then. The woman stared at me for a moment before she asked, "What threats?"

"You don't know that Mrs. Angeles and her children have been threatened because she's to testify against the man who shot your husband?"

She shook her head and stepped back, shivering slightly—whether from the cold outside or the memory of the murder, I couldn't tell. "I ... don't get out much these days."

"May I come in, talk with you about the shooting?"

She shrugged, unhooked the chain, and opened the door. "I don't know what good it will do. Amor's a damned fool for saying she'd testify in the first place."

"Aren't you glad she did? The man killed your husband."

She shrugged again and motioned me into a living room the same size as that in the Angeles house. All resemblance stopped there, however. Dirty glasses and dishes, full ashtrays, piles of newspapers and magazines covered every surface; dust balls the size of rats lurked under the shabby Danish furniture. Madeline Dawson picked up a heap of tabloids from the couch and dumped it on the floor, then indicated I should sit there and took a hassock for herself.

I said, "You *are* glad that Mrs. Angeles was willing to testify, aren't you?"

"Not particularly."

"You don't care if your husband's killer is convicted or not?"

"Reg was asking to be killed. Not that I wouldn't mind seeing the Dragon get the gas chamber—he may not have killed Reg, but he killed plenty of other people—"

"What did you say?" I spoke sharply, and Madeline Dawson blinked in surprise. It made me pay closer attention to her eyes; they were glassy, their pupils dilated. The woman, I realized, was high.

"I said the Dragon killed plenty of other people."

"No, about him not killing Reg."

"Did I say that?"

"Yes."

"I can't imagine why. I mean, Amor must know. She was up there in the window watching for sweet Isabel like always."

"You don't sound as if you like Isabel Angeles."

"I'm not fond of flips in general. Look at the way they're taking over this area. Daly City's turning into another Manila. All they do is buy, buy, buy—houses, cars, stuff by the truckload. You know, there's a joke that the first three words their babies learn are 'Mama, Papa, and Serramonte.'" Serramonte was a large shopping mall south of San Francisco.

The roots of the resentment she voiced were clear to me. One of our largest immigrant groups today, the Filipinos are highly westernized and by and large better educated and more affluent than other recently arrived Asians—or many of their neighbors, black or white. Isabel Angeles, for all her bright, cheap clothing and excessive makeup, had behind her a tradition of industriousness and upward mobility that might help her to secure a better place in the world than Madeline Dawson could aspire to.

I wasn't going to allow Madeline's biases to interfere with my line of questioning. I said, "About Dragón not having shot your husband—"

"Hey, who knows? Or cares? The bastard's dead, and good riddance."

"Why good riddance?"

"The man was a pig. A pusher who cheated and gouged people—people like me who need the stuff to get through. You think I was always like this, lady? No way. I was a nice Irish Catholic girl from the Avenues when Reg got his hands on me. Turned me on to coke and a lot of other things when I was only thirteen. Liked his pussy young, Reg did. But then I got old—I'm all of nineteen now—and I needed more and more stuff just to keep going, and all of a sudden Reg didn't even *see* me anymore. Yeah, the man was a pig, and I'm glad he's dead."

"But you don't think Dragón killed him."

She sighed in exasperation. "I don't know what I think. It's just that I always supposed that when Reg got it it would be for something more personal than driving his car into a stupid shrine in a parking space. You know what I mean? But what does it matter who killed him, anyway?"

"It matters to Tommy Dragón, for one."

She dismissed the accused man's life with a flick of her hand. "Like I said, the Dragon's a killer. He might as well die for Reg's murder as for any of the others. In a way, it'd be the one good thing Reg did for the world."

Perhaps in a certain primitive sense she was right, but her offhandedness made me uncomfortable. I changed the subject. "About the threat to Mrs. Angeles—which of the *Kabalyeros* would be behind them?"

"All of them. These guys in the gangs, they work together."

But I knew about the structure of street gangs—my degree in sociology from U. C. Berkeley hadn't been totally worthless—to be reasonably sure that wasn't so. There is usually one dominant personality, supported by two or three lieutenants; take away these leaders, and the followers become ineffectual, purposeless. If I could turn up enough evidence against the leaders of the *Kabalyeros* to have them arrested, the harassment would stop.

I asked, "Who took over the *Kabalyeros* after Dragón went to jail?"

"Hector Bulis."

It was a name that didn't appear on my list; Amor had claimed not to know who was the current head of the Filipino gang. "Where can I find him?"

"There's a fast-food joint over on Geneva, near the Cow Palace. Fat Robbie's. That's where the *Kabalyeros* hang out."

The second person I'd intended to talk with was the young man who had reportedly taken over the leadership of the Victors after Dawson's death, Jimmy Willis. Willis could generally be found at a bowling alley, also on Geneva Avenue near the Cow Palace. I thanked Madeline for taking the time to talk with me and headed for the Daly City line.

The first of the two establishments that I spotted was Fat Robbie's, a cinderblock-and-glass relic of the early sixties whose specialties appeared to be burgers and chicken-in-a-basket. I turned into a parking lot that was half-full of mostly shabby cars and left my MG beside one of the defunct drive-in speaker poles.

The interior of the restaurant took me back to my high school days: orange leatherette booths beside the plate glass windows, a long Formica counter with stools, laminated color pictures of disgusting-looking food on the wall above the pass-through counter from the kitchen. Instead of a jukebox there was a bank of video games along one wall. Three Filipino youths in jeans and denim jackets gathered around one called "Invader!" The *Kabalyeros,* I assumed.

I crossed to the counter with only a cursory glance at the trio, sat, and ordered coffee from a young woman who looked to be Eurasian. The *Kabalyeros* didn't conceal their interest in me; they stared openly, and after a moment one of them said something that sounded like "tick-tick," and they all laughed nastily. Some sort of Tagalog obscenity, I supposed. I ignored them, sipping the dishwater-weak coffee, and after a bit they went back to their game.

I took out the paperback that I keep in my bag for protective coloration and pretended to read, listening to the few snatches of conversation that drifted over from the three. I caught the names of two: Sal and Hector—the latter presumably Bulis, the gang's leader. When I glanced covertly at him, I saw he was tallish and thin, with long hair caught back in a ponytail; his features were razor-sharp and slightly skewed, creating the impression of a perpetual sneer. The trio kept their voices low, and although I strained to hear, I could make out nothing of what they were saying. After about five minutes Hector turned away from the video machine. With a final glance at me he motioned to his companions, and they all left the restaurant.

I waited until they'd driven away in an old green Pontiac before I called the waitress over and showed her my identification. "The three men who just left," I said. "Is the tall one Hector Bulis?"

Her lips formed a little "O" as she stared at the I. D. Finally she nodded.

"May I talk with you about them?"

She glanced toward the pass-through to the kitchen. "My boss, he don't like me talking with the customers when I'm supposed to be working."

"Take a break. Just five minutes."

Now she looked nervously around the restaurant. "I shouldn't—"

I slipped a twenty-dollar bill from my wallet and showed it to her. "Just five minutes."

She still seemed edgy, but fear lost out to greed. "Okay, but I don't want anybody to see me talking to you. Go back to the restroom—it's through that door by the video games. I'll meet you there as soon as I can."

I got up and found the ladies' room. It was tiny, dimly lit, with a badly cracked mirror. The walls were covered with a mass of graffiti; some of it looked as if it had been painted over and had later worked its way back into view through the fading layers of enamel. The air in there was redolent of grease, cheap perfume, and stale cigarette and marijuana smoke. I leaned against the sink as I waited.

The young Eurasian woman appeared a few minutes later. "Bastard gave me a hard time," she said. "Tried to tell me I'd already taken my break."

"What's your name?"

"Anna Smith."

"Anna, the three men who just left—do they come in here often?"

"Uh-huh"

"Keep pretty much to themselves, do they?"

"It's more like other people stay away from them." She hesitated. "They're from one of the gangs; you don't mess with them. That's why I wanted to talk with you back here."

"Have you ever heard them say anything about Tommy Dragón?"

"The Dragon? Sure. He's in jail; they say he was framed."

Of course they would claim that. "What about a Mrs. Angeles—Amorfina Angeles?"

"... Not that one, no."

"What about trying to intimidate someone? Setting fires, going after someone with a gun?"

"Uh-uh. That's gang business; they keep it pretty close. But it wouldn't surprise me. Filipinos—I'm part Filipina myself, my mom met my dad when he was stationed at Subic Bay—they've got this saying, *kumukuló ang dugó*. It means, 'the blood is boiling.' They can get pretty damn mad 'specially the men. So stuff like what you said—sure they do it."

"Do you work on Fridays?"

"Yeah, two to ten."

"Did you see any of the *Kabalyeros* in here last Friday around six?" That was the time when Isabel had been accosted.

Anna Smith scrunched up her face in concentration. "Last Friday ... oh, yeah, sure. That was when they had the big meeting all of them."

"*All* of them?"

"Uh-huh. Started around five-thirty, went on a couple of hours. My boss, he was worried something heavy was gonna go down, but the way it turned out, all he did was sell a lot of food."

"What was the meeting about?"

"Had to do with the Dragon, who was gonna be character witnesses at the trial, what they'd say."

The image of the three I'd seen earlier—or any of their ilk—as character witnesses was somewhat ludicrous, but I supposed in Tommy Dragón's position you took what you could get. "Are you sure they were all there?"

"Uh-huh."

"And no one at the meeting said anything about trying to keep Mrs. Angeles from testifying?"

"No. That lawyer the Dragon's got, he was there too."

Now that was odd. Why had Dragón's public defender chosen to meet with his witnesses in a public place? I could think of one good reason: he was afraid of them, didn't want them in his office. But what if the *Kabalyeros* had set the time and place—as an alibi for when Isabel was to be assaulted?

"I better get back to work," Anna Smith said. "Before the boss comes looking for me."

I gave her the twenty dollars. "Thanks for your time."

"Sure." Halfway out the door she paused, frowning. "I hope I didn't get any of the *Kabalyeros* in trouble."

"You didn't."

"Good. I kind of like them. I mean, they push dope and all, but these days, who doesn't?"

These days, who doesn't? I thought. *Good Lord ...*

The Starlight Lanes was an old-fashioned bowling alley girded by a rough cliff face and an auto dismantler's yard. The parking lot was crowded, so I left the MG around back by the garbage cans. Inside, the lanes were brightly lit and noisy with the sound of crashing pins, rumbling balls, shouts, and groans. I paused by the front counter and asked where I might find Jimmy Willis. The woman behind it directed me to a lane at the far end.

Bowling alleys—or lanes, as the new upscale bowler prefers to call them—are familiar territory to me. Up until a few years ago my favorite uncle Jim was a top player on the pro tour. The Starlight Lanes reminded me of the ones where Jim used to practice in San Diego—from the racks full of tired-looking rental shoes to the greasy-spoon coffeeshop smells to the molded plastic chairs and cigarette-burned scorekeeping consoles. I walked along it, soaking up the ambience—some people would say lack of it—until I came to lane 32 and spotted an agile young black man bowling alone. Jimmy Willis was a left-hander, and his ball hooked out until it hung on the edge of the channel, then hooked back with deadly accuracy and graceful form. His concentration was so great that he didn't notice me until he'd finished the last frame and retrieved his ball.

"You're quite a bowler," I said. "What's your average?"

He gave me a long look before he replied, "Two hundred."

"Almost good enough to turn pro."

"That's what I'm looking to do."

Odd, for the head of a street gang that dealt in drugs and death. "You ever heard of Jim McCone?" I asked.

"Sure. Damned good in his day."

"He's my uncle."

"No kidding." Willis studied me again, now as if looking for a resemblance.

Rapport established, I showed him my ID and explained that I wanted to talk about Reg Dawson's murder. He frowned, hesitated, then nodded. "Okay, since you're Jim McCone's niece, but you'll have to buy me a beer."

"Deal."

Willis toweled off his ball, stowed it and his shoes in their bag, and led me to a typical smoke-filled, murkily lighted bowling alley bar. He took one of the booths while I fetched us a pair of Buds.

As I slid into the booth I said, "What can you tell me about the murder?"

"The way I see it, Dawson was asking for it."

So he and Dawson's wife were of a mind about that. "I can understand what you mean, but it seems strange, coming from you. I hear you were his friend, that you took over the Victors after his death."

"You heard wrong on both counts. Yeah, I was in the Victors, and when Dawson bought it, they tried to get me to take over. But by then I'd figured out—never mind how, doesn't matter—that I wanted out of that life. Ain't nothing in it but what happened to Benny Crespo and Dawson—or what's going to happen to the Dragon. So I decided to put my hand to something with a future." He patted the bowling bag that sat on the banquette beside him. "Got a job here now—not much, but my bowling's free and I'm on my way."

"Good for you. What about Dragón—do you think he's guilty?"

Willis hesitated, looking thoughtful. "Why do you ask?"

"Just wondering."

"... Well, to tell you the truth, I never did believe the Dragon shot Reg."

"Who did, then?"

He shrugged.

I asked him if he'd heard about the *Kabalyeros* trying to intimidate the chief prosecution witness. When he nodded, I said, "They also threatened the life of her daughter last Friday."

He laughed mirthlessly. "Wish I could of seen that. Kind of surprises me, though. That lawyer of Dragón's, he found out what the *Kabalyeros* were up to, read them the riot act. Said they'd put Dragón in the gas chamber for sure. So they called it off."

"When was this?"

"Week, ten days ago."

Long before Isabel had been accosted. Before the dead dog and the shooting incidents, too. "Are you sure?"

"It's what I hear. You know, in a way I'm surprised that they'd go after Mrs. Angeles at all."

"Why?"

"The Filipinos have this macho tradition. 'Specially when it comes to their women. They don't like them messed with, 'specially by non-Filipinos. So how come they'd turn around and mess with one of their own?"

"Well, her testimony *would* jeopardize the life of one of their fellow gang members. It's an extreme situation."

"Can't argue with that."

Jimmy Willis and I talked a bit more, but he couldn't—or wouldn't— offer any further information. I bought him a second beer, then went out to where I'd left my car.

And came face-to-face with Hector Bulis and the man called Sal.

Sal grabbed me by the arm, twisted it behind me, and forced me up against the latticework fence surrounding the garbage cans. The stench from them filled my nostrils; Sal's breath rivaled it in foulness. I struggled, but he got hold of my other arm and pinned me tighter. I looked around, saw no one, nothing but the cliff face and the high board fence of the auto dismantler's yard. Bulis approached, flicking open a switchblade, his twisty face intense. I stiffened, went very still, eyes on the knife.

Bullis placed the tip of the knife against my jawbone, then traced a line across my cheek. "Don't want to hurt you, bitch," he said. "You do what I say, I won't have to mess you up."

The Tagalog phrase that Anna Smith had translated for me— *kumukuló ang dugó*—flashed through my mind. *The blood is boiling.* I sensed Bullis's was—and dangerously so.

I wet my dry lips, tried to keep my voice from shaking as I said, "What do you want me to do?"

"We hear you're asking around about Dawson's murder, trying to prove the Dragon did it."

"That's not—"

"We want you to quit. Go back to your own part of town and leave our business alone."

"Whoever told you that is lying. I'm only trying to help the Angeles family."

"They wouldn't lie." He moved the knife's tip to the hollow at the base of my throat. I felt it pierce my skin—a mere pinprick, but frightening enough.

When I could speak, I did so slowly, phrasing my words carefully. "What I hear is that Dragón is innocent. And that the *Kabalyeros* aren't behind the harassment of the Angeleses—at least not for a week or ten days."

Bullis exchanged a look with his companion—quick, unreadable.

"Someone's trying to frame you," I added. "Just like they did Dragón."

Bullis continued to hold the knife to my throat, his hand firm. His gaze wavered, however, as if he was considering what I'd said. After a moment he asked, "All right—who?"

"I'm not sure, but I think I can find out."

He thought a bit longer, then let his arm drop and snapped the knife shut. "I'll give you till this time tomorrow," he said. Then he stuffed the knife into his pocket, motioned for Sal to let go of me, and the two quickly walked away.

I sagged against the latticework fence, feeling my throat where the knife had pricked it. It had bled a little, but the flow already was clotting. My knees were weak and my breath came fast, but I was too caught up in the possibilities to panic. There were plenty of them—and the most likely was the most unpleasant.

Kumukuló ang dugó. The blood is boiling....

Two hours later I was back at the Angeles house on Omega Street. When Amor admitted me, the tension I'd felt in her earlier had drained. Her body sagged, as if the extra weight she carried had finally proved to be too much for her frail bones; the skin of her face looked flaccid, like melting putty; her eyes were sunken and vague. After she shut the door and motioned for me to sit, she sank into the recliner, expelling a sigh. The house was quiet—too quiet.

"I have a question for you," I said. "What does 'tick-tick' mean in Tagalog?"

Her eyes flickered with dull interest. *"Tiktik."* She corrected my pronunciation. "It's a word for detective."

Ever since Hector Bulis and Sal had accosted me I'd suspected as much.

"Where did you hear that?" Amor asked.

"One of the *Kabalyeros* said it when I went to Fat Robbie's earlier. Someone had told them I was a detective, probably described me. Whoever it was said I was trying to prove Tommy Dragón killed Reg Dawson."

"Why would—"

"More to the point, *who* would? At the time, only four people knew that I'm a detective."

She wet her lips, but remained silent.

"Amor, the night of the shooting, you were standing in your front window, watching for Isabel."

"Yes."

"Do you do that often?"

"... Yes."

"Because Isabel is often late coming home. Because you're afraid she may have gotten into trouble."

"A mother worries—"

"Especially when she's given good cause. Isabel is running out of control, isn't she?"

"No, she—"

"Amor, when I spoke with Madeline Dawson, she said you were standing in the window watching for 'sweet Isabel, like always.' She didn't say 'sweet' in a pleasant way. Later, Jimmy Willis implied that your daughter is not ... exactly a vulnerable young girl."

Amor's eyes sparked. "The Dawson woman is jealous."

"Of course she is. There's something else: when I asked the waitress at Fat Robbie's if she'd ever overheard the *Kabalyeros* discussing you, she said, 'No, not that one.' It didn't register at the time, but when I talked to her again a little while ago, she told me Isabel is the member of your family they discuss. They say she's wild, runs around with the men in the gangs. You know that, so does Alex. And so does Madeline Dawson. She just told me the first man Isabel became involved with was her husband."

Amor seemed to shrivel. She gripped the arms of the chair, white-knuckled.

"It's true, isn't it?" I asked more gently.

She lowered her eyes, nodding. When she spoke her voice was ragged. "I don't know what to do with her anymore. Ever since that Reg Dawson got to her, she's been different, not my girl at all."

"Is she on drugs?"

"Alex says no, but I'm not so sure."

I let it go; it really didn't matter. "When she came home earlier," I said, "Isabel seemed very interested in me. She asked questions, looked me over carefully enough to be able to describe to the *Kabalyeros*. She was afraid of what I might find out. For instance, that she wasn't accosted by any men with guns last Friday."

"She was!"

"No, Amor. That was just a story, to make it look as if your life—and your children's—were in danger if you testified. In spite of what you said early on, you haven't wanted to testify against Tommy Dragón from the very beginning.

"When the *Kabalyeros* began harassing you a month ago, you saw that as the perfect excuse not to take the stand. But you didn't foresee that Dragón's lawyer would convince the gang to stop the harassment. When that happened, you and Isabel, and probably Alex, too, manufactured incidents—the shot-out window, the dead dog on the doorstep, the men with the guns—to make it look as if the harassment was still going on."

"Why would I? They're going to put me in jail."

"But at the time you didn't know they could do that—or that your employer would hire me. My investigating poses yet another danger to you and your family."

"This is ... why would I do all that?"

"Because basically you're an honest woman, a good woman. You didn't want to testify because you knew Dragón didn't shoot Dawson. It's my guess you gave the police his name because it was the first one that came to mind."

"I had no reason to—"

"You had the best reason in the world: a mother's desire to protect her child."

She was silent, sunken eyes registering despair and defeat.

I kept on, even though I hated to inflict further pain on her. "The day he died, Dawson had let the word out that he was going to desecrate Benny's space. The person who shot him knew there would be fighting and confusion, counted on that as a cover. The killer hated Dawson—"

"Lots of people did."

"But only one person you'd want to protect so badly that you'd accuse an innocent man."

"Leave my mother alone. She's suffered enough on account of what I did."

I turned. Alex had come into the room so quietly I hadn't noticed. Now he moved midway between Amor and me, a Saturday night special clutched in his right hand.

The missing murder weapon.

I tensed, but one look at his face told me he didn't intend to use it. Instead he raised his arm and extended the gun, grip first.

"Take this," he said. "I never should of bought it. Never should of used it. I hated Dawson on account of what he did to my sister. But killing him wasn't worth what we've all gone through since."

I glanced at Amor; tears were trickling down her face.

Alex said, "Mama, don't cry. I'm not worth it."

When she spoke, it was to me. "What will happen to him?"

"Nothing like what might have happened to Dragón; Alex is a juvenile. You, however—"

"I don't care about myself, only my children."

Maybe that was the trouble. She was the archetypal selfless mother: living only for her children, sheltering them from the consequences of their actions—and in the end doing them irreparable harm.

There were times when I felt thankful that I had no children. And there were times when I was thankful that Jack Stuart was a very good criminal lawyer. This was a time I was thankful on both counts. I went to the phone, called Jack, and asked him to come over here. At least I could leave the Angeles family in good legal hands.

After he arrived, I went out into the gathering dusk. An old yellow VW was pulling out of Benny's space. I walked down there and stood on the curb. Nothing remained of the shrine to Benny Crespo. Nothing remained to show that blood had boiled and been shed here. It was merely a stretch of cracked asphalt, splotched with oil drippings, littered with the detritus of urban life. I stared at it for close to a minute, then turned away from the bleak landscape of Omega Street.

THE LOST COAST

California's Lost Coast is at the same time one of the most desolate and beautiful of shorelines. Northerly winds whip the sand into dustdevil frenzy; eerie, stationary fogs hang in the trees and distort the driftwood until it resembles the bones of prehistoric mammals; bruised clouds hover above the peaks of the distant King Range, then blow down to sea level and dump icy torrents. But on a fair day the sea and sky show infinite shadings of blue, and the wildflowers are a riot of color. If you wait quietly, you can spot deer, peregrine falcons, foxes, otters, even black bears and mountain lions.

A contradictory and oddly compelling place, this seventy-three-mile stretch of coast southwest of Eureka, where—as with most worthwhile things or people—you must take the bad with the good.

Unfortunately, on my first visit there I was taking mostly the bad. Strong winds pushed my MG all over the steep, narrow road, making hairpin turns even more perilous. Early October rain cut my visibility to a few yards. After I crossed the swollen Bear River, the road continued to twist and wind, and I began to understand why the natives had dubbed it The Wildcat.

Somewhere ahead, my client had told me, was the hamlet of Petrolia—site of the first oil well drilled in California, he'd irrelevantly added. The man was a conservative politician, a former lumber-company attorney, and given what I knew of his voting record on the environment, I was certain we disagreed on the desirability of that event, as well as any number of similar issues. But the urgency of the current situation dictated that I keep my opinions to myself, so I'd simply written down the directions he gave me—omitting his travelogue-like asides—and gotten under way.

I drove through Petrolia—a handful of new buildings, since the village had been all but leveled in the disastrous earthquake of 1992—and turned toward the sea on an unpaved road. After two miles I began looking for the orange post that marked the dirt track to the client's cabin.

The whole time I was wishing I was back in San Francisco. This wasn't my kind of case; I didn't like the client, Steve Shoemaker; and even though the fee was good, this was the week I'd scheduled to take off a few personal business days from All Souls Legal Cooperative, where I'm chief investigator. But Jack Stuart, our criminal specialist, had asked me to take on the job as a favor to him. Steve Shoemaker was Jack's old friend from college in Southern California, and he'd asked for a referral to a private detective. Jack owed Steve a favor; I owed Jack several, so there was no way I could gracefully refuse.

But I couldn't shake the feeling that something was wrong with this case. And I couldn't help wishing that I'd come to the Lost Coast in summertime, with a backpack and in the company of my lover—instead of on a rainy fall afternoon, with a .38 Special and soon to be in the company of Shoemaker's disagreeable wife, Andrea.

The rain was sheeting down by the time I spotted the orange post. It had turned the hard-packed earth to mud, and my MG's tires sank deep in the ruts, its undercarriage scraping dangerously. I could barely make out the stand of live oaks and sycamores where the track ended; no way to tell if another vehicle had traveled over it recently.

When I reached the end of the track I saw one of those boxy four-wheel-drive wagons—Bronco? Cherokee?—drawn in under the drooping branches of an oak. Andrea Shoemaker's? I'd neglected to get a description from her husband of what she drove. I got out of the MG, turning the hood of my heavy sweater up against the downpour; the wind promptly blew it off. So much for what the catalog had described as "extra protection on those cold nights." I yanked the hood up again and held it there, went around and took my .38 from the trunk and shoved it into the outside flap of my purse. Then I went over and tried the door of the four-wheel drive. Unlocked. I opened it, slipped into the driver's seat.

Nothing identifying its owner was on the seats or in the side pockets, but in the glove compartment I found a registration in the name of Andrea Shoemaker. I rummaged around, came up with nothing else of interest. Then I got out and walked through the trees, looking for the cabin.

Shoemaker had told me to follow a deer track through the grove. No sign of it in this downpour; no deer, either. Nothing but wind-lashed trees, the oaks pelting me with acorns. I moved slowly through them, swiveling my head from side to side, until I made out a bulky shape tucked beneath the farthest of the sycamores.

As I got closer, I saw the cabin was of plain weathered wood, rudely constructed, with the chimney of a woodstove extending from its composition shingle roof. Small—two or three rooms—and no light showing in its windows. And the door was open, banging against the inside wall

I quickened my pace, taking the gun from my purse. Alongside the door I stopped to listen. Silence. I had a flashlight in my bag; I took it out. Moved to where I could see inside, then turned the flash on and shone it through the door.

All that was visible was rough board walls, an oilcloth-covered table and chairs, an ancient woodstove. I stepped inside, swinging the light around. Unlit oil lamp on the table; flower-cushioned wooden furniture of the sort you always find in vacation cabins; rag rugs; shelves holding an assortment of tattered paperbacks, seashells, and drift wood. I shifted the light again, more slowly.

A chair on the far side of the table was tipped over, and a woman's purse lay on the edge of the woodstove, its contents spilling out. When I got over there I saw a .32 Iver Johnson revolver lying on the floor.

Andrea Shoemaker owned a .32. She'd told me so the day before.

Two doors opened off the room. Quietly I went to one and tried it. A closet, shelves stocked with staples and canned goods and bottled water. I looked around the room again, listening. No sound but the wail of wind and the pelt of rain on the roof. I stepped to the other door.

A bedroom, almost filled wall-to-wall by a king-sized bed covered with a goosedown comforter and piled with colorful pillows. Old bureau pushed in one corner, another unlit oil lamp on the single nightstand. Small travel bag on the bed.

The bag hadn't been opened. I examined its contents. Jeans, a couple of sweaters, underthings, toilet articles. Package of condoms. Uh-huh. She'd come here, as I'd found out, to meet a man. The affairs usually began with a casual pickup; they were never of long duration; and they all seemed to culminate in a romantic weekend in the isolated cabin.

Dangerous game, particularly in these days when AIDS and the prevalence of disturbed individuals of both sexes threatened. But Andrea Shoemaker had kept her latest date with an even larger threat hanging over her: for the past six weeks, a man with a serious grudge against her husband had been stalking her. For all I knew, he and the date were one and the same.

And where was Andrea now?

This case had started on Wednesday, two days ago, when I'd driven up to Eureka, a lumbering and fishing town on Humboldt Bay. After I passed the Humboldt County line I began to see huge logging trucks toiling through the mountain passes, shredded curls of redwood bark trailing in their wakes. Twenty-five miles south of the city itself was the company-owned town of Scotia, mill stacks belching white smoke and filling the air with the scent of freshly cut wood. Yards full of logs waiting to be fed to the mills lined the highway. When I reached Eureka itself, the downtown struck me as curiously quiet; many of the stores were out of business, and the sidewalks were mostly deserted. The recession had hit the lumber industry hard, and the earthquake hadn't helped the area's strapped economy.

I'd arranged to meet Steve Shoemaker at his law offices in Old Town, near the waterfront. It was a picturesque area full of renovated warehouses and interesting shops and restaurants, tricked up for tourists with the inevitable horse-and-carriage rides and t-shirt shops, but still pleasant. Shoemaker's offices were off a cobblestoned courtyard containing a couple of antique shops and a decorator's showroom.

When I gave my card to the secretary, she said Assemblyman Shoemaker was in conference and asked me to wait. The man, I knew, had lost his seat in the state legislature this past election, so the term of address seemed inappropriate. The appointments of the waiting room struck me as a bit much: brass and mahogany and marble and velvet, plenty of it, the furnishings all antiques that tended to the garish. I sat on a red velvet sofa and looked for something to read. *Architectural Digest, National Review, Foreign Affairs*—that was it, take it or leave it. I left it. My idea of waiting-room reading material is *People;* I love it, but I'm too embarrassed to subscribe.

The minutes ticked by: ten, fifteen, twenty. I contemplated the issue of *Architectural Digest,* then opted instead for staring at a fake Rembrandt on the far wall. Twenty-five, thirty. I was getting irritated now. Shoemaker had asked me to be here by three; I'd arrived on the dot. If this was, as he'd claimed, a matter of such urgency and delicacy that he couldn't go into it on the phone, why was he in conference at the appointed time?

Thirty-five minutes. Thirty-seven. The door to the inner sanctum opened and a woman strode out. A tall woman, with long chestnut hair, wearing a raincoat and black leather boots. Her eyes rested on me in passing—a cool gray, hard with anger. Then she went out, slamming the door behind her.

The secretary—a trim blond in a tailored suit—started as the door slammed. She glanced at me and tried to cover with a smile, but its edges were strained, and her fingertips pressed hard against the desk. The phone at her elbow buzzed; she snatched up the receiver. Spoke into it, then said to me, "Ms. McCone, Assemblyman Shoemaker will see you now." As she ushered me inside, she again gave me her frayed-edge smile.

Tense situation in this office, I thought. Brought on by what? The matter Steve Shoemaker wanted me to investigate? The client who had just made her angry exit? Or something else entirely ...?

Shoemaker's office was even more pretentious than the waiting room: more brass, mahogany, velvet, and marble; more fake Old Masters in heavy gilt frames; more antiques; more of everything. Shoemaker's demeanor was not as nervous as his secretary's, but when he rose to greet me, I noticed a jerkiness in his movements, as if he was holding himself under tight control. I clasped his outstretched hand and smiled, hoping the familiar social rituals would set him more at ease.

Momentarily they did. He thanked me for coming, apologized for making me wait, and inquired after Jack Stuart. After I was seated in one of the clients' chairs, he offered me a drink; I asked for mineral water. As he went to a wet bar tucked behind a tapestry screen, I took the opportunity to study him.

Shoemaker was handsome: dark hair, with the gray so artfully interwoven that it must have been professionally dyed. Chiseled features; nice, well-muscled body, shown off to perfection by an expensive blue suit. When he handed me my drink, his smile revealed white, even teeth that I, having spent the greater part of the previous month in the company of my dentist, recognized as capped. Yes, a very good-looking man, politician handsome. Jack's old friend or not, his appearance and manner called up my gut-level distrust.

My client went around his desk and reclaimed his chair. He held a drink of his own—something dark amber—and he took a deep swallow before speaking. The alcohol replenished his vitality some; he drank again, set the glass on a pewter coaster, and said, "Ms. McCone, I'm glad you could come up here on such short notice."

"You mentioned on the phone that the case is extremely urgent—and delicate."

He ran his hand over his hair—lightly, so as not to disturb its styling. "Extremely urgent and delicate," he repeated, seeming to savor the phrase.

"Why don't you tell me about it?"

His eyes strayed to the half-full glass on the coaster. Then they moved to the door through which I'd entered. Returned to me. "You saw the woman who just left?"

I nodded.

"My wife, Andrea."

I waited.

"She's very angry with me for hiring you."

"She did act angry. Why?"

Now he reached for the glass and belted down its contents. Leaned back and rattled the ice cubes as he spoke. "It's a long story. Painful to me. I'm not sure where to begin. I just ... don't know what to make of the things that are happening."

"That's what you've hired me to do. Begin anywhere. We'll fill in the gaps later." I pulled a small tape recorder from my bag and set it on the edge of his desk. "Do you mind?"

Shoemaker eyed it warily, but shook his head. After a moment's hesitation, he said, "Someone is stalking my wife."

"Following her? Threatening her?"

"Not following, not that I know of. He writes notes, threatening to kill her. He leaves ... things at the house. At her place of business. Dead things. Birds, rats, one time a cat. Andrea loves cats. She ..." He shook his head, went to the bar for a refill.

"What else? Phone calls?"

"No. One time, a floral arrangement—suitable for a funeral."

"Does he sign the notes?"

"John. Just John."

"Does Mrs. Shoemaker know anyone named John who has a grudge against her?"

"She says no. And I ..." He sat down, fresh drink in hand. "I have reason to believe that this John has a grudge against me, is using this harassment of Andrea to get at me personally."

"Why do you think that?"

"The wording of the notes."

"May I see them?"

He looked around, as if he were afraid someone might be listening. "Later. I keep them elsewhere."

Something, then, I thought, that he didn't want his office staff to see. Something shameful, perhaps even criminal.

"Okay," I said, "how long has this been going on?"

"About six weeks."

"Have you contacted the police?"

"Informally. A man I know on the force, Sergeant Bob Wolfe. But after he started looking into it, I had to ask him to drop it."

"Why?"

"I'm in a sensitive political position."

"Excuse me if I'm mistaken, Mr. Shoemaker, but it's my understanding that you're no longer serving in the state legislature."

"That's correct, but I'm about to announce my candidacy in a special election for a senate seat that's recently been vacated."

"I see. So after you asked your contact on the police force to back off, you decided to use a private investigator, and Jack recommended me. Why not use someone local?"

"As I said, my position is sensitive. I don't want word of this getting out in the community. That's why Andrea is so angry with me. She claims I value my political career more than her life."

I waited, wondering how he'd attempt to explain that away.

He didn't even try, merely went on, "In our ... conversation just prior to this, she threatened to leave me. This coming weekend she plans to go to a cabin on the Lost Coast that she inherited from her father to, as she put it, sort things through. Alone. Do you know that part of the coast?"

"I've read some travel pieces on it."

"Then you're aware how remote it is. The cabin's very isolated. I don't want Andrea going there while this John person is on the loose."

"Does she go there often?"

"Fairly often. I don't; it's too rustic for me—no running water, phone, or electricity. But Andrea likes it. Why do you ask?"

"I'm wondering if John—whoever he is—knows about the cabin. Has she been there since the harassment began?"

"No. Initially she agreed that it wouldn't be a good idea. But now ..." He shrugged.

"I'll need to speak with Mrs. Shoemaker. Maybe I can reason with her, persuade her not to go until we've identified John. Or maybe she'll allow me to go along as her bodyguard."

"You can speak with her if you like, but she's beyond reasoning with. And there's no way you can stop her or force her to allow you to accompany her. My wife is a strong-willed woman; that interior decorating firm across the courtyard is hers, she built it from the ground up. When Andrea decides to do something, she does it. And asks permission from no one."

"Still, I'd like to try reasoning. This trip to the cabin—that's the urgency you mentioned on the phone. Two days to find the man behind the harassment before she goes out there and perhaps makes a target of herself."

"Yes."

"Then I'd better get started. That funeral arrangement—what florist did it come from?"

Shoemaker shook his head. "It arrived at least five weeks ago, before either of us noticed a pattern to the harassment. Andrea just shrugged it off, threw the wrappings and card away."

"Let's go look at the notes, then. They're my only lead."

Vengeance will be mine. The sudden blow. The quick attack.
Vengeance is the price of silence.

Mute testimony paves the way to an early grave. The rest is silence.

A freshly turned grave is silent testimony
to an old wrong and its avenger.

There was more in the same vein—slightly biblical-flavored and stilted.

But chilling to me, even though the safety-deposit booth at Shoemaker's bank was overly warm. If that was my reaction, what had these notes done to Andrea Shoemaker? No wonder she was thinking of leaving a husband who cared more for the electorate's opinion than his wife's life and safety.

The notes had been typed without error on an electric machine that had left no such obvious clues as chipped or skewed keys. The paper and envelopes were plain and cheap, purchasable at any discount store. They had been handled, I was sure, by nothing more than gloved hands. No signature—just the typed name "John."

But the writer had wanted the Shoemakers—one of them, anyway—to know who he was. Thus the theme that ran through them all: silence and revenge.

I said, "I take it your contact at the E.P.D. had their lab go over these?"

"Yes. There was nothing. That's why he wanted to probe further—something I couldn't permit him to do."

"Because of this revenge-and-silence business. Tell me about it."

Shoemaker looked around furtively. My God, did he think bank employees had nothing better to do with their time than to eavesdrop on our conversation?

"We'll go have a drink," he said. "I know a place that's private."

We went to a restaurant a few blocks away, where Shoemaker had another bourbon and I toyed with a glass of iced tea. After some prodding, he told me his story; it didn't enhance him in my eyes.

Seventeen years ago Shoemaker had been interviewing for a staff attorney's position at a large lumber company. While on a tour of the mills, he witnessed an accident in which a worker named Sam Carding was severely mangled while trying to clear a jam in a bark-stripping machine. Shoemaker, who had worked in the mills summers to pay for his education, knew the accident was due to company negligence, but accepted a handsome job offer in exchange for not testifying for the plaintiff in the ensuing lawsuit. The court ruled against Carding, confined to a wheelchair and in constant pain; a year later, while the case was still under appeal, Carding shot his wife and himself. The couple's three children were given token settlements in exchange for dropping the suit and then were adopted by relatives in a different part of the country.

"It's not a pretty story, Mr. Shoemaker," I said, "and I can see why the wording of the notes might make you suspect there's a connection between it and this harassment. But who do you think John is?"

"Carding's oldest boy. Carding and his family knew I'd witnessed the accident; one of his coworkers saw me watching from the catwalk and told him. Later, when I turned up as a senior counsel ..." He shrugged.

"But why, after all this time—?"

"Why not? People nurse grudges. John Carding was sixteen at the time of the lawsuit; there were some ugly scenes with him, both at my home and my office at the mill. By now he'd be in his forties. Maybe it's his way of acting out some sort of midlife crisis."

"Well, I'll call my office and have my assistant run a check on all three Carding kids. And I want to speak with Mrs. Shoemaker—preferably in your presence."

He glanced at his watch. "It can't be tonight. She's got a meeting of her professional organization, and I'm dining with my campaign manager."

A potentially psychotic man was threatening Andrea's life, yet they both carried on as usual. Well, who was I to question it? Maybe it was their way of coping.

"Tomorrow, then," I said. "Your home. At the noon hour."

Shoemaker nodded. Then he gave me the address, as well as the names of John Carding's siblings.

I left him on the sidewalk in front of the restaurant: a handsome man whose shoulders now slumped inside his expensive suitcoat, shivering in the brisk wind off Humboldt Bay. As we shook hands, I saw that shame made his gaze unsteady, the set of his mouth less than firm.

I knew that kind of shame. Over the course of my career, I'd committed some dreadful acts that years later woke me in the deep of the night to sudden panic. I'd also *not* committed certain acts—failures that woke me to regret and emptiness. My sins of omission were infinitely worse than those of commission, because I knew that if I'd acted, I could have made a difference. Could even have saved a life.

I wasn't able to reach Rae Kelleher, my assistant at All Souls, that evening, and by the time she got back to me the next morning—Thursday—I was definitely annoyed. Still, I tried to keep a lid on my irritation. Rae is young, attractive, and in love; I couldn't expect her to spend her evenings waiting to be of service to her workaholic boss.

I got her started on a computer check on all three Cardings, then took myself to the Eureka P.D. and spoke with Shoemaker's contact, Sergeant Bob Wolfe. Wolfe—a dark haired, sharp featured man whose appearance was a good match for his surname told me he'd had the notes processed by the lab, which had turned up no useful evidence.

"Then I started to probe, you know? When you got a harassment case like this, you look into the victims' private lives."

"And that was when Shoemaker told you to back off."

"Uh-huh."

"When was this?"

"About five weeks ago."

"I wonder why he waited so long to hire me. Did he, by any chance, ask you for a referral to a local investigator?"

Wolfe frowned. "Not this time."

"Then you'd referred him to someone before?"

"Yeah, guy who used to be on the force—Dave Morrison. Last April."

"Did Shoemaker tell you why he needed an investigator?"

"No, and I didn't ask. These politicians, they're always trying to get something on their rivals. I didn't want any part of it."

"Do you have Morrison's address and phone number handy?"

Wolfe reached into his desk drawer, shuffled things, and flipped a business card across the blotter. "Dave gave me a stack of these when he set up shop," he said. "Always glad to help an old pal."

Morrison was out of town, the message on his answering machine said, but would be back tomorrow afternoon. I left a message of my own, asking him to call me at my motel. Then I headed for the Shoemakers' home, hoping I could talk some common sense into Andrea.

But Andrea wasn't having any common sense.

She strode around the parlor of their big Victorian—built by one of the city's lumber barons, her husband told me when I complimented them on it—arguing and waving her arms and making scathing statements punctuated by a good amount of profanity. And knocking back martinis, even though it was only a little past noon.

Yes, she was going to the cabin. No, neither her husband nor I was welcome there. No, she wouldn't postpone the trip; she was sick and tired of being cooped up like some kind of zoo animal because her husband had made a mistake years before she'd met him. All right, she realized this John person was dangerous. But she'd taken self-defense classes and owned a .32 revolver. Of course she knew how to use it. Practiced frequently, too. Women had to be prepared these days, and she was.

But, she added darkly, glaring at her husband, she'd just as soon not have to shoot John. She'd rather send him straight back to Steve and let them settle this score. May the best man win—and she was placing bets on John.

As far as I was concerned, Steve and Andrea Shoemaker deserved each other.

I tried to explain to her that self-defense classes don't fully prepare you for a paralyzing, heart-pounding encounter with an actual violent stranger. I tried to warn her that the ability to shoot well on a firing range doesn't fully prepare you for pumping a bullet into a human being who is advancing swiftly on you.

I wanted to tell her she was being an idiot.

Before I could, she slammed down her glass and stormed out of the house.

Her husband replenished his own drink and said, "Now do you see what I'm up against?"

I didn't respond to that. Instead I said, "I spoke with Sergeant Wolfe earlier."

"And?"

"He told me he referred you to a local private investigator, Dave Morrison, last April."

"So?"

"Why didn't you hire Morrison for this job?"

"As I told you yesterday, my—"

"Sensitive position, yes."

Shoemaker scowled.

Before he could comment, I asked, "What was the job last April?"

"Nothing to do with this matter."

"Something to do with politics?"

"In a way."

"Mr. Shoemaker, hasn't it occurred to you that a political enemy may be using the Carding case as a smoke screen? That a rival's trying to throw you off balance before this special election?"

"It did, and ... well, it isn't my opponent's style. My God, we're civilized people. But those notes ... they're the work of a lunatic."

I wasn't so sure he was right—both about the notes being the work of a lunatic and politicians being civilized people—but I merely said, "Okay, you keep working on Mrs. Shoemaker. At least persuade her to let me go to the Lost Coast with her. I'll be in touch." Then I headed for the public library.

After a few hours of ruining my eyes at the microfilm machine, I knew little more than before. Newspaper accounts of the Carding accident, lawsuit, and murder-suicide didn't differ substantially from what my client had told me. Their coverage of the Shoemakers' activities was only marginally interesting.

Normally I don't do a great deal of background investigation on clients, but as Sergeant Wolfe had said, in a case like this where one or both of them was a target, a thorough look at careers and lifestyles was mandatory. The papers described Steve as a straightforward, effective assemblyman who took a hard, conservative stance on such issues as welfare and the environment. He was strongly pro-business, particularly the lumber industry. He and his "charming and talented wife" didn't share many interests: Steve hunted and golfed; Andrea was a "generous supporter of the arts" and a "lavish party-giver." An odd couple, I thought, and odd people to be friends of Jack Stuart, a liberal who'd chosen to dedicate his career to representing the underdog.

Back at the motel, I put in a call to Jack. Why, I asked him, had he remained close to a man who was so clearly his opposite?

Jack laughed. "You're trying to say politely that you think he's a pompous, conservative ass."

"Well ..."

"Okay, I admit it: he is. But back in college, he was a mentor to me. I doubt I would have gone into the law if it hadn't been for Steve. And we shared some good times, too: one summer we took a motorcycle trip around the country, like something out of *Easy Rider* without the tragedy. I guess we stay in touch because of a shared past."

I was trying to imagine Steve Shoemaker on a motorcycle; the picture wouldn't materialize. "Was he always so conservative?" I asked.

"No, not until he moved back to Eureka and went to work for that lumber company. Then ... I don't know. Everything changed. It was as if something had happened that took all the fight out of him."

What had happened, I thought, was trading another man's life for a prestigious job.

Jack and I chatted for a moment longer, and then I asked him to transfer me to Rae. She hadn't turned up anything on the Cardings yet, but was working on it. In the meantime, she added, she'd taken care of what correspondence had come in, dealt with seven phone calls, entered next week's must-do's in the call-up file she'd created for me, and found a remedy for the blight that was affecting my rubber plant.

With a pang, I realized that the office ran just as well—better, perhaps—when I wasn't there. It would keep functioning smoothly without me for weeks, months, maybe years.

Hell, it would probably keep functioning smoothly even if I were dead.

In the morning I opened the Yellow Pages to Florists and began calling each that was listed. While Shoemaker had been vague on the date his wife received the funeral arrangement, surely a customer who wanted one sent to a private home, rather than a mortuary, would stand out in the order-taker's mind. The listing was long, covering a relatively wide area; it wasn't until I reached the R's and my watch showed nearly eleven o'clock that I got lucky.

"I don't remember any order like that in the past six weeks," the clerk at Rainbow Florists said, "but we had one yesterday, was delivered this morning."

I gripped the receiver harder. "Will you pull the order, please?"

"I'm not sure I should—"

"Please. You could help to save a woman's life."

Quick intake of breath, then his voice filled with excitement; he'd become part of a real-life drama. "One minute. I'll check." When he came back on the line, he said, "Thirty-dollar standard condolence arrangement, delivered this morning to Mr. Steven Shoemaker—"

"*Mister?* Not Mrs. or Ms.?"

"Mister, definitely. I took the order myself." He read off the Shoemakers' address.

"Who placed it?"

"A kid. Came in with cash and written instructions."

Standard ploy—hire a kid off the street so nobody can identify you.

"Thanks very much."

"Aren't you going to tell me—"

I hung up and dialed Shoemaker's office. His secretary told me he was working at home today. I dialed the home number. Busy. I hung up, and the phone rang immediately. Rae, with information on the Cardings.

She'd traced Sam Carding's daughter and younger son. The daughter lived near Cleveland, Ohio, and Rae had spoken with her on the phone. John, his sister had told her, was a drifter and an addict; she hadn't seen or spoken to him in more than ten years. When Rae reached the younger brother at his office in L.A., he told her the same, adding that he assumed John had died years ago.

I thanked Rae and told her to keep on it. Then I called Shoemaker's home number again. Still busy; time to go over there.

Shoemaker's Lincoln was parked in the drive of the Victorian, a dusty Honda motorcycle beside it. As I rang the doorbell I again tried to picture a younger, free-spirited Steve bumming around the country on a bike with Jack, but the image simply wouldn't come clear. It took Shoemaker a while to answer the door, and when he saw me, his mouth pulled down in displeasure.

"Come in, and be quick about it," he told me. "I'm on an important conference call."

I was quick about it. He rushed down the hallway to what must be a study, and I went into the parlor where we'd talked the day before. Unlike his offices, it was exquisitely decorated, calling up images of the days of the lumber barons. Andrea's work, probably. Had she also done his offices? Perhaps their gaudy decor was her way of getting back at a husband who put his political life ahead of their marriage?

It was at least half an hour before Shoemaker finished with his call. He appeared in the archway leading to the hall, somewhat disheveled, running his fingers through his hair. "Come with me," he said. "I have something to show you."

He led me to a large kitchen at the back of the house. A floral arrangement sat on the granite-topped center island: white lilies with a single red rose. Shoemaker handed me the card: "My sympathy on your wife's passing." It was signed "John."

"Where's Mrs. Shoemaker?" I asked.

"Apparently she went out to the coast last night. I haven't seen her since she walked out on us at the noon hour."

"And you've been home the whole time?"

He nodded. "Mainly on the phone."

"Why didn't you call me when she didn't come home?"

"I didn't realize she hadn't until mid-morning. We have separate bedrooms, and Andrea comes and goes as she pleases. Then this arrangement arrived, and my conference call came through...." He shrugged, spreading his hands helplessly.

"All right," I said, "I'm going out there whether she likes it or not. And I think you'd better clear up whatever you're doing here and follow. Maybe your showing up there will convince her you care about her safety, make her listen to reason."

As I spoke, Shoemaker had taken a fifth of Tanqueray gin and a jar of Del Prado Spanish olives from a Safeway sack that sat on the counter. He opened a cupboard, reached for a glass.

"No," I said. "This is no time to have a drink."

He hesitated, then replaced the glass, and began giving me directions to the cabin. His voice was flat, and his curious travelogue-like digressions made me feel as if I were listening to a tape of a *National Geographic* special. Reality, I thought, had finally sunk in, and it had turned him into an automaton.

I had one stop to make before heading out to the coast, but it was right on my way. Morrison Investigations had its office in what looked to be a former motel on Highway 101, near the outskirts of the city. It was a neighborhood of fast-food restaurants and bars, thrift shops and marginal businesses. Besides the detective agency, the motel's cinderblock units housed an insurance brokerage, a secretarial service, two accountants, and a palm reader. Dave Morrison, who was just arriving as I pulled into the parking area, was a bit of a surprise: in his mid-forties, wearing one small gold earring and a short ponytail. I wondered what Steve Shoemaker had made of him.

Morrison showed me into a two-room suite crowded with computer equipment and file cabinets and furniture that looked as if he might have hauled it down the street from the nearby Thrift Emporium. When he noticed me studying him, he grinned easily. "I know, I don't look like a former cop. I worked undercover Narcotics my last few years on the force. Afterwards I realized I was comfortable with the uniform." His gesture took in his lumberjack's shirt, work-worn jeans and boots.

I smiled in return, and he cleared some files off a chair so I could sit.

"So you're working for Steve Shoemaker," he said.

"I understand you did, too."

He nodded. "Last April and again around the beginning of August."

"Did he approach you about another job after that?"

He shook his head.

"And the jobs you did for him were—"

"You know better than to ask that."

"I was going to ask, were they completed to his satisfaction?"

"Yes."

"Do you have any idea why Shoemaker would go to the trouble of bringing me up from San Francisco when he had an investigator here whose work satisfied him?"

Headshake.

"Shoemaker told me the first job you did for him had to do with politics."

The corner of his mouth twitched. "In a matter of speaking." He paused, shrewd eyes assessing me. "How come you're investigating your own client?"

"It's that kind of case. And something feels wrong. Did you get that sense about either of the jobs you took on for him?"

"No." Then he hesitated, frowning. "Well, maybe. Why don't you just come out and ask what you want to? If I can, I'll answer."

"Okay—did either of the jobs have to do with a man named John Carding?"

That surprised him. After a moment he asked a question of his own. "He's still trying to trace Carding?"

"Yes."

Morrison got up and moved toward the window, stopped and drummed his fingers on top of a file cabinet. "Well, I can save you further trouble. John Carding is untraceable. I tried every way I know—and that's every way there is. My guess is that he's dead, years dead."

"And when was it you tried to trace him?"

"Most of August."

Weeks before Andrea Shoemaker had begun to receive the notes from "John." Unless the harassment had started earlier? No, I'd seen all the notes, examined their postmarks. Unless she'd thrown away the first ones, as she had the card that came with the funeral arrangement?

"Shoemaker tell you why he wanted to find Carding?" I asked.

"Uh-uh."

"And your investigation last April had nothing to do with Carding?"

At first I thought Morrison hadn't heard the question. He was looking out the window; then he turned, expression thoughtful, and opened one of the drawers of the filing cabinet beside him. "Let me refresh my memory," he said, taking out a couple of folders. I watched as he flipped through them, frowning.

Finally he said, "I'm not gonna ask about your case. If something feels wrong, it could be because of what I turned up last spring—and that I don't want on my conscience." He closed one file, slipped it back in the cabinet, then glanced at his watch. "Damn! I just remembered I've got to make a call." He crossed to the desk, set the open file on it. "I better do it from the other room. You stay here, find something to read."

I waited until he'd left, then went over and picked up the file. Read it with growing interest and began putting things together. Andrea had been discreet about her extramarital activities, but not so discreet that a competent investigator like Morrison couldn't uncover them.

When Morrison returned, I was ready to leave for the Lost Coast.

"I hope you weren't bored," he said.

"No, I'm easily amused. And, Mr. Morrison, I owe you a dinner."

"You know where to find me. I'll look forward to seeing you again."

And now that I'd reached the cabin, Andrea had disappeared. The victim of violence, all signs indicated. But the victim of whom? John Carding—a man no one had seen or heard from for over ten years? Another man named John, one of her cast-off lovers? Or ...?

What mattered now was to find her.

I retraced my steps, turning up the hood of my sweater again as I went outside. Circled the cabin, peering through the lashing rain. I could make out a couple of other small structures back there: outhouse and shed. The outhouse was empty. I crossed to the shed. Its door was propped open with a log, as if she'd been getting fuel for the stove.

Inside, next to a neatly stacked cord of wood, I found her.

She lay facedown on the hard-packed dirt floor, blue-jeaned legs splayed, plaid-jacketed arms flung above her head, chestnut hair cascading over her back. The little room was silent, the total silence that surrounds the dead. Even my own breath was stilled; when it came again, it sounded obscenely loud.

I knelt beside her, forced myself to perform all the checks I've made more times than I could have imagined. No breath, no pulse, no warmth to the skin. And the rigidity ...

On the average—although there's a wide variance—rigor mortis sets in to the upper body five to six hours after death; the whole body is usually affected within eighteen hours. I backed up and felt the lower portion of her body. Rigid; rigor was complete. I straightened, went to stand in the doorway. She'd probably been dead since midnight. And the cause? I couldn't see any wounds, couldn't further examine her without disturbing the scene. What I should be doing was getting in touch with the sheriff's department.

Back to the cabin. Emotions tore at me: anger, regret, and—yes—guilt that I hadn't prevented this. But I also sensed that I *couldn't* have prevented it. I, or someone like me, had been an integral component from the first.

In the front room I found some kitchen matches and lit the oil lamp. Then I went around the table and looked down at where her revolver lay on the floor. More evidence; don't touch it. The purse and its spilled contents rested near the edge of the stove. I inventoried the items visually: the usual makeup, brush, comb, spray perfume; wallet, keys, roll of postage stamps; daily planner that had flopped open to show pockets for business cards and receipts. And a loose piece of paper ...

Safeway, it said at the top. Perhaps she'd stopped to pick up supplies before leaving Eureka; the date and time on this receipt might indicate how long she'd remained in town before storming out on her husband and me. After I picked it up. At the bottom I found yesterday's date and the time of purchase: 9:14 p.m.

"KY SERV DELI ... CRABS ... WINE ... DEL PRAD OLIVE ... LG RED DEL ... ROUGE ET NOIR ... BAKERY... TANQ GIN—"

A sound outside. Footsteps slogging through the mud. I stuffed the receipt into my pocket.

Steve Shoemaker came through the open door in a hurry, rain hat pulled low on his forehead, droplets sluicing down his chiseled nose He stopped when he saw me, looked around. "Where's Andrea?"

I said, "I don't know."

"What do you mean you don't know? Her Bronco's outside. That's her purse on the stove."

"And her weekend bag's on the bed, but she's nowhere to be found."

Shoemaker arranged his face into lines of concern. "There's been a struggle here."

"Appears that way."

"Come on, we'll go look for her. She may be in the outhouse or the shed. She may be hurt—"

"It won't be necessary to look." I had my gun out of my purse now, and I leveled it at him. "I know you killed your wife, Shoemaker."

"What!"

"Her body's where you left it last night. What time did you kill her? How?"

His faked concern shaded into panic. "I didn't—"

"You did."

No reply. His eyes moved from side to side—calculating, looking for a way out.

I added, "You drove her here in the Bronco, with your motorcycle inside. Arranged things to simulate a struggle, put her in the shed then drove back to town on the bike. You shouldn't have left the bike outside the house where I could see it. It wasn't muddy out here last night, but it sure was dusty."

"Where are these baseless accusations coming from? John Carding—"

"Is untraceable, probably dead, as you know from the check Dave Morrison ran."

"He told you— What about the notes, the flowers, the dead things—"

"Sent by you."

"Why would I do that?"

"To set the scene for getting rid of a chronically unfaithful wife who had potential to become a political embarrassment."

He wasn't cracking, though. "Granted, Andrea had her problems. But why would I rake up the Carding matter?"

"Because it would sound convincing for you to admit what you did all those years ago. God knows it convinced me. And I doubt the police would ever have made the details public. Why destroy a grieving widower and prominent citizen? Particularly when they'd never find Carding or bring him to trial. You've got one problem, though: me. You never should have brought me in to back up your scenario."

He licked his lips, glaring at me. Then he drew himself up, leaned forward aggressively—a posture the attorneys at All Souls jokingly refer to as their "litigator's mode."

"You have no proof of this," he said firmly, jabbing his index finger at me. "No proof whatsoever."

"Deli items, crabs, wine, apples," I recited. "Del Prado Spanish olives, Tanqueray gin."

"What the hell are you talking about?"

"I have Andrea's receipt for the items she bought at Safeway yesterday, before she stopped home to pick up her weekend bag. None of those things is here in the cabin."

"So?"

"I know that at least two of them—the olives and the gin—are at your house in Eureka. I'm willing to bet they all are."

"What if they are? She did some shopping for me yesterday morning—"

"The receipt is dated yesterday *evening,* nine-fourteen p.m. I'll quote you, Shoemaker: 'Apparently she went out to the coast last night. I haven't seen her since she walked out on us at the noon hour.' But you claim you didn't leave home after noon."

That did it; that opened the cracks. He stood for a moment, then half collapsed into one of the chairs and put his head in his hands.

The next summer, after I testified at the trial in which Steve Shoemaker was convicted of the first-degree murder of his wife, I returned to the Lost Coast—with a backpack, without the .38, and in the company of my lover. We walked sand beaches under skies that showed infinite shadings of blue; we made love in fields of wildflowers; we waited quietly for the deer, falcons, and foxes.

I'd already taken the bad from this place; now I could take the good.

THE HOLES IN THE SYSTEM
A RAE KELLEHER STORY

There are some days that just ought to be called off. Mondays are always hideous: The trouble starts when I dribble toothpaste all over my clothes or lock my keys in the car and doesn't let up till I stub my toe on the bedstand at night. Tuesdays are usually when the morning paper doesn't get delivered. Wednesdays are better, but if I get to feeling optimistic and go to aerobics class at the Y, chances are ten to one that I'll wrench my back. Thursdays—forget it. And by five on Friday, all I want to do is crawl under the covers and hide.

You can see why I love weekends.

The day I got assigned to the Boydston case was a Tuesday.

Cautious optimism, that was what I was nursing. The paper lay folded tidily on the front steps of All Souls Legal Cooperative— where I both live and work as a private investigator. I read it and drank my coffee, not even burning my tongue. Nobody I knew had died, and there was even a cheerful story below the fold in the Metro section. By the time I'd looked at the comics and found all five strips that I bother to read were funny, I was feeling downright perky.

Well why not? I wasn't making a lot of money, but my job was secure. The attic room I occupied was snug and comfy. I had a boyfriend, and even if the relationship was about as deep as a desert stream on the Fourth of July, he could be taken most anyplace. And to top it off, this wasn't a bad hair day.

All that smug reflection made me feel charitable toward my fellow humans—or at least my coworkers and their clients—so I refolded the paper and carried it from the kitchen of our big Victorian to the front parlor and waiting-room so others could partake. A man was sitting on the shabby maroon sofa: bald and chubby, dressed in lime green polyester pants and a strangely patterned green, blue, and yellow shirt that reminded me of drawings of sperm cells. One thing for sure, he'd never get run over by a bus while he was wearing that getup.

He looked at me as I set the paper on the coffee table and said, "How ya doin', little lady?"

Now, there's some contention that the word "lady" is demeaning. Frankly, it doesn't bother me: when I hear it I know I'm looking halfway presentable and haven't got something disgusting caught between my front teeth. No, what rankled was the word "little." When you're five foot three the word reminds you of things you'd just as soon not dwell on—like being unable to see over people's heads at parades, or the little-girly clothes that designers of petite sizes are always trying to foist on you. "Little," especially at nine in the morning, doesn't cut it.

I glared at the guy. Unfortunately, he'd gotten to his feet and I had to look up.

He didn't notice I was annoyed; maybe he was nearsighted. "Sure looks like it's gonna be a fine day," he said.

Now I identified his accent—pure Texas. Another strike against him, because of Uncle Roy, but that's another story.

"It *would've* been a nice day," I muttered.

"Ma'am?"

That did it! The first—and last—time somebody had gotten away with calling me "Ma'am" was on my twenty-eighth birthday two weeks before, when a bag boy tried to help me out of Safeway with my two feather-light sacks of groceries. It was not a precedent I wanted followed.

Speaking more clearly, I said, "It would've been a nice day, except for you."

He frowned. "What'd I do?"

"Try 'little,' a Texas accent, and 'ma'am'!"

"Ma'am are you all right?"

"Aaargh!" I fled the parlor and ran up the stairs to the office of my boss, Sharon McCone.

Sharon is my friend, mentor, and sometimes—heaven help me—custodian of my honesty. She's been all those things since she hired me a few years ago to assist her at the co-op. Not that our association is always smooth sailing: She can be a stern taskmaster and she harbors a devilish sense of humor that surfaces at inconvenient times. But she is always been there for me, even during the death throes of my marriage to my pig-selfish, perpetual-student husband, Doug Grayson. And ever since I've stopped referring to him as "that bastard Doug," she's decided I'm a grown-up who can be trusted to manage her own life—within limits.

That morning she was sitting behind her desk with her chair swiveled around so she could look out the bay window at the front of the Victorian. I've found her in that pose hundreds of times: sunk low on her spine, long legs crossed, dark eyes brooding. The view is of dowdy houses across the triangular park that divides the street, and usually hazed by San Francisco fog, but it doesn't matter; whatever she's seeing is strictly inside her head, and she says she gets her best insights into her cases that way.

I stepped into the office and cleared my throat. Slowly Shar turned, looking at me as if I were a stranger. Then her eyes cleared. "Rae, hi. Nice work on closing the Anderson file so soon."

"Thanks. I found the others you left on my desk; they're pretty routine. You have anything else for me?"

"As a matter of fact, yes." She smiled slyly and slid a manila folder across the desk. "Why don't you take this client?"

I opened the folder and studied the information sheet stapled inside. All it gave was a name—Darrin Boydston—and an address on Mission Street. Under the job description Shar had noted "background check."

"Another one?" I asked, letting my voice telegraph my disappointment.

"Uh-huh. I think you'll find it interesting."

"Why?"

She waved a slender hand at me. "Go! It'll be a challenge."

Now, that *did* make me suspicious. "If it's such a challenge, how come you're not handling it?"

For an instant her eyes sparked. She doesn't like it when I hint that she skims the best cases for herself—although that's exactly what she does, and I don't blame her. "Just go see him."

"He'll be at this address?"

"No. He's downstairs. I got done talking with him ten minutes ago."

"Downstairs? *Where* downstairs?"

"In the parlor."

Oh, God!

She smiled again. "Lime green, with a Texas accent."

"So," Darrin Boydston said, "Did y'all come back down to chew me out some more?"

"I'm sorry about that." I handed him my card. "Ms. McCone has assigned me to your case."

He studied it and looked me up and down. "You promise to keep a civil tongue in your head?"

"I said I was sorry."

"Well, you damn near ruint my morning."

How many more times was I going to have to apologize?

"Let's get goin', little lady." He started for the door.

I winced and asked, "Where?"

"My place. I got somebody I want you to meet."

Boydston's car was a white Lincoln Continental—beautiful machine, except for the bull's horns mounted on the front grille. I stared at them in horror.

"Pretty, aren't they?" he said, opening the passenger's door.

"I'll follow you in my car," I told him.

He shrugged. "Suit yourself."

As I got into the Ramblin' Wreck—my ancient, exhaust-belching Rambler American—I looked back and saw Boydston staring at *it* in horror.

Boydston's place was a storefront on Mission a few blocks down from my Safeway—an area that could do with some urban renewal and just might get it, if the upwardly mobile ethnic groups that're moving in to the neighborhood get their way. It shared the building with a Thai restaurant and a Filipino travel agency. In its front window red neon tubing spelled out THE CASH COW, but the bucking outline letters was a bull. I imagined Boydston trying to reach a decision: call it the Cash Cow and have a good name but a dumb graphic; call it the Cash Bull and have a dumb name and a good graphic; or just say the hell with it and mix genders.

But what kind of establishment was this?

My client took the first available parking space, leaving me to fend for myself. When I finally found another and walked back two blocks he'd already gone inside.

Chivalry is dead. Sometimes I think common courtesy's obit is about to be published too.

When I went into the store, the first thing I noticed was a huge potted barrel cactus, and the second was dozens of guitars hanging from the ceiling. A rack of worn cowboy boots completed the picture.

Texas again. The state that spawned the likes of Uncle Roy was going to keep getting in my face all day long.

The room was full of glass showcases that displayed an amazing assortment of stuff: rings, watches, guns, cameras, fishing reels, kitchen gadgets, small tools, knickknacks, silverware, even a metronome. There was a whole section of electronic equipment like TVs and VCRs, a jumble of probably obsolete computer gear, a fleet of vacuum cleaners poised to roar to life and tidy the world, enough exercise equipment to trim down half the population, and a jukebox that just then was playing a country song by Shar's brother-in-law, Ricky Savage. Delicacy prevents me from describing what his voice does to my libido.

Darrin Boydston stood behind a high counter, tapping on a keyboard. On the wall behind him a sign warned CUSTOMERS MUST PRESENT TICKET TO CLAIM MERCHANDISE. I'm not too quick most mornings, but I did manage to figure out that the Cash Cow was a pawnshop.

"Y'all took long enough," my client said. "You gonna charge me for the time you spent parking?"

I sighed. "Your billable hours start now." Then I looked at my watch and made a mental note of the time.

He turned the computer off, motioned for me to come around the counter, and led me through a door into a warehouse area. Its shelves were crammed with more of the kind of stuff he had out front. Halfway down the center aisle he made a right turn and took me past small appliances: blenders, food processors, toasters, electric woks, pasta makers, even an ancient pressure cooker. It reminded me of the one the grandmother who raised me used to have, and I wrinkled my nose at it, thinking of those sweltering late-summer days when she'd make me help her with the yearly canning. No wonder I resist the womanly household arts!

Boydston said, "They buy these gizmos 'cause they think they need 'em. Then they find out they don't need and can't afford 'em. And then it all ends up in my lap." He sounded exceptionally cheerful about this particular brand of human folly, and I supposed he had good reason.

He led me at a fast clip toward the back of the warehouse—so fast that I had to trot to keep up with him. One of the other problems with being short is that you're forever running along behind taller people. Since I'd already decided to hate Darrin Boydston, I also decided he was walking fast to spite me.

At the end of the next-to-last aisle we came upon a thin man in a white T-shirt and black work pants who was moving boxes from the shelves to a dolly. Although Boydston and I were making plenty of noise, he didn't hear us come up. My client put his hand on the man's shoulder, and he stiffened. When he turned I saw he was only a boy, no more than twelve or thirteen, with the fine features and thick black hair of a Eurasian. The look in his eyes reminded me of an abused kitten my boyfriend Willie had taken in: afraid and resigned to further terrible experiences. He glanced from me to Boydston, and when my client nodded reassuringly, the fear faded to remoteness.

Boydston said to me, "Meet Daniel."

"Hello, Daniel." I held out my hand. He looked at it, then at Boydston. He nodded again, and Daniel touched my fingers, moving back quickly as if they were hot.

"Daniel," Boydston said, "doesn't speak or hear. Speech therapist I know met him, says he's prob'ly been deaf and mute since he was born."

The boy was watching his face intently. I said, "He reads lips or understands signing, though."

"Does some lip reading, yeah. But no signing. For that you gotta have schooling. Far as I can tell, Daniel hasn't. But him and me, we worked out a personal kind of language to get by."

Daniel tugged at Boyston's sleeve and motioned at the shelves, eyebrows raised. Boydston nodded, then pointed to his watch, held up five fingers, and pointed to the front of the building. Daniel nodded and turned back to his work. Boydston said, "You see?"

"Uh-huh. You two communicate pretty well. How'd he come to work for you?"

My client began leading me back to the store—walking slower now. "The way it went, I found him all huddled up in the back doorway one morning 'bout six weeks ago when I opened up. He was damn near froze but dressed in clean clothes and a new jacket. Was in good shape, 'cept for some healed-over cuts on his face. And he had this laminated card ... wait, I'll show you." He held the door for me, then rummaged through a drawer below the counter.

The card was a blue three-by-five—encased in clear plastic; on it somebody had typed I WILL WORK FOR FOOD AND A PLACE TO SLEEP. I DO NOT SPEAK OR HEAR, BUT I AM A GOOD WORKER. PLEASE HELP ME.

"So you gave him a job?"

Boydston sat down on a stool. "Yeah. He sleeps in a little room off the warehouse and cooks on a hotplate. Mostly stuff outta cans. Every week I give him cash; he brings back the change—won't take any more than what his food costs, and that's not much."

I turned the card over. Turned over my opinion of Darrin Boydston, too. "How d'you know his name's Daniel?"

"I don't. That's just what I call him."

"Why Daniel?"

He looked embarrassed and brushed at a speck of lint on the leg of his pants. "Had a best buddy in high school down in Amarillo. Daniel Atkins. Got killed in 'Nam." He paused. "Funny, me giving his name to a slope kid when they were the ones that killed him." Another pause. "Of course, this Daniel wasn't even born then, none of that business was his fault. And there's something about him ... I don't know, he must reminds me of my buddy. Don't suppose old Danny would mind none."

"I'm sure he wouldn't." Damn, it was getting harder and harder to hate Boydston! I decided to let go of it. "Okay," I said, "my casefile calls for a background check. I take it you want me to find out who Daniel is."

"Yeah. Right now he doesn't exist—officially, I mean. He hasn't got a birth certificate, can't get a social security number. That means I can't put him on the payroll, and he can't get government help. No classes where he can learn the stuff I can't teach him. No SSI payments or Medicare, either. My therapist friend says he's one of the people that slip through the cracks in the system."

The cracks are more like yawning holes, if you ask me. I said, "I've got to warn you, Mr. Boydston: Daniel may be in the country illegally."

"You think I haven't thought of that? Hell, I'm one of the people that voted for Prop One-eighty-seven. Keep those foreigners from coming here and taking jobs from decent citizens. Don't give 'em nothin' and maybe they'll go home and quit using up my tax dollar. That was before I met Daniel." He scowled. "*Damn*, I hate moral dilemmas! I'll tell you one thing, though: This is a good kid, he deserves a chance. If he's here illegally ... well, I'll deal with it somehow."

I liked his approach to his moral dilemma; I'd used it myself a time or ten. "Okay," I said, "tell me everything you know about him."

"Well, there're the clothes he had on when I found him. They're in this sack; take a look." He hauled a grocery bag from under the counter and handed it to me.

I pulled the clothing out: rugby shirt in white, green, and navy; navy cords; navy-and-tan down jacket. They were practically new, but the labels had been cut out.

"Lands' End?" I said. "Eddie Bauer?"

"One of those, but who can tell which?"

I couldn't, but I had a friend who could, "Can I take these?"

"Sure, but don't let Daniel see you got them. He's real attached to 'em, cried when I took 'em away to be cleaned the first time."

"Somebody cared about him, to dress him well and have this card made up. Laminating like that is a simple process, though; you can get it done in print shops."

"Hell, you could get it done *here*. I got in one of those laminating gizmos a week ago; belongs to a printer who's having a hard time of it, checks his shop equipment in and out like this was a lending library."

"What else can you tell me about Daniel? What's he like?"

Boydston considered. "Well, he's proud—the way he brings back the change from the money I give him tells me that. He's smart; he picked up on the warehouse routine easy, and he already knew how to cook. Whoever his people are, they don't have much; he knew what a hotplate was, but when I showed him a microwave it scared him. And he's got a tic about labels—cuts 'em out of the clothes I give him. There's more, too." He looked toward the door; Daniel was peeking hesitantly around its jamb. Boydston waved for him to come in and added, "I'll let Daniel do the telling."

The boy came into the room, eyes lowered shyly—or fearfully. Boydston looked at him till he looked back. Speaking very slowly and mouthing the words carefully, he asked, "Where are you from?

Daniel pointed at the floor.

"San Francisco?"
Nod.
"This district?"
Frown.
"Mission district? Mis-sion?"
Nod.
"Your momma, where is she?"
Daniel bit his lip.
"Your momma?"
He raised his hand and waved.
"Gone away?" I asked Boydston.
"Gone away or dead. How long, Daniel?" When the boy didn't respond, he repeated, "How long?"
Shrug.
"Time confuses him." Boydston said. "Daniel, your daddy—where is he?"
The boy's eyes narrowed and he made a sudden violent gesture toward the door.
"Gone away?"
Curt nod.
"How long?"
Shrug.
"How long, Daniel?"
After a moment he held up two fingers.
"Days?"
Headshake.
"Weeks?"
Frown.
"Months?"
Another frown.
"Years?"
Nod.
"Thanks, Daniel." Boydston smiled at him and motioned to the door, "You can go back to work now." He watched the boy leave, eyes troubled, then asked me, "So what d'you think?"
"Well—he's got good linguistic abilities; somebody bothered to teach him—probably the mother. His recollections seem scrambled. He's fairly sure when the father left, less sure about the mother. That could mean she went away or died recently and he hasn't found a way to mesh it with the rest of his personal history. Whatever happened, he was left to fend for himself."
"Can you do anything for him?"

"I'm sure going to try."

My best lead on Daniel's identity was the clothing. There had to be a reason for the labels being cut out—and I didn't think it was because of a tic on the boy's part. No, somebody had wanted to conceal the origins of the duds, and when I found out where they'd come from I could pursue my investigation from that angle. I left the Cash Cow, got in the Ramblin' Wreck, and when it finally stopped coughing, drove to the six-story building on Brannan Street south of Market where my friend Janie labors in what she calls the rag trade. Right now she works for a T-shirt manufacturer—and there've been years when I would've gone naked without her gifts of overruns—but during her career she's touched on every area of the business; if anybody could steer me toward the manufacturer of Daniel's clothes, she was the one. I gave them to her and she told me to call later. Then I set out on the trail of a Mission district printer who had a laminating machine.

Print and copy shops were in abundant supply there. A fair number of them did laminating work, but none recognized—or would own up to recognizing—Daniel's three-by-five card. It took me nearly all day to canvass them, except for the half-hour when I had a beer and a burrito at La Tacqueria, and by four o'clock I was totally discouraged. So I stopped at my favorite ice cream shop, called Janie and found she was in a meeting, and to ease my frustration had a double-scoop caramel swirl in a chocolate chip cookie cone.

No wonder I'm usually carrying five spare pounds!

The shop had a section of little plastic tables and chairs, and I rested my weary feet there, planning to check in at the office and then call it a day. If turning the facts of the case over and over in my mind all evening could be considered calling it a day ...

Shar warned me about that right off the bat. "If you like this business and stick with it," she'd said, "you'll work twenty-four hours a day, seven days a week. You'll think you're not working because you'll be at a party or watching TV or even in bed with your husband. And then all of a sudden you'll realize that half your mind's thinking about your current case and searching for a solution. Frankly, it doesn't make for much of a life."

Actually it makes for more than one life. Sometimes I think the time I spend on stakeouts or questioning people or prowling the city belongs to another Rae, one who has no connection to the Rae who goes to parties and watches TV and—now—sleeps with her boyfriend. I'm divided, but I don't mind it. And if Rae-the-investigator intrudes on the off-duty Rae's time, that's okay. Because the off-duty Rae gets to watch Rae-the-investigator make her moves—fascinated and a little envious.

Schizoid? Maybe. But I can't help but live and breathe the business. By now that's as natural as breathing air.

So I sat on the little plastic chair savoring my caramel swirl and chocolate chips and realized that the half of my mind that wasn't on sweets had come up with a weird little coincidence. Licking ice cream dribbles off my fingers, I went back to the phone and called Darrin Boydston. The printer who had hocked his laminating machine was named Jason Hill, he told me, and his shop was Quik Prints, on Mission near Geneva.

I'd gone there earlier this afternoon. When I showed Jason Hill the laminated card he'd looked kind of funny but claimed he didn't do that kind of work, and there hadn't been any equipment in evidence to brand him a liar. Actually, he wasn't a liar; he didn't do that kind of work *anymore*.

Hill was closing up when I got to Quik Prints, and he looked damned unhappy to see me again. I took the laminated card from my pocket and slapped it into his hand. "The machine you made this on is living at the Cash Cow right now," I said. "You want to tell me about it?"

Hill—one of those bony-thin guys that you want to take home and fatten up—sighed. "You from Child Welfare or what?"

"I'm working for your pawn broker, Darrin Boydston." I showed him the ID he hadn't bothered to look at earlier. "Who had the card made up?"

"I did."

"Why?"

"For the kid's sake." He switched the Open sign in the window to Closed and came out onto the sidewalk. "Mind if we walk to my bus stop while we talk?"

I shook my head and fell in next to him. The famous San Francisco fog was in, gray and dirty, making the gray and dirty Outer Mission even more depressing than usual. As we headed toward the intersection of Mission and Geneva, Hill told me about his story.

"I found the kid on the sidewalk about seven weeks ago. It was five in the morning—I'd come in early for a rush job—and he was dazed and banged up and bleeding. Looked like he'd been mugged. I took him into the shop and was going to call the cops, but he started crying—upset about the blood on his down jacket. I sponged it off, and by the time I got back from the restroom, he was sweeping the print-room floor. I really didn't have time to deal with the cops, so I just let him sweep. He kind of made himself indispensable."

"And then?"

"He cried when I tried to put him outside that night, so I got him some food and let him sleep in the shop. He had coffee ready the next morning and helped me take out the trash. I still thought I should call the cops, but I was worried: He couldn't tell them who he was or where he lived; he'd end up in some detention center or a foster home and his folks might never find him. I grew up in foster homes myself; I know all about the system. He was a sweet kid and deserved better than that. You know?"

"I know."

"Well, I couldn't figure *what* to do with him. I couldn't keep him at the shop much longer—the landlord's nosy and always on the premises. And I couldn't take him home—I live in a tiny studio with my girlfriend and three dogs. So after a week I got an idea: I'd park him someplace with a laminated card asking for a job; I knew he wouldn't lose it or throw it away because he loved the laminated stuff and saved all of the discards."

"Why'd you leave him at the Cash Cow?"

"Mr. Boydston has a reputation for taking care of people. He's helped me out plenty of times."

"How?"

"Well, when he sends out the sixty-day notices saying you should claim your stuff or it'll be sold, as long as you go in and make a token payment, he'll hang onto it. He sees you're hurting, he'll give you more than the stuff's worth. He bends over backward to make a loan." We got to the bus stop and Hill joined the rush-hour line. "And I was right about Mr. Boydston helping the kid, too. When I took the machine in last week, there he was, sweeping the sidewalk."

"He recognize you?"

"Didn't see me. Before I crossed the street, Mr. Boydston sent him on some errand. The kid's in good hands."

Funny how every now and then when you think the whole city's gone to hell, you discover there're a few good people left ...

Wednesday morning: cautious optimism again, but I wasn't going to push my luck by attending an aerobics class. Today I'd put all my energy into the Boydston case.

First, a call to Janie, whom I hadn't been able to reach at home the night before.

"The clothes were manufactured by a company called Casuals, Incorporated," she told me. "They only sell by catalogue, and their offices and factory are on Third Street."

"Any idea why the labels were cut out?"

"Well, at first I thought they might've been overstocks that were sold through one of the discounters like Ross, but that doesn't happen often with the catalogue outfits. So I took a close look at the garments and saw they've got defects—nothing major, but they wouldn't want to pass them off as first quality."

"Where would somebody get hold of them?"

"A factory store, if the company has one. I didn't have time to check."

It wasn't much of a lead, but even a little lead's better than nothing at all. I promised Janie I'd buy her a beer sometime soon and headed for the industrial corridor along Third Street.

Casuals, Inc. didn't have an on-site factory store, so I went into the front office to ask if there was one in another location. No, the receptionist told me, they didn't sell garments found to be defective.

"What happens to them?"

"Usually they're offered at a discount to employees and their families."

That gave me an idea, and five minutes later I was talking with a Mr. Fong in personnel. "A single mother with a deaf-mute son? That would be Mae Jones. She worked here as a seamstress for ... let's see ... a little under a year."

"But she's not employed here anymore?"

"No. We had to lay off a number of people, and those with the least seniority are the first to go."

"Do you know where she's working now?"

"Sorry, I don't."

"Mr. Fong, is Mae Jones a documented worker?"

"Green card was in order. We don't hire illegals."

"And you have an address for her?"

"Yes, but I'm afraid I can't give that out."

"I understand, but I think you'll want to make an exception in this case. You see, Mae's son was found wandering the Mission seven weeks ago, the victim of a mugging. I'm trying to reunite them."

Mr. Fong didn't hesitate to fetch Mae's file and give me the address, on Lucky Street in the Mission. Maybe, I thought, this was my lucky break.

The house was a Victorian that had been sided with concrete block and painted a weird shade of purple. Sagging steps led to a porch where six mailboxes hung. None of the names on them was Jones. I rang all the bells and got no answer. Now what?

"Can I help you?" An Asian-accented voice said behind me. It belonged to a stooped old woman carrying a fishnet bag full of vegetables. Her eyes, surrounded by deep wrinkles, were kind.

"I'm looking for Mae Jones." The woman had been taking out a keyring. Now she jammed it into the pocket of her loose-fitting trousers and backed up against the porch railing. Fear made her nostrils flare.

"What?" I asked. "What's wrong?"

"You are from them!"

"Them? Who?"

"I know nothing."

"Please don't be scared. I'm trying to help Mrs. Jones's son."

"Tommy? Where is Tommy?"

I explained about Jason Hill finding him and Darrin Boydston taking him in.

When I finished the woman had relaxed a little. "I am so happy one of them is safe."

"Please, tell me about the Joneses."

She hesitated, looking me over. Then she nodded as if I'd passed some kind of test and took me inside to a small apartment furnished with things that made the thrift-shop junk in my nest at All Souls look like Chippendale. Although I would've rather she tell her story quickly, she insisted on making tea. When we were finally settled with little cups like the ones I'd bought years ago at Bargain Bazaar in Chinatown, she began.

"Mae went away eight weeks ago today. I thought Tommy was with her. When she did not pay her rent, the landlord went inside the apartment. He said they left everything."

"Has the apartment been rented to someone else?"

She nodded. "Mae and Tommy's things are stored in the garage. Did you say it was seven weeks ago that Tommy was found?"

"Give or take a few days."

"Poor boy. He must have stayed in the apartment waiting for his mother. He is so quiet and can take care of himself."

"What d'you suppose he was doing on Mission Street near Geneva, then?"

"Maybe looking for her." The woman's face was frightened again.

"Why there?" I asked.

She stared down into her teacup. After a bit she said, "You know Mae lost her job at the sewing factory?"

I nodded.

"It was a good job, and she is a good seamstress, but times are bad and she could not find another job."

"And then?"

"... There is a place on Geneva Avenue. It looks like an apartment house, but it is really a sewing factory. The owners advertise by word of mouth among the Asian immigrants. They say they pay high wages, give employees meals and a place to live, and do not ask questions. They hire many who are here illegally."

"Is Mae an illegal?"

"No. She was married to an American serviceman and has her permanent green card. Tommy was born in San Francisco. But a few years ago her husband divorced her and she lost her medical benefits. She is in poor health, she has tuberculosis. Her money was running out, and she was desperate. I warned her, but she wouldn't listen."

"Warned her against what?"

"There is talk about that factory. The building is fenced and the fences are topped with razor wire. The windows are boarded and barred. They say that once a worker enters she is not allowed to leave. They say workers are forced to sew eighteen hours a day for very low wages. They say that the cost of food is taken out of their pay, and that ten people sleep in a room large enough for two."

"That's slavery! Why doesn't the city do something?"

The old woman shrugged. "The city has no proof and does not care. The workers are only immigrants. They are not important."

I felt a real rant coming on and fought to control it. I've lived in San Francisco for seven years, since I graduated from Berkeley, a few miles and light years across the Bay, and I'm getting sick and tired of the so-called important people. The city is beautiful and lively and tolerant, but there's a core of citizens who think nobody and nothing counts but them and their concerns. Someday when I'm in charge of the world (an event I fully expect to happen, especially when I've had a few beers), they'll have to answer to *me* for their high-handed behavior.

"Okay," I said, "tell me exactly where this place is, and we'll see what we can do about it."

"Slavery, plain and simple," Shar said.

"Right."

"Something's got to be done about it."

"Right."

We were sitting in a booth at the Remedy Lounge, our favorite tavern down the hill from All Souls on Mission Street. She was drinking white wine, I was drinking beer, and it wasn't but three in the afternoon. But McCone and I have found that some of our best ideas come to us when we tilt a couple. I'd spent the last four hours casing—oops, I'm not supposed to call it that—conducting a surveillance on the building on Geneva Avenue. Sure looked suspicious—trucks coming and going, but no workers leaving at lunchtime.

"But what can be done?" I asked. "Who do we contact?"

She considered. "Illegals? U.S. Immigration and Naturalization Service. False imprisonment? City police and district attorney's office. Substandard working conditions? OSHA, Department of Labor, State Employment Development Division. Take your pick."

"Which is best to start with?"

"None—yet. You've got no proof of what's going on there."

"Then we'll just have to get proof, won't we?"

"Uh-huh."

"You and I both used to work in security. Ought to be a snap to get into that building."

"Maybe."

"All we need is access. Take some pictures. Tape a statement from one of the workers. Are you with me?"

She nodded. "I'm with you. And as backup, why don't we take Willie?"

"*My* Willie? The diamond king of northern California? Shar, this is an investigation, not a date!"

"Before he opened those discount jewelry stores Willie was a professional fence, as you may recall. And although he won't admit it, I happen to know he personally stole a lot of the items he moved. Willie has talents we can use."

"My tennis elbow hurts! Why're you making me do this?"

I glared at Willie. "Shh! You've never played tennis in your life."

"The doc told me most people who've got it have never played."

"Just be quiet and cut the wire."

"How d'you know there isn't an alarm?"

"Shar and I have checked. Trust us."

"I trust you two, I'll probably end up in San Quentin."

"Cut!"

Willie snipped a fair segment out of the razor wire topping the chain-link fence. I climbed over first, nearly doing myself grievous personal injury as I swung over the top. Shar followed, and then the diamond king—making unseemly grunting noises. His tall frame was encased in dark sweats tonight, and they accentuated the beginnings of a beer belly.

As we each dropped to the ground, we quickly moved into the shadow of the three-story frame building and flattened against its wall. Willie wheezed and pushed his longish hair out of his eyes. I gave Shar a look that said, *Some asset you invited along.* She shrugged apologetically.

According to plan we began inching around the building, searching for a point of entry. We didn't see any guards. If the factory employed them, it would be for keeping people in; it had probably never occurred to the owners that someone might actually *want* in.

After about three minutes Shar came to a stop and I bumped into her. She steadied me and pointed down. A foot off the ground was an opening that had been boarded up; the plywood was splintered and coming loose. I squatted and took a look at it. Some kind of duct—maybe people-size. Together we pulled the board off.

Yep. A duct. But not very big. Willie wouldn't fit through it—which was fine by me, because I didn't want him alerting everybody in the place with his groaning. I'd fit, but Shar would fit better still.

I motioned for her to go first.

She made an after-you gesture.

I shook my head.

It's your case, she mouthed.

I sighed, handed her the camera loaded with infrared film that I carried, and started squeezing through.

I've got to admit that I have all sorts of mild phobias. I get twitchy in crowds, and I'm not fond of heights, and I hate to fly, and small places make my skin crawl. This duct was a *very* small space. I pushed onward, trying to keep my mind on other things—such as Tommy and Mae Jones.

When my hands reached the end of the duct I pulled hard, then moved them around till I felt a concrete floor about two feet below. I wriggled forward, felt my foot kick something, and heard Shar grunt. *Sorry.* The room I slid down into was pitch black. I waited till Shar was crouched beside me, then whispered, "D'you have your flashlight?"

She handed me the camera, fumbled in her pocket, and then I saw streaks of light bleeding around the fingers she placed around its bulb. We waited, listening. No one stirred, no one spoke. After a moment, Shar took her hand away from the flash and began shining its beam around. A storage room full of sealed cardboard boxes, with a door at the far side. We exchanged glances and began moving through the stacked cartons.

When we got to the door I put my ear to it and listened. No sound. I turned the knob slowly. Unlocked. I eased the door open. A dimly lighted hallway. There was another door with a lighted window set into it at the far end. Shar and I moved along opposite walls and stopped on either side of the door. I went up on tiptoe and peeked through the corner of the glass.

Inside was a factory: row after row of sewing machines, all making jittery up-and-down motions and clacking away. Each was operated by an Asian woman. Each woman slumped wearily as she fed the fabric through.

It was twelve-thirty in the morning, and they still had them sewing!

I drew back and motioned for Shar to have a look. She did, then turned to me, lips tight, eyes ablaze.

Pictures'? she mouthed.

I shook my head. *Can't risk being seen.*

Now what?

I shrugged.

She frowned and started back the other way, slipping from door to door and trying each knob. Finally she stopped and pointed to one with a placard that said STAIRWAY. I followed her through it and we started up. The next floor was offices—locked up and dark. We went back to the stairwell, climbed another flight. On the landing I almost tripped over a small, huddled figure.

It was a tiny gray-haired woman, crouching there with a dirty thermal blanket wrapped around her. She shivered repeatedly. Sick and hiding from the foreman. I squatted beside her.

The woman started and her eyes got big with terror. She scrambled backwards toward the steps, almost falling over. I grabbed her arm and steadied her; her flesh felt as if it was burning up. "Don't be scared," I said.

Her eyes moved from me to Shar. Little cornered bunny-rabbit eyes, red and full of the awful knowledge that there's no place left to hide. She babbled something in a tongue that I couldn't understand. I put my arms around her and patted her back—universal language. After a bit she stopped trying to pull away.

I whispered, "Do you know Mae Jones?" She drew back and blinked.

"Mae Jones?" I repeated.

Slowly she nodded and pointed to the door off the next landing.

So Tommy's mother *was* here. If we could get her out, we'd have an English-speaking witness who, because she had her permanent green card, wouldn't be afraid to go to the authorities and file charges against the owners of this place. But there was no telling who or what was beyond that door. I glanced at Shar. She shook her head.

The sick woman was watching me. I thought back to yesterday morning and the way Darrin Boydston had communicated with the boy he called Daniel. It was worth a try.

I pointed to the woman. Pointed to the door. "Mae Jones." I pointed to the door again, then pointed to the floor.

The woman was straining to understand. I went through the routine twice more. She nodded and struggled to her feet. Trailing the ratty blanket behind her, she climbed the stairs and went through the door.

Shar and I released sighs at the same time. Then we sat down on the steps and waited.

It wasn't five minutes before the door opened. We both ducked down, just in case. An overly thin woman of about thirty-five rushed through so quickly that she stumbled on the top step and caught herself on the railing. She would have been beautiful, but lines of worry and pain cut deep into her face; her hair had been lopped off short and stood up in dirty spikes. Her eyes were jumpy, alternately glancing at us and behind her. She hurried down the stairs.

"You want me?"

"If you're Mae Jones." Already I was guiding her down the steps.

"I am. Who are—"

"We're going to get you out of here, take you to Tommy."

"Tommy! Is he—"

"He's all right, yes."

Her face brightened, but then was taken over by fear. "We must hurry. Lan faked a faint, but they will notice I'm gone very soon."

We rushed down the stairs, along the hall toward the storage room. We were at its door when a man called out behind us. He was coming from the sewing room at the far end.

Mae froze. I shoved her, and then we were weaving through the stacked cartons. Shar got down on her knees, helped Mae into the duct, and dove in behind her. The door banged open.

The man was yelling in a strange language. I slid into the duct, pulling myself along on its riveted sides. Hands grabbed for my ankles and got the left one. I kicked out with my right foot. He grabbed for it and missed. I kicked upward, hard, and heard a satisfying yelp of pain. His hand let go of my ankle and I wriggled forward and fell to the ground outside. Shar and Mae were already running for the fence.

But where the hell was Willie?

Then I saw him: a shadowy figure, motioning with both arms as if he were guiding an airplane up to the jetway. There was an enormous hole in the chain-link fence. Shar and Mae ducked through it.

I started running. Lights went on at the corners of the building. Men came outside, shouting. I heard a whine, then a crack.

Rifle, firing at us!

Willie and I hurled ourselves to the ground. We moved on elbows and knees through the hole in the fence and across the sidewalk to the shelter of a van parked there. Shar and Mae huddled behind it. Willie and I collapsed beside them just as sirens began to go off.

"Like 'Nam all over again," he said.

I stared at him in astonishment. Willie had spent most of the war hanging out in a bar in Cam Ranh Bay.

Shar said, "Thank God you cut the hole in the fence!"

Modestly he replied, "Yeah, well, you gotta do something when you're bored out of your skull."

Because a shot had been fired, the SFPD had probable cause to search the building. Inside they found some sixty Asian women—most of them illegals—who had been imprisoned there, some as long as five years, as well as evidence of other sweatshops the owners were running, both here and in southern California. The INS was called in, statements were taken, and finally at around five that morning Mae Jones was permitted to go with us to be reunited with her son.

Darrin Boydston greeted us at the Cash Cow, wearing electric-blue pants and a western-style shirt with the bucking-bull emblem embroidered over its pockets. A polyester cowboy. He stood watching as Tommy and Mae hugged and kissed, wiped a sentimental tear from his eye, and offered Mae a job. She accepted, and then he drove them to the house of a friend who would put them up until they found a place of their own. I waited around the pawnshop till he returned.

When Boydston came through the door he looked down in the mouth. He pulled up a stool next to the one I sat on and said, "Sure am gonna miss that boy."

"Well, you'll probably be seeing a lot of him, with Mae working here."

"Yeah." He brightened some. "And I'm gonna help her get him into classes. Stuff like that. After she lost her Navy benefits when that skunk of a husband walked out on her, she didn't know about all the other stuff that's available." He paused, then added, "So what's the damage?"

"You mean, what do you owe us? We'll bill you."

"Better be an honest accounting, little lady," he said. "Ma'am, I mean," he added in his twangiest Texas accent. And smiled.

I smiled, too.

KNIVES AT MIDNIGHT

My eyes were burning, and I felt not unlike a creature that spends a great deal of its life underground. I marked the beat-up copy of last year's *Standard California Codes* that I'd scrounged up at a used bookstore on Adams Avenue, then shut it. When I stood up, my limbs felt as if I were emerging from the creature's burrow. I stretched, smiling. *Well, McCone,* I told myself, *at last one of your peculiarities is going to pay off.*

For years, I'd taken what many considered a strange pleasure in browsing through the tissue-thin pages of both the civil and penal codes. I had learned many obscure facts. For instance: it is illegal to trap birds in a public cemetery; anyone advertising merchandise that is made in whole or in part by prisoners must insert the words "convict-made" in the ad copy; stealing a dog worth $400 or less is petty theft, while stealing a dog worth more than $400 is grand theft. Now I could add another esoteric statute to my store of knowledge, only this one promised a big payoff.

Somebody who thought himself above the law was about to go down—and I was the one who would topple him.

Two nights earlier, I'd flown into San Diego's Lindbergh Field from my home base in San Francisco. Flown in on a perilous approach that always makes me, holder of a both single- and a multi-engine rating, wish I didn't know quite so much about pilot error. On top of a perfectly natural edginess, I was aggravated with myself for giving in to my older brother John's plea. The case he wanted me to take on for some friends sounded like one where every lead comes to a dead end; besides, I was afraid that in my former hometown I'd become embroiled in some family crisis. The McCone clan attracts catastrophe the way normal people attract stray kittens.

John was waiting for me at the curb in his old red International Scout. When he saw me, he jumped out and enveloped me in a bear hug that made me drop both my purse and my briefcase. My travel bag swung around and whacked him on his back; he released me, grunting.

"You're looking good," he said, stepping back.

"So're you." John's a big guy—six-foot-four—and sometimes he bulks up from the beer he's so fond of. But now he was slimmed down to muscle and sported a new closely trimmed beard. Only his blond hair resisted taming.

He grabbed my bag, tossed it into the Scout, and motioned for me to climb aboard. I held my ground. "Before we go anyplace—you didn't tell Pa I was coming down, did you?"

"No."

"Ma and Melvin? Charlene and Ricky?"

"None of them."

"Good. Did you make me a motel reservation and reserve a rental car?"

"No."

"I asked you—"

"You're staying at my place."

"John! Don't you remember—"

"Yeah, yeah. Don't involve the people you care about in something that could get dangerous. I heard all that before."

"And it *did* get dangerous."

"Not very. Anyway, you're staying with me. Get in."

John can be as stubborn as I when he makes up his mind. I opted for the path of least resistance. "Okay, I'll stay tonight—only. But what am I supposed to drive while I'm here?"

"I'll loan you the Scout."

I frowned. It hadn't aged well since I last borrowed it.

He added, "I could go along, help you out."

"John!"

He started the engine and edged into the flow of traffic.

"You know, I've missed you." Reaching over and ruffling my hair, he grinned broadly. "McCone and McCone—the detecting duo. Together again."

I heaved a martyred sigh and buckled my seat belt.

The happy tone of our reunion dissipated when we walked into the living room of John's little stucco house in nearby Lemon Grove. His old friends, Bryce and Mari Winslip, sat on the sofa in front of the corner fireplace; their hollow eyes reflected weariness and pain and—when they saw me—a kind of hope that I immediately feared was misplaced. While John made the introductions and fetched wine for me and freshened the Winslips' drinks, I studied them.

Both were a fair number of years older than my brother, perhaps in their early sixties. John had told me on the phone that Bryce Winslip was the painting contractor who had employed him during his apprenticeship; several years ago, he'd retired and they'd moved north to Oregon. Bryce and Mari were white-haired and had the bronzed, tough-skinned look of people who spent a lot of time outdoors. I could tell that customarily they were clear-eyed, mentally acute, and vigorous. But not tonight.

Tonight the Winslips were gaunt-faced and red-eyed; they moved in faltering sequences that betrayed their age. Tonight they were drinking straight whiskey, and every word seemed an effort. Small wonder: they were hurting badly because their only child, Troy, was violently dead.

Yesterday morning, twenty-five-year-old Troy Winslip's body had been found by the Tijuana, Mexico, authorities in a parking lot near the bullring at the edge of the border town. He had been stabbed seventeen times. Cause of death: exsanguination. Estimated time of death: midnight. There were no witnesses, no suspects, no known reason for the victim to have been in that place. Although Troy was a San Diego resident and a student at San Diego State, the SDPD could do no more than urge the Tijuana authorities to pursue an investigation and report their findings. The TPD, which would have been overworked even if it wasn't notoriously corrupt, wasn't about to devote time to the murder of a *gringo* who shouldn't have been down there in the middle of the night anyway. For all practical purposes, case closed.

So John had called me, and I'd opened my own case file.

When we were seated, I said to the Winslips, "Tell me about Troy. What sort of person was he?"

They exchanged glances. Mari cleared her throat. "He was a good boy ... man. He'd settled down and was attending college."

"Studying what?"

"Communications. Radio and TV."

"You say he'd 'settled down.' What does that mean?"

Again the exchanged glances. Bryce said, "After high school, he had some problems that needed to be worked through—one of the reasons we moved north. But he's been fine for at least five years now."

"Could you be more specific about these problems?"

"Well, Troy was using drugs."

"Marijuana? Cocaine?"

"Both. When we moved to Oregon, we put him into a good treatment facility. He made excellent progress. After he was released, he went to school at Eugene, but three years ago he decided to come back to San Diego."

"A mistake," Mari said.

"He was a grown man; we couldn't stop him," her husband responded defensively. "Besides, he was doing well, making good grades. There was no way we could have predicted that ... this would happen."

Mari shrugged.

I asked, "Where was Troy living?"

"He shared a house on Point Loma with another student."

"I'll need the address and the roommate's name. What else can you tell me about Troy?"

Bryce said, "Well, he is ... was athletic. He liked to sail and play tennis." He looked at his wife.

"He was very articulate," she added. "He had a beautiful voice and would have done well in radio or television."

"Do you know any of his friends here?"

" ... No. I'm not even sure of the roommate's name."

"What about women? Was he going with anyone? Engaged?"

Head shakes.

"Anything else?"

Silence.

"Well," Bryce said after a moment, "he was a very private person. He didn't share many of the details of his life with us, and we respected that."

I was willing to bet that the parents hadn't shared many details of their life with Troy, either. The Winslips struck me as one of those couples who have formed a closed circle that admits no one, not even their own offspring. The shared glances, their body language, the way they consulted nonverbally before answering my questions—all that pointed to a self-sufficient system. I doubted they'd known their son very well at all, and probably hadn't even realized they were shutting him out.

Bryce Winslip leaned forward, obviously awaiting some response on my part to what he and Mari had told me.

I said, "I have to be frank with you. Finding out what happened to Troy doesn't look promising. But I'll give it a try. John explained about my fee?"

They nodded.

"You'll need to sign one of my standard contracts, as well as a release giving me permission to enter Troy's home and go through his personal effects." I took the forms from my briefcase and began filling them in.

After they'd put their signatures on the forms and Bryce had written me a check as a retainer, the Winslips left for their hotel. John had fetched me another glass of wine and a beer for himself and sat in the place Mari had vacated, propping his feet on the raised hearth.

"So," he said, "how're we going to go about this?"

"You mean how am *I* going to go about this. First *I* will check with the SDPD for details on the case. Do you remember Gary Viner?"

"That dumb-looking friend of Joey's from high school?"

All of our brother Joey's friends had been dumb-looking. "Sandy-haired guy, one of the auto shop crowd."

"Oh, yeah. He used to work on Joey's car in front of the house and ogle you when he thought you weren't looking."

I grinned. "That's the one. He used to ogle me during cheerleading, too. When I was down here on that kidnaping case a couple of years ago, he told me I had the prettiest bikini pants of anybody on the squad."

John scowled indignantly, like a proper big brother. "So what's this underwear freak got to do with the Winslip case?"

"Gary's on Homicide with the SDPD now. It's always best to check in with the local authorities when you're working a case on their turf, so I'll stop by his office in the morning, see what he's got from the TJ police."

"Well, just don't wear a short skirt. What should I do while you're seeing him?"

"Nothing. Afterward, *I* will visit Troy's house, talk with the roommate, try to get a list of his friends and find out more about him. Plus go State and see what I can dig up there."

"What about me?"

"You will tend to Mr. Paint." Mr. Paint was the contracting business he operated out of his home shop and office.

John's lower lip pushed out sulkily.

I said, "How about dinner? I'm starving."

He brightened some. "Mexican?"

"Sure."

"I'll drive."

"Okay."

"You'll pay."

"John!"

"Consider it a finder's fee."

Gary Viner hadn't changed since I'd seen him a couple of years earlier, but he was very different from the high school kid I remembered. Gaining weight and filling out had made him more attractive; he'd stopped hiding his keen intelligence and learned to tone down his ogling to subtly speculative looks that actually flattered me. Unfortunately, he had no more information on the Winslip murder than what John had already told me.

"Is it okay if I look into this for the parents?" I asked him.

"Feel free. It's not our case, anyway. You go down there"—he motioned in the general direction of Baja California—"you might want to check in with the TJ authorities."

"I won't be going down unless I come up with nothing good up here."

"Well, good luck, and keep me posted." As I started out of his cubicle, Gary added, "Hey, McCone—the last time I saw you, you never did answer my question."

"Which is?"

"Can you still turn a cartwheel?"

I grinned at him. "You bet I can. And my bikini pants are still the prettiest ever."

It made me feel good to see a tough homicide cop blush.

My first surprise of the day was Troy Winslip's house. It was enormous, sprawling over a double lot that commanded an impressive view of San Diego Bay and Coronado Island. Stucco and brick and half-timbers, with a terraced yard landscaped in brilliantly flowering iceplant, it must have been at least six thousand square feet, give or take a few.

A rich roommate? Many rich roommates? Whatever, it sure didn't resemble the ramshackle brown-shingled house that I'd shared with what had seemed a cast of thousands when I was at UC Berkeley.

I rang the bell several times and got no response, so I decided to canvass the neighbors. No one was home at the houses to either side, but across the street I got lucky. The stoop-shouldered man who came to the door was around seventy and proved to like the sound of his own voice.

"Winslip? Sure, I know him. Nice young fellow. He's owned the place for about a year now."

"You're sure he owns it?"

"Yes. I knew the former owners. Gene and Alice Farr—nice people, too, but that big house was too much for them, so they sold it and bought one of those condos. They told me Winslip paid cash."

Cash? Such a place would go for many hundreds of thousands. "What about his roommate? Do you also know him?"

The old man leered at me. "Roommate? Is that what you call them these days? Well, he's a she. The ladies come and go over there, but none're very permanent. This last one, I'd say she's been there eight, nine weeks?"

"Do you know her name?"

He shook his head. "She's a good-looking one, though—long red hair, kind of willowy."

"And do you know what either she or Mr. Winslip do for a living?"

"Not her, no. And if he does anything, he's never talked about it. I suspect he inherited his money. He's home a lot, when he's not sailing his boat."

"Where does he keep his boat?"

"Glorietta Bay Marina, over on Coronado." The man frowned now, wrinkles around his eyes deepening. "What's this about, anyway?"

"Troy Winslip's been murdered, and I'm investigating it."

"What?"

"You didn't read about it in the paper?"

"I don't bother with the paper. Don't watch TV, either. With my arthritis, I'm miserable enough; I don't need other humans' misery heaped on top of that."

"You're a wise man," I told him, and hurried back to where I'd left the Scout.

Glorietta Bay Marina sits at the top of the Silver Strand, cattycorner from the Victorian towers of the Hotel Del Coronado. It took me more than half an hour to get there from Point Loma, and when I drove into the parking lot, I spotted John leaning against his motorcycle. He waved and started toward me.

I pulled into a space and jumped out of the Scout. "What the hell are *you* doing here?"

"Nice way to greet somebody who's helping you out. While you were futzing around at the police department and Troy's place, I went over to State. Talked with his adviser. She says he dropped out after one semester."

"So how did that lead you here?"

"The adviser sails, and she sees him here off and on. He owns a boat, the *Windsong*."

"And I suppose you've already checked it out."

"No, but I did talk with the marina manager. He says he'll let us go aboard if you show him your credentials and the release from Bryce and Mari."

"Good work," I said grudgingly. "You know," I added as we started walking toward the manager's office, "it's odd that Troy would berth the boat here."

"Why?"

"He lived on Point Loma, not far from the Shelter Island yacht basin. Why would he want to drive all the way around the bay and across the Coronado Bridge when he could have berthed her within walking distance of his house?"

"No slips available over there? No, that can't be; I've heard the marinas're going hungry in this economy."

"Interesting, huh? And wait till you hear what else—" I stopped in my tracks and glared at him. "Dammit, you've done it again!"

"Done what? I didn't do anything! What did I do?"

"You know *exactly* what you've done."

John's smile was smug.

I sighed. "All right, other half of the 'detecting duo'—lead me to the manager."

My unwanted assistant and I walked along the outer pier toward the *Windsong's* slip. The only sounds were the cries of seabirds and the rush of traffic on the Strand. Our footsteps echoed on the aluminum walkways and set them to bucking on a slight swell. No one was around this Wednesday morning except for a pair of artists sketching near the office; the boats were buttoned up tightly, their sails furled in sea-blue covers. Troy Winslip's yawl was a big one, some thirty feet. I crossed the plank and stepped aboard; John followed.

"Wonder where he got his money," he said. "Bryce and Mari're well off, but not wealthy."

"I imagine he had his ways." I tried the companionway door and found it locked.

"What now?" my brother asked. "Standing around on deck isn't going to tell us anything."

"No." I felt through my bag and came up with my set of lock picks.

John's eyes widened. "Aren't those illegal?"

"Not strictly." I selected one with a serpentine tip and began probing the lock. "It's a misdemeanor to possess lock picks with intent to feloniously break and enter. However, since I intend to break and enter with permission from the deceased owner's next of kin, we're in kind of a gray area here."

John looked nervously over his shoulder. "I don't think cops recognize gray areas."

"For God's sake, do you see any cops?" I selected a more straight-tipped pick and resumed probing.

"Where'd you get those?" John asked.

"An informant of mine made them for me; he even etched my initials on the finger holds. Wiley 'the Pick' Pulaski. He's currently doing four-to-six for burglary."

"My little sister, consorting with known criminals."

"Well, Wiley wasn't exactly known when I was consorting with him. Good informants can't keep a high profile, you know." I turned the lock with a quick flick of my wrist. It yielded, and I removed the pick and opened the door. "After you, big brother."

The companionway opened into the main cabin—a compactly arranged space with a galley along the right bulkhead and a seating area along the left. I began a systematic search of the lockers but came up with nothing interesting. When I turned, I found John sitting at the navigator's station, studying the instruments.

"Big help you are," I told him. "Get up; you're blocking the door to the rear cabin."

He stood, and I squeezed around him and went inside.

The rear cabin had none of the teak-and-brass accoutrements of the main; in fact, it was mostly unfinished. The portholes were masked with heavy fabric, and the distinctive trapped odor of marijuana was enough to give me a contact high. I hadn't experienced its like since the dope-saturated seventies in Berkeley.

John, who cultivated a small crop in his backyard, smelled it, too. "So that's what pays the mortgage!"

"Uh-huh." My eyes were becoming accustomed to the gloom, but not fast enough. "You see a flashlight anyplace?"

He went away and came back with one. I flicked it on and shined it around. The cabin was tidy, the smell merely a residue of the marijuana that had been stored there, but crumbled bits of grass littered the floor. I handed John the flashlight, pulled an envelope from my bag, and scraped some of the waste matter into it. Then I moved forward, scrutinizing every surface. Toward the rear under the sharp cant of the bulkhead, I found a dusting of white powder. After I tasted it, I scraped it into a second envelope.

"Coke, too?" John asked.

"You got it."

"Mari and Bryce aren't going to like this. They thought he'd kicked his habit."

"He wasn't just feeding a habit here, John. Or dealing on a small scale. He was distributing, bringing it in on this boat in a major way."

"Yeah." He fell silent, staring grimly at the littered floor. "So what're you going to do—call the cops?"

"They'll have to know eventually, but not yet. The dealing in itself isn't important anymore; its bearing on Troy's murder is."

Back on Point Loma, I waited just out of sight of Troy Winslip's house in the Scout. John had wanted to come along and help me stake the place out, so in order to otherwise occupy him, I'd sent him off on what I considered a time-consuming errand. The afternoon waned. Behind me, the sky's blue deepened and the lowering sun grew bright gold in contrast. Tall palms bordering the Winslip property cast long easterly shadows. At around six, a white Dodge van rounded the corner and pulled into Troy's driveway. A young woman—red-haired, willowy, clad in jeans and a black-and-white African print cape—jumped out and hurried into the house. By the time I got to the front door, she was already returning, arms full of clothing on hangers. She started when she saw me.

I had my identification and the release from Troy's parents ready. As I explained what I was after, the woman barely glanced at them. "All I want is my things," she said. "After I get them out of here, I don't care what the hell you do."

I followed her, picking up a purple silk tunic that had slipped from its hanger. "Please come inside. We'll talk. You lived with Troy; don't you care why he was killed?"

She laughed bitterly, tossed the armload of clothing into the back of the van, and took the tunic from my outstretched hand. "I care. But I also care about myself. I don't want to be around here any longer than necessary."

"You feel you're in danger?"

"I'd be a fool if I didn't." She pushed around me and hurried up the walk. "Those people don't mess around, you know."

I followed her. "What people?"

She rushed through the door, skidding on the polished marble of the foyer. A few suitcases and cartons were lined up at the foot of a curving staircase. "You want to talk?" the woman said. "We'll talk, but you'll have to help me with this stuff."

I nodded, picked up the nearest box, and followed her back to the van. "I know that Troy was dealing."

"Dealing?" She snorted. "He was supplying half the county. He and Daniel were taking the boat down to Baja three, four nights a week."

"Who's Daniel?"

"Daniel Pope, Troy's partner." She took the box from my hands, shoved it into the back of the van, and started up the walk.

"Where can I find him?"

"His legit business is a surf shop on Coronado—Danny P's."

"And the people who don't mess around—who are they?"

We were back in the foyer now. She thrust two suitcases at me.

"Oh, no, you're not getting me involved in *that*."

"Look—what's your name?"

"I don't have to tell you." She hefted the last carton, took a final look around, and tossed her hair defiantly. "I'm out of here."

Once again, we were off at a trot toward the van. "You may be out of here," I said, "but you're still afraid. Let me help you."

She stowed the carton, took the suitcases from me, and shook her head. "Nobody can help me. It's only a matter of time. I know too much."

"Then share it—"

"No!" She slammed the van's side door, slipped quickly into the driver's seat, and locked the door behind her. For a moment, she sat with her head bowed, her hands on the wheel; then she relented and rolled down the window a few turns. "Why don't you go talk to Daniel? If he's not at the surf shop, he'll be at home; he's the only Pope on C Street in Coronado. Ask him ..." She hesitated, looking around as if someone could hear her.

"Ask him about Renny D."

"Ronny D?"

"No, Renny, with an e. It's short for Reynaldo." Quickly, she cranked up the window and started the van. I stepped back in time to keep from getting my toes squashed.

The woman had left the front door of the house open and the keys in the lock. For a moment, I considered searching the place, then concluded it was more important to talk to Daniel Pope. I went back up the walk, closed the door, turned the deadbolt, and pocketed the keys for future use.

Daniel Pope wasn't at his surf shop, and he wasn't at his home on C Street. But John was waiting two houses down, perched on his cycle in the shade of a jacaranda tree.

I raised my eyes to the heavens and whispered to the Lord, "Please, not again!"

The Lord, who in recent years had been refusing to listen to my pleas, failed to eradicate my brother's presence.

I parked the Scout behind the cycle. John sauntered back and leaned on the open window beside me. "Daniel Pope owns a half interest in the *Windsong*," he said out of the corner of his mouth, eyes casing the house like an experienced thief.

I'd assigned him to check into the yawl's registry, but I hadn't expected him to come up with anything this quickly.

John went on, "He and Troy bought the boat two years ago for 90,000 dollars cash from the yacht broker at Glorietta Bay. They took her out three or four times a week for about eight hours a stretch. In between, they partied. Men would come and go, carrying luggage. Some of the more conservative—read that 'bigoted'—slip holders complained that they were throwing 'fag parties.'"

"But we know they were holding sales meetings."

"Right."

"Where'd you get all that?"

"The yacht broker. I pretended I was interested in buying the *Windsong*. He's probably got the commission spent already. Shit, I feel really guilty about it."

A blue Mercedes was approaching. It went past us, slowed, and turned into the driveway of the white Italianate house we'd been watching. I unbuckled my seat belt and said, "Ease your guilt by telling yourself that if you ever do buy a boat, you'll use that broker."

He ignored me, straightening and watching the car pull into an attached garage. "Daniel Pope?"

"Probably."

"So now what do we do?"

Thoughtfully, I looked him over. My brother is a former bar brawler and can be intimidating to those who don't know him for the pussycat he is. And at the moment, he was in exceptionally good shape.

"We," I said, "are going in there and talk with Pope about somebody called Renny D."

Daniel Pope was suffering from a bad case of nerves. His bony, angular body twitched, and a severe tic marred his ruggedly handsome features. When we'd first come to the door, he'd tried to shut it in our faces; now that he was reasonably assured that we weren't going to kill him, he wanted a drink. John and I sat on the edge of a leather sofa in a living room filled with sophisticated sound equipment while he poured three fingers of single-malt Scotch. Then I began questioning him.

"Who's Renny D?"

"Where'd you get that name?"

"Who is he?"

"I don't have to talk about—"

"Look, Pope, we know all about the *Windsong* and your trips to Baja. And about the dealers who come to the yawl in between. The rear cabin is littered with grass and coke; I can have the police there in—"

"Jesus! I thought you were working for Troy's parents."

"I am, but Troy's dead, and they're more interested in finding out who killed him than in covering up your illegal activities."

"Oh, Jesus." He took a big drink of whiskey.

I repeated, "Who's Renny D?"

Silence.

"I'm not going to ask again." I moved my hand toward a phone on the table beside me. John grinned evilly at Pope.

"Don't! Don't do that! Christ, I'll... Renny Dominguez is the other big distributor around here. He didn't want Troy and me cutting into his territory."

"And?"

"That's it."

"No, it's not." I moved my hand again. John did a fair imitation of a villain's leer. Maybe, I thought, he should have taken up acting.

"Okay, all right, it's not. I'll tell you, just leave the phone alone. At first, Troy and I tried to work something out with Renny D. Split the territory, cooperate, you know. He wasn't having any of that. Things've been getting pretty intense over the last few months: there was a fire at my store; somebody shot at Troy in front of his house; we both had phone threats."

"And then?"

"All of a sudden, Renny D decides he wants to make nice with us. So we meet with him at this bar where he hangs out in National City, and he proposes we work together, kick the business into really high gear. But now it's Troy who isn't having any of that."

"Why not?"

"Because Troy's convinced himself that Renny D is small-time and kind of stupid. He thinks we should kick *our* business into high gear and take over Renny's turf. I took him aside, tried to tell him that what he saw as small-time stupidity was only a matter of different styles. I mean just because Renny D doesn't wear Reeboks or computerize his customer list doesn't mean he's an idiot. I tried to tell Troy that those people were dangerous, that you at least had to try to humor them. But did Troy listen? No way. He went back to the table and make Renny look bad in front of his *compadres,* and that's bad shit, man."

"So then what happened?"

"More threats. Another drive-by. And that only made Troy more convinced that Renny and his pals were stupid, because they couldn't pick him off at twenty feet. Well, this kind of stuff goes on until it's getting ridiculous, and finally Renny issues a challenge: the two of them'll meet down in TJ near the bullring and settle it one-on-one, like honorable men."

"And Troy fell for that?"

"Sure. Like I said, he'd convinced himself Renny D was stupid, so he had me set it up with Renny's number two man, Jimmy. It was supposed to be just the four of us, and only Renny and Troy would fight."

"You didn't try to talk him out of it?"

"All the way down there, I did. But Troy—stubborn should've been his middle name."

"And what happened when you got there?"

"It was just the four of us, like Jimmy said. But what he didn't say was that he and Renny would have knives. The two of them moved damn fast, and before I knew what was happening, they'd stabbed Troy."

"What did you do?"

Pope looked away. Went to get himself another three fingers of scotch.

"What did you do, Daniel?"

"I froze. And then I ran. Left Troy's damned car there, ran off, and spent half the night wandering, the other half hiding behind an auto body shop near the port of entry. The next morning, I walked back over the border like any innocent tourist."

"And now you think Renny and his friends'll come after you."

"I was a witness, it's only a matter of time."

That was what Troy's girlfriend had said, too. "Are you willing to tell your story to the police?"

Silence.

"Daniel?"

He ran his tongue over dry lips. After a moment, he said, "Shit, what've I got to lose? Look at me." He held out a shaky hand. "I'm a wreck, and it's all Troy's fault. He had fair warning of what was gonna go down. When I think of the way he ignored it, I want to kill him all over again."

"What fair warning?"

"Some message Renny D left on his answering machine. Troy thought it was funny. He said it was so melodramatic, it proved Renny was brain-damaged."

"Did he tell you what the message was?"

Daniel Pope shook his head. "He was gonna play it for me when we got back from TJ. He said you had to hear it to believe it."

The message was in a weird Spanish-accented falsetto, accompanied by cackling laughter: "Knives at midnight, Winslip. Knives at midnight."

I popped the tape from Troy's answering machine and turned to John. "Why the hell would he go down to TJ after hearing that? Did he think Renny D was joking?"

"Maybe. Or maybe he took along his own knife, but Renny and Jimmy were quicker. Remember, he thought they were stupid." He shook his head. "Troy was a dumb middle-class kid who got in over his head and let his own high opinion of himself warp his judgment. But he still sure as hell didn't deserve to die in a parking lot of seventeen stab wounds."

"No, he didn't." I turned the tape over in my hands. "Why do you suppose Renny D left the message? You'd think he'd have wanted the element of surprise on his side."

John shrugged. "To throw Troy off balance, make him nervous? Some twisted code of drug dealers' honor? Who knows?"

"This tape isn't the best of evidence, you know. There's no proof that it was Renny D who called."

"Isn't there?" He motioned at another machine that looked like a small video display terminal.

"What's that?"

"A little piece of new technology that allows you to see what number an incoming call was dialed from. It has a memory, keeps a record." He pressed a button, and a listing of numbers, dates, and times appeared. After scrolling through it, he pointed to one with a 295 prefix. "That matches the time and date stamp on the answering machine tape."

I lifted the receiver and dialed the number. A machine picked up on the third ring: "This is Renny D. Speak."

I hung up. "Now we've got proof."

"So do we go see Gary Viner?"

"Not just yet. First I think we'd better report to Mari and Bryce, ask them if they really want all of this to come out."

"I talked with them earlier; they were going to make the funeral arrangements and then have dinner with relatives. Maybe we shouldn't intrude."

"Probably not. Besides, there's something I want to do first."

"What?"

"Get a good look at this Renny D."

An old friend named Luis Abrego frequented the Tradewinds tavern in National City, halfway between San Diego and the border. The first time I'd gone there two years before, John had insisted on accompanying me for protection; tonight he insisted again. I didn't protest, since I knew he and Luis were fond of each other.

Fortunately, business was slow when we got there; only half a dozen Hispanic patrons stopped talking and stared when they saw two Anglos walk in. Luis hunched in his usual place at the end of the bar, nursing a beer and watching a basketball game on the fuzzy TV screen. When I spoke his name, he whirled, jumped off his stool, and took both my hands in his. His dark eyes danced with pleasure.

"Amiga," he said, "it's been much too long."

"Yes, it has, *amigo.*"

Luis released me and shook John's hand. He was looking well. His mustache swooped bandit-fashion, and his hair hung free and shiny to his shoulders. From the nearly black shade of his skin, I could tell he'd been working steadily on construction sites these days. Late at night, however, Luis plied a very different and increasingly dangerous trade; "helping my people get where they need to go," was how he described those activities.

We sat down in a booth, and I explained about Renny D and Troy Winslip's murder. Luis nodded gravely. "The young man was a fool to underestimate Dominguez," he said. "I don't know him personally, but I've seen him, and I hear he's one evil *hombre.*"

"Do you know where he hangs out down here?"

"A bar two blocks over, called the Gato Gordo. You're not planning on going up against him, *amiga?*"

"No, nothing like that. I just want to get a look at him. Obviously, I can't go there alone. Will you take me?"

Luis frowned down into his beer. "Why do you feel you have to do this?"

"I like to know who I'm up against. Besides, this is going to be a difficult case to prove; maybe seeing Renny D in the flesh will inspire me to keep at it."

He looked up at my face, studied it for a moment, then nodded. "Okay, I'll do it. But he"—he pointed at John—"waits for us here."

John said, "No way."

"Yes," Luis told him firmly. "Here you're okay; everybody knows you're my friend. But there, a big Anglo like you, we'd be asking for trouble. On the other hand, me and the *chiquita* here, we'll make a damn handsome couple."

Reynaldo Dominguez was tall and thin, with razor-sharp features that spoke of *indio* blood. There were tattoos of serpents on his arms and knife scars on his face, and part of one index finger was missing. He sat at a corner table in the Gato Gordo, surrounded by admirers. He leaned back indolently in his chair and laughed and joked and told stories. When Luis and I sat down nearby with our drinks, he glanced contemptuously at us; then he focused on Luis's face and evidently saw something there that warned him off. There was not a lot that Luis Abrego hadn't come up against in his life, and there was nothing and no one he feared. Renny D, I decided, was a good judge of character.

Luis leaned toward me, taking my hand as a lover would and speaking softly. "He is telling them how he single-handedly destroyed the Anglo opposition. He is laughing about the look on Winslip's face when he died, and at the way the other man ran. He is bragging about the cleverness of meeting them in TJ, where he has bribed the authorities and will never be charged with a crime." He paused, listened some more. "He is telling them how he will enjoy striking and destroying the other man and Winslip's woman—bit by bit, before he finally puts the knife in."

I started to turn to look at Dominguez.

"Don't." Luis tightened his grip on my hand.

I looked anyway. My eyes met Renny D's. His were black, flat, emotionless—devoid of humanity. He stared at me, thin lip curling.

Luis's fingernails bit into my flesh. "Okay. you've had your look at him. Drink up, and we'll go."

I could feel those soulless eyes on my back. I tried to finish my drink, but hatred for the creature behind me welled up and threatened to make me choke. Troy Winslip had in many respects been a useless person, but he'd also been young and naive and hadn't deserved to die. Nor did Daniel Pope or Troy's woman deserve to live, and perhaps die, in terror.

Luis said softly, "Now he is bragging again. He is telling them he is above the law. No one can touch him, he says. Renny D is invincible."

"Maybe not."

"Let's go now, *amiga*."

As we stood, I looked at Dominguez once more. This time, when our eyes met a shadow passed over his. What was that about? I wondered. Not suspicion. Not fear. What?

Of course—Renny D was puzzled. Puzzled because I didn't shy away from his stare. Puzzled and somewhat uneasy.

Well, good.

I said to Luis, "We'll see who's invincible."

I'd expected the Winslips to pose an obstacle to bringing Renny D to justice, but they proved to be made of very strong stuff. The important thing, they said, was not to cover up their son's misdeeds but to ensure that a vicious murderer didn't go free to repeat his crime. So, with their blessing, I took my evidence downtown to Gary Viner.

And Gary told me what I'd been fearing all along: "We don't have a case."

"Gary, there's the tape. Dominguez as good as told Winslip he was going to stab him. There's the record of where the call originated. There's the eyewitness testimony of Daniel Pope—"

"There's the fact that the actual crime occurred on Mexican soil. And that Dominguez has the police down there in his hip pocket. No case, McCone."

"So what're you going to do—sit back and wait till he kills Pope and Winslip's woman, or somebody else?"

"We'll keep an eye on Dominguez. That's all I can promise you. Otherwise, my hands're tied."

"Maybe *your* hands are tied."

"What's that supposed to mean? What're you going to do? Don't give me any trouble, McCone—please."

"Don't worry. I'm going to go off and think about this, that's all. When I do give you something, I guarantee it won't be trouble."

When I'm upset or need to concentrate, I often head for water, so I drove north to Torrey Pines State Beach and walked by the surf for an hour. Something was nagging at the back of my mind, but I couldn't bring it forward. Something I'd read or heard somewhere. Something ...

Knives at midnight, Winslip. Knives at midnight.

Renny D's high-pitched, cackling voice in the answering machine tape kept playing and replaying for me.

After a while, I decided to do some research and drove to Adams Avenue to find a used bookshop with a large legal section.

Crimes against the person: homicide. Express and implied malice ... burden of proving mitigation—no.

Second degree ... penalty for person previously convicted—no.

Manslaughter committed during operation of a vessel—certainly not.

Death of victim within three years and a day—forget it.

What the hell was I combing the penal code for, anyway?

Mayhem? Hardly. Kidnaping? No, Troy went willingly, even eagerly. Conspiracy? Maybe. No, the situation's too vague. Nothing there for me.

Knives at midnight, Winslip. Knives at midnight.

Can't get it out of my head. Keep trying to connect it with something. Melodramatic words, as Troy told Pope. A little old-fashioned, as if Dominguez was challenging him to a—

That's it!

Duels. Duels and challenges. Penal code, 225.

Defined: Combat with deadly weapons, fought between two or more persons, by previous agreement ...

Punishment when death ensues: state prison for two, three, or four years.

Not much, but better than nothing.

I remember reading this now, one time when I was browsing through statutes that had been on the books for a long time. It's as enforceable today as it was then in 1872. Especially section 231; that's the part I really like.

Gotcha, Renny D.

"I'll read it to you again," I said to Gary Viner. He was leaning toward me across his desk, trying to absorb the impact of the dry, formal text from 1872.

"'Dueling beyond State. Every person who leaves this State with intent to evade any provisions of this chapter, and to commit any act out of the State as is prohibited by this chapter, and who does any act, although out of this State, which would be punishable by such provisions if committed within this State, is punishable in the same manner as he would have been *in case such act had been committed within this State.*'

"And there you have it." I closed the heavy tome with an emphatic thump.

Gary nodded. "And there we have it."

I began ticking off items on my fingers. "A taped challenge to a duel at knifepoint. A probable voiceprint match with the suspect. A record of where the call was made from. An eyewitness who, in order to save his own sorry hide, will swear that it actually *was* a duel. And, finally, a death that resulted from it. Renny D goes away for two, three, or four years in state prison."

"It's not much time. I'm not sure the DA'll think it's worth the trouble of prosecuting him."

"I remember the DA from high school. He'll be happy with anything that'll get a slimeball off the streets for a while. Besides, maybe we'll get lucky and somebody'll challenge Renny D to a duel in prison."

Gary nodded thoughtfully. "I remember our DA from high school, too. Successfully prosecuting a high-profile case like this would provide the kind of limelight he likes—and it's an election year."

By the time my return flight to San Francisco left on Saturday, the DA had embraced the 1872 statute on duels and challenges with a missionary-like zeal and planned to take the Winslip case to the grand jury. Daniel Pope would be on hand to give convincing testimony about traveling to Tijuana primed for hand-to-hand combat with Dominguez and his cohort. Renny D was as yet unsuspecting but would soon be behind bars.

And at a Friday-night dinner party, the other half of the "detecting duo" had regaled the San Diego branch of the McCone family with his highly colored version of our exploits.

I accepted a cup of coffee from the flight attendant and settled back in the seat with my beat-up copy of *Standard California Codes*. I had a more current one on the shelf in my office, but somehow I couldn't bring myself to part with this one. Besides, I needed something to read on the hour-and-a-half flight.

Disguised Firearms or Other Deadly Weapons. Interesting.

Lipstick Case Knife. Oh, them deadly dames, as they used to say.

Shobi-zue: a staff, crutch, stick, rod, or pole with a knife enclosed. Well, if I ever break a leg ...

Writing Pen Knife. That's a good one. Proves the pen can be mightier than the sword.

But wait now, here's one that's *really* fascinating ...

UP AT THE RIVERSIDE
A TED SMALLEY STORY

"Duck if you see a cop, Ted."

And so we were off an our mission: my boss, Sharon McCone; my partner, Neal Osborn; and me. Ted Smalley. She, the issuer of my orders, drove her venerable MG convertible. He sat slouched and rumpled beside her. I was perched on the backseat, if you could call it that, which you really can't because it's nothing more than a shelf for carrying one's groceries and such. And illegal for passengers, which is why I had to keep a keen eye out for the law.

I think our minor vehicular transgression made Shar feel free—far away from her everyday concerns about clients and caseloads at the investigative agency she owns. I knew our excursion was taking Neal's mind off the rising rent and declining profits of his used bookstore. And even though I entertained an image of myself as a sack from Safeway, my thinning hair ruffling like the leaves of a protruding bunch of celery, I still felt like a kid cutting school. A kid who had freed himself from billing and correspondence, to say nothing of keeping five private investigators and the next-door law firm in number-two pencils and scratch pads.

Soon we were across the Golden Gate Bridge and speeding north on Highway 101. It was a summer Friday and traffic was heavy, but Shar made the MG zip from lane to lane and we outdistanced them all. Our mission was a pleasurable one: a stop along the Russian River to look at and perhaps purchase the jukebox of Neal's and my dreams, then a picnic on the beach at Jenner.

Our plans had been formulated that morning when Shar called us at the ungodly hour of six, all excited. "One of those jukeboxes you guys want is advertised in today's classified," she said. "Seeburg Trashcan, and you won't believe this: It's almost within your price range."

While I primed my brain into running order, Neal went to fetch our copy of the paper. "Phone number's in the 707 area code," he said into the downstairs extension "Sonoma County."

"Nice up there," Shar said wistfully.

"Maybe Ted and I can take a drive on Sunday, check it out."

I issued a Neanderthal grunt of agreement Till I have at least two cups of coffee, I'm not verbal. "I've a feeling somebody'll snap it up before then," she said.

"Well, if you'll give Ted part of the day off, I can ask my assistant to mind the store."

"I ... oh hell, why don't the three of us take the whole day off? I'll pack a picnic. You know that sourdough loaf I make, with all the melted cheese and stuff?"

"Say no more."

Shar exited the freeway at River Road and we sped through vineyards toward the redwood forest. When we rolled into the town of Guerneville, its main street mirrored our holiday spirits. People roamed the sidewalks in shorts and t-shirts, many eating ice cream cones or by-the-slice pizza; a flea market in the parking lot of a supermarket was doing a brisk business; rainbow flags flapped in the breeze outside gay-owned businesses.

The town has been the hub of the resort area for generations; rustic cabins and summer homes line the riverbank and back up onto the hillsides. In the seventies it became a vacation-time mecca for gays, and the same wide-open atmosphere as in San Francico's Castro district prevailed, but by the late eighties the AIDS epidemic, a sagging economy, and a succession of disastrous floods had taken away the magic. Now it appeared that Guerneville was bouncing back as an eclectic and bohemian community of hardy folk who are willing to yearly risk cresting flood waters and mud slides. I, the grocery sack, smiled benevolently as we cruised along.

Outside of town the road wound high above the slow-moving river. At the hamlet of Monte Rio, we crossed the bridge and turned down a narrow lane made narrower by encroaching redwoods and vehicles pulled close to the walls of the mainly shabby houses. Neal began squinting at the numbers. "Dammit, why don't they make them bigger?" he muttered.

I refrained from reminding him that he was overdue for his annual checkup at the optometrist's.

Shar was the one who spotted the place, a large sagging three-story dirty-white clapboard structure with a parking area out front. The roof was missing a fair number of its shingles, the windows were hopelessly crusted with grime, and one column of the wide front porch leaned alarmingly. On the porch, to either side of the double front door, sat identical green wicker rockers, and in each sat a scowly-looking man. Between them, extending from the door and down the steps, was a series of orange cones such as highway department crews use. A yellow plastic tape strung from cone to cone bore the words DANGER DO NOT CROSS

DANGER DO NOT CROSS DANGER DO NOT CROSS ...

In as reverent a tone as I'd ever heard him use, Neal said, "Good God, it's the old Riverside Hotel!"

While staring at it Shar had overshot the parking area. As she drove along looking for a place to turn around she asked, "You know this place?"

"From years ago. Was built as a fancy resort in the twenties. People would come up from the city and spend their entire vacations here. Then in the seventies the original owner's family sold it to a guy named Tom Atwater, who turned it into a gay hotel. Great restaurant and bar, cottages with individual hot tubs scattered on the grounds leading down to the beach, anything-goes atmosphere."

"You stayed there?" I asked.

Neal heard the edge in my voice. He turned his head and smiled at me, laugh lines around his eyes crinkling. It amuses and flatters him that I'm jealous of his past. "I had dinner there. Twice."

Shar turned the MG in a driveway and we coasted back toward the hotel. The men were watching us. Both were probably in their mid fifties, dressed in shorts and t-shirts, but otherwise—except for the scowls—they were total opposites. The one on our left was a scarecrow with a shock of long gray-blond hair; the one on the right reminded me of Elmer Fudd. and had just as bald a pate.

When we climbed out of the car—the grocery sack needing a firm tug—Neal called, "I phoned earlier about the jukebox."

The scarecrow jerked his thumb at Fudd and kept scowling. Fudd arranged his face into more pleasant lines and got up from the rocker.

"I'm Chris Fowler," he said. "You Neal and Ted?"

"I'm Neal, this is Ted, and that's Sharon."

"Come on in, I'll show you the box."

"'Come on in, I'll show you the box,'" the scarecrow mimicked in a high nasal whine.

"Jesus!" Chris Fowler exclaimed. He led us through his side of the double front door.

Inside was a reception area that must've been magnificent before the oriental carpets faded and the flocked wallpaper became water stained and peeling. In its center stood a mahogany desk backed by an old fashioned pigeonhole arrangement, and wide stairs on either side led up to the second story. The yellow tape continued, from the door to the pigeonholes, neatly bisecting the room.

Shar stopped and stared at it, frowning. I tugged her arm and shook my head. Sometimes the woman can be so rude. Chris Fowler didn't notice though, just turned right into a dimly lighted barroom. "There's your jukebox," he said.

A thing of beauty, it was. Granted, a particular acquired-taste kind of beauty: shaped like an enormous trash can of fake blond wood, with two flaring red plastic side panels and a gaudy gilt grille studded with plastic gems. Tiny mirrored squares surrounded the grille, and the whole thing was decked out with enough chrome as a 1950s Cadillac. I went up to it and touched the coin slot. Five plays for a quarter, two for a dime, one for a nickel. Those were the days.

Instantly I fell in love.

When I looked at Neal his eyes were sparkling. "Can we play it?" he asked Chris.

"Sure." He took a nickel from his pocket and dropped it into the slot. Whirrs, clicks, and then mellow tones crooned, "See the pyramids across the Nile …"

Shar shook her head, rolled her eyes, and wandered off to inspect a pinball machine. She despairs of Neal's and my campy tendencies.

"So what d'you think?" Chris asked.

I said, "Good sound tone."

Neal said, "The price is kind of steep for us, though."

Chris said, "I'll throw in a box of extra 78s."

Neal said, "I don't know …"

And then Shar wandered back over. "What's with the tape?" she asked Chris. "And what's with the guy on the other side of it?"

Neal looked as if he wanted to strangle her. I stifled a moan. A model of subtlety, Shar, and right when we were trying to strike a deal.

Chris grimaced. "That's my partner of many years, Ira Sloan. We've agreed to disagree. The tape's my way of indicating my displeasure with him."

"Disagree over what?"

"This hotel. We jointly inherited it six months ago from Tom Atwater. Did either of you guys know him?"

I shook my head, but Neal nodded. He said, "I met him." Grinned at me and added, "Twice."

"Well," Chris said, "Tom was an old friend. In fact, he introduced Ira and me, nearly twenty years ago. When he left the place to us we said, 'What a great way to get out of the city, have our own business in an area that's experiencing a renaissance.' So we sold our city house, moved up here, called in the contractors, and got estimates of what it would take to go upscale and reopen. The building's run down, but the construction's solid. All it needs outside is a new roof and paint job. The cottages were swept away in the floods, but eventually they can be rebuilt. Inside here, all it would take is redecorating, a new chimney and fireplace in the common room on the other side, and updated kitchen equipment. So then what does my partner decide to do?"

All three of us shook our heads, caught up in his breathless monologue.

"My loving partner decides we're to do nothing. Even though we've got more than enough money to fix the place up, he wants to leave it as is and live out our golden years here in Faulkneresque splendor while it falls down around us!"

Neal and I looked properly horrified, but Shar asked, "So why'd you put up the tape?" Maybe a singleminded focus is an asset in a private investigator, but it seems to me it plays hell with interpersonal relations.

Chris wanted to talk about the tape, however. "Ira and I divided the place, straight down the middle. He took the common room, utility room, and the area on the floors above it. I took the restaurant, kitchen, bar, and above. I prepare the meals and slip his under the tape on the reception desk. He washes our clothes and pushes mine over here to me. I'll tell you, it's quite a life!"

"And in the meantime, you're selling off the fixtures in your half?"

"Only the ones that won't fit the image I want to create here."

"How can you create it in half a hotel?"

"I can't, but I'm hoping Ira'll come around eventually. I wish I knew why he has this tic about keeping the place the way it is. If I did, I know I could talk him out of the notion."

Shar was looking thoughtful now. She walked around the jukebox, examining its lovely lines and gnawing at her lower lip. She peered through the glass at the turntable where the 78 of "You Belong to Me" now rested silently. She glanced through the archway at the yellow plastic tape.

"Chris," she said, "what would it be worth to you to find out what Ira's problem is?"

"A lot."

"A reduction of price on this jukebox to one my friends can afford?"

I couldn't believe it! Yes, she was offering out of the goodness of her heart, because she'd seen how badly Neal and I wanted the jukebox, and she knew the limits of our budget. But she was also doing it because she never can resist a chance to play detective.

Chris looked surprised, then grinned. "A big reduction, but I don't see how—"

She took one of her business cards from her purse and handed it to him. Said to me, "Come on, Watson. The game's afoot."

"Mr. Sloan?" Shar was standing at the tape on the porch. I was trying to hide behind her.

Ira Sloan's eyes flicked toward us, then straight ahead.

"Oh, Mr. Sloan!" Now she was waving, for heaven's sake, as if he wasn't sitting a mere five feet away!

His scowl deepened.

Shar stepped over the tape. "Mr. Sloan, d'you suppose you could give Ted and me a tour of your side of the hotel? We love old places like this, and we both think it's a shame your partner wants to spoil it."

He turned his head, looking skeptical but not as ferocious.

Shar reached back and yanked on my arm so hard that I almost tripped over the tape. "Ted's partner, Neal, is in there with Chris, talking upscale. I had to remove Ted before they end up with a tape down the middle of their apartment."

Ira Sloan ran his hand through his longish hair and stood up. He was very tall—at least six-four—and so skinny he seemed to have no ass at all. Had he always been so thin, or was it the result of too many cooling meals shoved across the reception desk?

He said, "The tape was his idea."

"So he told us."

"Thinks it's funny."

"It's not."

"I like people who appreciate old things. It'll be a pleasure to show you around."

The common room was full of big maple furniture with wide wooden arms and thick floral chintz-covered cushions, faded now. The chairs and sofas would've been fashionable in the thirties and forties, campy in the seventies. Now they just looked tired. Casement windows overlooked the lawn and the river, and on the far side of the room was a deep stone fireplace whose chimney showed chinks where the mortar had crumbled. Against the stones hung an oval stained-glass panel in muddy looking colors. It reminded me of the stone in one of those mood rings that were popular in the seventies.

By the time we'd inspected the room, Shar and Ira Sloan were chattering up a storm. By the time we got upstairs to the guestrooms, they were old friends.

The guestrooms were furnished with waterbeds, another cultural icon of the sybaritic decade. Now their mattresses were shriveled like used condoms. The suites had Jacuzzi tubs set before the windows, once brightly colored porcelain, but now rust-stained and grimy. The balconies off the third-story rooms were narrow and cobwebby, and the webbing on their lounge chairs had been stripped away, probably by nesting birds.

Shar asked, "How long was the hotel in operation?"

"Tom closed it in 'eighty-three."

"Why?"

"Declining business. By then ... well, a lot of things were over."

It made me so sad. The Riverside Hotel's brief time in the sun had been a wild, tumultuous, drug-hazed era—but also curiously innocent. A time of experimentation and new found freedom. A time to adopt new lifestyles without fear of reprisal. But now the age of innocence was over, harsh reality had set in. Many of the men who had stayed here were dead, many others decaying like this structure.

Why would Ira Sloan want to keep intact this monument to the death of happiness?

Back downstairs Shar whispered to me, "Stay here. Talk with him." Then she was gone into the reception room and over the tape.

I turned, trying to think of something to say to Ira Sloan, but he'd vanished into some dark corner of the haunted place, possibly to commune with his favorite ghost. I sat down on one of the chairs amid a cloud of rising dust to see if he'd return. Against the chimney the stained-glass mood-ring stone seemed to have darkened. My mood darkened with it. I wanted out of this place and into the sun.

In about ten minutes Ira Sloan still hadn't reappeared. I heard a rustling behind the reception desk. Shar—who else? She was removing a ledger from a drawer under the warning tape and spreading it open.

"Well, that's interesting," she muttered after a couple of minutes. "Very interesting."

A little while more and she shut the ledger and stuffed it into her tote bag. Smiled at me and said, "Let's go now. You look as though you can use some of my famous sourdough loaf and a walk by the sea."

When we were ensconced on the sand with our repast spread before us, I asked Shar, "What'd you take from the desk?"

"The guest register." She pulled it from her tote and handed it to me.

"You stole it?"

Her mouth twitched—a warning sign. "Borrowed it, with Chris's permission."

"Why?"

"Well, when I went back to talk with him some more, I asked how the two of them decided who got what. He said Ira insisted on his side of the hotel, and Chris was glad to divide it that way because he likes to cook."

Neal poured wine into plastic glasses and handed them around. "Bizarre arrangement, if you ask me."

Shar was cutting the sourdough loaf, in imminent danger of sawing off a finger as well. I took the knife from her and performed culinary surgery.

"Anyway," she went on, "then I asked Chris if Ira had insisted on getting anything else. He said only the guest register. But by then Chris'd gotten his back up, and he pointed out that the ledger was kept in a drawer of the desk that's bisected by the tape. So they agreed to leave it there and hold it in common. Ira wasn't happy with the arrangement."

I filled paper plates with slices of the loaf. Its delicious aroma was quickly dispelling my hotel-induced funk.

"And did the register tell you anything?" Neal asked.

"Only that somebody—I assume Ira—tore the pages out for the week of August 13, 1978. Recently."

"How d'you know it was recent?"

"Fresh tears look different than old ones. The edges of these aren't browning." She flipped the book open to where the pages were missing.

"So now what?"

"I try to find out who was there and what happened that week. Maybe some well known who was still in the closet stayed there. Or somebody who was with a person he wasn't supposed to be."

I asked, "How're you going to find out, if the pages're missing?"

She stabbed her finger at the first column on the ledger page, then at the last. "Date checked in, date checked out. Five individuals who checked in before the thirteenth checked out on the eighteenth. My job for this weekend is to try to locate and talk with them."

"Hey, Ted, come along with me!"

Shar was in the driver's seat of the agency van parked on the floor of Pier 24½, where we have our offices. I was dragging tail down the iron stairway from the second level, intent on heading home after a perfectly outlandish Monday. I went over to the van and leaned in the open window. "What's happening?"

"With any luck, you and I are going to collect your jukebox this evening and have it back at your place by the time Neal closes the store." Neal's used bookstore, Anachronism, is open till nine on Mondays.

I jumped into the van, the day's horrors forgotten. "You find out what Ira Sloan's problem is?"

"Some of it. The rest is about to unfold."

I got my seatbelt on just as she swerved into traffic on the waterfront boulevard outside the pier. Thanked God I was firmly strapped in, a grocery sack no longer.

The house was on a quiet street on the west side of Petaluma, a small city some forty minutes north of the Golden Gate. It used to be called the Egg Basket of the World, before the chicken boom went bust. From what

I hear lately, it's turning into Yuppie Heaven.

As we got out of the van I looked up at the gray Victorian. It had a wide porch, high windows, and a fan-like pediment over the door that was painted in the colors of the rainbow. This, Shar had told me, was the home of Mark Curry, one of the men who had stayed at the Riverside during the second week of August, 1978. Surprisingly, given the passage of time, she'd managed to locate three of the five who'd signed the register before the missing week, and to interview two so far.

"Ted," she said, "how long have gays been doing that rainbow thing?"

"You mean the flags and all? Funny—since 1978. The first rainbow flag was designed by a San Francisco artist, Gilbert Baker, as a sign of the gay community's solidarity. A version of it was flown in the next year's Pride Parade."

"I didn't realize it went back that far." She started up the walk, and I followed.

The man who answered the door was slender and handsome, with a fine-boned face and a diamond stud in one nostril, and a full head of wavy gray hair that threatened to turn me green with envy. His wood-paneled parlor made me envious too: full of Chippendale furniture, with a gilt harp in the front window. Mark Curry seated us there, offered coffee, and went to fetch it.

Shar saw the way I was looking at the room. "It's not you," she said. "In a room like this that jukebox would look—"

"Like a wart on the face of an angel. But in our place—"

"It'll still look like a trashcan."

Mark Curry came back with a silver coffee service, and got down to business while he poured. "After you phoned, Ms. McCone, I got in touch with Chris Fowler. He's an old friend, from the time we worked as volunteers at an AIDS hospice. He vouched for you, so I dug out my journal for 1978 and refreshed my memory about August's stay at the Riverside."

"You arrived there August eleventh?"

"Yes."

"Alone?"

"No, with my then partner, Dave Howell. He's been dead ... do you believe nearly sixteen years now?"

"I'm sorry."

"Thanks. Sometimes it seems like yesterday."

"Were you and Mr. Howell staying in a cottage or the main building?"

"Main building, third floor, river side. Over the bar."

"D'you recall who else was there?"

"Well, the place was always full in the summertime, and a lot of the men I didn't know. And even more people came in over the weekend. There was to be a canoeing regatta on Wednesday the sixteenth, with a big barbecue on the beach that evening, and they were gearing up for it."

I said, "*Canoeing* regatta?"

Mark Curry winked at me. "A bunch of guys, stoned and silly, banging into each other and capsizing and having a great time of it."

"Sounds like fun."

Shar said, "So who do you remember?"

"Well, Tom Atwater, of course. His lover, Bobby Gardena, showed up on Tuesday. Bobby had a house in the city, divided his time between there and the river. Ira Sloan, one of Tom's best friends, and the guy who inherited that white elephant along with Chris. He was alone, had just broken off a relationship, and seemed pretty unhappy, but a few months later Tom introduced him to Chris, and they've been together ever since. Then there was Sandy Janssen. Darryl Williams. And of course there was ..."

Shar dutifully noted the names, but I sensed she'd lost interest in them. No well known who customarily hid in the closet, no scandalous mispairing. When Mark Curry ran out of people, she said, "Tell me about the week of the thirteenth. Did anything out of the ordinary happen?"

Mark Curry laughed. "Out of the ordinary was de rigeur at the Riverside."

"More out of the ordinary than usual."

Her serious—and curiously intense—tone sobered him. He stared into his coffee cup, recapturing his memories. When he spoke, his voice was subdued.

"The night of the regatta, you know? Everybody was on the beach, carrying on till all hours. A little before two Dave and I decided we wanted to have a couple of quiet drinks alone, so we slipped away from the party. I remember walking up the slope from the beach and across the lawn to the hotel. Everything was so quiet. I suppose it was just the contrast to the commotion on the beach, but it gave me the shivers. Dave, too. And when we went inside, it was still quiet, but ..."

"But what, Mr. Curry?"

"There was a ... an undercurrent. A sense of whispers and footfalls, but you couldn't really identify whose or where they were. Like something was going on, but not really. You know how that can be?"

Shar's face was thoughtful. She's had a lot of unusual experiences in her life, and I was sure she did know how that could be.

Mark Curry added, "Dave and I went into the bar and sat down. Nobody came. We were about to make our own drinks—you could do that, so long as you signed a chit—when Ira Sloan stepped out of the kitchen and told us the bar was closed."

"But this was after legal closing time."

He shook his head. "The bar at the Riverside never closed. It was immune to the dictates of the state lawmakers—some of whom were its frequent patrons."

"I see. Did Ira give you any explanation?"

"No. He asked if we wanted to buy a bottle, so we did, and took it up to our room and consumed it on our balcony. And all night the noisy party on the beach went on. But the quiet in the hotel was louder than any cacophony I've ever experienced."

When we got back to the van, Shar took out her phone and made a call. "Hi, Mick," she said. "Anything?"

Mick Savage, her nephew, computer specialist, and fastest skiptracer in the west.

"I see ... Uh-huh ... Right ... No evidence about a gas leak on Friday the eighteenth?... Yes, I thought as much ... No, nothing else. And thanks."

She broke the connection, stuffed the phone back into her bag, and looked at me. Her expression was profoundly sad.

"You've got yourself a jukebox," she said.

"Before I go into this," Shar said to Chris Fowler, "there's something I ought to say."

The three of us were seated at a table in the bar at the Riverside. The dim lighting made Chris look curiously young and hopeful.

"Secrets," Shar went on, "are not necessarily harmful, so long as they remain secrets. But once you put them into words, they can't be taken back. Ever."

Chris nodded. "I understand what you're trying to tell me, but I need to know."

"All right, then. I spoke with three men who were present at the hotel on Wednesday, August 16, 1978. Each gave me bits and pieces of a story, that led me to suspect what happened. A check I had run on a fourth man pretty much confirmed my suspicions.

"On August sixteenth of that year, a canoeing regatta was held at this hotel—a big yearly event. The cottages and rooms were all full, but we're only concerned with a few people: Tom Atwater and his lover, Bobby Gardena. Ira. And my witnesses: Mark Curry, Darryl Williams, and Sandy Janssen.

"All three witnesses came up here the Friday before the regatta. Ira arrived on Sunday, Bobby Gardena on Tuesday. It soon became apparent to everybody that Tom and Bobby weren't getting on. Bobby was baiting

Tom. They quarreled frequently and publicly. Bobby confided to Sandy Janssen that he'd told Tom he'd quit his job and put his San Francisco house up for sale, with the intention of moving to New Orleans. Tom accused him of being involved with somebody else, and Bobby wouldn't confirm or deny it. He taunted Tom with the possibility.

"After the regatta there was a barbecue on the beach. Everybody was there except for Tom, Bobby, and Ira. Bobby had told Darryl Williams he planned to pack and head back to the city that night. Ira was described by Mark Curry as alone and unhappy."

I heard a noise in the reception area and looked that way. A thin scarecrow's shape stood deep in shadow on the other side of the desk. Ira Sloan. I started to say something, then thought, No. Shar and Chris are discussing him. He has a right to hear, doesn't he?

"Something unusual happened that night," Shar continued. "Mark Curry noticed it when he returned to the hotel around two. Sandy Janssen described a strange atmosphere that kept him from sleeping well. Darryl Williams talked about hearing whispers in the corridors. The next morning Tom told everybody that Bobby had left early for the city, but Darryl claims he saw Bobby's car in the lot when he looked out his window around nine. An hour later it was gone. None of my three witnesses ever heard from or saw Bobby again. The skip trace I had run on him turned up nothing. The final closing on the sale of his city house was handled by Tom, who had his power-of-attorney."

Chris Fowler started to say something, but Shar held up her hand. "And here's the most telling point: On Thursday night, all the guests received notice that they had to vacate the premises on Friday morning, due to a potentially dangerous gas leak that needed to be worked on. A leak that PG&E has no record of. The only men who remained behind were Tom and Ira."

Chris sat very still, breathing shallowly. I looked at the reception area. The scarecrow figure in the shadows hadn't moved.

"I think you can draw your own conclusions," Shar added. She spoke gently and sadly—not the usual trumpeting and crowing that I hear from her when she solves a case.

Slowly Chris said, "God, I can't believe Tom killed Bobby! He was a gentle man. I never saw him raise his hand to anybody."

"It may have been self defense," Shar said. "Darryl Williams told me one of his friends had an earlier relationship with Bobby, an abusive one. Bobby always threw the first punches."

"So an argument, a moment of violence ..."

"Is all it takes."

"Naturally he would've turned to Ira to help him cover up. They were best friends, had been since grade school. But that doesn't make Ira a murderer."

"No, it doesn't."

"Anyway, you can't prove it."

"Not without Bobby's remains—which are probably somewhere in this hotel."

Chris glanced around, shivering slightly. "And as long as they're here, Ira and I will be at a stalemate, estranged for the rest of our lives. That's how long he'll guard them."

I was still staring at Ira Sloan's dark figure, but now I looked beyond it, into the common room. The stained-glass oval hanging on the fireplace chimney, that I'd fancifully thought of as the stone in a mood ring, gleamed in the rays from a nearby floor lamp: pink, red, orange, yellow, green, blue, indigo. The seven colors of the rainbow.

I said, "I know where Bobby's buried."

"When I saw this stained glass yesterday," I said, "I couldn't tell the colors, on account of it being hung where no light could pass through. A strange place, and that should've told Shar or me something right then. Tonight, with the lamp on, I see that it's actually the seven colors of the rainbow."

We—Shar, Chris, and I—were standing in front of the fireplace. I could feel Ira Sloan's presence in the shadows behind us.

"It's the only rainbow symbol in the hotel," I went on, "and it was probably commissioned by Tom Atwater sometime in 1978."

"Why then?" Shar asked.

"Remember I told you that the first rainbow flag was designed in 78? And that a version of it was flown in the 79 Pride Parade?"

She nodded.

"The 78 flag was seven colors, like this panel. Respectively, they symbolized sexuality, life, healing, sun, nature, art, harmony, and spirit. But the flag that was flown at the parade only had six colors. They dropped indigo so there would be exactly three stripes on either side of the street. That's the one that's become popular and is recognized by the International Congress of Flag Makers."

Chris said, "So Tom and Ira put Bobby's body someplace temporary the night of the murder—maybe the walk-in freezer—and after Tom closed the hotel, they walled him in behind the fireplace. But Tom was a sentimental guy, and he loved Bobby. He'd've wanted some monument."

Behind us there was a whisper of noise, such as I imagined had filled this hotel the night of August 16, 1978. Shar heard it—I could tell from the way she cocked her head—but Chris didn't.

Bitterly he said, "It couldn't've been self defense. If it was, Tom or Ira would've called the county sheriff."

"It wasn't self defense," Ira's voice said. "It was an accident. I was there. I saw it."

Slowly we turned toward the reception area. Ira Sloan had come out of the shadows and was backed up against the warning tape, his face twisted with the despair of one who expects not to be believed.

"Bobby was leaving to go back to the city," he added. "He was taunting Tom about how he'd be seeing his new lover. They were at the top of the stairs. Tom called Bobby an ugly name, and Bobby went to hit him. Tom ducked, Bobby lost his balance. He fell, rolled over and over, and hit his head on the base of the reception desk." He motioned at the sharp corner near the stairway.

Shar asked, "Why didn't you call the sheriff?"

"Tom had been outspoken about gay rights. Outspoken and abrasive. He had enemies on the county board of supervisors and in the sheriff's department. They'd have seen to it that he was charged with murder. Tom was afraid, so I did what any friend would do."

Chris said, "For God's sake, Ira, why didn't you tell me this when we inherited the hotel?"

"I wanted to preserve Tom's memory. And I was afraid what you might think of me. What you might do about it."

His partner was silent for a moment. Then he said, "I should've let you keep your secret."

"Maybe not," Shar told him. "Secrets that tear two people apart are destructive and potentially dangerous."

"But—"

"The fact is, Chris, that secrets come in all varieties. What you do about them, too. You can expose them, and then everybody gets hurt. You can make a tacit agreement to keep them, and by the time they come out, nobody cares, but keeping them's still exacted its toll on you. Or you can share them with a select group of trusted people and agree to do something about them."

"What're you trying to tell me?"

"The group of people in this room is a small and closed-mouthed one. We all know Ira can keep his own counsel. Bobby Gardena's been in his tomb a long time, but I doubt he's rested easily. Perhaps it would release him if you moved his remains to a more suitable place on the property, and created a better monument to him."

I said, "A better monument, like a garden in the colors of the rainbow."

Chris nodded. A faint ray of hope touched Ira's tortured features.

I added, "Of course, a fitting monument to both Bobby and Tom would be if you renovated this hotel like you planned and reopened it to the living."

Chris nodded again. Then he went to Ira, grasped the warning tape, and tore it free from where it was anchored to the pigeonholes.

I rode in the back of the van on our way home to the city, making sure the Seeburg Trashcan didn't slip its moorings. Both Shar and I were quiet as we maneuvered it up my building's elevator and into the apartment.

Later, after Neal promised to become the fifth party to a closely held secret, I told him the story of August 16, 1978. He was quiet too.

But still later, when we'd jockeyed the Trashcan into position in our living room and plugged it in, the nostalgic tunes of happier times played long into the night, heralding happy times to come.

IRREFUTABLE EVIDENCE

I tossed the pine cone from hand to hand and looked up at the tree it had fallen from. It was perhaps twenty feet tall and very dense, with branches that swept the ground except on its left-hand side, where they were bent and sheared off. A young bristlecone pine, hundreds of years old and still growing. In the high elevations of California's White Mountains, where the tule elk and wild mustangs range, there are bristlecones over four thousand years old—some say the oldest living things on the face of the earth. Years ago, I'd made one of the better decisions of my life while lying under such a pine; today I'd been hoping this tree would yield evidence that would help me identify a killer.

No such luck.

After a time I turned away and, still holding the pine cone, retraced my steps to my rented Jeep. I tossed the cone on the passenger's seat, got in, and cranked up the air conditioning. The temperature was in the mid nineties—August heat. I eased the vehicle over the rocky, sloping ground to the secondary road, bumped along it for two miles, then turned southwest onto Route 168 toward Big Pine, a town of 1,350 nestled in a valley between the Whites and the John Muir Wilderness Area. My motel was on the wide main street, a homey place with a tree-shaded lawn and picnic tables. No high-speed Internet access or other amenities that my operatives at McCone Investigations would have deemed necessities, but plenty good enough for their boss.

I tell my operatives I believe in the simple life. They claim I'm living in the Dark Ages.

Dark Ages, indeed. I had a cell phone, which I took out as soon as I entered my unit and dialed the agency in San Francisco. Ted Smalley, our office manager, sounded relieved when he heard my voice. That morning I'd flown down to Bishop, some fifteen miles north of here, in the Cessna 170B I jointly owned with my significant other, Hy Ripinsky; Ted, ever nervous about what he called my "dangerous hobby," had probably been fretting all day.

"Shar, it's after five o'clock. Where are you?" he asked.

"The motel in Big Pine."

"Why didn't you check in with me from the airport? I've been waiting—"

"There was somebody at the airport who offered me a ride to the dealer I'm renting a car from, so I couldn't take the time. Then I had to stop by the local sheriff's substation to let them know I'd be working in the area, check in here, and— Why am I explaining all this to you?"

"I don't know. Why are you?"

"Sometimes you remind me of my mother."

"God help me. She's a nice lady, but ..."

"Yeah. So what's going on there?"

"Quiet day, except for the trouble with the UPS guy."

"Trouble?"

"You don't want to know."

"Probably not. Is Mick in?" Mick Savage, my nephew and chief computer expert.

"No, he left for the day, but he said to tell you he e-mailed the files on the research job you assigned him."

Which I would access on my laptop—another rebuttal to the claim that the boss was living in the Dark Ages.

I read through the files Mick had sent me, then walked down to a steakhouse I'd spotted on the way in. After dinner I went back to the motel and sat at one of the picnic tables, enjoying the cool of the evening and planning a course of action for the next day. The air was sweet with sage and dry grass; crickets chorused in a field behind the motel, and somewhere far off, a dog was barking. I felt relaxed, mellow, even; it was good to get out of the city.

The case I was working had been brought to me by Glenn Solomon, a criminal-defense attorney who threw a lot of business my way. His client, Tom Worthington, had been indicted here in Inyo County for the brutal murder of his lover, Darya Adams. Worthington was a wealthy man, an olive rancher from over near Fresno; it was natural he would turn to one of the stars of San Francisco's legal community for his defense.

I thought back to the briefing Glenn had given me in his office high atop Embarcadero Four the previous afternoon.

"Tom Worthington is a family man," he'd begun, folding his hands over the well-tailored expanse of his stomach. "Wife, two college-age children. Good reputation. No indications that he's ever strayed before. Darya Adams, he apparently couldn't resist. Former beauty queen—Miss California, I believe—and widowed. Ran a tourist boutique at Mammoth Lakes. They met when he was on a ski trip there. Before long, they were meeting on a regular basis at a country cabin he bought for her outside Chelsea."

I looked up from the notes I was taking. "Where's Chelsea? I've never heard of it."

"You know Big Pine, Inyo County?"

"As a matter of fact, I do. One of Hy's friends used to have a cabin in the mountains near there."

"Well, Chelsea is a wide place on the road some seven miles into the hills above Big Pine."

"Okay, now, the murder ...?"

"As close as the medical examiner could pinpoint it, it occurred on July thirty-first. Worthington and Adams had met at the cabin on the twenty-eighth, according to the employee who was minding the boutique in her absence. When Adams didn't return on August first as scheduled, the employee called the cabin, received no answer, then asked the sheriff to check. Place was closed up. On August third, a hiker came across Adams's body in the foothills of the White Mountains several miles from Big Pine. She'd been beaten and strangled. There were signs that the body had been moved there from the place she was killed, but the sheriff's department hasn't been able to determine where that was."

"And they're calling this a crime of passion, perpetrated by your client?"

"Right. One of Darya Adams's friends claimed she was fed up with the arrangement and had threatened to go to his wife if he didn't initiate divorce proceedings. He claims that wasn't true."

"What's the evidence pointing to Worthington?"

Glenn shifted in his chair, reached for the bottled water on the desk.

"Two pieces. One, a key chain near the body, containing a miniature of his Safeway Rewards Club card—you know, the ones they give you so if you lose your keys, whoever finds them can turn them in to the store, and they'll call you. And two, a pine cone in the bed of Worthington's truck."

"A *pine cone?*"

"A bristlecone, from the tree Adams's body was found under."

"How do they know it was from that particular tree?"

"Ah, my friend, that's where it gets interesting. Human beings, as you know, can be identified by their DNA. Animals, too. But are you aware that plants also have DNA?"

"No."

"Well, they do, and, as with humans, the DNA of one plant is unlike the DNA of any other."

"Wait a minute—you're saying they ran a DNA test on a pine cone?"

"They did, and it came up a match for those on the tree."

I paused for a moment, letting that sink in. "So what do you expect me to do with this? DNA is a conclusive test."

"Oh, there's no doubt the cone in Tom Worthington's truck came from the place where Darya Adams was found. No doubt it was his key ring near the body. But he insists he's innocent, that she was alive when he left for home the morning of July thirty-first. Says he'd misplaced the key ring at the cabin during a previous visit. Says he doesn't know how the cone came to be in the truck."

"I can see someone planting the keys, but it seems far-fetched that someone would be knowledgeable and clever enough to plant that pine cone."

"Not really. D'you watch any of those true-crime shows on TV?"

"No. They resemble my real life too closely."

"Well, I watch them, and so do millions of others. On July fifteenth, just two weeks before Darya Adams's murder, *Case Closed* did a segment in which a murder conviction hinged on DNA testing of seed pods."

"So someone could've gotten the idea of planting the pine cone from the show."

"Right."

"And you believe Tom Worthington's being truthful with you?"

"I do. My instincts don't lie."

"That's good enough for me."

"Then what I expect you to do, my friend, should be clear: Find out who left that key ring near the body, and the cone in Worthington's truck. When you do, we'll have our line of defense: Darya Adams's real murderer."

As full dark settled in, I returned to my motel room and again looked over the files Mick had sent me. Background on Tom Worthington and Darya Adams. Background on friends and associates, scattered throughout Inyo and Fresno counties. Tomorrow I'd begin interviewing them, starting with those in the Big Pine area, and then visit Worthington at the county jail in Independence.

Finding a lead to Darya Adams's killer wasn't going to be easy. Inyo is California's third largest county—over ten thousand square miles, encompassing mountains, volcanic wasteland, timber, and desert. Its relatively small communities are scattered far and wide. In addition to its size, the county has a reputation for harboring a strange and often violent population. People vanish into the desert; bodies turn up in old mine shafts; bars are shot up by disgruntled customers. It's not uncommon for planes carrying drugs from south of the border to land at isolated airstrips; desert rats and prospectors and cults with bizarre beliefs hole up in nearly inaccessible canyons. I'd have no shortage of potential suspects here.

Too bad my visit to the bristlecone pine under which Darya Adams died hadn't offered a blinding flash of inspiration.

The red sun over the mountains told me the day was going to be hot. I dressed accordingly, in shorts and a tank top, with a looseweave shirt for protection against the sun. After a big breakfast at a nearby cafe—best to fortify myself since I didn't know when the next opportunity to eat would present itself—I set off for the offices of Ace Realty, a block off the main street.

According to my background checks, Jeb Barkley, the agent who had handled the sale of the cabin near Chelsea last year, was an old friend of Tom Worthington's, had played football with him at Fresno State. A big man with a round, balding head that looked too small for his body, he was at his desk when I arrived. The other desks were unoccupied and dust-covered; business must not be good.

Barkley greeted me, brought coffee, then sat in his chair, leaning forward, hands clasped on the desktop, a frown furrowing his otherwise baby-smooth brow. "I sure hope you can do something to help Tom, Ms. McCone," he said.

"I'm going to try. Did you see him on his last visit?"

"Oh no. He and Darya ... they liked their privacy."

"When was the last time you saw him?"

"Couple of months ago. He came alone, to go fishing, and when he got to the cabin he discovered he didn't have his keys. So he called me and I drove out to let him in with the spare we keep on file here."

That would support Worthington's claim that he'd misplaced the keys that had been found near Adams's body. "How did he seem?"

"Seem? Oh ..." Barkley considered, the furrows in his brow deepening. "I'd say he was just Tom. Cheerful. Glad to be there. He asked if I'd like to go fishing with him, but I couldn't get away."

"Mr. Barkley, when Tom Worthington bought the cabin, was it clear to you that he was buying it for Darya Adams?"

"From the beginning. I mean, they looked at a number of properties together. And the offer and final papers were drawn up in her name, as a single woman."

"As an old friend of Tom's, how did you feel about the transaction?"

"I don't understand."

"Tom Worthington was cheating on his wife. Buying property for another woman. How did that make you feel?"

He hesitated, looking down at his clasped hands. "Ms. McCone," he said after a moment, "Tom has had a lot of trouble with his wife. A lot of trouble with those kids of his, too. Darya was a nice woman, and I figured he deserved a little happiness in his life. It wasn't as if he was just fooling around, either. They were serious about each other."

"Serious enough that he would leave his family for her?"

"He said he was thinking of it."

"But so far he hadn't taken any steps toward a divorce?"

"Not that I know of."

"Let me ask you this, Mr. Barkley: Are you convinced of Tom Worthington's innocence?"

"I am."

"Any ideas about who might have killed Darya Adams?"

"I've given that some thought. There're a lot of weird characters hanging out in the hills around Chelsea. Screamin' Mike, for one."

"Who's he?"

"Headcase, kind of a hermit. Has a shack not too far from Tom and Darya's cabin. Comes to town once a month when his disability check arrives at general delivery. Cashes it at Gilley's Saloon, gets drunk, and then he starts screaming nonsense at the top of his voice. How he got his name."

"Is he dangerous to others?"

"Not so far. Ed Gilley runs him off, he goes back to his shack and sobers up. But you never know."

I made a note about Screamin' Mike. "Anyone else you can think of?"

"There's a cult up one of the canyons—Children of the Perpetual Life. Some of their members've had run-ins with the sheriff, and a couple of years ago one of their women disappeared, was never found. Maybe Ed Gilley could help you; running a saloon, he's hooked in with the local gossip."

I noted the cult's and Gilley's names. "Well, thank you, Mr. Barkley," I said. "When I spoke with your local sheriff's deputy yesterday, he told me they have no objection to my examining the cabin, and I have Mr. Worthington's permission as well. Has he contacted you about giving me the keys?"

"Yes. But why do you want to go there? If the sheriff's department didn't find anything—"

"Even so, there may be something that will give me a lead."

He rose, then hesitated. "The cabin—it's kind of hard to find. How about I drive you there, let you in myself?"

At first I balked at the idea, but I sensed a reserve in Jeb Barkley; he might volunteer something useful in a less structured situation. "Okay," I said. "I'd appreciate it."

We went outside to a parking area behind the real-estate office, and Barkley unlocked the doors of a blue Subaru Outback whose left side was badly scratched. He saw me looking at it and said, "Damn kids. Keyed it while the wife and I were at the movies last week."

"I guess kids in small towns aren't any different from those in big cities." I slid into the passenger seat, wincing as the hot vinyl burned the back of my thighs.

"Makes me glad I never had any." Barkley eased his big body behind the wheel.

"You mentioned that Tom Worthington had trouble with his children."

"Yeah. Jeannie, the older one, got into drugs in high school. Tom had her in and out of schools for troubled teens, but it didn't do any good. She's out on her own now, only shows up when she wants money. The boy, Kent, has ... I guess they call them anger-management problems. Did jail time for beating up his girlfriend. He's in college now and doing well, but Tom says he's still an angry young man."

I made a mental note to find out more about Worthington's troubled offspring. "And his wife—what kind of trouble did he have with her?"

"... I'm not sure I should be talking about that."

"You'll save me from having to ask him."

'Well, okay, then. Betsy, that's the wife's name, she drinks. It's gotten so that she doesn't go out of the house, just drinks from morning till night. Wine after breakfast, the hard stuff in the afternoon, more wine during and after dinner. And then she passes out. They don't have much of a life together."

"Do you think she knew about Darya Adams?"

"Doubt the woman knows much about anything. I mean, when you're in the bag all the time ..."

"I hear you."

Barkley drove north on the highway for about three miles, then looped off onto a secondary road that twisted and branched, twisted again, and began climbing into the hills between rocky outcroppings to which pines and sage and manzanita stubbornly clung. The road flattened briefly, and a scattering of buildings appeared—grocery store, propane firm, diner, and several small private homes.

"Chelsea," Barkley said, and turned into a side road.

"Not much to it."

"Nope. Of course, it suited Tom and Darya. As I said, they liked their privacy."

"Why here, though? Why didn't they buy a place nearer to Mammoth Lakes, where she had her shop?"

"Darya wasn't comfortable with that. She's...she was a prominent businesswoman, active in civic organizations and charities. Until Tom could see his way clear to divorcing Betsy, Darya preferred to keep their relationship secret."

"Exactly why couldn't he see his way clear?"

Barkley glanced at me, lips twisting wryly. "Money—what else? Community-property state, lots of assets at stake. He was trying to figure out a way to minimize the divorce's impact on his holdings. I've been advising him how to do that."

"You mean you've been advising him on a way to hide his assets."

Barkley shrugged, turned his eyes back on the road.

After about a mile, he braked and made a sharp right turn into a graveled driveway. Clumps of dry grass stubbled the ground to either side, and ahead, tucked under tall pines and backing up to a rocky hill, stood the cabin. It was small, of stone and logs, with a wide porch running along the front and a dormer window peeking out from under its eaves. Barkley pulled the car up near the steps.

I got out and climbed to the porch. It was refreshingly cool there. Barkley followed, taking out a set of keys, and opened the front door. The interior of the cabin was even cooler.

The main floor was one big room: kitchen with a breakfast bar separating it from an informal dining area, sitting area centering around a stone fireplace. Rustic furnishings, the kind you expect in a vacation place. Stuffed animal heads on the walls; I could feel their glassy eyes watching me.

"Worthington's a hunter?" I asked.

"What? No, the place came furnished."

A spiral staircase led up to a loft. I climbed it, found two bedrooms with a connecting bath. In the larger of the two, the bed was unmade, the blanket and sheets tangled. In the bathroom, towels were draped crookedly over their bars; a silk robe in a red- and-black floral pattern lay on the edge of the tub.

I thought about the vacation place Hy and I owned on the Mendocino coast. At the end of every visit, we took time to tidy it, so we'd be greeted by a clean home when we returned. Tom Worthington claimed he had left the cabin on the morning of July thirty-first—apparently delegating the cleanup to Darya. Darya was due back at her shop in Mammoth Lakes on August first, and she probably would have wanted to go home and get settled in the night before, but there was no sign she'd been preparing to depart. I went down to the kitchen. Dirty dishes were piled in the sink, and a trash receptacle was overflowing. Barkley stood at the counter, his back to me, looking out a greenhouse window.

"Poor hummingbirds," he said. "Their feeder's empty. I think I'll fill it." He reached into a cabinet next to the sink as I went back to the living area.

There were two grass-cloth placemats and pewter salt-and-pepper shakers on the table, and the chairs had been neatly pushed in. The cushions on the sofa in front of the fireplace were rumpled, but I saw no books, magazines, or anything else of a personal nature. There were no knickknacks, photographs, or pictures on the wall.

Who are you people? I thought, standing by the fireplace. *Or, in Darya's case, who were you?* With the exception of the disarray upstairs and in the kitchen, the cabin might have been a set for a TV movie. I couldn't begin to fathom how the woman had died unless I knew how she had lived. And—with due apologies to Glenn's instincts—I couldn't fully assess Tom Worthington's guilt or innocence until I knew what kind of man he was.

I decided to take a run up Highway 395 to Mammoth Lakes, in Mono County, right away. I'd speak to Adams's employee there. Then, in the afternoon, I'd drive down to the Inyo County jail in Independence.

When Jeb Barkley dropped me off at my rental car, I called the office and asked Mick to start background searches on Tom Worthington's son and daughter. Then I phoned Darya Adams's employee, Kathy Bledsoe, and made an appointment to meet her at Adams's shop, High Desert Mementoes. As I drove northwest on 395, I reviewed what I knew of the woman.

Kathy, according to Mick's files, was an artist, in her mid thirties, around Darya's age. She'd enjoyed some success selling her landscapes through a gallery in Mammoth Lakes. For a number of years she'd been employed as a ski instructor at one of the area's resorts, but had quit in order to devote more time to her painting; it must have been the right move, for a review of a showing of her works at the gallery last year predicted that her career was due to take off.

Mammoth Lakes struck me as an upscale community for Mono County. Hy owned a ranch to the north, near Tufa Lake, that he'd inherited from his stepfather, and I was accustomed to the small towns and open countryside of that area. But here you had good motels (presumably equipped with all the amenities my operatives would find desirable), a variety of restaurants, and shopping centers. A lot of shopping centers. I located Darya Adams's establishment in one of them, not far from 395. Its windows displayed a better class of merchandise than usually found in tourist shops: obsidian sculptures, lava rock, dried desert plants, coffee-table books. The sign on the door said the shop was closed, but when I tapped on the glass, a slender, dark-haired woman admitted me and identified herself as Bledsoe.

When we were seated in a small office behind the selling floor, she said, "Truthfully, I don't know what I can tell you that might help Tom. I mean, I was just here minding the store when Darya ... Well, I just don't know."

"Basically I'm after background. I take it you knew about Ms. Adams's relationship with Mr. Worthington?"

"*Knew* about it? I introduced them."

"Tell me about that."

"Tom was a friend of my former husband's. They'd known each other forever, fished together. About two years ago, I had an opening at the Lakes Gallery—I'm a painter, landscapes, mainly. Tom was up skiing and came to the show; Darya was there, too. They hit it off, and the rest, as they say, is history." Her dark eyes clouded. "A good history, until last week."

"The relationship was harmonious, then?"

"Very. Darya never mentioned so much as a harsh word."

"So she was open about it with you?"

"Of course. Why d'you ask?"

"I've heard she tried to keep it a secret."

"From people who had no business knowing, yes. But not from me."

"Was Tom planning to divorce his wife?"

"Eventually."

"And Darya had no problem with the delay?"

Kathy Bledsoe smiled faintly. "If anything, she was in favor of waiting. Darya was very independent—she'd had to be, since her husband—a marine—was killed on a military training exercise when she was twenty-three. Darya loved Tom, but I sensed she was having trouble getting used to the idea of giving up some of that independence. The cabin was a sort of compromise for them, a place where they could give living together a trial run."

"Have you ever been to the cabin?"

"Only once. The boutique was closed because some repairs were being done, and Darya wanted to go down to the cabin because she had an appointment with a plumber who was going to install a new hot-water heater. But she didn't want to be there alone, so she asked me along. I had a good time." Bledsoe's eyes filled with tears. "God, it's so damn unfair!"

I waited till she'd gotten herself under control, then asked, "Why didn't she want to go alone? Because of the isolation?"

"No. Her house here is fairly isolated, and she'd never had a problem with that." Bledsoe frowned. "Now that you mention it, I remember thinking it strange at the time. She seemed on edge the whole time we were there."

Interesting. "Think about that weekend. Did anything unusual happen? Anyone drop by, or call, besides the plumber?"

She thought, shook her head.

"Did Ms. Adams ever mention a man called Screamin' Mike?"

"I'm sure I'd remember if she had."

"Anyone else in the area?"
"No."
"But you're sure she was on edge that weekend."
"Yes, I'm sure. Darya was afraid of something or someone down there."

Tom Worthington was a handsome man. Even in the jail jumpsuit, his eyes shadowed and puffy from lack of sleep, his gray-frosted dark hair touseled, he would have turned female heads. We sat in a little visiting room, guard outside, and went over everything he'd told the sheriff's people and Glenn Solomon. Then we went over it again; I found no inconsistencies.

"Mr. Worthington," I said, "were you and Ms. Adams getting along at the time of her death?"

"Better than ever. That last weekend we spent together was ... well, I'll never forget it."

"I understand you were planning to leave your wife, marry Ms. Adams."

"I had hoped to."

"And the delay was because of your marital situation?"

He rubbed his hand across his stubbled chin, nodded. "My wife ... has her problems. I was trying to find a way to leave the marriage without exacerbating them."

"She drinks."

"Yes. I've been trying to convince her to get help, so has our family doctor. Until she does ..." He spread his hands.

"I understand. Is your wife the sort of person who becomes violent when she drinks?"

"Betsy? God no! She's constantly sedated."

"Perhaps she's drinking to sublimate anger?"

"I don't ... oh, I see where you're going. No, Ms. McCone, Betsy didn't find out about Darya and kill her. She hasn't left the house, except when I've forced her to accompany me, in five years. And those occasions were not successful ones."

"What about your children—did they know about your affair with Ms. Adams?"

"Jeannie, my daughter, didn't. She's too caught up in her drugged-out little world. Kent did. He's visited at the cabin, and he liked Darya. She had a calming effect on him."

"I understand he has anger-management problems."

"Yes. Anger toward his mother, primarily. But he's working on them."

"Mr. Worthington, are you aware that Ms. Adams was afraid of something or someone? And that it was connected with your cabin?"

"Darya? Afraid?"

I explained what Kathy Bledsoe had told me.

Worthington shook his head in a bewildered way. "Why didn't she confide in me? Or in Jeb? If somebody'd been bothering her while she was down there, he would've taken care of them."

"Jeb's a good friend?"

"The best. He'd do anything for me. Or Darya."

"He claims he was advising you on how to conserve your assets in the event of a divorce."

Worthington had been grim-faced through most of our meeting, but now he smiled. "Jeb? *He's* the one who needs advice when it comes to financial matters."

"Why d'you say that?"

"Jeb nearly lost his shirt in a real-estate deal a couple of years ago. High-risk, and I warned him not to get into it, but he wouldn't listen. Now he's got a big balloon payment coming due, and he can't cover it. Jeb's a sweet guy, but ..." He spread his hands. "He introduced Darya and me, you know."

"I thought Kathy Bledsoe did."

"We deliberately gave her that impression. I went up to meet Darya at an opening at the Lakes Gallery; turned out Kathy was the artist. I was taken aback to see an old acquaintance, and find out she worked for Darya. Darya sensed my discomfort and played along when Kathy introduced us. But no, I met Darya about six months before that at Jeb's house in Big Pine."

"And how long had Jeb known her?"

"His whole life. Darya was his cousin."

"No, Shar," Mick said over the phone. "Jeb Barkley has no cousin. And neither does Darya Adams."

"Are you sure?"

"My computer doesn't lie."

"Why not? Mine does, all the time."

"That's because you don't use the right databases."

That was probably true. I sighed.

"Shar? Anything else?"

"Yes. I need deep background on Jeb Barkley and Darya Adams. Specifically, if either has a criminal record."

The scenario that came together in my mind as I drove back to Big Pine was a disturbing one. Jeb Barkley had no cousin; Darya Adams had none, either. But Tom Worthington was under the impression they were related.

Barkley had introduced Adams to him as his cousin. Why?

Wealthy man with an unhappy home life. Young, attractive single woman. Old friend who has lost money in a real-estate deal and has a large balloon payment coming up in a year and a half. He introduces the woman as his cousin. The wealthy man is induced to leave his wife for her. The woman then has a community-property stake in those assets—which she can share with her "cousin."

Not cousins—partners in crime.

But something had gone wrong.

My phone buzzed. I pulled to the side of the road, picked up. Mick.

"Shar, I called Adah Joslyn at the SFPD."

Adah, an inspector on the Homicide detail, and a good friend. "And?"

"She accessed Barkley's and Adams's criminal records for me. The two of them—Adams was Darya Dunn then, her maiden name before she married the marine—were arrested over in Nevada fifteen years ago on a bunko charge. Barkley did time; from what I'm reading between the lines, he took the rap for Adams."

"Why didn't this show up in your original backgrounding?"

A silence. Then, reproachfully, "You didn't specify *deep* back-grounding, Shar. Criminal records're hard to access unless you want to use contacts like Adah. And you've warned me not to abuse the privilege."

I sighed. "Well, it didn't occur to me to go deep on an old friend who sold them a house—or on the victim."

"Which leads us to private investigator's lesson number one—"

"Right. Suspect everyone." I thanked Mick and broke the connection. Pulled back onto the road.

Jeb Barkley finds his former partner in crime running a boutique up in Mammoth Lakes. He needs money badly, and his friend Tom Worthington has refused to help him out. Darya is attractive, just the sort of woman who might attract a man like Worthington, who is trapped in a dead marriage. So Barkley reminds Adams of the old days and puts pressure on her to begin a relationship with Worthington, with an eye to getting her hands on his assets. Adams agrees, because she values her reputation and position in her community. But then Adams and Barkley have a falling-out, maybe because she'd actually fallen in love with her victim. Now she's afraid of someone down at the cabin.

Barkley, who demonstrated this morning that he was familiar with the place—so much so that he even knew where she kept the hummingbird food—and who also had a set of keys.

And she'd had good reason to be afraid. He'd found her alone on July thirty-first, they'd quarreled, and he'd killed her. Then he'd planted evidence to implicate his friend.

Now what I needed was concrete evidence to implicate him.

As I drove the rest of the way to Big Pine, I kept thinking about the tree that Darya Adams's body had been found under. On impulse, when I reached the intersection of Routes 395 and 168, I turned east into the foothills.

The bristlecone stood alone on the rocky slope, clinging to the poor, coarse soil. I got out of the Jeep and walked around it, ducked under its low-hanging branches. Even though the sun was dipping below the ridge to the west, it felt uncomfortably warm there, and the air was dusty enough to make me sneeze. I went out the other side where the branches were bent and sheared off sap congealing on their broken tips.

Emergency vehicles, I thought. They did this damage getting the body out.

Or ...

I took out my cell phone, called the local sheriff's department substation. The officer I'd spoken with the previous afternoon, who had been one of the first at the murder scene, took a look at the official photographs and confirmed my suspicion.

"Our people did some damage after the photos were taken," he told me, "but the tree was already ripped up on that side, probably by your client's truck when he dumped the body."

"Was there damage to Mr. Worthington's truck? Chipped paint, scratches?"

A pause. "I don't see any photos or mention of it."

"In your opinion, if his truck was scratched, would the paint contain traces of the tree's DNA?"

"Well, I'm not a lab technician, Ms. McCone, but I'll hazard a guess that it would."

"Thanks. I'll be in touch."

Jeb Barkley's house was on a quiet side street in Big Pine: a small stucco bungalow on a small lot with a patch of lawn out front. A sprinkler was throwing out lazy arcs of water, and light glowed behind blinds in the windows. Barkley's Outback stood before the closed doors of a single-car garage. I parked down the block and waited until it was full dark before I approached.

Armed with a paint scraper and one of the plastic bags I'd earlier purchased at a hardware store, I crept up to the passenger side of the car. I switched on my pencil flashlight and, holding it between my teeth, began removing flecks of paint from the scratched area on the door. When I had a respectable amount, I sealed the bag.

I glanced at the house. No visible activity there. Slowly I began to move around the car, shining the beam over it. Nothing distinctive about the tires—and the sheriff's people hadn't been able to take any impressions at the scene, anyway. A few more scratches on the front panel, nothing lodged under the bumper.

The outside vent below the windshield, maybe. He would have removed anything obvious that was caught there, probably had washed the car, but deep down inside ...

Yes!

I glanced over at the house. Still no activity. I fumbled in my bag for the pouch where I keep miscellaneous objects—chapstick, nail clippers, tweezers for the splinters I'm always getting. Took out the tweezers and fished around in the vent, until I found a slender wood fragment.

Ten to one it came from the bristlecone pine. There was another fragment lodged down there, but I'd leave it for the sheriff's technicians.

I slipped back to the Jeep, headed for the substation.

Overconfidence, I thought, that's what always brings them down. Jeb Barkley hadn't counted on anyone looking into his past and discovering his connection with Darya Adams. He hadn't bothered to have his car repainted because who would suspect him—a small-town real-estate agent, and Tom Worthington's friend—of killing anyone? He hadn't even bothered to conceal from me his knowledge of where things were kept in the cabin.

All of that, and irrefutable DNA evidence as the clincher.

Glenn Solomon was going to love this. Maybe he'd even pay a bonus for my getting results in record time.

TELEGRAPHING

I have become the operator of a major way station on the moccasin telegraph.

Not by choice; gossip doesn't interest me much, and that's what we Indians mainly do on the wire. But as an investigative tool, it sometimes beats out the Internet.

"We Indians." The phrase still doesn't come easily. For most of my life, I thought my looks were a throwback to my Shoshone great-grandmother, and that I was mainly Scotch-Irish. But then I found out I'd been adopted and discovered a huge new Shoshone family—some related by blood, some by virtue of just plain friendliness and acceptance. Mentally and emotionally I'm not Indian yet, and sometimes I doubt I ever will be; but I'm learning the legends and traditions, making friends, and becoming closer to my birth parents.

The latter of which sometimes is not all that easy.

Oh, Saskia Blackwater, my birth mother, is no problem. She's an attorney in Boise, Idaho, and active in many Native causes. My half-sister, Robin, is following in her mother's footsteps, going to law school at Berkeley. And my half-brother, Darcy, is just your garden-variety screwed-up kid. Then there's Elwood ...

Elwood Farmer. A painter of national reputation. He lives on the Flathead Reservation in Montana, where he funds and teaches art programs in the schools. Elwood's traditional, lives simply, and in the beginning was very hard to know. Now that he and I have gotten closer, I realize he can be cantankerous, obstinate, opinionated, and downright mean. But he's also thoughtful, wise, insightful, and downright charming. Elwood's the reason I've become a moccasin telegraph operator.

In case you don't know, the moccasin telegraph is nothing more than a large group of Indians throughout the country who are connected by bloodlines, friendships, or past histories. And they love to gossip. The telegraph is a great investigative tool; at my San Francisco agency, McCone Investigations, it's a fallback when all else fails. Here's an example, from a morning last week, of how it works—and it's only a small part of what I've recently been through.

"Hi, Elwood. It's Sharon."

"You're calling early, daughter." A match scraped; he inhaled. Smoking is Elwood's only vice.

"I've been up all night working on this investigation for you."

Exhaled. "Not good. You need your sleep. Have you found out anything?"

"A little. I need you to call Jane Nomee in Arlee. Ask her if she knows the whereabouts of an Eric Yatz. She can get back to me on my cellular."

"Who's Eric Yatz?"

"I'll tell you later. Just call Jane, will you?"

"If you'd had more sleep, daughter, you wouldn't be so surly."

"Sharon? Jane Nomee. Your dad just called. I remember Eric Yatz from here in town, but haven't heard of him in years. He does have a cousin, though—Carol Yatz, in McMinnville, Oregon. Here's her number."

"No, I haven't heard from Cousin Eric in years. He was very close to one of our aunts, Bella Wilford, in Minneapolis. Let me look up her number."

"Last Christmas Eric sent me a card postmarked Plymouth, California.... No, there was no return address.... You're welcome."

Plymouth was in the Gold Country. A small town; if Eric Yatz was still there, I was pretty sure I could find him.

Amador County is not usually considered Indian country. Most of those unfamiliar with the area in the Sierra foothills identify it with gold mining and, nowadays, quaint Old West tourist towns and vineyards. But the Indian presence is there, most notably in the Jackson Rancheria, a twenty-four-hour gambling casino and hotel on Miwok tribal lands near the small city of Jackson. Amador is not hospitable to casinos: Not long ago, county supervisors rejected a proposal from the Buena Vista Rancheria that would have put many millions of dollars into the public coffers as compensation for police and fire and water services—at the same time leaving the county free to continue the fight against the casino in court.

The majority of residents of Amador prefer to preserve the rural ambience. Meanwhile, Miwoks, Iones, and other small tribes continue to fight for their piece of the great gambling pie.

I drove past the town of Plymouth, where I had visited before, in a couple of eyeblinks. There was a Best Western on Highway 49 near there, and I'd made a reservation. The first-floor room looked out on an idyllic scene: an oak-dotted pasture with cows grazing. I sat down at the table by the window and took out the notes on the investigation I was conducting—gratis—for my birth father.

One of Elwood's art students, a nine-year-old named Marcus Fourwinds, possessed an exceptional talent. He and his mother, Elise, had moved to

St. Ignatius, near where Elwood lives, three years ago. Their origins were vague; they had no relatives in the area, and Marcus had little recollection of where they'd lived before. On that subject his mother was reticent, saying only that they "had some trouble with the tribe" and had been forced to move.

Then, two weeks ago Elise had been brutally knifed at their home. In order to keep Marcus from being made a ward of the county youth authorities, Elwood had taken him in. Marcus said that a friend of his mother's, Don Dixon, had been at their house the day she was killed. The tribal police had not been able to track Dixon down so, with their permission, Elwood turned to me.

The Internet databases that my agency subscribes to turned up a criminal record on Dixon, mostly for kiting checks and petty theft. Moccasin telegraph informed me he was a drifter who had appeared in St. Ignatius about six months before, taken a job at a convenience store in Arlee, and been staying at the Fourwinds place on and off the whole time. I then traced Dixon to Reno, where he was in jail once more for petty theft. He admitted to having seen Elise Fourwinds that day, but claimed a man named Eric Yatz was responsible for her death. Dixon wouldn't say why, except that it had something to do with Indian gaming rights.

Which was strange, because Montana is considered one of the worst places in the nation for tribal casinos. Most of the bars there allow gambling—slot machines, live poker, and keno—but the tribes' efforts to persuade the state to permit them to offer such other games of chance as blackjack have fallen on deaf ears.

So what did Elise Fourwinds' murder have to do with Indian gaming? I'd have to locate Eric Yatz to find the answer to that question.

Internet research on Yatz told me little: no criminal record, no record of employment, no previous addresses. I asked my nephew and computer whiz, Mick Savage, to run a highly sophisticated search, and he came up with a birthplace and date: Newark, New Jersey, on March 8, 1983. After that, Yatz became an invisible man: no Social Security number, no record of education or military service.

How did he stay so far below the radar?

Another thing I'd have to ask Yatz.

Yatz was not listed in the Amador County phone book. I drove toward town, turned at the rodeo grounds and then along the main street: small homes, an old hotel with an upstairs galleria, a handsome Queen Anne Victorian; various false-fronted buildings, a deli with tables on the sidewalk, a derelict, boarded-up brick warehouse; some shops, a trendy-looking restaurant called Taste, a barbecue place, Incahoots, that smelled wonderful and had a line out the door. Where to start?

Deli. I was hungry, and there were tables free.

Some two hours later, and I'd canvassed the business establishments in town. No one knew—or admitted to knowing—Eric Yatz. Finally, footsore and thirsty, I retreated to the tavern at the old hotel—dimly lighted with old mirrors whose silvering was patchy and cracked, with a wood-inlaid bar, well worn floor, and a string of crushed beer cans behind the bar, attached to a sign that read "Trailer Trash Art." The place was crowded, both with locals and tourists; I could tell them apart by the way they dressed. The tourist men looked as if they were ready to tee off on the golf course; the women wore outfits in bright shades of polyester. The locals were in jeans. I spotted a woman in a T-shirt decorated with three wineglasses and a caption that said "Therapy Session." My therapy arrived in the form of a schooner of IPA.

For a while I studied the antics of the crowd in the back bar mirror. A tourist at the table behind me put a straw up either nostril and made growling sounds, and the people with him laughed hysterically. What was he supposed to be? An elephant? Elephants don't growl. A local couple got into a spat, and she slapped him and stalked out. He sat there, stunned, then shrugged and took a swallow of his drink. Another couple, obviously more in sync, kissed on a settee built into the front wall.

After a while a man with a guitar came in from the ell at the back that contained pool tables. He proceeded to perch on a stool and play. The guitar was badly tuned, his voice even more so. A cowboy next to him covered his ears, took a slug of his drink, and shouted, "Shut up, Willard!" Willard shut up and slunk away.

Then suddenly a tension invaded the room, as two slight, dark-haired and -skinned men entered and took seats at the table near the door. They were Indian, but then so was I; nobody had reacted negatively to my presence. But with the appearance of the pair, voices dropped to a low level, spines went stiff, and eyes focused on them.

"Here comes trouble," the bartender said.

A tall, lanky man at the far end of the bar got off his stool. He pressed his cowboy hat firmly down and strode toward them—loose-limbed, dangerous. When he stopped beside their table, he loomed over them.

"You boys aren't welcome here," he said.

The taller of the two looked up. "Last I heard, this was a free country."

"Last *I* heard, your tribe was trying to take a free ride on it."

"Our land. We can do what we want with it."

"It's not your land. Belongs to the Gilardis. Has since—"

"They stole it from us."

The tall man drew back, balling up his right fist. "Gilardis didn't steal—"

"We got the documentation. The papers that show the land belongs to our tribe. That gives us the right to do what we want with it, and what we're gonna do is build a casino."

The bar had grown still during the conversation, but now there was an angry stirring among the patrons. The tall man drew back his fist; one of the other locals restrained him before he could throw a punch. The bartender rushed up to the table and spoke softly with the two Indians; they nodded, got up, and left. As a collective sigh of relief came from the customers, I left money on the bar and followed them.

The two men were nearing the derelict warehouse when I caught up with them. "Please, may I talk with you?" I said.

They stopped, regarded me with wary eyes. The more slender of the two, whose long hair was pulled back by a blue bandana, said, "Talk about what?"

"The casino you're going to establish here. Your tribal lands. Are you Miwok?"

"Amador Band of the Iones. You?"

"Shoshone."

They exchanged glances. The man who hadn't spoken—thin faced, with a baseball cap pulled low on his brow—seemed to defer to the other, who said, "No Shoshone around here. Where you from?"

"San Francisco." I extended one of my cards. "I'm working a case for my father, who lives on the Flathead rez in Montana. He's an artist—Elwood Farmer. Maybe you've heard of him?"

Shrugs.

"I'm looking for a man named Eric Yatz, who's rumored to live in Plymouth."

Both men stiffened. "Don't know anybody of that name," the spokesman said.

"Okay, tell me about this casino. The tribal lands you're reclaiming—"

"Why don't you go back to the bar—yeah, we saw you there—and ask the white people about that? We got nothing to say."

They turned in unison and walked away.

So I'd go back to the bar and ask the white people.

Willard, the dreadful guitar player, looked to be the most sober person in the room. He sat nursing a soda on the settee where the amorous couple had been. I got my own soda from the bartender and asked Willard if I could join him. He shrugged and motioned for me to sit down.

"How's the music business?" I asked.

"Shitty."

"Tough way to make a living."

"I don't. Work construction when I can get hired on."

"Much of that going on here?"

"Nope. I'm hanging in on unemployment, waiting to see if the casino deal's gonna go through."

"Most people don't seem to want that."

"Well, I do. My girlfriend's gonna have a baby this fall; she and the kid're gonna need a lot of things."

"So what's the deal with the casino?"

I listened as Willard told me.

The Amador Ione tribe had for centuries lived on the land around Plymouth, peaceably hunting and gathering. But the Gold Rush in the late 1840s flooded the area with treasure seekers, and white men forced the Indians off their lands, resulting in violent disputes and deadly confrontations.

"Indians always came out sucking hind titty," Willard said, "so finally the government stepped in and made treaties with them, gave 'em land. Congress never got around to approving those treaties, though. Iones moved away, joined up with other tribes. Finally the BIA stepped up to the plate and gave ten tribe members the right to a hundred acres in the Shenandoah Valley. Didn't do no good; none of those ten people was able to get title to that land, and a family named Gilardi took it over and started a winery."

Now I knew where I'd heard the name. "Gilardi Oaks?"

"Right. But trouble came along two years ago when the county decided the hundred acres belonged to those ten Iones or their descendants after all, if they could produce the original document from the seventies giving them rights to the land. They couldn't find the document. Some say Ed Jakes, first head of the tribal council they set up in the nineties, was careless, but there was a rumor it got stolen."

"By?"

Shrug. "Some say Gilardis, others say one of their own tribe members."

"Why would a tribe member take it?"

Willard's eyes shifted away from mine. "I said too much already. Hear those Iones've got big Las Vegas connections backing the casino. You know what that means. And I don't want folks in here to think I'm an Indian-lover. No offense meant, ma'am."

"None taken. Where can I find this Ed Jakes?"

"He's in the old Ione burial ground up the hill toward Fiddletown. But his son Junior Jakes is head of the tribal council now. Lives out the Old

Shenandoah Road. You might talk to him."

It was nearly eleven, so I decided to do that in the morning.

Back at my motel I couldn't sleep, so I set up my laptop, thinking to check my e-mail. The place only had dial-up—fortunately I have an AOL account for just those occasions—and it took a long time to connect. I had to smile at my impatience. Not too many years ago I wouldn't have known the difference between dial-up and *Dialing for Dollars*.

I had little mail. My husband, Hy Ripinsky, and my office manager, Ted Smalley, usually call when I'm traveling, and what was in the box wasn't important. I checked my voice mail, having turned off the ringtone while canvassing Plymouth: routine report from Ted on the agency's day; message from Hy saying he was in New York on a sudden business trip and could call again in the morning. That was it.

I turned back to the laptop and began a more thorough search on the Amador Ione.

The land that they couldn't prove rights to—although, according to the tribe members I'd spoken with earlier, they now had documents to prove ownership—sat at the gateway to the Amador wine country. I'd been there before: It was rural, with widely spaced vineyards on rolling hillsides and bucolic views; I could understand why the locals didn't want a casino there, but I also could understand why the tribe, landless and impoverished, hoped to tap into the new California gold rush.

I continued visiting sites that mentioned the Amador Ione, and one April article in the *San Francisco Chronicle* caught my attention: "Tribes Toss Out Members in High-Stakes Conflict."

The story stated that many California tribes, in anticipation of profits from casinos, had been purging their rolls of those individuals whose lineage and membership was held in doubt. The tribal spokespersons claimed that as sovereign nations they had a right to "readjust" their records as they saw fit. Many of the fifty-seven tribes sharing in annual 7.7 billion dollar gaming revenues had expelled people as prominent as former officials of their councils.

All in the pursuit of the almighty dollar, the banished Indians said.

An accompanying piece outlined how the wealth generated on Indian lands reached few of the state's Indian residents because of tribal enrollment status.

I leaned back in my chair, thinking of what Elwood had said of Elise Fourwinds: *She had some trouble with her tribe.*

Trouble—as in being removed from the rolls?

Was Elise Fourwinds a former member of the Amador Ione?

I'd have to ask Junior Jakes about that—and about the Las Vegas connection.

Junior Jakes lived in a doublewide on a small lot surrounded by vineyards. An oak tree shaded the trailer, and chickens pecked at the packed-dirt yard. Jakes was a lean, muscular man of about sixty; his long white hair was tied back in a ponytail.

He greeted me cordially and led me to a pair of lawn chairs under the oak. The day was already hot, but a light breeze rustled the tree's leaves and brought some relief. I showed my credentials and told him I was working on behalf of Elise Fourwinds' son Marcus.

"Marcus? But he's only a little boy."

"Little boys sometimes require the services of an investigator—especially when their mothers have been murdered."

What I'd said sank in slowly. Junior Jakes's lips moved, mouthing the word "murder." Then he sat very still, his gaze turned inward.

I said, "I understand Elise Fourwinds was a member of your tribe."

"She was."

"But she was taken off the rolls and moved to Montana." It was an educated guess that proved valid.

"Is that where she went? I had no idea."

I studied his lined face, trying to determine if he was telling the truth, but it wasn't an easy one to read.

I asked, "Why was she removed from the rolls?"

"Just setting our records straight."

"How many other people were removed?"

"I don't recall. A number."

"So Marcus isn't a tribal member, either. He won't benefit from the casino?"

"No."

"I hear the casino project's going to happen. That your tribe now has the documentation to prove the hundred acres were ceded to the ten individuals or their heirs."

He nodded.

"How'd you acquire the documentation?"

"It was handled by the Las Vegas company that is consulting with us on building and running the casino—Slater and Associates. I don't know the details."

"That would be Eric Yatz you're working with?"

Slowly he turned his head. "You know Mr. Yatz?"

"Not personally, but I'd like to meet him."

I waited by the side of the road in the shelter of an oak a hundred yards from Junior Jakes's driveway. The August heat was intense, with no breeze now; cicadas buzzed in the dry grass. Jakes had agreed to set up a meeting between Yatz and me, and then to call me on my cellular, but I hadn't liked what I'd seen in his eyes before I'd walked back to my car: a gathering anger and steely resolve. Elise Fourwinds had meant something to him. Jakes hadn't known she was dead or how Yatz had gone about getting his hands on the stolen document, but he'd probably known she'd taken it, and he'd unwittingly steered Yatz to her.

Half an hour later, Jakes drove out in a red pickup I'd seen parked to the side of the doublewide. There was a rifle in the gun rack.

I followed him to Highway 49, past Plymouth and south toward Jackson. A mile or so outside of town he turned off on Jackson Gate Road. I knew the area some, since my Uncle Jim and Aunt Susan lived on a small ranch near there; a former pro bowler, Jim for years had owned the local bowling center and had only recently turned it over to his son Bill.

Jackson Gate Road wound past small homes and occasional businesses, a cemetery and vegetation-choked lots. It was a convenient, if slow, way around the stoplights and clogged intersections leading into town. I assumed that was why Jakes was taking it, and was surprised to see him turn off after about a mile.

The driveway he entered was newly paved and bordered by an attractive stone wall. At its bottom was a sign: Old Mine Inn. I allowed him some distance, before following.

An amazing edifice loomed up before me: the shaft of an old gold mine dug back into the hill's slope, with a group of buildings spread around it. The buildings were intended, I supposed, to replicate the iron-and-timber style of the mine, but they were too shiny and new to blend in properly. In a parking lot surrounded by lush plantings sat two limousines and a scattering of luxury cars.

Junior Jakes's pickup was pulled in at an odd angle in one of the parking spaces. Its door was open, and he and the rifle I'd glimpsed earlier were gone. I looked around, spotted his lean figure disappearing behind the far right wing of the building.

Careful, McCone. Go slow. What you do here could save a good man and bring a bad one down.

I unlocked the glove box of my car and took my .357 Magnum from inside. Checked its load. I've always been opposed to handguns in the possession of the average citizen but—perhaps hypocritically—I consider myself above average, at least in that respect. I'm licensed by the state to carry a handgun, am a good shot, and practice at the range once or twice a month. Anyway, I was damned glad to have the weapon along now.

I moved quickly through the plantings and slipped to the far side of the wing where Jakes had gone. The building's wall was hot on my hand—corrugated iron to match the mine shaft. I moved along it, listening. When I came to the corner I stuck my head around: four patios with french doors faced a fenced garden; voices came from the open door of the second. I moved closer.

"... You killed her, you bastard!"

Unintelligible response—a man's voice.

"I gave you the information in good faith! I didn't know there would be killing involved."

"You didn't ask, either." Deep, raspy tones. "Besides, she came at me like a crazy woman, screaming and fighting for that paper. What did you expect me to do?"

"You didn't *have* to kill her, Yatz."

The curtains on the first unit were closed; I moved quickly past them.

"Maybe not. But why're you getting so worked up? You've got what you wanted, haven't you? We're going to be able to build your casino."

I risked a quick glance into the room. Junior Jakes stood with his back to the door pointing his rifle at a burly brown-haired man wearing shorts and a sport shirt. Yatz stood oddly at ease, arms loose at his sides, as if being held at gunpoint was nothing unusual. His eyes were a cold, unblinking blue.

Jakes's hands shook—with fury, I thought. He said, "I'm worked up because she was my daughter, that's why."

Yatz's expression didn't change. "You removed your own daughter from the tribal rolls?"

"My illegitimate daughter. Her mother was a white woman."

"You poor son of a bitch. Forced to kick out your own daughter and grandson." Yatz laughed.

Jakes raised his rifle. I leaped through the door and rammed into his back just as he pulled the trigger; the bullet clanged off the metal wall behind Yatz. Jakes struggled to maintain his footing, but I managed to trip him; he went down on his side, dropping the rifle.

I kicked it out of both men's reach, covering Yatz with the Magnum.

My ears were ringing from the blast, but I could hear cries and running feet. I backed up, called out, "The situation's under control. Will somebody get security, please?"

A man's voice said, "Will do."

I then shut the french doors against prying eyes. Said to Yatz, "You—go over and sit down on that chair."

He did as told, still calm and controlled. Even the close call with the rifle bullet didn't seem to faze him. He returned my gaze steadily.

Typical enforcer. He's here to keep an eye on the situation till the higher-ups arrive and take over.

Still on the floor, Jakes moaned.

"You all right?" I asked.

"Yeah, mostly."

"That rifle—Yatz jumped you, and it went off by accident."

"... Right."

"You brought it along only for protection."

"I get you."

"The rest of it you tell as it happened."

I glanced at Yatz. Still unconcerned; his firm could afford the best lawyers money can buy. But what he hadn't realized—yet—was that he'd been flying under the radar for many years, and a court case would destroy his anonymity. At the least it would put him out of work and possibly expose additional crimes for which he might be prosecuted. Maybe even make him the target of another well-paid enforcer.

He'd pay for his crimes, one way or the other.

"Daughter? This is Elwood. I hear you found the man who killed Elise Fourwinds and that he is in custody."

I pushed hair off my face and looked at the illuminated numbers of the bedside clock in my room at the Best Western. It was nearly two in the morning.

"How did you ...?"

"Moccasin telegraph works round the clock. Sylvia Wilson, an Ione who lives in Jackson, found out what happened and this afternoon she called her nephew, Rich Three Wings, who lives up near that ranch of yours in Mono County. I believe he knows you. Rich called a cousin of Junior Jakes in Jackson, who knew about the arrest but not where you were staying. The cousin couldn't reach Jakes, and your agency was already closed, so he called his stepdaughter in Oakland. She happens to know that office manager of yours—"

My God, now non-Indians are on the wire!

"Daughter? Are you listening?"

I yawned. "Yes, Elwood."

"The office manager didn't answer his phone, but the man he lives with did, and he gave the cousin's stepdaughter the number of one of your employees and ..."

TELL ME WHO I AM

Tell me who I am.
Those were the first words Debra Judson said to me. "Tell me who I am."

As I motioned her toward one of the clients' chairs, I studied her. Thin, stringy blond hair; no makeup on her round face; a trifle overweight for her five-and-a-half-foot frame, but not obese; ripped, tattered jeans and a rumpled pink blouse with two buttons missing. But that's the style for twentysomethings here in San Francisco's tech-savvy canyons South of Market. To the casual observer she might have seemed to be unclean and smell bad. But no, her face was recently scrubbed and a faint gardenia scent drifted around her.

"I guess I arrived at the right time, getting right in to see the boss lady," she said without making eye contact.

She had a faint regional accent—Midwestern, maybe.

I didn't want to tell her that she'd gotten in to see me because business was so slow that the "boss lady" was terminally bored and had been dozing on her couch. My husband and partner, Hy Ripinsky, who handles more of McCone & Ripinsky International's far-flung cases, had been in Asia for a week, so I didn't even have him in the office next door to divert me.

Ted Smalley, our office manager, who calls himself the Grand Poobah and shares a friendship with me that goes back to the Stone Age, had actually told me the other day that I needed to get a life. No, I'd insisted, what I needed to get was a case. Something I could really get involved with. Was that what this raggedy young woman was bringing to me?

"You identified yourself as Debra Judson," I said to the prospective client. "Isn't that who you are?"

"Oh, sure. I've had that name all my life. I've got a Social Security number too. High school diploma, job résumé, letters of recommendation from past employers. But something's missing—my identity."

"True identity?"

"Right."

"Who recommended you to M&R?"

"Nobody. A couple of years ago I read a human interest feature about you—how you found out you were adopted and tracked down your real parents. I thought maybe you could help me do the same."

I hesitated, studying her.

"Ms. McCone, if you're not interested, I can pick another firm just as easy. I guess you think I can't afford you. I know I don't look too great on account of the airline losing my luggage when I flew in last night from Michigan. But I've got plenty of money—"

"It's not about money, and I *am* interested. Tell me your story." I motioned her to one of the chairs in the grouping by the high bay-view windows and took one opposite her.

She relaxed visibly, but still wouldn't make eye contact. "It all started two weeks ago. In Westland, Michigan, where I was raised. My dad, Dennis Judson, died three years ago in an auto accident, but Mom—her name was Marla—and I were doing fine. She had a good job as a business analyst with Ford, and I was learning the ropes so I could get on there too. Then, one day she came home with what she called one of her sick headaches, and when I checked on her the next morning, she was gone. A stroke, the doctor said."

"I'm sorry for your loss."

Now she did look me straight in the eyes; hers were gray-green, suffused with coppery flares of anger. "Sorry?" she said. "You didn't even know her. You don't even know *me*."

"It was a conventional, reflexive comment. Go on, please."

She wriggled uncomfortably in the chair. "Okay, the house was a rental, and the landlord wanted me out so he could charge more, and he could evict me because we'd lived there so long we'd never thought we needed to renew the lease. And he wanted me out *fast*. Quick evictions are happening all the time now."

"How much time did he give you?"

"A week."

"I'm not familiar with Michigan law, but I have a friend—"

"Screw it. I'm through with that house and with Michigan too. So, anyway, I packed some of my stuff up in my car, got rid of the rest. And in the back of Mom's closet off her bedroom, I found this box." She pulled it from the tote bag she'd set on the floor beside the chair. It was a small box, about the size replacement checks from your bank come in.

But, as I remembered all too vividly, the size of those life-altering boxes doesn't matter.

Years before, when my father died, his will had stipulated that I be the one to clear out his possessions from the famed McCone garage—a structure so crammed with junk that no car had fit there in at least twenty years. Pa had probably been depending on my nosy inclinations when he wrote the will, because there I'd uncovered a box containing all sorts of official documents—including my own adoption papers. For all my life I'd been a dark, strong-featured child in a family of blond Scotch-

Irish siblings; my parents had told me I was a "throwback" to distant Indian relatives. But something about that explanation had never felt right. There was just enough information in those papers to allow me to locate my birth parents and other relatives, as well as tell me I was a full-blooded member of the Shoshone tribe. Now I had two families whom I liked and connected with on a more or less regular basis. But not all such boxes contain pleasurable information.

"May I open this?" I asked Debra Judson as she handed hers to me.

"Please do."

It contained the usual items parents save: a certificate from Sparrow Lake Hospital in Colusa County, California, giving the birth date of a female child named Pamela Stanton as twenty-two years ago last August 17, parents Rodney and Carol Stanton. A few photographs of a crawling infant and a toddling preschooler, smiling in all of them. And a number of news clippings from a paper called the *Colusa Express*, yellowed and tattered as if they'd been unfolded and read many times.

When I came to the clippings I looked up at Debra Judson and she nodded for me to go on reading.

SPARROW LAKE TODDLER MISSING
SEARCH FOR STANTON TODDLER INTENSIFIED
UNSEASONAL RAIN HAMPERS SEARCH FOR CHILD
SEARCH FOR MISSING STANTON CHILD SCALED BACK
PAMELA STANTON FEARED DEAD

There were other items, the usual notices that a child has disappeared and the authorities are still searching for her or him, but which essentially mean that they believe the victim is dead and that the case has been back-burnered.

"That birth date on the certificate," Debra Judson said, "is not mine. Neither is the name of the hospital nor those of my parents." She reached into her tote bag. "These documents, which have been available to me my whole life, state who I am."

She handed me a manila envelope. In it was her birth certificate, showing she'd been born to Dennis and Marla Judson twenty-two years ago at Beaumont Hospital in Royal Oak, Michigan. There were also photographs showing a child as she matured to a teenager and then to a young woman. Report cards from schools in the city of her birth. Clippings attesting to her proficiency in soccer at Dondero High School. A high school diploma; she'd graduated with honors, and the seals and ribbons indicating her excellence were still attached, if a bit faded. There were letters and postcards, presumably from friends and relatives, boyfriends too. And two acceptances from small but excellent state colleges.

She saw me studying the acceptance notices. "I didn't get to go. They came about the time Dad was killed. Mom needed me."

"All these papers indicate you had a fairly happy, successful life until your parents died."

"Yeah, I did."

"And you say that you've been left financially secure."

"I have."

"Then why not let go of this other information? For all you know, it may have nothing to do with you."

"Do you really think so, Ms. McCone?"

The odd, coppery flares of anger in her eyes were stronger now. I met them with my own gaze, felt an anger that I'd thought I'd years ago put to rest.

"*Do* you think so?" she repeated.

"… No, I don't."

Our mutual anger was understandable. When you enter adulthood thinking you're a unique person with your own unique history, and all of that individuality is suddenly in jeopardy, you feel as if you're sinking into quicksand. Nothing to grab on to, no solid ground to rest upon, no one to extend a hand and drag you to safety. For me, my investigator's skills had provided aid and comfort; now, perhaps, they might do the same for Debra.

I gave my secretary—one in a sequence of many short-lived employees—the clippings for copying. Then I asked Debra Judson for photographs of her parents; she was prepared for the request, had already had extras made. After she signed a contract and provided a retainer, I sent her back to her hotel—the Stanford Court, proving she hadn't been left badly off—and read the clippings carefully. Then I turned to the computer.

The websites I visited fleshed out the story of the Stanton child that had been skimpily covered in the print media. She'd had six older siblings—four boys and two girls, their ages ranging from four to thirteen. Their father, Rodney, worked as a caretaker in a mobile home park near Sparrow Lake in exchange for the rent on their space; their mother, Carol, was a part-time convenience store clerk and occasional waitress, but her poor health and pregnancies—she'd also had two miscarriages after Pamela was born—prevented her from taking regular jobs. The Stantons were described by neighbors who seemed genuinely fond of them as good parents, even though stressed and desperately poor. Abuse was never hinted at.

On the day over twenty years ago when Pamela disappeared it had rained hard—one of those sudden deluges that used to happen in the pre-drought years of our state. The wet ground should have made it easier to track a child who might have wandered outdoors at the wrong moment, become disoriented or panicked. But the rural sheriff's department—not summoned until dinnertime, when the mother realized her youngest was missing—could identify no footprints or other telltale traces in the gathering dusk. And by first light the next day, a second storm had obliterated any other possible traces.

Where had Pamela's parents been that day? Rodney had driven Carol to a nearby mobile-health unit for tests on her thyroid. Their eldest, thirteen-year-old Jackson, was deputized to look after the younger children, but uncharacteristically he'd gone off with his friends and left the other kids alone. It was a mistake that apparently haunted Jackson to this very day: he'd begun drinking heavily at fourteen and twice attempted suicide.

The Stantons blamed Jackson for shirking his familial duties, but in actuality they'd put too much responsibility on a young teenager. Had put too much trust in the rest of their brood to obey the rules. Of course the press had labeled the parents with all the sins of our judgmental society, including caring more about themselves and Carol's perilous health than their children, and being too poor to hire a babysitter. In the face of this castigation, the family had fled farther into the wilderness—northeast to Lassen County on the California/Nevada border—and then scattered.

I'd need to locate as many of them as I could, probe more into the events of that rainy day. In the meantime, I'd have one of my research staff verify the two sets of documents my client had provided.

The Stanton documents turned out to be originals. But the Judson documents proved false. Debra's birth certificate was in reality that of a child who had died two days after her birth at the Michigan hospital; it had been requested from the state nearly two years after the baby's death. It reminded me of the decades-old ploy for obtaining false identification, generally used by college students to verify that they were old enough to drink alcoholic beverages. But it could be used for major crimes as well.

The first crime that occurred to me was kidnapping. There had been no hint about kidnapping in the rural press: the child was pretty, but the family dirt-poor. No calls had come to the local bar through which they routed their infrequent phone messages; no ransom note had ever arrived. It seemed highly unlikely that Pamela Stanton had been snatched by anyone who preyed on kids for sex or porn. There was no indication that Debra Judson had been molested; she'd described a normal, happy childhood.

I went down the hall to the office of Craig Morland, a former FBI agent who had been lured away from the Bureau by another of my operatives, Adah Joslyn, now his wife.

"Twenty years ago if a child disappeared in a rural county here, would the FBI be called in?" I asked him.

"Probably not, unless there was clear evidence of a kidnapping, such as a ransom demand or an eyewitness to the abduction."

Nothing of the sort had been mentioned.

"Could you check with your contacts at the Bureau?" I gave him the specifics.

"Shouldn't take long."

Fifteen minutes later he came to my office. "My contacts couldn't find anything in the available files. The disappearance must've been handled by local law enforcement."

Okay, what about another form of kidnapping: a couple desperately seeking a child—and God knows there are many—picking up a youngster from the street, a park, wherever, and claiming her or him as their own? The child, like Pamela, would be too young to remember any prior life, easily lulled by love and care.

I buzzed Mick Savage, my nephew and computer genius, and explained about the case, asked that he run a background check on the Judsons. Even if they were upstanding citizens, the fact didn't necessarily absolve them of having taken the child. But an unresolved twenty-year-old crime is a very cold case. I'd solved cold cases before; maybe I'd get lucky again. Anyway, I'd give it my best shot.

Once I'd gathered and studied all the background data available, the next step in my investigation was on-site interviews with those who had witnessed or otherwise been involved in the pertinent events. After calling Debra Judson for authorization of the additional expense, I set out at dawn the next morning in Hy's and my Cessna 170B for Sparrow Lake.

Colusa County is sparsely populated, located in the Central Valley northwest of Sacramento. The general aviation airport is three miles south of the town of Colusa, and I'd arranged with a ride-service company similar to Uber that the agency uses throughout the state to pick me up and supply a car I could use on my drive seventeen miles to Sparrow Lake, near the northeastern county line.

The lake itself was picture-postcard material, surrounded by tall old pines through which rustic cabins on the shoreline could be glimpsed. The town itself looked like a set from an old Western movie—an old and neglected one. False-fronted buildings, their paint blistered and peeling; decaying wooden sidewalks; cars and trucks parked helter-skelter at angles to the edges of a potholed main street. As I drove along I noted two saloons that were obviously tricked up for tourists but didn't appear to be doing much business; a Wells Fargo bank; a small grocery; a hardware store; and an office calling itself the *Sparrow Sun*. Newspaper? Possibly. Good place to start.

The office contained two desks, only one occupied. A woman sat there, pushing her fingers through her short dark hair. She looked up from a page she was penciling and said, "You want to place an ad? I can be with you in a second."

"Thanks." I moved around the waiting area, examining the framed clippings that were posted on the walls. A few were from the *Colusa Express* and concerned the missing Stanton child.

The woman behind the desk slapped the copy she'd been editing into an out-box and came over to me. "Tricia Prine," she said, extending a hand. "Editor and owner."

I introduced myself, told her why I was there.

"That story." She motioned me to a chair beside her desk and sat back down. "Every few years we get somebody nosing around here about it. Nothing ever comes of it."

"What my client has found may constitute a break in the case." I studied Prine: she was in her mid- to late twenties, too young to have any true memories of the Stanton disappearance. "Did you live here then?" I asked.

She shook her head. "We ... I only moved here five years ago. My husband Ned and I bought this piece-of-shit newspaper with these stereotypical dreams about being award-winning country muckrakers. Sort of like the *Point Reyes Light* people, you know? Only there wasn't any muck to rake, and after a while Ned got fed up and moved back to LA. Now he's with the *Times* there and building a great career. And I'm ... just here." She gestured around weakly.

"You get the paper in the divorce settlement?"

"Oh, yeah. He was fair about all our assets, such as they were. He just wanted out. I don't blame him. Your dreams can only stretch so far."

I like women—and men—who don't want to put the blame for their out-of-control lives on others. And I liked Tricia Prine.

I said, "Let's see if you and I can develop a story that'll put some life into this old rag."

Tricia and I went over the details we had on the Stanton family. Jackson, the brother who had been told to watch his siblings, had returned to the area and was living in an isolated cabin near the lake.

"You'd better be real wary of approaching him," she told me. "He can be a mean drunk, and he's drunk most of the time."

"Where can I find him?"

"Well, I wouldn't recommend you go to his cabin. Better the Desert Rat Saloon. He hangs out there."

"Any other family members?"

"A sister, Ramona Pitts. Was ten when the kid disappeared. Runs that raggedy-ass gift shop down the street. She's okay, especially if you buy something."

"What about friends?"

Tricia considered. "Angie Ellis was close to the other older sister—I forget her name. She lives on Willow Way, an artist, works out of her garage."

I thanked her and told her I'd check in later.

The "raggedy-ass" gift shop was closed, so I asked a passerby for directions to Willow Way. It was a dusty side street with no trees, especially not a willow, in sight. The woman who came to the door of the small stucco house wore paint-stained clothing and a discouraged look.

"Tricia Prine called to say you might be by," she said. "I've got time to talk—it's been a bad day creatively. Time for a beer. Join me?"

"Why not?"

The heat in the shabby front room Angie Ellis showed me to was oppressive. She raised a pair of old-fashioned windows, went through a door, and returned with a couple of cans of Bud Light. Normally I dislike the stuff, but I happily let it slip down my parched throat.

I showed Angie Ellis the photos of the Judsons. She didn't recognize them.

"Were you friends with Pamela Stanton?" I asked.

"I was friends with her older sister, Katie. She's dead, couple of years now. Anyway, we were out fishing ... oh, hell ... messing around by the river with a couple of guys from school the day the kid disappeared. The parents were gone, and old Jackson had gone off someplace, even though he was supposed to watch the kids. All hell broke loose later that night: phone calls, sheriff's deputies. And later, reporters. I couldn't tell them a thing. I can't tell *you* a thing."

"Think back. Did anything unusual happen before all hell broke loose?"

She closed her eyes for a moment. "Well, there was one ... I guess you'd call it an oddity. Mr. Stanton was this big, easygoing guy. But that morning he seemed kind of nervous. He kept asking Mrs. Stanton if Pamela was ready."

"Ready for what?"

She shook her head. "I don't know—ready."
"What did Mrs. Stanton say?"
"Just gave him a look. The old what's-the-matter-with-you look. And then they were off to the medical unit."
"Where was Pamela when they left?"
"Around, I guess. I mean, Jackson was supposed to be watching her. Me and Katie, we took off for the river."

Ramona Pitts tried to sell me a dozen items—one of which, a fake handlebar mustache, I bought as a joke gift for Ted—before she would settle down and talk about the day her younger sister went missing. She didn't recognize the photos of the Judsons and was vague on the details of the disappearance.
"I don't recall."
"I was only ten, you know."
"I can't remember."
When she asked if there was a reward for any information, I gave up on her. She couldn't have cared less about her sister's fate because there was nothing in it for her.

Jackson Stanton wasn't at the Desert Rat Saloon, although the barkeeper informed me I could count on finding him there later. In the meantime I canvassed the business section and many of the nearby houses, showing people pictures of the Judson couple and asking if they'd ever seen them in the area. All the answers were negative. The Judsons were attractive and affluent-looking; they would have stood out in people's minds, even after twenty years. I had to conclude they hadn't been involved in Pamela Stanton's disappearance.

The Desert Rat Saloon looked like a set from *Gunsmoke*; I half expected to see Miss Kitty and Marshal Matt Dillon descend the stairs from the upper story. But there was no one in the saloon except for a bartender—not the one I'd spoken to earlier—in a stained apron watching a Giants game on the big-screen TV and a man in a straw hat and plaid shirt, whom the barkeep identified as Stanton.

As I approached, he pushed a stool toward me and said in a gravelly voice, "Sit. I know who you are and why you're here. News travels fast in a place like this. Want a drink?"

"Uh, sure."

He signaled the bartender without asking me what the drink should be.

"Let's get this settled right away," Jackson added. "I did not see who took my sister. I did not harm her in any way. Folks around here have whispered about me and tried to shame me ever since it happened. But all I've ever been guilty of is being a neglectful teenager."

"Your family moved away because of that kind of talk."

"Ran away is more like it."

Two Bud Lights in their bottles appeared before us.

I sipped mine, said, "But you came back."

He shrugged. "The lake's my home. Maybe by coming back I was trying to prove something. Can't say as I have."

"My client thinks she may be Pamela. She's located papers that indicate it."

"Papers can be bought any day of the week. Besides, why would any decent person want to latch on to a family like ours? We're worthless: a drunk like me; another brother who was shot dead by the cops in a convenience store robbery; another who OD'd on the street in LA; another who's been disappeared from the face of the earth for more than twenty years, probably's been lying in a grave next to a dope farm the whole time. Then there's Ramona with her godawful gift shop. And Katie's dead."

"My client ..." I described her.

"Now I *know* she doesn't want to connect with me," he said. "Nobody like that would."

"Jackson, please try to remember anything unusual about that day."

His cool gray eyes focused on mine. He might've been a drunk, but the alcohol abuse hadn't destroyed his intelligence.

"Okay," he said, "there were a couple of things. For one, Pammie was dressed up that morning. Little flowered ... what did they call 'em? Pinafores. One I'd never seen before. Better than the usual stuff Ma bought for us at Kmart too. Why would a kid be dressed up when it's just supposed to be an ordinary day going into town?"

"And?"

"And?" He looked at me blankly.

"What's the other thing you remember?"

"Oh, right. For a while afterwards we seemed to have more money than usual. More food. Sure, friends brought casseroles and cakes and stuff after Pammie went missing, but we went out for pizza a lot and Ma had some new dresses. Then the money wasn't there. Dad spent a lot of time in the bars drinking money up when we had any."

"Are you sure Pamela didn't go with your parents to ... where were they headed for?"

"Colusa. One of those medical health trailers was supposed to be there. Ma needed regular checks on her thyroid."

We talked a bit more, but there wasn't anything else he could tell me. After a while his attention wandered to the Giants game, and I left.

Ramona Pitts had given me a list of addresses where she thought other members of her family could be found, but they were all at a distance, and it was getting on toward midafternoon. So I went back to the airport, got the overnight kit I always carry in the plane's baggage compartment, and checked into the tidy-looking Shady Grove motel. I updated my office on my whereabouts by e-mail, then lay back on the bed to think over the bits and pieces I'd gleaned about Pamela Stanton's disappearance.

Mr. Stanton was this big, easygoing guy. But that morning he seemed kind of nervous.

He kept asking Mrs. Stanton if Pamela was ready.

Why would a kid be dressed up when it's just supposed to be an ordinary day playing around the house?

... mobile-health unit for tests on her thyroid ...

I got up and went to my laptop. Googled hospitals and found the number of the Colusa Regional Medical Center. The switchboard directed my inquiry to a Mr. Henry in administration. He was friendly and helpful, saying, "Let me see if I can access the information you need. Thanks to a generous benefactor, we have a new automated system, and our volunteers have put records on it that go back many years." Tippety-tapping of a keyboard.

"Yes, here it is," Mr. Henry said. "We still use the same mobile-health testing company as we did in the period you're asking about."

He read off the phone number and gave me a contact name, Felicia Parr.

The mobile-health firm put me through to Ms. Parr with a minimum of delay.

God, I thought, how pleasant it is to be operating in this kind of environment instead of the urban areas, where every request is met with suspicion!

Felicia Parr also had a fully automated system. There had been no mobile unit testing for the thyroid in Colusa on the date I asked her about.

I lay back on the bed again.

The Stantons—father and mother—had gone somewhere on the day their daughter Pamela vanished. But not their stated destination.

... dressed up ...

For a while afterwards we seemed to have more money than usual ...

I reached for my folder on the case, turned to the newspaper clippings with the two-year-old's photo. She had been an exceptionally pretty child. The word "marketable" came to mind.

Back to the laptop. For a few minutes I couldn't come up with an appropriate term for what I was looking for. "Adoption." No, I needed to refine it. "Adoption agencies." Too broad a category, and there were thousands of them.

What about private adoption? That was what mine had been. It was a perfectly legal method of placing an unwanted infant or even an older child in the home of a family who did want her or him. Or an infant such as I had been, whose mother couldn't care for her and relinquished her to distant relatives who could.

But the case of Pamela Stanton didn't have the feel of either category.

An illegal adoption? What else did they call that?

Black-market adoption.

My fingers were flying over the keyboard now.

Such adoptions violated state and federal law. Usually large sums of money were involved. They were often arranged by an attorney, an adoption agency, something termed an "adoption facilitator," or another intermediary. There was another name for such facilitators or intermediaries.

Baby brokers.

This was getting too complicated for me. I called the agency. Fortunately Mick had not left yet, and when I told him what I was looking for he said he'd get right on it.

I was down the street in a diner having a burger when he called back. I took my phone outside and listened to his findings.

"Sometimes they call them 'baby mills'—like puppy mills, you know. There're thousands of them; the demand for kids is high, since a lot of people today are all wound up in their careers and wait too long to be able to produce their own families. Most provide full documentation of the baby's birth, but in the name of the adoptive parents. Legitimate adoption procedures are discouraged."

"Was that true twenty years ago, about the documentation, I mean?"

"Not like it is now."

"So the family Pamela Stanton was sold to might've needed a birth certificate and used that old dodge of requesting one of a child who had died from the state."

"Right. But here's an interesting fact: you said the child was two?"

"Yes."

"Then the crime wasn't baby brokering. She was too old. It was human trafficking."

"What's the penalty for that?"

"In California, it varies. And our laws are designed for cases where the victims are sold into slavery—particularly sexual slavery. Your investigation takes us into murky territory. I put a call in to Hank and Anne-Marie"—the agency's affiliated attorneys—"but I haven't heard back yet."

I thanked him and asked him to call me when one of them got in touch. Then went back inside to my cold burger and thought of the day Pamela Stanton had disappeared into that murky territory. Wherever her parents had taken her, they'd been back home in time to prepare dinner. It hadn't been a long trip.

Someplace in the county?

Well, the Yellow Pages weren't going to help me. There wouldn't be listings for "baby brokers" or "human traffickers." I needed an inside source, someone who would know about illegal activities and—more important—would talk about them. My mind sifted through the people I'd met here and kept coming back to the newspaper owner, Tricia Prine.

Prine was still in her office when I arrived. "I've been having a lot of trouble with a story I'm working on," she told me.

When I finished telling her what I'd found out, she said, "Interesting, the difference between baby broker and human trafficker. I wasn't aware of that."

"I guess few people are. Do you recall anyone in the county, particularly in Colusa, who might match either description?"

Prine was silent for a moment. Then she said, "Two. An attorney named Jerome Page and an orphanage called Home Sweet Home. The orphanage is long gone, but Page is still practicing in Colusa." She read off the phone number, home, and office addresses.

Okay, Mr. Page, Esquire.

Jerome Page's office was in a faux adobe building near the Colusa city hall. When I arrived at nine the next morning, a slender woman in a black business suit and high stiletto heels was unlocking its door. She showed me in, told me Mr. Page usually appeared between then and nine thirty, and began making coffee; the cup she brought me was very good—some sort of vanilla bean blend.

Page arrived at nine twenty. A short man, somewhat heavy, with a clipped mustache and receding brown hair. When I mentioned the Pamela Stanton case, he turned away from me. "Give me a few minutes to get organized," he told the secretary.

When she showed me into his office some ten minutes later, Page was seated behind a light-oak desk, shuffling some papers. He didn't rise or offer his hand, nor did he invite me to sit down. I sat anyway and slid my card over to him. A faint flush colored his cheeks as he looked at it. He pushed it aside.

"Now what's this about, Ms. McCone?" he asked.

"As I said before, the Pamela Stanton case."

"Little girl who disappeared some twenty years ago? It was big news here for a while, but I can't say as I recall much about it."

"Let me refresh your memory." I went over the details.

"But what does all that have to do with me?"

"At that time, according to local sources who prefer to remain anonymous, you fulfilled the role of an adoption facilitator."

He swallowed, picked up a pencil that was lying on his desk blotter, and began turning it between his thick fingers. "I admit I may have placed one or two unwanted babies with adoptive parents, but such procedures are perfectly legal under state law."

"You *may have?*"

"... I did."

"How many was it—one or two?"

"Um ... two."

"I suppose you have records of those proceedings?"

"In storage, yes."

"I'd like to see them."

"They're strictly confidential. And would take days, even weeks, to find."

I studied him. Beads of sweat were beginning to appear on his high forehead, although it was cool here in his office.

I took out my notebook—a little leather one I seldom use for anything more than grocery lists—and flipped through it.

"Does the name Judson have any meaning for you? In particular Dennis and Marla Judson?" I showed him the photos; he barely glanced at them.

"No." He replied too quickly and a nervous tic appeared at the corner of his mouth.

"Not names that might appear in those old confidential files?"

"Absolutely not."

"Aren't you curious about why I'm asking you about them?"

"Not especially. But who are they and what do they want from me?"

"They don't want a thing from you, Mr. Page. They're both dead."

"Then why ...?"

"Their daughter, Debra Judson, is my client. And she has evidence that suggests she is—or formerly was—Pamela Stanton."

"Impossible!"

"Why?"

"Pamela Stanton was a child who wandered off into the woods. Her body was never found."

I looked at my notebook again. The page I'd turned it to read "orange juice, salmon, dishwasher soap."

"My client has documents that indicate otherwise." When Page flushed again I added, "Memories too."

"She couldn't possibly remember anything, she was only two—"

"Some children—especially exceptional ones—retain memories from early childhood."

"What does she remember?"

I shook my head. "What do *you* remember, Mr. Page?"

"Nothing. Absolutely nothing!" He stood. "And now, Ms. McCone, I want you to leave my offices—at once."

The man, I decided, wouldn't be budged from his story. Not by me. But my client's history of growing up in Michigan was another thing entirely: interstate human trafficking is under the jurisdiction of the FBI. I was quite certain that Page wouldn't be able to stonewall them. I called Craig and asked him to hand over the case to his contacts there. Then I went to collect Jackson Stanton from the bar.

Jackson was horrified when I explained how his parents had sold his little sister. "How could they've done that?" he asked. "She was such a little sweetheart."

I just shook my head.

"But you say she had a good life with these Judson people?"

"Yes, but they're both gone, and now she's searching for family. Would you like to fly back to San Francisco with me and meet her?"

Jackson hesitated, then studied his image in the mirror on the backbar. "Would she want to see me like this, an old hairy drunk in ratty clothes?"

"She wants to see you. We can deal with the hair and ratty clothes. The drunk part is up to you."

He looked wistfully at his beer, then pushed it away. Stood and said, "Then let's get a move on."

Later that day when Jackson—a cleaned-up and barbered man in brand-new clothing—and my client met in my office, the resemblance between them was totally apparent: same facial shape; same eye color; similar features. His had been roughened by too many bad years; hers were toned and smooth, but the worry lines around the eyes were the same. I was sure a DNA test would prove they were brother and sister.

At first they were shy, exchanging pleasantries but holding back in a way that decidedly would not make a good TV movie. I ordered in sandwiches from Angie's Deli downstairs, then found an excuse to leave them alone. When I peeked through the office video cam an hour later, they were sitting close, talking earnestly. I ordered up dessert. And when they emerged an hour after that, they were holding hands. After they'd left, I felt lonely for my own relatives.

Mick was out somewhere on a case. John didn't answer any of his phones. Sister Charlene, I knew, was overseas and probably in lengthy conferences with bankers and venture capitalists. Sister Patsy answered her cellular but said she'd have to call me back; she was supervising the installation of a pizza oven at her restaurant in Napa County.

Who else? Robin Blackhawk, my half sister in law school at UC Berkeley? No, she was in Cozumel for a long-deserved vacation. Saskia Blackhawk, my birth mother, had told me she'd be in Washington, DC, for the week. Ma, my adoptive mother, was jurying an art show in Mendocino County and hadn't left a number. Of course, there was my birth father, Elwood Farmer.

After three rings he answered at his home on the Flathead Reservation in Montana. I started babbling about solving the cold case and telling my client who she was, as I'd been hired to do.

"Relax, my daughter," he said. And then added a variation of the first phrase he'd ever delivered to me, "Wait a moment, until you've assembled your thoughts."

I waited and assembled. I could hear Elwood's patient breathing.

Finally I said, "You know, Elwood," then corrected myself, using the name he now preferred I call him, "Father, a lot of the things that I'm required to do in my work don't make me feel proud. In fact, some of them are downright distasteful."

"So you've told me."

"Well, today I did something that makes me proud. I reunited a sister and brother who had been lost to each other since they were quite young." Then I proceeded to tell him about the case.

"This should be no surprise to you," he said when I'd finished. "It's what you did when you located your mother and your half brother and sister and me. Along with us and your adoptive relatives, you've created a whole new family. Be glad of it, and depend on it, as we depend on you."

APRIL 13

April 13. Anniversary number five. A ridiculous ritual, I admit.

Normally I'm not a superstitious individual. Black cats don't bother me—I have two. I skip happily under ladders, don't eat an apple a day, and have broken more mirrors than I can remember. But I couldn't get loose from this April thirteenth obsession.

It was eleven in the morning. I'd cleared up all my paperwork, held a staff meeting, and conferred one-on-one with various of my operatives. Hy Ripinsky, my husband and partner in McCone & Ripinsky Investigations, was back east at our Chicago field office, and I had nothing urgent to share with him anyway. I wasn't currently working a case myself. No reason to remain in my office in the M&R building. After all, I was the boss!

But still I remained at my desk and turned to my computer, opened up the older case files section, and scrolled down to "Voss, Judith." And there it was—the cold case that I'd reviewed obsessively every April 13 for five years now. Maybe this year something would stand out—a fact or scrap of information that I had somehow missed or failed to internalize before.

Judith Voss, according to her parents, had been one of those too-good-to-be-true daughters: the kind who make good grades—in her case, at SF State—never cause trouble in the home, date the appropriate boys, have ambitions appropriate to their family's station in life. In fact, for them *appropriate* was a good word to sum up her character. She was conventionally pretty, excelled at soccer and swimming, wanted to be a physical therapist. In order to finance her higher education, she banked money from a part-time job clerking at a small flower shop near the home she shared with her parents in the inner Sunset District near Golden Gate Park. She claimed she loved San Francisco and would never leave it, but apparently she had.

Five years ago on April 13, Judith had left home at 7:00 p.m., supposedly for a French club meeting. She went out the door calling out, "Goodbye, Mom, goodbye, Dad," instead of her usual "See you later." When she didn't return by the time her parents normally went to bed, they didn't think much of her absence. They assumed she had decided to stay over with a friend from the club, as she sometimes did. But when she hadn't returned by late the next afternoon, Mrs. Voss called the friend and found there had been no club meeting; in fact, the friend hadn't seen

Judith in a month or more.

The officers on SFPD's Missing Persons detail hadn't seen much cause for alarm. Young people disappeared in the city all the time; they usually turned up unscathed. Detectives went through the motions, which included contacting outlying jurisdictions, but finally concluded that Judith had left the city of her free will. She was over eighteen and had every right to come and go as she pleased—not like the decades-long plague of underage runaways who flocked to such places as the Haight, Taos, Seattle, New York, and Florida. The parents were referred to me by their attorney and they asked me to see if I could find something the police had missed. I tried for two weeks, but the record was straightforward; we finally terminated our professional relationship, and Judith remained missing.

I've never considered any of my agency's relatively few unsolved cases closed. Years ago when I'd been changing offices, I'd unearthed an open file that dealt with the disappearance of a young couple. I read it, put a couple of neglected facts together, and by night the couple were reunited with their families.

That was why, every April 13, I picked through the Voss file. An exercise in futility so far.

All the transcripts of my interviews were there, starting with my clients, the parents. Emily Voss was blonde, thin, and nervous; her fingers picked at her clothing and she constantly twisted her wedding ring. I suspected the nervousness was habitual rather than related to the problem at hand. When she spoke of her daughter, I heard a wisp of envy in her voice: "Judy was so smart—she could achieve whatever she wanted to in her life. She wouldn't be ordinary..." At that point she let her words trail off and glanced at her husband. His thick lips twisted, acknowledging the unsaid, "Ordinary like me."

Doug Voss, stocky in his neatly pressed chinos and checked sport shirt, was a high school basketball coach. His big hands swooped around as he talked. "That girl, there's no way she's in serious trouble. I trained her well. She's strong, got her head together. Whatever she's up to, she's got a reason."

"You think she disappeared deliberately?" I asked.

He nodded. "That girl, she's up to something, is what I say."

Judith hadn't had many friends—"Too competitive," her father claimed—but I interviewed them all. And they all offered opinions that conflicted with her parents' views.

Nancy Melton told me, "Judy could be a lot of fun. She had a wild side. Nothing dangerous, just pranks. Like stealing her boyfriend's jock from his gym locker and leaving it on the math teacher's desk."

"Judy dated a lot," a former boyfriend, Gary Cramer said. "You wanted some, you knew where to get it. She loved to fuck, the more the better."

"She was a very spiritual person," Cindy Stafford remarked. "It was always up to God. 'God's gonna get me for this.' 'God'll handle this problem.'"

Art Gallo commented, "Girl knew—and used—more swearwords than I do."

The friend who had the most penetrating insights into Judith Voss was classmate Barbie Jennings, a big, graceless woman in bib overalls and a T-shirt who, in the course of our talk at her apartment, tripped over a hassock, bruised her upper arm on the corner of a bookcase, and knocked over a tall stack of paperback books.

From the Jennings transcript:

BJ: If you asked me to come up with one word that described Jude, I'd say it would be *wanting,* as in aching for stuff. She needed ... I don't know what she needed. But whatever it was, she wasn't going to get it on a physical therapist's salary.

SM: She wanted something in a monetary sense?

BJ: Yeah. It's like what we used to do on Sundays sometimes when the real estate ads came out. Jude would go over the open homes section and circle ones that looked good. Then we'd go tour them.

SM: You weren't thinking of buying or renting?

BJ: God, no. Even back then, the prices were outrageous. And the places she wanted to look—Cow Hollow, Pacific Heights, Russian Hill—were out of sight. I asked her once why didn't we look at inexpensive condos or apartment rentals. Maybe something nice would turn up and we could go halves on it. She said no. The way things were, she'd have to go it alone.

SM: The way things were?

BJ: Yeah. I asked her what she meant, but she just smiled like I was supposed to know.

SM: Did she have a boyfriend—this Gary Kramer, for instance— whom she might've been planning on moving in with?

BF: Did she have a boyfriend? Who-eee! Guys were calling all the time, but as far as I knew she didn't go with any one for very long. And she didn't talk about them.

SM: No one steady at all?

BJ: No. She'd say, "He's strictly temporary" or "I can't be bothered with him." That was it. Once, not long before she disappeared, she found a house she really liked on Russian Hill. It was an odd little place, but she was very taken with it. As she was looking around I heard her mutter, "This would be perfect for—" and then she saw me looking at her and smiled in that weird, secret way she had and refused to talk about it. After that ... well, I decided she wasn't much of a friend, and we saw less of each other. Then suddenly she was gone, and I never heard from her again.

Next I looked at the transcripts of my talks with Judith's teachers.

Lynda Holman, English literature, found Judith "very studious. Most of the kids, well, you see vacant stares and you know they're far away, into something else entirely. But I'd be giving a lecture on Chaucer—which even bored me—and I'd catch Judy watching me with an intense look, almost as if she wanted something more from me. But the few times I called on her and asked, 'Yes, Judy?' she waved the question aside."

Mark Bolton, statistics, had a similar take on her: "Most students take my courses to satisfy a requirement for a program like the MBA, but Judy was into them for the content. She wanted to know what statistics could do for her, personally. It's hard to say why, but it was as if she was working on a problem and needed proof of the solution."

Emma Carpenter, biology, said, "When she disappeared, I thought, 'Well, isn't that just like her.' I mean, she was so remote. She performed the class and lab work all right, but she was ... well, mechanical. Just filling up space until she could get to what was really important to her."

Valerie Mott, women's athletic director, commented, "God, could that girl run." Then she smiled and shook her head. "Sorry, the pun was unintentional. But I guess that's what this is all about—she ran, and nobody ever knew why."

More transcripts. Older people, friends and associates of Judith's parents, all of whom had widely varying opinions of her.

"I wish I had a kid like her."

"Sneaky."

"Sincere."

"Very helpful to her mother."

"I don't think she was very close to her father."

"Physical therapist? I thought she wanted to be an interior decorator, or do something in real estate."

"She wouldn't just up and run away. She's got to be dead. Someday they'll find her body in a ditch someplace."

"She gave off a strange sexual aura."

"She went out with my son Jeff. Just a few dates. He found her boring."

"I never caught her in a lie, but she sometimes seemed untruthful."

"Gossipy—but most of what she talked about was untrue. I wouldn't be surprised if she made it all up."

"She made me uncomfortable."

"I'm not sure that there wasn't something abnormal about the girl."

"Flirtatious? Yes. But a lot of girls like to flirt with older men. And we like them to flirt."

"Bright. She could hold up her end of conversations on many complicated issues."

"Poised and socially at ease."

More of the same from the Vosses' neighbors:

"She'd sneak out of the house in the middle of the night," Mrs. Polly Gilbert said. "I know because I'm unwell and sit up in my chair next to our bedroom window most of the time. There'd usually be this man waiting for her."

"A man, not a boy?" I asked.

"I'm sure I'd know the difference."

"Can you describe him?"

"Not very well. Just tall and well built."

"Did you hear them talking? Maybe she mentioned his name."

"Talk? The two of them? Not hardly."

"Yes, I'd see Judy slipping out of the house all the time," an elderly woman who wouldn't give me her name told me. "Out the window, and gone. It's lucky that's a one-story house. If she'd had to climb down a drainpipe, she might've broken her neck."

"Men? Nonsense!" Mrs. Olivia Johnson shook her head vehemently. "They weren't all men. Some of them were teenagers, too."

"Do you remember any of them?"

"Well, the man who came the most, he had a red Porsche—one of the old ones that look like an upside-down spoon—that he'd park down the street, and then he'd lean against the car, bold as brass. She'd go to him, and they'd take off. I can still hear the sound of that car growling away into the night."

"When was this?"

"It went on for four months, right before Judith disappeared."

"Did you ever overhear any conversation between them? The man's name, for instance?"

"No."

"What about the car's license plate?"

"It was in-state. But I didn't notice the numbers. I've never been good with numbers." She shook her head and added, "I warned my Margaret to stay away from the Voss girl. Her midnight escapades set a bad example. Let's just say that Judith Voss never came around here selling Girl Scout cookies."

That first April 13, the grown man with the red Porsche had seemed my only starting point. From my contact at the Department of Motor Vehicles, I learned that there were twenty-three such models in the Greater Bay Area that had been licensed over five years previously. Nine of them I could rule out because they were registered to women. Two were on planned nonoperation. Another had been in a wreck and consigned to the junkyard.

Ten cars, then, in various locations around the area.

I'd begun by phoning.

Owner #1 had been deceased for over a year. "I just can't get around to selling that Porsche," his widow said.

Owner #2 had been in Thailand on sabbatical five years ago. "Car was up on blocks in his garage," his secretary told me. "He made me go over and check on it once a month. That's how much he loved that car."

Owner #3's phone was disconnected.

Owner #4 had moved to Utah.

Two more deceased owners. At the second number a woman said, "I always told my husband that car would be the death of him."

Owner #7 was annoyed. "I sold it to a kid a year ago. Don't tell me he didn't reregister it!" Apparently he hadn't.

Three owners to go. None of them answered the phone. I decided to wait until evening, then show up at their addresses.

Eldon McFeeney lived in a bad section of Oakland: men wearing gang colors congregated around a corner drugstore; most of the dilapidated houses had security gates on the doors and windows, while others were boarded up. I parked in front of the McFeeney garage and mounted the rickety stairs to knock. In a few moments, when I'd just about given up on getting a reply, a skinny black man on crutches answered. His skin was dry and clung to his fragile-looking cheekbones; his hair had receded to two small spots above his large ears; a strong odor of alcohol surrounded him.

"Yes, what is it?" he asked.

I handed him one of my cards. He looked at it, shook his head, and muttered something that sounded like, "What next?"

"I'm interested in the Porsche 912 you have registered under your name," I said.

"The Porsche ... that's not mine. Can you see an old wreck like me driving that baby?" He smiled faintly. "It's my younger brother's, registered in my name because ... well, Donny has trouble with traffic cops. They took his license away permanently years ago."

"How many years?"

"Seven? Eight? My memory's not so good."

"Does Donny live here with you?"

"No, ma'am. I don't know where he crashes these days. The car lives with me—he's too messed up to drive it."

"How long has the Porsche been living with you?"

"Five years. It needs a lot of work, but since I don't drive it, I'm not putting any money into it."

"Does your brother drive it at all?"

"Not since he parked it in my garage. I suppose I'll get around to selling it when he ... goes."

I knew what he meant by "goes." I myself had had a brother who died of drug addiction.

Arthur Harris, the next Porsche owner, was an entrepreneur of sorts. His office was a cubicle in a shared workspace in an old building on Fourth Street south of Market. The lettering on the door said Entertainers Collective.

The cubicle was tiny: a single desk and two chairs, one of which was piled with files, and a bookcase full of reference works that were mostly collapsed on one another. Harris himself was fifty at the outside and energetic, judging from the way he sprang from his chair when I entered. His blond handlebar mustache twitched as he examined my card, and he then studied me with keen blue eyes.

"I don't believe this," he exclaimed. "A private eye masquerading as an entertainer. What is it you do—act, sing, play the xylophone?"

"None of the three." I took the chair he indicated. "Actually, this is an inquiry about a disappearance. Are you familiar with the name Judith Voss?"

Pause. "Can't say as I am. Does she act, sing—"

"No, and she doesn't play the xylophone. I understand you own a red Porsche 912, license number—"

"So what if I do?"

"And you've owned it since ...?"

"Oh, maybe seven years. What the hell does that matter?"

"Judith Voss had a friend who owned one. She was seen with him shortly before she disappeared last month."

"Well, that friend wasn't me."

"I see. I'm curious—what exactly is it you do, Mr. Harris?"

He began fiddling with objects on his desk—a stapler, letter opener, calculator. "I'm an agent—I put my clients together—actor with director, scriptwriter with producer, that sort of thing."

"And you take a fee from them?"

"Of course."

"Sounds like interesting work. How long have you been doing this?"

"Forever, it seems. At least fifteen years."

"Would I know any of your clients?"

He hesitated. "Well, there's Sandra Adams and Kiki Charles and Lissa Sloane."

I'd never heard of them.

"And Sam Sills."

Sam was an artist; I knew him slightly, in the way you become familiar with someone you bump into around clubs and galleries and gatherings associated with the art world. I hadn't seen him in quite some time.

I mentioned as much, and judging by the look on Harris's face, he hadn't, either.

Getting back to the subject, I asked, "Are you sure you have no recollection of Judith Voss?"

"No, sorry but I don't." His gaze avoided mine. I was sure he was lying.

The last red Porsche owner was Evan Draper, what the newspapers used to call a metrosexual: trendy, stylish, and thoroughly caught up in his own appearance. When he answered the door of his high-rise condo in the SoMa area, he automatically pushed back an errant curl of his dark hair and straightened the jacket of an expensive pin-striped suit. "Yes?" he said.

I gave him my card and explained my reason for being there.

He motioned me into a stylized modern living room—slingback chairs and glass tables with spindly metal legs, carefully placed globes that caught the light from recessed fixtures and spread varicolored beams in all directions. Large uncurtained windows afforded a view from the Ferry Building and Alcatraz to the Oakland shipping terminals.

Draper was a gracious host: he offered tea or coffee and, when I refused, settled me into one of the chairs, which proved to be surprisingly comfortable.

"A missing person case, you said?" he asked, perching on the edge of a sofa.

"Yes. Are you familiar with the name Judith Voss?"

"The woman who disappeared recently?"

"That's the one. How do you know her?"

"I've been following the case in the papers. Disappearances fascinate me—Judge Crater, Hoffa, you know. But why have you come to me, a stay-at-home accountant?"

I explained about the red Porsche.

"Amazing how you can trace people. Detective work is so compelling. I watch all the TV shows."

Just what I needed, a detective junkie.

"I've been thinking," Draper added. "This Judith Voss—did she have money?"

"Only what she earned at a part-time job."

"Too bad. But she could've saved up and left the country."

"Passport control says she didn't."

"But she could've gone to Mexico or Canada. I read someplace about how there're places along the Canadian border where you can just hike up a trail, open a gate, and be in Canada scot-free. Or there's always the old trick of stowing away in a moving van or a UPS truck. They say FedEx apprehends dozens of free riders a month."

His eyes were bright and his face was turning red; Draper was really getting into his game.

I said, "Those are two interesting takes on the situation. I'll have to think about them."

"What about her parents? What does her father do?"

"He teaches school."

"Too bad. I was thinking he might be connected, you know. She could've been taken hostage by the mob—"

"I doubt it."

"Well, kidnapped by somebody."

"There's been no ransom note."

"But there could be a conspiracy. A friend of mine, he's very into conspiracies. He has a fine collection on the subject, and I've read a lot of it."

God save me from conspiracy theories! Next we'd be talking alien abduction.

"Mr. Draper," I said, standing up, "our conversation has been very enlightening. I'll get back to you if—"

"Do you want I should send you some of the literature?"

"Sure, why not?" I headed for the door. It would make interesting reading by the fireplace.

So there I was: three red Porsches, their owners claiming no connection to Judith Voss. During the next few days I ran more checks on possible owners but came up with nothing useful. Second interviews with Judith's friends and neighbors proved equally fruitless. Finally I had to admit I was wasting the Voss family's money and my time.

File closed.

Late afternoon, April 13, five years later. My eyes were burning from reading off the computer screen, so I hunted up the paper file and took it to my comfy leather armchair next to the window. The chair, which had been with me since my days at All Souls Legal Cooperative, had been shabby and butt-sprung for most of those years. But then, in honor of M&R.'s splendid new offices, Ted Smalley, our office manager, had smuggled it out to an upholstery shop. When it returned, it was outfitted in soft brown leather and had acquired a matching footstool; now both resided in front of the broad window of my corner office beneath a ficus tree, also a gift from Ted and, appropriately, called Mr. T.

Okay, I told myself, *go over the file one more time. If you don't find anything, there's always next April 13.*

The impressions of Judith I'd gathered from friends, teachers, and other adults varied widely: studious, sneaky, poised, highly sexed, spiritual, a lot of fun. Who was she, really? After a moment I turned back to my lengthy interview with her former best friend, Barbie Jennings. The word she'd used to describe Judith was *needing.* Needing in terms of "aching for stuff." Stuff she was unlikely to acquire on a physical therapist's salary.

Then the red Porsche came into the picture. A man had frequently met Judith, a man who could afford a classic car. Much as my friend at the DMV had searched—and much as the lunch I bought her every year as payment for her services would cost—only the three individuals I'd spoken with had matched the time frame.

Eldon McFeeney. Could the brother or someone else have taken it out of McFeeney's garage without him noticing? I'd doubted it five years ago and I still doubted it; McFeeney might be disabled, but he was mentally sharp. It was something to check on, though, and I called McFeeney's number. The woman who answered told me she was his niece and that her uncle had died the previous year. The Porsche was still in the garage.

"Nobody ever showed up looking for it," she said, "and since it wasn't taking up any space I needed—I don't have a car myself—I just left it there. I keep thinking I ought to have it fixed up and sell it. How much do you think I could get for it?"

I referred her to her local Porsche dealer.

Evan Draper. A "mere stay-at-home accountant" and detective buff, to say nothing of conspiracy theorist. He knew of Judith's disappearance, had advanced his ideas on what happened to her. A very enthusiastic man, Mr. Draper. But what if his enthusiasm was manufactured to mask other, darker motives?

Might as well see how Evan was doing this year. I left a message on his voice mail.

Arthur Harris. The agent who had named clients I'd never heard of. I'd checked on Harris on past April 13s. Harris was no longer listed in any of the Bay Area directories. How long had he been out of the agenting business? None of the clients he'd mentioned except for artist Sam Sills were listed, either. In the entertainment section of last Sunday's *Chronicle* I'd noticed Sills was having a showing at a gallery in Dogpatch this week. Had Harris set that up for him? Well, why not go to his showing tonight and ask him? I had nothing better to do.

The NewSpace Gallery occupied part of an old warehouse in the eclectic Dogpatch neighborhood. A trendy part of the city between Potrero Hill and the Bay, the former shipbuilding center had been transformed by live-work lofts, cafes, specialty shops, brew pubs, and wine bars. Although it was early—only five—Third Street, its main artery, was crowded with strollers and shoppers. I stopped to admire a Peruvian cape in a window, imagined its outrageous price tag, and pressed forward.

The gallery was doing a brisk business. Sills's space was a large one at the front and there were tags affixed to some of the paintings indicating a sale had been made. I couldn't say I liked them much: he must have been in his gray period, because most of them were muddied, with occasional splotches of bright primary colors peeking through. They struck me as real downers.

"That painting," a voice said over my shoulder, "does it speak to you?"

I turned. Sam Sills hadn't changed at all. Short, brown-haired, with a fluffy beard and a thick mustache that someone had once opined made him look as if he was "trying to eat a cat."

"Sharon McCone! I haven't seen you since ... when?" he exclaimed. "Forget my words—I wouldn't attempt to sell you any of this tripe."

"Tripe?"

He took my arm and drew me aside. "That's just what it is—folks like it, buy it, keep me in food and drink. Fuck 'em if they can't take a joke."

"In the interviews I read you used to seem so serious about your work."

"I used to be serious about a lot of things. But I was only publicly serious. When I stopped with the self-praise I took a good look at my work and realized I'd better get a real job or go broke. Real jobs and going broke have never appealed to me, so I altered my technique and aimed for a less sophisticated audience. That's why I don't praise my work anymore. But you, I hear about you and your agency all the time. What brings you here tonight? Just slumming?"

"I wanted to talk to you about your agent, Arthur Harris—"

"Former agent. He took me on when I was a starving artist and kept me poor by stealing from me. I left him as soon as I could attract better representation. Is the old bugger still in the business?"

"Apparently not. He's no longer listed anywhere."

"How come you're interested in him?"

I explained about Judith Voss.

Sills smiled knowingly. "You should've come to me five years ago, darlin'. I can't tell you where your missing woman is now, but I can make a pretty good guess why she went missing. Along with his agenting career, Artie Harris was a pimp."

For a moment I was taken aback. "A pimp!"

"Right. And not your small-timer. He set his ladies up in fancy places, trained them in the high-class call girl business. He had half a dozen or more in his stable at one time."

"What happened? His agent's office was pretty downscale when I saw him five years ago."

"That was his cover. He figured the law wouldn't suspect anybody that unsuccessful could have been doing so well in an illicit trade."

A blonde woman in a black dress with an official-looking name tag came up behind Sam. "Mr. Sills, I have a customer who's serious about purchasing *Summer Dawn.*"

"All right!" To me he said, "Good luck with your search, Sharon. If you need anything else, call me." He hurried away with the blonde woman.

Okay, I thought, *now maybe I have the lead I need to finally solve the April 13 cold case.* The probable scenario: Judith Voss, a woman who reputedly "loved to fuck" and "wanted stuff," had somehow encountered Artie Harris, a high-class pimp and the owner of the red Porsche she'd been seen in, and he'd set her up in luxurious digs. When Harris was forced to quit pimping, if Judith was smart—and I knew she was—she would have continued with her clientele and kept the fees for her services for herself.

The question was, where was Judith now plying her trade?

Somewhere here in the city that she'd vowed she would never leave? It was entirely possible. She'd surely changed her appearance—dyed and restyled hair, expensive cosmetics, expensive clothes—and would be living a lifestyle far removed from her former one. San Francisco is a big city; she could have been lucky enough not to have crossed paths with any of her former acquaintances.

As soon as I left the gallery, I called Barbie Jennings, who expressed surprise at hearing from me. "Is this about Judith after all this time?"

"Yes. I have a few questions for you."

"Okay, shoot."

"You mentioned a house on Russian Hill that Judith fell in love with on one of your excursions. Where was it?"

"I remember the house, but ... Wait a minute. I kept a diary back then. I'll hunt it up."

It took her a few minutes to get back to me. "Here it is," she said somewhat breathlessly. "End of March. Yes. Sunday. The house was on Taylor Street. It was unique, set way back from the street. You had to approach it down a little alley."

There couldn't be that many such houses in a district where millionaires had been putting up mansions since the Gold Rush days. "Do you recall what the cross streets were?"

"Umm ... I'm pretty sure it was between Filbert and Union. Why is this important—"

"I'll get back to you."

The house was an original, for San Francisco. Tucked halfway down an alley between two looming redbrick apartment houses, and overgrown by tough old wisteria vines that looked as if they were reaching for the sun. Probably a converted outbuilding for one of the mansions that had once crowned the hill. There were lights on inside.

The woman who answered my knock at the front door could not possibly have been Judith Voss. Too old, too tall, with long red hair tied in a ponytail and trailing down her back to her waist. She wasn't unattractive, but she didn't strike me as the call girl type.

"Yes?" she said pleasantly.

I showed her my ID. "Do you have a roommate, by any chance, Ms. ...?"

"Kelly. No, I don't."

"May I ask how long you've lived here?"

"Six months. Why do you want to know?"

"I'm looking for a young woman who may have been a former occupant—"

"You must mean Jennifer Vail. She lived here for about five years before I took over the lease."

J.V—same initials.

"And she moved out six months ago?"

"Closer to eight. But she didn't exactly move out."

"Oh?"

"She disappeared just before the lease came up for renewal. Here one day, gone the next."

"Do you have any idea where she went?"

"No. Nobody does, apparently. Not even the police."

"The police?"

"Somebody called them and reported her missing. One of her johns, I suppose."

"Then you're aware of her profession. Did you know Jennifer?"

"No, I never met her. Her profession became apparent almost as soon as I moved in. Men kept coming by, asking for her. I finally contacted the police, and the detective I talked to confirmed that she was a call girl. He didn't seem particularly interested that she'd disappeared."

I didn't suppose he had been. People are prone to disappear in a big city, and unless they're prominent in one way or another, or there's evidence of foul play, it's just business as usual.

"Did she take all her possessions with her when she went away?" I asked.

"No, and it's kind of odd that she didn't. She had a lot of jewelry and clothing that she left behind."

"Do you know what happened to it?"

"It's all still here. The real estate agent had it boxed up and put it in the storage closet. It'll all be sold if she doesn't claim it after a year."

"There was nothing that might indicate where she'd gone or why?"

"Not according to the agent or the police," Ms. Kelly said. "But you're welcome to look through the boxes, if you'd like."

"I would."

There were three big boxes full of carefully folded underwear, lounging outfits, formal dresses, and informal wear. A velvet pouch held earrings, rings, bracelets, and necklaces. I wasn't any expert on jewelry, but it all looked expensive to me.

I thanked Ms. Kelly and walked down the alley, but stopped midway, staring at the little vine-covered cottage. My search for Judith Voss had ended here tonight. And so had my April 13 obsession. I had found her at last, only to have her elude me again, and there was nothing more I could or wanted to do to find her a second time. Nor would I share what I'd discovered with her parents. They must have come to terms with their loss by this time; I was not about to bring more hurt to them by revealing what their daughter had chosen to do with her life.

Maybe her disappearance had been a willful one, and if so, she'd found what she was looking for someplace else. But a call girl's existence is precarious at best. And it seemed out of character that a successful one with expensive tastes would abandon her material possessions on a sudden whim.

It just might be that Judith had found her Mr. Goodbar.

SCAMMING THE SCAMMER

"I lost my life savings to that scammer. Thirty thousand dollars. Everything I had," Ana Emery told me.

"This was an internet scam?" I asked.

"No, Ms. McCone. I don't have a computer, don't much like them. It happened on the phone."

I frowned. Internet scammers are fairly easy to trace; I have an employee at my agency—Derek Frye—who can identify one with a few strokes of his keyboard. But phone scammers are not as simple: they change their number often, re-route their calls deviously, assume identities with the artistry of Academy Award-winning actors.

"Tell me how it happened," I said.

She fiddled with the edge of her Irish-knit sweater, uncrossed and recrossed her legs.

Ashamed of her foolishness, I thought.

My new client struck me as someone who was very concerned with projecting a confident image as an executive assistant in one of San Francisco's high-powered law firms. She'd been referred to me by her boss, my old friend criminal defense attorney Glenn Solomon, who'd called her—in retro-speak manner—"one sharp cookie." But the cookie appeared to be crumbling now as she sat across my desk from me in one of the clients' chairs. She looked around the office at everything but me.

"Ms. Emery?" I prompted.

She roused herself and sighed. "I just feel so stupid."

"No need for that. Thousands of people are scammed every day. Why don't you start at the beginning?"

She sighed again, ran her fingers through her short, feather-cut hair. It was almost as black as my own, except for feint reddish highlights. "This woman called. I don't normally pick up the phone unless I know who's calling, but I was cooking and expecting to hear from my friend Janey, so I did. She said, 'Hi, this is Daniela.' Now, I *do* have a friend called Daniela, but I was surprised to hear from her since she lives in Paris. So surprised that I said, 'Hey, what's happening?' We chatted; she asked me about my job and my new car and recommended a few investment opportunities, which I decided to take her up on."

"And when did you act on that decision?"

"The very next morning. They sounded too good to pass up."

"Let me guess: these opportunities involved cryptocurrency."

"Yes. I wish I'd never heard that term."

I know a good amount about cryptocurrency. It's been around a few years now, to very mixed reviews. Hailed as the new wave of high-earning investment, it is purely digital, bypassing banks and other financial institutions, and since its inception has been plagued by serious drawbacks. Purchases in such currencies as Bitcoin, Etherium, Litcoin and SafeTcoin are uninsured, hard to convert, and subject to extreme volatility. Huge price swings can wipe out fortunes in nanoseconds.

"Which crypto exchange did you have your account with?"

"SafeTcoin. Daniela recommended it."

SafeTcoin was the least reliable of all the exchanges.

"Did you talk with Glenn before you invested?"

"No. I wanted to, but he's been involved in a high-profile murder trial, and I didn't feel I should bother him. Plus, I wanted to prove I could do something on my own."

Pride goeth before, I thought.

"When did you realize your funds had been wiped out?" I asked.

"The second day after I transferred them in. I called Daniela's number in Paris. And then I knew."

"It wasn't Daniela you'd been speaking with."

"As soon as she answered, I knew it hadn't been her voice on the phone. The voice had been close but a little off."

I'd expected this. "What information did you share with the fake Daniela?"

"Everything. She said she needed it to help set up a wallet—one of those digital things where they store your information—for me."

"Even your social security number?"

She nodded. "I know they say you should never give it out, but Daniela—the real one—has been my friend forever. I felt safe with her."

I hesitated, doodling on the legal pad where I'd been taking notes. "Okay," I said, "I'll need one of my staff to get in touch with Daniela in Paris so he can get a voiceprint on her. Also copies of your savings and investment statements and any communications with the fraud departments you contacted. And anything else you may feel is pertinent to the investigation."

She nodded and stood up, clearly relieved the interview was at an end.

After she was gone, I moved from the desk to one of the sofas in the conversation area of my office. Stared out at the flurries of late February rain that washed the plate glass window. Thought about how I'd pursue this new investigation. Before I left to go home to my house in the Marina district—and to my husband Hy's great chicken cacciatore—I made a list of additional questions to ask Ana Emery.

The morning was as gloomy as the day before. I drove my Miata to the McCone & Ripinsky Building in the financial district, parked in the underground garage, and took the elevator to the top floor. Ana Emery was already there, a typed list of the answers to my questions and a sheaf of documents in hand. I poured coffee from the carafe on the table and seated Ana in the conversation area, where—as I'd supposed—she seemed more at ease than in the formal setting across my desk. While we sipped, I glanced over the list. No surprises there; I'd turn it over to Derek for fact-checking. After a moment I said to Ana, "The voiceprint from Daniela came in last night. I didn't think it could possibly be a match. As you probably realize most scammers don't know their victims, which makes them so hard to trace. But from what you've told me, this woman seemed to have a lot of your personal information. I think we need to take a look at your other women friends."

"Oh, I don't believe any of them could be responsible ..."

"It's still a possibility. Who are they?"

"Well, I ... I don't actually have many. I'm not what you'd call gregarious. There's Janey Woodman, who I was expecting a call from when I first heard from the fake Daniela. Lee Leveroni. Becca Sissel. That's about it."

"Are they work friends?"

"No. I went to high school with Becca. Lee I met at a book group about three years ago. It bored me, so I quit. Janey used to live in my old building on Arguello; we've kept in touch."

I wrote down the names and contact information, then asked, "Any male friends?"

"No." She colored slightly. "I used to date a guy named Mark Evans, but he moved to Silicon Valley a few months ago. Besides, aren't you looking for a woman?"

"Or a man who put her up to this scam."

She pressed her fingertips to her lips. "I hadn't thought of that."

It seemed to me there were a lot of things she hadn't thought of.

"Besides," she added, "Mark doesn't need money. He's independently wealthy."

"To some people, any amount of wealth isn't enough." I made a check mark beside the next item on my list. "Okay, Ms. Lewis, what do you do for fun?"

"Fun?" She made it sound like a foreign term.

"Do you play sports? Take classes? Take photographs or paint or travel? You mentioned a book group—anything else like that?"

"Why do you need to know those things?"

"Just trying to get a picture of your life."

"Oh. Well, I *did* take a cooking class at Le Ecole a while back, but it didn't work out so well. Turns out I've got no talent as a cook."

"What about going to nightclubs?"

"I don't drink."

"Not even to listen to music? Or dance?"

"Well, I went once to Jude's Tavern—that place on Van Ness—with Janey, but I hated it. It was crowded and hot, and the music was loud. I never went back."

I wanted to snap, "Is there anything you do *do?*" but I held back. The client, I always proclaim to my employees, must always be coddled and cosseted.

"Your administrative assistant," I told Glenn, "is a real nothing woman."

We were seated over drinks in Rosanna's, on the 31st floor of Embarcadero Three, his favorite after-work venue. The rain had worsened, slashing at the windows, and neither of us had cared to venture out.

"I said she was a smart cookie, not Miss Personality."

"More appropriately—in your vernacular—Miss Wet Blanket."

"Give the girl a break."

"I'm trying to. But what the hell is wrong with her?"

"Difficult childhood."

"How so?"

He frowned, ran his fingers through his thick white hair. "Her father left the family when Ana was ten. Went to live with a friend of her mother's down the street from them and later divorced the mother and married the new woman. The mother became an alcoholic and died of an overdose of sleeping pills three years later. The father took Ana in, but his new wife treated her badly. Ana left at sixteen—underage, but her father didn't try to stop her."

"And after that?"

"Surprisingly, Ana pulled herself together. Moved in with a friend's family and exchanged babysitting services for her room and board. Graduated high school early and attended paralegal classes while holding what she calls 'a string of nothing jobs.' Came to me two, two and a half years ago. She's been an excellent employee."

"I see she gave her address as a studio apartment south of Market, not too far from the M&R building."

"Singles place. She could have afforded better before this scam occurred, but she said she was saving to buy a house."

"She's still there?"

"Rent is paid up until the end of the month."

"And then?"

Glenn looked embarrassed, as he always does when caught in a kindness. "I'll cover it until this mess is cleaned up."

"I notice none of the three friends whose names she gave to me live at that address. I'd have thought she'd connect with more people in a singles place."

"Friends don't seem to be big on her agenda."

"Nothing else does, either."

"McCone, you seem to have taken a dislike to Ana."

"Not a dislike. It's just that passionless people irritate me."

He considered that. "Come to think of it, me too."

I spent a couple of hours setting up appointments to interview Ana's three friends: Janey Woodman, Lee Leveroni, and Becca Sissel. Before I'd called the women I'd listened to the voiceprint of the real Daniela: the register was low, but strong, with a silent French accent. The women's voices were all low and strong, but none had an accent. Of course, accents can easily be faked.

Becca worked at home in interior design. Her office was in a spacious condo on Scott Street, crowded with three drawing boards for her assistants. She took me into a glassed-in conference room and gave me coffee. From her surroundings I assumed she was affluent and worked hard at it—I doubted she had the need or the time to pull off a complicated scam.

She seemed genuinely concerned about Ana's problem. "I wish she'd let me know. I could easily have helped tide her over. Is there any way she can recover the money?"

"It's doubtful. Scams like this—especially ones involving cryptocurrency—are designed to move funds very quickly. What I'm primarily concerned with now is to prevent any more losses, and we're monitoring her few existing accounts—like credit cards—on an hourly basis. She provided information to the scammer that might make it possible for her to tap into whatever little remains."

"I'm going to phone her, see if there's anything I can do."

"I'm sure she'll appreciate that."

Ana didn't; she called me shortly before I left for home, railing at my invading her privacy. "I brought this problem to you because Glenn stressed your high value on confidentiality!"

"The women you named are your friends."

"They won't be if they find out what a fool I've been."

"Becca sounded as if she was anxious to help."

"Anxious to look down her nose at me! She's already wired five thousand dollars into my bank account, as if I were some poor relation."

"I'd say that was a very kind gesture."

"The hell it was! You don't know Becca."

"I guess not. Ana, do you want me to go on with this inquiry?" I'd have been delighted if she'd said no.

But instead, she said grudgingly, "Yes, of course—go ahead."

Damn! I told her I'd be in touch.

I met Janey Woodman the next morning at a coffee shop on Haight Street. The neighborhood—long ago known as the birthplace of the hippie movement—has undergone various changes over the past few decades and is now gentrified. The coffee shop was shiny with chrome and plush with leather, an oasis from the rain that still pelted the city.

Janey Woodman, who lived upstairs from the shop and clerked at a nearby bed-and-bath store, reminded me of the quintessential earth mother: long brown hair gathered at the nape of her neck; no makeup; plain shapeless clothing. Her earrings were clusters of some kind of seed and matched a double strand around her neck. She ordered a cinnamon latte while I opted for black coffee.

"Ana and I went to parochial school together—Saint Mary's," she told me. "Actually, we lived together the last two years after she moved out on her father and new stepmother. She traded babysitting services with my folks in exchange for room and board."

"So you've been close a long time."

She frowned. "Not close, actually. Ana doesn't get close to anybody. Never has. But we've kept in touch. I've tried to be a friend, and the past couple of years, I've concentrated on breaking her out of her shell—getting her to do stuff like take classes, go to concerts, go clubbing. I haven't been real successful."

"She mentioned not liking Jude's Tavern very much."

"She *hated* it. Even though she met Mark Evans there."

The boyfriend who moved to Silicon Valley. "That was a serious relationship?"

"He wanted it to be, asked her to marry him and move to Santa Clara. She refused. He still comes up to the city, and I see him around Jude's Tavern now and then. He always asks about her."

I'd try to contact Mark Evans later.

"Anything else you could tell me about Ana?" I asked.

Janey considered, spooning up the last of her latte. "Not really. I've given her gifts from the store where I work, even offered her a place to stay till she gets on her feet. But to tell the truth, I've soured on the friendship. You go out of your way to try to help somebody, and they don't appreciate it—that's kind of a losing situation, isn't it?"

So Becca Sissel had helped to the extent of five thousand dollars. Janey Woodman hadn't been successful in bringing her out of her shell and was cooling on the friendship. Had Lee Leveroni been similarly repulsed? I'd have to ask her, but Lee was a flight attendant and I couldn't meet with her until after her four o'clock return on Southwest. I hadn't visited my office in the M&R building yet that day, so I stopped there and spent a few hours going over the numerous operatives' reports that were clogging my in box.

Missing persons: two of them, no progress. Easy to get lost in this city. Check forgery, but the family didn't want the police involved, just wanted to confront the cheating son and probably beat the hell out of him. Petty thefts from a small clothing store; owner merely wanted photographs of the light-fingered employee. Missing grandchildren of legal age. Threatening calls in the Sunset district, probably from a neighbor. Car vandalism. Missing electric bike. Graffiti on sidewalk. Surveillance on Pickleball courts as a possible basis for a nuisance suit. Missing Pickleball paddles....

Finally, it was time to meet Lee Leveroni at her apartment on Russian Hill. It was in a small wood-shingled building sandwiched between two nondescript highrises that must have provided good views of the Bay. Lee—blonde, well-groomed—had changed from her airline uniform to blue sweats and seemed to be glad to be at home. She offered me a glass of wine—which I gratefully accepted—and seated me on a black sofa whose fabric was shot with gold threads.

"So Ana's up to her old tricks," she said.

"I'm not sure what you mean by that."

"Poor mouthing."

"She's been the victim of a scam—"

"Ana is a perpetual victim."

"Her entire assets have been wiped out in a cryptocurrency confidence scheme."

"What assets?"

"Stocks, bonds, pension fund, bank accounts."

Lee Leveroni looked surprised. "I didn't think she was so prudent with her money. I've never known her to save. Ana spends and spends. Always has. Always will."

Somebody was lying to me.

Lee Leveroni? She was a distant friend from a book club she and Ana had once attended. I'd questioned her more thoroughly about that. The club had focused on how-to volumes about finance. "Ana didn't seem to grasp the concepts," Lee told me. "She took detailed notes, but the questions she asked didn't address the issues we were all talking about."

"Did she attend for very long?"

"Three weeks, maybe. Frankly, I'm surprised she gave my name to you as a reference."

Janey Woodman? She'd known Ana the longest. Their high school years were long behind them, so why had Janey recently taken an interest in breaking Ana out of her shell? Janey hadn't struck me as a woman who needed old friends in her life; several people had greeted her enthusiastically in the coffee shop, and she'd introduced one of them to me as her "bestie." Of course, Janey also seemed to be the type who liked to be helpful.

Becca Sissel? She seemed sincere about wanting to help Ana, had indeed sent her the five thousand—unappreciated—dollars. But Ana had been upset with me for contacting Becca, claimed she would be "looking down her nose" at her. Why? Was there some dynamic there that I was missing?

Seven o'clock. I'd called Mark Evans earlier and when I'd mentioned Ana's name, he'd eagerly agreed to meet at Jude's Tavern. The club was on Van Ness Avenue, sandwiched between a new car dealership and a bank. Rock music filtered out onto the sidewalk, and the interior—as Ana described it—was hot, crowded, and noisy. Big-screen TVs showed reruns of football games in three corners. I asked the hostess for Evans, and she pointed me to a booth near the rear.

Evans was sandy-haired, one of the baby-faced men who would never look old. He rose, asked what I would like to drink, and signaled to a waitress for my glass of wine. Then he asked eagerly, "Ana—is she all right?"

"She's had some difficulty." I explained about the cryptocurrency scam.

"Damn!" He slapped a hand on the table. "I should've warned her about investing in stuff like that! I'm an analyst for Citibank. I know the risks. But it never occurred to me that she would take that kind of plunge. Why did she?"

"Bad advice. Tell me, do you know anything about her friend Daniela?"

His mouth turned down. "The expatriate? Oh sure. Ana adores her. So free, she says. So worldly. But I can't imagine Daniela would set her up like that."

"Apparently, she didn't. But someone who could mimic Daniela convinced her to move her money."

"Someone who could mimic Daniela." He stared into the distance for a moment. "Let me check with a buddy of mine." He took out his phone, got up, and moved toward the door. "Be right back."

While I waited, I studied the crowd. They were a mixture of young and middle-aged, dressed in casual business attire. Long blonde hair predominated among the women; the men favored shorter cuts and were mostly clean-shaven. From the quality of their clothing—to say nothing of the prices on the drink menu—I assumed they were fairly affluent. They gathered in large booths or at long tables, calling out to friends and newcomers. At a nearby table, I spotted a pair of men, one at either end, holding an enthusiastic conversation with each other via their cell phones.

Mark was back in about five minutes. "Had to go outside; it's hard to make yourself heard in here. I was calling a friend of mine who's a sound engineer with one of the cable companies. He says it's easy to mimic a person's voice if you vary the levels and introduce enough background noise to distract the listener."

"Ana told me the connection was 'spotty'—one of the reasons she actually thought she was talking with Daniela in Paris."

"That could have been done deliberately."

"Did you ever meet Daniela?"

"No. Ana's always been very guarded about her friends."

"Someone also has told me that Ana never saved money."

"That I wouldn't know about. From her clothing, I'd say she spent a lot."

"She furnished my office with copies of statements from the various accounts that were looted."

Mark was looking bored with the conversation. "What I really want to know," he said, "is if there's a chance she'll come back to me. Money doesn't matter; I have plenty of my own."

"Why don't you ask her?" I surveyed the crowded bar, then blinked in surprise.

"How can I do that when she won't see me?"

"Look right over there." I gestured at a space near the hostess stand where Ana had suddenly appeared.

As I rose, Mark turned. When I reached the hostess, Ana had already slipped out the door.

She was nowhere on the street—not that I could have spotted her through the driving rain. I ran around the corner to where I'd parked my car, fumbled with my keys, and slipped inside, squeezing water out of my hair and reaching for a cap I kept in the back carrying space. I was severely pissed off at my client—so angry that normally I would have dumped her case on the spot. But not yet; it had piqued my curiosity, and

I had too many questions to let them go unasked.

From the car I called Derek Ford. Still at the office, the unceasing workaholic. When I asked about the documents Ana had provided us, he said, "Can you come over here? There's something I want to show you."

Traffic from Van Ness to the financial district was slow on a rainy late afternoon. I drummed my fingers on the steering wheel and grumbled. When I was finally seated across the desk in Derek's office, I pulled off my cap and used it to wipe moisture from my face. "So what have you found?" I asked.

He slid a sheaf of papers over to me. "Take a look at the numbers on these accounts," he told me.

They were the account statements showing zero balances that Ana had provided. I scanned them, shook my head. "They look okay to me."

"They're not. An extra zero has been added to each. No such account exists at any of the financial institutions. Someone's faked them to show no balances."

"Ana?"

"Most likely."

"But why?"

"Think, Shar, of what she's gained since she claimed to have been cleaned out."

I considered. "Glenn Solomon plans to pay her rent. Her interior decorator friend sent cash. Her flight attendant friend is offering frequent flyer miles in case she needs to travel to look for a new job. Her pal Janey gave her gifts from the store where she works and also offered her a place to stay. Her old boyfriend is determined to marry her."

"To say nothing of her getting free investigative services from M&R." Dammit, I'd been had. Had like the most gullible victim of a simple scam.

I gritted my teeth, growled something along the lines of wanting to kill her.

Derek tried to hide a smile, but didn't quite succeed. "Don't get murderous," he said. "Get even."

We went to the conference room, met with my operatives Patrick Neilan and Julia Rafael, as well as my nephew Mick Savage, Hy, and a couple of operatives from his side of the business. Officer manager Ted Smalley obliged with a couple of pots of coffee. He also sat in and contributed avidly as we began to plan what we called Scamming the Scammer.

Ana called around noon the next day. "Sharon, I think I may have a line on the scammer"

"You *do?*" My surprised tone was disingenuous, given what I now knew.

"Yes. A man phoned this morning and claimed he knows who the woman is. He wants money before he'll tell me anymore."

"How much money?"

"He wouldn't say."

"Who is he?"

"He wouldn't tell me that either. He wanted to arrange a meeting."

"Where? When?"

"You know the Grove?"

It was a parklet near our building. An appropriate place, since the rain had yielded to a brilliantly clear day.

"Yes, I do."

"He'll be there at four-thirty. Can you come too?"

"Yes, but I may be a little late. Don't let that bother you, though; it's a perfectly safe location."

"I won't agree to anything till you get there."

You bet she wouldn't.

Our office manager, Ted Smalley, had volunteered to play the role of blackmailer and made the call to Ana last night. He'd really gotten into it, so much so that I'd had to ask him to tone down his villainous pose. A wiry, goateed man with streaks of silver in his dark hair, for years he'd indulged in periodic changes of costume: grunge, Edwardian, hip-hop, Botany 500, Hawaiian, caftans. You name it, he'd tried them all. Fortunately, under the influence of his husband, antiquarian book dealer Neal Osborne, he'd settled on more normal attire, although today, I'd had to restrain him from trading his coat for a cape worthy of Jack the Ripper.

I watched from the corner of our building as Ted crossed the parklet. Awnings had been let down over the little tables scattered there, and he approached the one where a slumped figure sat. Ana. From her posture, I assumed she wasn't taking the news of her "recovered money" well.

Ted's voice came over the open line between our cell phones. "Ms. Emery?"

"Yes."

"Ted Smalley. May I sit down?"

"If you wish."

Scraping of a chair as he sat.

"I understand you've been the victim of a crypto currency scheme."

"—One that you perpetrated."

"I'll neither confirm nor deny that."

"So what do you want?"

"To return your finds to you—for a percentage, of course."

"How much percentage?"

"Fifty."

She was silent.

I crossed the street, entered the parklet.

Ted went on, "I have here the most recent statements from your bank and brokerage accounts. Would you care to look at them?"

Grudgingly: "All right."

Rustle of papers.

"These aren't mine."

"It's your name on them."

"But they show the full balances that were scammed! They must be outdated."

"Look at the date—it's yesterday's." Yesterday's, when Derek had created them using actual statements as templates.

"But I gave my investigator the most recent statements."

"The most recently *doctored* statements."

"What does that mean? I don't know what you're talking about!"

More rustling of paper.

Ted said, "Look at the numbers on the statements you gave, er, your investigator."

Silence. Then: "Oh. There's an extra zero."

"Meaning the documents were faked."

"But who would do such a thing?"

I stepped up to the table. "Who, Ana? You."

She twisted in her chair, eyes wide with shock. "It's about time you got here. Who is this Ted Smalley person anyway?"

"A member of my staff. He volunteered to pose as a scammer."

"Why? And what's this about me faking those documents? Why would I?"

"To prove you'd been a victim of a scam."

"But why?"

"Because of the things you collected or are about to collect from people who care about you. Rent subsidies, cash, gifts, frequent flyer miles. And I've wasted a hell of a lot of my valuable time chasing around on your so-called case.

She pushed her chair back.

"Stay right where you are," I said. "There's no use rushing out and cashing in your accounts. I've already contacted the district attorney and he's put a hold on the funds."

She sank back, shaking her head. "I don't see why what I did was a crime. It was a game, that's all. Just a game."

"My agency has been playing a game, too. It's called Scamming the Scammer."

THE McCONE FILES

Part 1 — The First

The big Victorian slumped between its neighbors on a steeply sloping sidestreet in San Francisco's Bernal Heights district: tall, shabby, and strangely welcoming in spite of its sagging roofline and blistered chocolate paint. I got out of my battered red MG and studied the house for a moment, then cut across the weedy triangular park that bisected Coso Street and climbed the front steps. A line of pigeons roosted on the peak above the door; I glanced warily at them before slipping under and obeying a hand-lettered sign that told me to "Walk Right In!"

It seemed an unnecessary risk to leave one's door open in this low-rent area, but when I entered I came face-to-face with a man sitting at a desk. He had fine features and a goatee, and was dressed in the flannel-shirt-and-Levi's uniform of the predominantly gay Castro district; although his dark eyes were mild and friendly, he was scrutinizing me very carefully. I presented my business card—one of the thousand I'd had printed on credit at my friends Daphne's and Charlie's shop—and his expression became less guarded. "You're Sharon McCone, Hank's detective friend!" he exclaimed.

I nodded, although I didn't feel much like a detective any more. For the past few years I'd worked under the license of one of the city's large investigative firms; the day I'd received my own ticket from the state department of consumer affairs, my boss had fired me for insubordination. At first I'd seen it as an opportunity to strike out on my own, but operating out of my studio apartment on Guerrero Street was far from an ideal situation; jobs were few, I was about to run out of cards, and my rent was due next Thursday. Yesterday I'd run into Hank Zahn, a former housemate from my college days at U. C. Berkeley. He'd asked me to stop by his law firm for a talk.

I'd hoped the talk would be about a job, but from the looks of this place I doubted it.

The man at the desk seemed to be waiting for more of a response. Inanely I said, "Yes," to reinforce the nod.

He got up and stuck out his hand. "Ted Smalley—secretary, janitor, and—occasionally—court jester. Welcome to All Souls Legal Cooperative."

I clasped his slender fingers, liking his smile.

"Hank's in conference with a client right now," Ted went on. "Why don't you make yourself comfortable in the parlor." He motioned to his right, at a big blue room with a fireplace and a butt-sprung maroon sofa and chair. "I'll tell him you're here."

I went in there, noting an old-fashioned upright piano and a profusion of books and games on the coffee table. A tall schefflera grew in the window bay; its pot was a pink toilet. I sat on the couch and immediately a coil of spring prodded my rump. Moving over, I glared at where it pushed through the upholstery.

Make myself comfortable, indeed!

Ted Smalley had disappeared down the long central hall off the foyer. I looked around some more, wondering what the hell Hank was doing in such a place.

Hank Zahn was a Stanford grad and had been at the top of his law school class at Berkeley's Boalt Hall. When I'd last seen him he was packing his belongings prior to turning over his room in the brown-shingled house we'd shared on Durant Street to yet another of an ongoing chain of tenants that stretched back into the early sixties and for all I knew continued unbroken to this very day. At the time he was being courted by several prestigious law firms, and he'd joked that the salaries and benefits they offered were enough to make him sell out to the establishment. But Hank was a self-styled leftist and social reformer, a Vietnam vet weaned from the military on Berkeley's radical politics; selling out wasn't within his realm of possibility. I could envision him as a public defender or an ACLU lawyer or a loner in private practice, but what was this cooperative business?

As I waited in the parlor, though, I had to admit the place had the same feel as the house we'd shared in Berkeley: laid-back and homey, brimming with companionship, humming with energy and purpose. Several people came and went, nodding pleasantly to me but appearing focused and intense. I'd come away from the Berkeley house craving solitude as strongly as when I'd left my parents' rambling, sibling-crowded place in San Diego. Not so with Hank, apparently.

Voices in the hallway now. Hank's and Ted Smalley's. Hank hurried into the parlor, holding out his hands to me. A tall, lean man, so loose-jointed that his limbs seemed linked by paperclips, he had a wiry Brillo pad of brown hair and thick horn-rimmed glasses that magnified the intelligence in his eyes; in the type of cords and sweaters that he'd always favored he looked more the college teaching assistant than the attorney. He clasped my hands, pulled me to my feet and hugged me. "I see you've already done battle with the couch," he said, gesturing at the protruding spring.

"Where did you get that thing—the city dump?"

"Actually, somebody left it and the matching chair and hassock on the sidewalk on Sixteenth Street. I recognized a bargain and recycled them."

"And the piano?"

"Ted's find. Garage sale. The same with the schefflera."

"Well, you guys are nothing if not resourceful. You want to tell me about this place?"

"In a minute." He steered me to the hallway. "Wait till you see the kitchen."

It was at the rear of the house: a huge room equipped with ancient appliances and glass-fronted cupboards; dishes cluttered the drainboard of the sink, a stick of butter melted on its wrapper on the counter, and a long red phone cord snaked across the floor and disappeared under a round oak table by a window that gave a panoramic view of downtown. A book titled *White Trash Cooking* lay broken-spined on a chair. Hank motioned for me to sit, fetched coffee, and pulled up a chair opposite me.

"Great, isn't it?" he said.

"Sure."

"You're probably wondering what's going on here."

I nodded.

"All Souls Law Cooperative works like a medical plan. People who can't afford the bloated fees many of my colleagues charge buy a membership, its cost based on a scale according to their incomes. The membership gives them access to consul and legal services all the way from small claims to the U. S. Supreme Court. Legal services plans're the coming thing, an outgrowth of the poverty law movement."

"How many people're involved?"

"Seventeen, right now."

"You making any money?"

"Does it look like we are? No. But we sure are having fun. Most of us live on the premises—offices double as sleeping quarters, and there're some bedrooms on the second floor—and that offsets the paltry salaries. We pool expenses, barter services such as cooking and taking out the trash. There're parties and potlucks and poker games. Right now a Monopoly tournament's the big thing."

"Just like on Durant."

"Uh-huh. You remember Anne-Marie Altman?"

"Of course." She'd been an off-and-on resident at Durant, and a classmate of Hank's.

"Well, she's our tax attorney, and one of the people who helped me found the co-op."

"Why, Hank?"

"Why a co-op? Because it's the most concrete way I can make a difference in a world that doesn't give a rat's ass about the little people. I learned at Berkeley that bombs and bricks aren't going to do a damned thing for society; maybe practicing law the way it was meant to be practiced will."

He looked idealistic and earnest and—in spite of the years he had on me—very young. I said, "I hope so, Hank."

He must have sensed my doubt and felt a twinge of his own, because for a moment his gaze muddied. Then he said briskly, "So, how's business?"

I made a rueful face, glancing down at my ratty sweater and faded jeans. The heels on my leather boots were worn down, and the last time it rained, water leaked through the right sole. "Bad," I admitted.

"Thinking of looking for permanent employment?"

"With my references?" I snorted. "'Doesn't take direction well, nonresponsive to authority figures, inflexible and overly independent. Can be pushy, severe, and dominant.' That was my last review before the agency canned me. Forget it."

"Jesus, that could describe any one of us at All Souls."

"Maybe it's a generational flaw."

"Maybe, but it's us. You want a job here?"

"Do I want ... *what?*"

"We're looking for a staff investigator."

"Since when?"

He grinned. "Since yesterday when I ran into you in front of City Hall and started thinking about all the nonlegal work we've been heaping on our paralegals."

"Such as?"

"Nothing all that exciting, I'm afraid. Filing documents; tracking down witnesses; interviewing same; locating people and serving subpoenas. Pretty dull work, when you get right down to it, but the after-hours company is good. We're all easygoing; we'd leave you alone to do your work in your own way."

"Salary?"

"Low. Benefits, practically nil."

"I couldn't live in; I've kind of o.d.'d on the communal stuff."

"We couldn't accommodate you, anyway. The only available space is a converted closet under the stairs—which, incidentally, would be your office. I might be able to raise the salary a little to help with your rent."

"What about expenses? My car—"

"Is a hunk of junk. But we'll pay mileage. Besides ..." he paused, eyes dancing wickedly. "I can offer you a first case that'll intrigue the hell out of you."

A steady job, bosses who would leave me alone, a first case that would intrigue the hell out of me. What more was I looking for?

"You've got yourself an investigator," I told him.

Hank's client, Marnie Morrison, was one of those soft, round young women who always remind me of puppy dogs—clingy and smiley and eager to please. A thinly veiled anxiety in her big blue eyes and the way most of her statements turned up as if she were asking a question told me that the puppy had been mistreated and wasn't too sure she wouldn't be mistreated again. She sat across from me at the round table and related her story—crossing and recrossing her bluejeaned legs, twisting a curl of fluffy blond hair around her finger, glancing up at Hank for approval. Her mannerisms were so distracting that it took me a few minutes to realize I'd read about her in the paper.

"His name, it was Jon Howard. I met him on the sorority ski trip to Mammouth over spring break. In the bar at the lodge where we were staying? He was there by himself and he looked nice and my roommate Terry, she kind of pushed me into going over and talking. He was kind of sweet? So we had some drinks and made a date to ski together the next day and after that we were together all the time."

"Jon was staying at the lodge?"

"No, this motel down the road. I thought it was kind of funny, since he told me he was a financier and sole owner of this company with holdings all over Europe and South America. I mean, the motel was cheap? But he said it was quieter there and he didn't like big crowds of people, he was a very private person. We spent a lot of time there because I was rooming with Terry at the lodge, and we did things like get take-out and drink wine?" Mamie glanced at Hank. He nodded encouragingly.

"Anyway, we fell in love. And I decided not to go back to USC after break. We came to San Francisco because it's our favorite city. And Jon was finalizing a big business deal, and after that we were going to get married." The hurt-puppy look became more pronounced. "Of course, we didn't."

"Back up a minute, if you would." I said. "What did you and Jon talk about while ... you were falling in love?"

"Our childhoods? Mine was good—I mean, my parents are nice and we've always had enough money. But Jon's? It was awful. They were poor and he always had to work and he never finished high school. But he was self-taught and he'd built this company with all these holdings up from nothing."

"What kind of company?"

Frown lines appeared between her eyebrows. "Well, a financial company, you know? It owned ... well, all kinds of stuff overseas."

"Okay," I said, "you arrived here in the city when?"

"Two months ago."

"And did what?"

"Checked into the St. Francis. We registered under my last name—Mr. and Mrs. Jon Morrison?"

"Why?"

"Because of Jon's business deal. He'd made some enemies, and he was afraid they'd get to him before he could wrap it up. Besides, the credit card we were using was in my name." Her mouth drooped. "The American Express card my father gave me when I went to college. I ... guess that was the real reason?"

"So you registered at the St. Francis and ...?"

"Jon was on the phone a lot on account of his business deal? I got my hair done and shopped. Then he hired a limo and a driver and we started looking at houses. As soon as the deal was finalized and his money was wire-transferred from Europe we were going to buy one. We found the perfect place on Vallejo Street in Pacific Heights, only it needed a lot of remodeling, we wanted to put in an indoor pool and a tennis court? So Jon wrote a postdated deposit check and hired a contractor and a decorator and then we went shopping for artwork because Jon said it was a good investment. We bought some nice paintings at a gallery on Sutter Street and they were holding them for us until the check cleared."

"What then?"

"There were the cars? We ordered a Mercedes for me and a Porsche for Jon. And we looked at yachts and airplanes, but he decided we'd better wait on those."

"And Jon wrote postdated checks for the cars?"

Marnie nodded.

"And the rest went on your American Express card?"

"Uh-huh."

"How much did you charge?"

She bit her lip and glanced at Hank. "The hotel bill was ten thousand dollars. The limo and the driver were over five. And there was a lot of other stuff? A lot." She looked down at her hands.

I met Hank's eyes. He shrugged, as if to say, "I told you she was naive."

"What did your parents have to say about the credit-card charges?" I asked.

"They paid them, at least that's what the police said. Or else I'd be in jail now?"

"Have you spoken with your parents?"

She whispered something, still looking down.

"I'm sorry, I didn't catch that."

"I said, I can't face them."

"And what about Jon?" I recalled the conclusion of Marnie's tale from the newspaper account I'd read, but I wanted to hear her version.

"A week ago? They came to our hotel room—the real-estate agent and the decorator and the salesman from the gallery. The checks Jon wrote? They'd all bounced, and they wanted him to make good on them. Only Jon wasn't there. I thought he'd gone downstairs for breakfast while I was in the shower, but he wasn't anyplace in the hotel, he'd packed his things and gone. All that was left was a pink carnation on my pillow."

It was difficult to feel sorry for her; she had, after all, refused to recognize the blatant signs of a con job. But when she raised her head and I saw the tears slipping over her round cheeks, I could feel her pain. "So what do you want me to do, Marnie?"

"Find him."

"Aren't the police trying to do that?"

She shook her head. "Since the checks were postdated they were only like ... promises to pay? The police say it's a civil matter, and all but one of the people Jon wrote them to have decided not to press charges. The decorator had already spent a lot of money out of pocket ordering fabric and stuff, so she hired a detective to trace Jon, but he's disappeared."

I thought for a moment. "Okay, Marnie, suppose I do locate Jon Howard. What then?"

"I'll go to him and get the money to pay my parents back. Then I can face them again."

"It doesn't sound as if he has any money."

"He must." To my astonished look she added, "All of this has been a terrible mistake. Maybe he ran away because his business rivals were after him? Maybe the big deal he was working on fell through and he was ashamed to tell me? When you find him, he'll explain everything."

"You sound as though you still believe in him."

"I do. I always will. I love him."

"She's got to be insane!" I said to Hank. Marnie Morrison had just left for the cheap residential hotel that was all she could afford on her temporary office worker's wages.

"No, she's naive and doesn't want to believe the great love of her life was a con artist. I figure meeting up with Jon Howard in his true incarnation'll cure her of that."

"Then you actually want me to find him?"

"Yeah. I'd like to get a look at him, find out what makes a guy like that tick."

As a matter of fact, so would I.

The recession-hungry merchants who had been taken in by the supposedly rich young couple were now engaged in various forms of facesaving.

Dealer Henry Richards of the Avant Gallery on Sutter Street: "Mr. Morrison was *very* knowledgeable about art. He asked all the right questions. He knew which paintings would appreciate and which would not. Had he followed through on the purchases, he would have had the beginnings of a top flight collection. He may not have been rich, but I could tell he was well educated, and there's no concealing good breeding."

Realtor Deborah Lakein of Bay Properties: "From the moment I set eyes on the Morrisons I knew something was wrong. At first I thought it was simply the silk-purse-out-of-sow's-ear effect: too much money, too little breeding. But they seemed serious and were very enthusiastic about the property—it's a gem, asking price one million three. In this market one doesn't pass up the opportunity to make such a sale. Of course his deposit check was postdated like the others he wrote all over town, and when I finally put it through it was returned for nonsufficient funds. The same was true of the checks to the contractor, decorator, and landscaper I recommended. Oh, I'm in hot water with them, I am!"

Salesman Donald Neditch of European Motors on Van Ness Avenue's auto row: "Well, our customers come in all varieties, if you know what I mean. You don't have to be a blueblood to drive one of these babies. All you need is the cash or the credit. The two of them were well dressed—casually but expensively—and they arrived in a limo. I could tell they hadn't had money for very long, though. He asked a lot of questions, but they were the kind you'd ask if you were buying a preowned model. About used cars, he was knowledgeable enough to sell them, but I'd bet the Mercedes for his wife was the first new car he ever looked at."

Claire Walks, clerk in the billing office at the St. Francis Hotel: "No one questioned their charges because American Express was honoring them. There was a lot of room service, a lot of champagne and fine wines. Fresh flowers every day for the three weeks they stayed here. Generous tips added to each check, too. The personnel who had dealings with them tell me she was young and sweet; he was more rough at the edges, as you'd expect a self-made man to be, but very polite. Security had no complaints about loud partying, so I assume they were as well behaved in private as in public."

Wallis referred me to an inspector in the Fraud Division of the SFPD, who had taken a list of calls made from the "Morrisons's" suite and checked it out before it became apparent that no criminal statutes had been violated. The copy of the list the inspector provided me showed that Jon Howard had called car dealerships from San Rafael to Walnut Creek, a yacht broker in Sausalito, aircraft dealers near SFO and Oakland Airport. The numbers for the real-estate agency and art gallery appeared frequently, as did those of the contractor, decorator, and landscaper. Restaurants, theater-ticket agencies, beauty shops, and a tanning salon figured prominently. There were no calls to Marnie Morrison's parents, or to anyone who might have been a personal friend.

By now I realized that Jon Howard had covered his tracks very well. I had no photograph of him, no descriptions beyond the one Marnie provided—and that was highly romanticized at best. I didn't even know if he had used his real name. I made my way down to the list of places he'd called, though, visiting the yacht broker ("He didn't know shit about boats."), the aircraft sales agencies ("I told him he'd better take flying lessons first, but he just laughed and said he had a pilot on call."), and all the auto dealerships—including Ben Rudolph's Chevrolet in Walnut Creek, where Howard had called nearly every day, but no one had any recollection of either him or Marnie. Finally I reached Lou Petrocelli, driver for Golden West Limousine Service.

"Sure, I got to know him pretty well, driving him around for almost three weeks," Petrocelli told me. "He was ... well, down-home, like a lot of the rock stars I've driven. When she came along he'd get in back with her and they'd hit the bar, watch some TV. When he was alone he'd hop up front and talk my ear off. Money, it was always money. Was this house in Pacific Heights a good investment? Did I think they oughta buy a van for the help to use for running errands? Which restaurants did the 'in' people eat at? Should he get season tickets for the opera? I thought it was funny, a guy who was supposed to be so rich and smart asking *me* for advice. He struck me as very insecure. But hell, I liked the guy. He was kind of wide-eyed and innocent in his way, and American Express was honoring the charges."

I asked Petrocelli to look over the list of establishments to which Howard had made phone calls. He confirmed he'd driven the couple to most of them, with the exception of the yacht brokers and the car dealership in Walnut Creek. They had traveled as far afield as the Napa Valley for wine tasting, and Marnie had insisted he share their hotel-catered picnic lunch. No, they'd never met with friends; Petrocelli didn't think they'd known anyone in the city except the merchants with whom they had dealings.

Around the time I reached the bottom of the list other cases began to claim my attention. I'd been ensconced long enough in the cubbyhole under the stairs that All Souls's attorneys believed I was there to stay and began heaping my desk with tasks. They ranged from filing documents with the recorder's office to serving subpoenas to interviewing a member of the San Francisco Mime Troupe about an accident he'd witnessed—no simple matter, since his replies to my questions were in pantomime. I made some effort on the Morrison case when I could, but Marnie had stopped calling to ask for reports. The last time I spoke with her she sounded so demoralized that three days later I stopped in at her hotel to see how she was doing; her room was empty, and the manager told me she'd checked out. Checked out in the company of a handsome young man driving an old Honda.

Jon Howard?

When I reported this latest development to Hank, he didn't seem surprised. "I had a call earlier," he said. "Some guy looking for Marnie. I was with a client, so Ted gave him her number."

"Then it probably was Howard. But how'd he know to call you?"

Hank shrugged. "You've been asking around about him, leaving your card. He could have talked to the limo driver, the real-estate broker—anybody."

"And of course she went away with him."

"She said she still loved him."

"I wonder if he plans to pull the same scam in some other city."

"Doubtful; he doesn't have her American Express card to bankroll it."

"What d'you suppose will happen to her?"

Hank shook his head. "Let's hope her dreams come true—whatever they might be."

A year later I added a follow-up note to the Marnie Morrison file: her parents, whom Hank had contacted following her disappearance, reported that they'd begun receiving periodic money orders for a hundred dollars apiece, mailed from various Bay Area cities. They were convinced they came from Marnie, in repayment of the credit-card charges. Since they'd long before paid the bill, they wanted to give Hank a message to pass on to their daughter, should she contact him.

The message was that they loved her, she was forgiven and always welcome at home. Hank was never able to tell her.

A couple of years after that I appended a newspaper clipping to the file: the Morrisons had been killed in a fire that swept the southern California canyon where their home was located. The article rehashed the bizarre scam their daughter and her boyfriend had perpetrated and mentioned the money orders. A further footnote to the story ran a while later: the money orders were now arriving at the office of the executor of the Morrisons's estate, earmarked "for my parents' favorite charity."

When I saw this last item, I was intrigued and wished I could take the time to locate Marnie. But in those early days at All Souls my caseload was heavy and soon I was caught up in other equally intriguing matters. The Morrison case still nagged at me, though; it was my first—and last—open file.

Part 2 — The Last

The movers had come for my office furniture. All that remained was for me to haul a few cartons to McCone Investigations' nearly new van. I hefted one and carried it down to the foyer of All Souls's big Victorian, then made three round trips for the others. Before I went downstairs for the last time I let my gaze wander around the front room that for years had been my home away from home. Empty, it looked battle-scarred and shabby: the wallpaper was peeling; the ceiling paint had blistered; the hardwood floors were scraped; there were gouges in the mantel of the nonworking fireplace.

A far cry from the new offices on the waterfront, I thought, but still I'd miss this room. Would miss sitting in my swivel chair in the window bay and contemplating the sagging rooflines of the Outer Mission district or the weedy triangular park below. Would miss pacing the faded Oriental carpet while talking on the phone. But most of all I would miss the familiar day-to-day sounds of the co-op that had assured me that I was among friends.

Only in the end friends here had been damned few. Now none were left. Time to say goodbye. Time to move on to McCone Investigations' new offices on one of the piers off the Embarcadero, next to the equally new offices of Altman & Zahn, Attorneys-at-Law.

I took the last carton downstairs.

Ted's old desk still stood in the foyer, but without his personal possessions—particularly the coffee mug shaped like Gertrude Stein's head and the campy lamp fashioned from a mesh-stockinged mannequin's legit was a slate wiped clean of the years he had presided there. Already he'd be arranging those treasures down at the pier. I set the box with the others and, both out of curiosity and nostalgia, went along the hall to the converted closet under the stairs that had been my first office.

Rae Kelleher, its recent occupant, had already taken her belongings to McCone Investigations. With relief I saw she'd left the ratty old armchair. For a moment I stood in the door looking at each familiar crack in the walls; then I stepped inside and ran my hand over the chair's back where stuffing sprouted. How many hours had I sat there, honing my fledgling investigator's skills?

A cardboard box tucked under the angle of the staircase caught my eye. I peered at it, wondering why Rae had left it behind, and saw lettering in her hand: "McCone Files." Early ones, they must be. I'd probably neglected to remove them from the cabinet when I transferred my things upstairs. I pulled the box toward me, sat down in the armchair, and lifted the lid. A dry, dusty odor wafted up. On the files' tabs I saw names: Albritton, DiCesare, Kaufmann, Morrison, Smith, Snelling, Whelan, and many more. Some I recognized immediately, others were only vaguely familiar, and about the rest I hadn't a clue. I scanned them, remembering—

Morrison! That damned case! It was the only file I hadn't been able to close in all my years at All Souls.

I pulled it from the box and flipped through. Interesting case. Marnie Morrison, the naive young woman with Daddy's American Express card. Jon Howard, the "financier" who had used her to help him scam half the merchants in San Francisco. And Hank in turn had used the case's promise to lure me into taking the job here.

But I hadn't been able to solve it.

Could I solve it now?

Well, maybe. I was a far better investigator than when I'd operated out of this tiny office. The hundreds of hours spent honing my skills had paid off; so had my life experiences, good and bad. I picked up on facts that I might not have noticed back then, could interpret them more easily, had learned to trust my gut-level instincts, no matter how farfetched they might seem.

I turned my attention to the file.

Well, there was one thing right off—the daily phone calls Jon Howard had made to the car dealership in Walnut Creek. When I'd driven out there and talked with its manager, neither he nor his salesmen could remember the memorable young couple.

I took a pen from my purse, made a note of the dealership's name, address, and phone number, then read on.

And there was something else—the conversation I'd had with the salesman at European Motors here in the city. My recent experience with buying a "pre-owned" van for the agency put a new light on his comments.

My office phone had been disconnected the day before, and the remaining partners would frown on me placing toll calls on All Souls's line. Quickly I hauled the file box out to where my other cartons sat, threw on my jacket, and headed downhill to the Remedy Lounge on Mission Street.

The Remedy had long been a favorite watering hole for the old-timers at All Souls. Brian, the owner, extended us all sorts of courtesies—

excluding table service for anyone but Rae, who reminded him of his dead sister, and including running tabs and letting us use his office phone. When I got there the place was empty and the big Irishman was watching his favorite soap opera on the TV mounted above the bar.

"Sure," he said in answer to my request, "use the phone all you want. Yours is turned off already?"

"Right. It's moving day."

Brian's fleshy face grew melancholy. He picked up a rag and began wiping down the already polished surface of the bar. "Guess I won't be seeing much of you guys any more."

"Why not? The bar's on a direct line between the new offices and the Safeway where we all shop."

He shrugged. "People always say stuff like that, but in the end they drift away."

"We'll prove you wrong," I told him, even though I suspected he was right.

"We'll see." He pressed the button that unlocked the door to his office.

At his desk I opened my notebook and dialed the number of Ben Rudolph Chevrolet in Walnut Creek. I reached their used-car department. The salesman's answer to my first question confirmed what I already suspected. His supervisor, who had worked there since the late seventies, was out to lunch, he told me, but would be back around two.

Five minutes later I was in the van and on my way to the East Bay.

Walnut Creek is a suburb of San Francisco, but a city in its own right, sprawling in a broad valley in the shadow of Mount Diablo. When I'd traveled there on the Morrison case more than a decade earlier, it still had a small-town flavor: few trendy shops and restaurants in the downtown district; only one office building over two stories; tracts and shopping centers, yes, but also semi-rural neighborhoods where the residents still kept horses and chickens. Now it was a hub of commerce, with tall buildings whose tinted and smoked glass glowed in the afternoon sun. There was a new cultural center, a restaurant on nearly every corner, and the tracts went on forever.

Ben Rudolph Chevrolet occupied the same location on North Main Street, although its neighbors squeezed more tightly against it. As I parked in the customer lot I wondered why years ago I had neglected to call the phone number the SFPD had supplied me. If I'd phoned ahead rather than just driven out here, I'd have discovered that the dealership maintained separate lines for its new- and used-car departments. And I'd have known that Jon Howard's daily calls weren't made because he was hot on the trail of a snappy new Corvette.

I went directly to the manager of the used-car department, a ruddyfaced, prosperous-looking man named Dave Swenson. Yes, he confirmed, he'd worked there since seventy-eight. "Only way to survive in this business is you stick with one dealership, dig in, create your own clientele."

"I'm looking for someone who might've been a salesman here in the late seventies and early eighties." I showed him my I. D. "Handsome man, dark hair and mustache, late twenties. Good build. Below average height. His name may have been Jon Howard."

"No, it wasn't."

"I'm sorry?"

"I know the fella you're talking about, but you got it backwards. His name was Howard John."

Howard John—simple transposition. The salesman at European Motors had told me he knew enough about used cars to sell them, and he'd been correct. "John's not working here any more?"

"Hell, no. He was fired over a dozen years ago. I don't recall exactly when." Swenson tapped his temple. "Sorry, the old memory's going."

"But you remembered him right off."

"Well, he was that kind of guy. A real screw-up, always talking big and never doing anything about it, but you couldn't help liking him."

"Talking big, how?"

"Ah, the usual. He was studying nights, gonna get his MBA, set up some financial company, be somebody. He'd have a big house in the city, a limo, boats and planes, hobnob with all the right people—you know. All smoke and no fire, Howie was, but you had to hand it to him, he could be an entertaining fellow."

"And then he was fired."

Yeah. It was stupid, it didn't have to happen. The guy was producing; he made sales when nobody else could. What Howie did, he took a vacation to Mammouth to ski. When his week was up, he started calling in, saying he was sick with some bug he caught down there. This went on for weeks, and the boss got suspicious, so he checked out Howie's apartment. The manager said he hadn't been back since he drove off with his ski gear the month before. So a few days after that when Howie strolled in here all innocent and business-as-usual, the boss had no choice but to can him."

"What happened to him? Do you know where he's working now?"

Swenson stared thoughtfully at me. "You know, I meant it when I said I liked the guy."

"I don't mean him any harm, Mr. Swenson."

"No?" He waited.

Quickly I considered several stories, rejected all of them, and told

Swenson the truth. He reacted with glee, laughing loudly and slapping his hand on his desk. "Good for Howie! At least he got a few weeks of the good life before everything went down the sewer."

"So will you tell me where I can find him?"

"I still don't know why you want him."

I hesitated, unsure myself as to why I did. No one was looking for Howard John any more, and the organization that had assigned me to find him had ceased to exist. Finally I said, "When you have a sale pending that you think is a sure thing and then it falls through, does it nag at you afterwards?"

"Sure, for years, sometimes. I wonder what I did wrong, why it didn't fly."

"I'm the same way about my cases. This is my last open file from the law firm where I used to work. Closing it will tie off some loose ends."

"Well ..." Swenson considered some more. "Okay. I don't know if Howie's still there, but I saw him working another lot about three months ago—Roy's Motors, up in Concord."

Concord was a city to the north. I thanked Swenson and hurried out to the van.

Concord, like Walnut Creek, had developed into a metropolis since I once worked a case at its performing arts pavilion, but the windswept frontage road where Roy's Motors was located was a throwback to the early sixties. An aging shopping center with a geodesic dome-type cinema and dozens of mostly dead stores adjoined the used-car lot; both were almost devoid of customers. Faded plastic flags fluttered limply above Roy's stock, which consisted mainly of vehicles that looked as though they'd welcome a trip to the auto dismantler's; a sign proclaiming it HOME OF THE BEST DEALS IN TOWN creaked disconsolately. I could make out the figure of a man sitting inside the small sales shack, but his features were obscured by the dirty window glass.

A young couple were wandering through the lot, stopping here and there to examine pick-up trucks. After a few minutes they displayed more than passing interest in a canary-yellow Ford, and the man got up and came out of the shack. He was on the short side and running to paunch, with thinning dark hair, a brushy mustache, and a face that once had been handsome. Howard John?

As he approached the couple, the salesman held himself more erect and sucked in his stomach; his step took on a jaunty rhythm and a charismatic smile lit up his face. He shook hands with the couple, began expounding on the truck. He laughed; they laughed. He helped the woman into the cab, urged the man in on the driver's side. The chemistry was working, the magic flowing. This, I was sure, was the man who years before had scammed the greedy merchants of San Francisco.

A few short weeks of living like the high rollers, I thought, then dismissal from a good job and a series of steps down to this. How did he go on, with the memory of those weeks ever in the back of his mind? How did he come to this windswept lot every day and put himself through the paces?

Well, maybe his dreams—improbable as they might seem—had survived intact. He'd done it once, his reasoning might go, and he could do it again. Maybe Howard John still believed that he was only occupying a waystation on the road to the top.

But what about Marnie Morrison?

I found Howard John's residence by a method whose simplicity and effectiveness have never ceased to amaze me: a look-see into the phone book. The listing was in two names, and the wife's was Marnie.

The shabby residential street was not far from the used-car lot: a two-block row of identical shoebox-style tract homes of the same vintage as the shopping center. The pavement was potholed and the houses on the west side backed up on a concrete viaduct, but big poplars arched over the street and, in spite of the hum of nearby freeway traffic, it had an aura of tranquility. The house I was looking for was painted mint green and surrounded by a low chain link fence. A sign on its gate said SUNNYSIDE DAYCARE CENTER, and in the yard beyond it sat an assortment of brightly colored playground equipment.

It was close to five o'clock; for the next hour I watched a steady stream of parents arrive and depart with their offspring. Ten minutes after the last had left a woman came out of the house and began collecting the playthings strewn in the yard. I peered through my shade-dappled windshield and recognized an older, heavier version of Marnie Morrison. Clad in an oversized sweatshirt and leggings that strained over her ample thighs, she moved slowly, stopping now and then to wipe sweat from her brow. When she finished she trudged inside.

So this was what Marnie had become since I'd last seen her: the overworked, prematurely aged wife of an unsuccessful used-car salesman, who operated a daycare center to make ends meet. And one of those ends was her periodic hundred-dollar atonement to her parents' favorite charity for the credit-card binge that had bought her a few weeks of high living and dreams.

Unsure as to why I was doing it, I continued to watch the mint green house. I'd found Marnie. Why didn't I give up and go back to the city? There were things I should be doing at the new offices, things I should be doing at home.

But I wanted an end to the story, so I stayed where I was.

Half an hour later a Ford Bronco passed me and pulled into the Johns's driveway. Howard got out carrying a bouquet of pink carnations. He let himself into the yard, stopping to pick up a stuffed bear that Marnie had missed. He held the bear at arm's length, gave it a jaunty grin, and tucked it under his arm. His step was light as he moved toward the door. Before he got it open his wife appeared, now dressed in a gauzy caftan, and enveloped him in a welcoming embrace.

I'd reached the end of the tale. Leaving Marnie and Howard to their surviving dreams and illusions, I drove back to All Souls for the last time.

The big Victorian was mostly dark and totally silent. Only the porchlight and another far back in the kitchen shone. It was about eight o'clock; none of the remaining partners lived in the building, and they rarely spent more time there than was necessary. The new corporation they'd formed had the property up for sale and would move downtown as soon as a buyer was found.

Moving on, all of us.

I was about to haul the cartons I'd left in the foyer down to the van when I heard a sound in the kitchen—the familiar creak of the refrigerator door. Curiosity aroused, I went back there, walking softly. The room was dim, the light coming from a single bulb in the sconce over the sink. A figure turned from the fridge, glass of wine in hand. Hank.

He started, nearly dropping the glass. "Jesus, Shar!"

"Sorry. I'm not up to talking to any of the new guard tonight, so I tiptoed. Why aren't you down at the pier helping everybody shove the new furniture around?"

"I was, but nobody could make up their mind where it should go, and I foresaw a long and unpleasant relationship with a chiropractor."

"So you came *here?*"

He shrugged. "Why not? You want some wine?"

"Sure. For old times' sake."

Hank went to the fridge and poured the last of the so-so jug variety that had been an All Souls staple. He handed it to me and motioned for me to sit at the round table by the window. As we took our places I realized that they were identical to those we'd occupied the first afternoon I'd come here.

I said, "You still haven't told me why you're here."

"You haven't told me why *you're* here."

"I meant to be gone hours ago, but wait till you hear my news!" I explained about closing the Morrison file.

He shook his head. "You *do* believe in tying up loose ends. So what about those two—do you think they're happy?"

I hesitated. "What's happy? It's all relative. The guy still brings her flowers. She still dresses up for him. Maybe that's enough."

"But after the scams they pulled, the style they lived?"

"It only lasted a few weeks. Maybe that was enough, too."

"Maybe." He took a long pull at his wine, took a longer look around the kitchen. His expression grew melancholy. This room and this table had been a big part of Hank's life since leaving law school.

"Don't," I said, "or you'll get me going."

His eyes moved to the window, scanning the lights of downtown. After a moment they stopped and his lips curved into a smile. I knew he was looking at the section of waterfront where the law firm of Altman & Zahn had recently rented offices next to McCone Investigations on a renovated pier.

"File closed," he said.

We finished our wine in silence. Around us the big house creaked and groaned, as it did every evening when the day's warmth faded. I felt my eyes sting, blinked hard. Only an incurable romantic would find significance in tonight's particular creaks and groans. And I, of course, had not a romantic bone in my body.

So why had that last creak sounded like "goodbye"?

Hank drained his glass and stood. Carried both to the sink, where he rinsed them carefully and set them on the drainboard. "In answer to your earlier question," he said, "I'm here because I forgot something."

"Oh? What?"

He came over and rapped his knuckles on the table where we'd eaten and drunk, played games and talked, celebrated and commiserated, fought and made up, and—now—let go. "This table and chairs're mine. Marin County Flea Market, the week after we founded All Souls. They're going along."

"To our joint conference room?"

"Mind reader. Is that okay with you?"

I nodded.

"Then give me a hand with them, will you?"

I stood, grinning. "Sure, but only if ..."

"If what?"

It was a stupid, sentimental decision—one I was sure to regret. "Only if you'll give me a hand with that ratty armchair in my former office. I can't imagine why Rae forgot it."

THE END

Marcia Muller Bibliography

Novels
The Rockspur Eleven (1978; a YA novel)
The Arborgate (1980)
The Lighthouse (1987; co-written with Bill Pronzini)

Sharon McCone series
Edwin of the Iron Shoes (October, 1977)
Ask the Cards A Question (May, 1982)
The Cheshire Cat's Eye (January, 1983)
Games to Keep the Dark Away (1984)
Leave A Message for Willie (September, 1984)
Double (October, 1984; co-written with Bill Pronzini, featuring the Nameless Detective)
There's Nothing to Be Afraid of (August, 1985)
Eye of the Storm (March, 1988)
There's Something in A Sunday (January, 1989)
The Shape of Dread (November, 1989)
Trophies and Dead Things (September, 1990)
Where Echoes Live (July, 1991)
Pennies on A Dead Woman's Eyes (July, 1992)
Wolf in the Shadows (July, 1993)
Till the Butchers Cut Him Down (July, 1994)
A Wild and Lonely Place (August, 1995)
The Broken Promise Land (June, 1996)
Both Ends of the Night (July, 1997)
While Other People Sleep (July, 1998)
A Walk Through the Fire (May, 1999)
Listen to the Silence (July, 2000)
Dead Midnight (July, 2002)
The Dangerous Hour (July, 2004)
Vanishing Point (July, 2006)
The Ever-Running Man (July, 2007)
Burn Out (October, 2008)
Locked In (October, 2009)
Coming Back (October, 2010)
City of Whispers (October, 2011)
Looking For Yesterday (November, 2012)
The Night Searchers (July, 2014)
Someone Always Knows (July, 2016)
The Color of Fear (August, 2017)
The Breakers (August, 2018)
Ice and Stone (August, 2021)
Circle in the Water (April, 2024)

Carpenter and Quincannon Mysteries
The Bughouse Affair (2013; co-written with Bill Pronzini)
The Spook Lights Affair (2013; co-written with Bill Pronzini)
The Body Snatchers Affair (2015; co-written with Bill Pronzini)
The Plagues of Thieves Affair (2016; co-written with Bill Pronzini)
Dangerous Ladies Affair (2017; co-written with Bill Pronzini)

Elena Oliverez series
The Tree of Death (1983)
The Legend of the Slain Soldiers (1985)
Beyond the Grave (1986; co-written with Bill Pronzini)

Joanna Stark series
The Cavalier in White (1986)
There Hangs the Knife (1988)
Dark Star (1989)

Soledad County series
Point Deception (2001)
Cyanide Wells (2003)
Cape Perdido (2005)

Short Stories

Deceptions (1991)
The McCone Files (1994)
Duo (1998; co-written with Bill Pronzini)
McCone and Friends (1999)
Time of the Wolves (2003; western stories)
Somewhere in the City (2007)
Crucifixion River (2007; co-written with Bill Pronzini)

Anthologies
The Web She Weaves (1983; co-edited with Bill Pronzini)
Witches Brew: Horror and Supernatural Stories by Women (1984; co-edited with Bill Pronzini)
Child's Ploy: An Anthology of Mystery and Suspense Stories (1984; co-edited with Bill Pronzini)
She Won the West: An Anthology of Western and Frontier Stories by Women (1985; co-edited with Bill Pronzini)
Dark Lessons: Crime and Detection on Campus (1985; co-edited with Bill Pronzini)
Kill or Cure: Suspense Stories About the World of Medicine (1985; co-edited with Bill Pronzini)
The Deadly Arts: A Collection of Artful Suspense (1985; co-edited with Bill Pronzini)
Chapter and Hearse: Suspense Stories About the World of Books (1985; co-edited with Bill Pronzini)
The Wickedest Show on Earth: A Carnival of Circus Suspense (1985; co-edited with Bill Pronzini)
Lady on the Case: 21 Stories and 1 Complete Novel Starring the World's Great Female Sleuths (1988; co-edited with Bill Pronzini & Martin H. Greenberg)
Detective Duos: The Best Adventures of Twenty-Five Crime-Solving Twosomes (1997; co-edited with Bill Pronzini)

Non-fiction
1001 Midnights: The Aficionado's Guide to Mystery and Detective Fiction (1986; co-edited with Bill Pronzini)

And from Mystery Writers of America Grand Master
Bill Pronzini

"Pronzini is a magnificent entertainer of the first rank."—Ed Gorman

Small Felonies 2
50 short-short crime stories in a variety of styles, something for everyone's tastes. "... this book has something for everyone who loves stories of crime, detection, psychological suspense, noir, fantasy, humor, and twists."—Ted Hertel, *Deadly Pleasures*

High Concepts
Thirty-four science fiction and fantasy stories. "... devilish-sly mechanisms calculated to pull you in, then yank the rug out from under your feet, sending you into an unexpected abyss."—Paul Di Filippo, *Locus*

Cream of the Crop: Best Mystery & Suspense Stories
Twenty-six stories personally selected by Bill Pronzini from over a half century's writing career. "... a marvelous collection you'll want to rush through, but it is best read slowly to better experience its savory taste."—Ben Boulden, *Dark City Underground*

The Hanging Man & Other Western Stories
An essential collection of Pronzini's western stories spanning 35 years and including the award-winning "Crucifixion River." "... represents the genre at its best and will be a welcome addition to western collections."—*Booklist*

Tales of the Impossible
Nineteen ingenious crime puzzle mysteries—tales involving locked rooms, bizarre vanishings, curious murder methods and ghostly apparitions. "Delightfully compact and devilishly constructed, these stories stand alongside Pronzini's best work."
—*Publishers Weekly* starred review

Available in trade paperback from...
Stark House Press, 1315 H Street, Eureka, CA 95501
griffinskye3@sbcglobal.net / www.StarkHousePress.com
Available from your local bookstore, or order direct via our website.

www.ingramcontent.com/pod-product-compliance
Lightning Source LLC
LaVergne TN
LVHW021806060526
838201LV00058B/3255